D0399305

BLOOD

OF A

THOUSAND

STARS

BLOOD

OF A

THOUSAND

STARS

RHODA BELLEZA

RAZORBILL®

An Imprint of Penguin Random House LLC
Penguin.com

RAZORBILL & colophon is a registered trademark
of Penguin Random House LLC.

First published in the United States of America by Razorbill,
an imprint of Penguin Random House LLC, 2018

Copyright © 2018 Glasstown Entertainment and Rhoda Belleza
Map by Diana Sousa

LIBRARY OF CONGRESS CATALOGING-IN-PUBLICATION DATA IS AVAILABLE

ISBN: 9781101999134

Printed in the United States of America

1 3 5 7 9 10 8 6 4 2

Interior design by Eric Ford

For Dad

DESUCO QUADRANT

Nau Fruma

KAL

HOUL

Rhest

Tinoppa

NAIDOZ

CHRAM

Navrum

Erawae

DERKATZ

PORTIIS

HERYL QUADRANT

RELLIA QUADRANT

DEMBOS

WRAETA

FONTIS

BAZORL QUADRANT

MAJOR CHARACTERS

KALUSIAN

Rhiannon Ta'an: Princess, sole surviving heir to the ruling Ta'an dynasty

Kara: Contested Ta'an princess and sister to Rhiannon

Tai Simone Reyanna: Governess to Crown Princess Rhiannon

Nero Cimna: Kalusian ambassador to the Crown Regent's office

WRAETAN

Alyosha Myraz: Former UniForce soldier, former DroneVision star of *The Revolutionary Boys*

Issa: Medic for the Wraetan Fontisian Coalition

FONTISIAN

Dahlen: Rogue warrior, associated with both the Order of the Light and Wraetan Fontisian Coalition

Lahna: Soldier on behalf of the Order of the Light

UNKNOWN

The Fisherman: Outlaw in the galaxy's Outer Belt

PLANETS

KALU: Most populated planet in the galaxy and ancestral home of the ruling Ta'an dynasty

KALUSIAN TERRITORIES

Navrum: Terraformed asteroid

Rhesto: Larger moon of Kalu, the site of a nuclear plant before the Great War

Tinoppa: Tiny asteroid equidistant from Kalu and Nau Fruma, home to the sacred crystals

Chram: Dwarf planet allied to Kalu

FONTIS: Largest planet in the galaxy

FONTISIAN TERRITORIES

Wraeta: Decimated planet, destroyed by a Kalusian attack ten years ago during the Great War

NEUTRAL TERRITORIES

Nau Fruma: Smaller moon of Kalu

Portiis: Outlying planet

Erawae: Domed city on an asteroid in the Bazorl Quadrant

Part One:

THE RETURNED

"An organic memory is an act of creation, of *re*-creation in fact—and by definition an imperfect copy, corrupted by emotion and an overload of sensory details. A memory recalled via the cube, however, is the exact memory perfectly preserved. It's argued such recollections are less visceral, or that something essential is lost. But it seems little cost for the truth in returning to the same moment, countless times, unchanged."

—G-1K Summit Appeal to the United Planets, the year 858

ONE

KARA

IF Kara was hot up here, it must've been hell down in the packed square. All of Nau Fruma was on a labor strike, and from her vantage point, the protesters looked like a single living organism— angry, undulating. For a historically neutral moon, Nau Fruma was not exactly peaceful these days.

Sweat stung Kara's eyes as she scanned the crowd below. She wiped it away with the back of her hand, smearing the moon-dust that had settled on her skin.

"Test," she said to Pavel, the small droid who sat beside her. The heat made everything shimmer in the distance. "Six o'clock."

A bright white light flashed across the terra-cotta brick building directly behind them. It was gone in a split second. Kara scratched at the surface of the rusty coin, the one she'd carried around always. It hadn't been anything more than a good-luck charm until Lydia told her otherwise.

This binds you to your family. There's history in this coin, she'd said with her dying breath.

Kara blinked away the memory. "Again, Pavel: nine o'clock."

Pavel swiveled west and used a small mirror attachment to reflect the sunlight.

"Again: two o'clock—"

"All right, all right, take it easy," Aly said as he climbed up the wire ladder that led to the roof. "You're more intense than half the souls I came up with in basic." He crouched down next to Kara, half-hidden by the ledge.

"Just trying to prep," she said, pocketing the coin. He had no idea how militant Lydia had been. The woman Kara had thought was her mother had a consummate work ethic. Language testing. Survival training. Ways to smuggle credits, and how to get a good read on a person. Kara had thought it was absurd and paranoid, which showed how much she knew. It had paid off, in a way. Kara had survived, even if Lydia hadn't.

"You keep 'prepping' and someone down there might notice our little operation."

"They're too busy watching the picket line."

It had been two days since Kara and Aly had gotten to Nau Fruma, and just one day since Empress Rhiannon Ta'an had come forward to announce she was alive. Since Nau Fruma was a moon of Kalu, news of her return home was all over the holos. Kara would have been relieved about her sister's safe return, but the holos were also buzzing with the newest speculation: where Josselyn Ta'an was. Rhiannon's older sister.

If anyone in the universe knew the answer to that question, it was Kara.

Because Kara *was* Josselyn. Or she had been once, even if she didn't remember.

After informing the galaxy that she was alive, Rhee had outed Kara, offering a reward for her safe return.

Actually, she had offered a reward for *Josselyn*, the missing royal sister and rightful empress, the one who everyone believed had died all those years ago in a spacecraft explosion, along with the rest of the Ta'an family.

Maybe Kara should've been moved by the gesture. She didn't have a single memory before the age of twelve. Lydia had told her it was a cube malfunction; Kara had believed it all those years, and filled in the big white blank space of her mind with made-up scenarios. And she'd gotten so good at it that soon she was spinning entire tales, fabricating alternate lives on the spot while kids at parties nodded their heads, wide-eyed and amazed.

Underneath all the lies she'd told, the lies she'd *been* told, she had a true family and a real home—but what did blood really matter? Rhiannon was a stranger in every other sense of the word, and seeing her on the holos brought on a slew of feelings about a lot of people, most of them dead and gone. Lydia, the scientist who had harbored her. Her *actual* parents, the late Emperor and Empress of Kalu, whom she hardly remembered. And Rhiannon, the girl who'd come back from the dead, who was in the process of assuming her crown . . . while Kara crouched on a hot roof hiding for her life.

Aly unscrewed a canteen and took a big gulp, his head tipped back, his mouth parted. Kara turned away and tried to focus. She squinted at the doorway across the way. Her bangs fell into her face, and she pawed at them, annoyed.

"These will help," Aly said. From his messenger bag he pulled out a bulky hunk of black metal that looked like two cups attached side by side. "They're called binoculars. Vintage military gear. They magnify your vision."

Apparently you could find anything on the black market. She took the binoculars and put them to her eyes. They were heavier than they looked, and everything came out blurry and small. "They don't work."

"You have them upside-down," he said, shaking his head and grinning in that way that made her forget her life was on fire.

"I knew that," she lied. Kara put the device to her eyes and immediately regretted it. The view was disorienting, claustrophobic, too narrow. She could only see a small cluster of people at a time. She ripped it away from her face and nearly dropped it.

"Whoa," Aly said, grabbing it from her hand. "Everything okay?"

She shook her head. "I feel kind of dizzy." She realized she had a headache, a light pulsing behind her eye. It wasn't the binoculars. The meds Lydia had given her were running low. Kara had been taking them for years; Lydia told her the pills were to help manage the severe headaches and nightmares from her cube malfunction. And even if they treated her symptoms just fine, Kara had discovered that the cause was a lie.

The pills did help with the headaches, but they were DNA suppressors too, meant to skew Josselyn's features—Lydia's own biological design, if Kara had to guess. For the last couple of weeks she'd been weaning herself off by taking half doses, then quarter doses, to fractions of a pill every other day. This morning she'd broken a pill apart without a knife, and most of it crumbled to dust.

Kara had almost cried. Not that she could tell you why. There was something about the end of one simple routine that tethered you to your past. Even if it was a lie.

"You take it," Kara said, handing the binoculars back. "Narrate for me."

"Well, you're not missing much," he said, staring into the binoculars. "Just a bunch of pissed-off Nauies." He rubbed the back of his neck like he always did when he was thinking. His shirt lifted up to reveal a strip of dark skin, his belly button a tiny outie, dimples on the inside of either hip.

"Are you well, Kara? I detect a sudden but minor change in your skin color." Pavel's eyelights went red. "The medical bible says this is a common physiological reaction to emotional stressors. Blood vessels open wide, flooding the skin with blood and reddening the face."

"It's called blushing," Aly said. He'd dropped the binoculars; the corners of his mouth had turned up just slightly.

"You're a rat." Kara nudged Pavel with the tip of her boot so that he rolled back with the force. She felt herself flushing more. "I'll open up that head of yours and rearrange all the inside bits," she threatened.

"Better watch out, little man."

"This is humor, correct?" Pavel's eyelights had gone red. "Because theoretically we're not too far off. There's new research to suggest that cube-to-cube transfers could be enhanced. Nearby neural pathways can give and receive the info without even being prepped, without even—"

Aly dropped the hand with the binoculars. "All right, P," he said, all the playfulness drained from his voice. "Chill out. She was just kidding."

"Have him try me," Kara tried to joke, but the mood had already shifted. Aly knew she didn't like talking about their cubes. The mere mention put her on edge, reminded her they had all turned theirs off in case Nero was trying to track them right now.

Aly closed the gap between them and slid his palm into hers. She tried to ignore the way it lit her skin on fire. "You okay?" he asked.

"I'm fine," she said, slipping her hand out of his grasp.

Aly gave her that look he made when he was trying to get a read on her—the slight pout in his full lips, his brown eyes opened wide so his thick lashes fanned out. He had a cut across his left eyebrow, the same spot where he'd nicked it when he was younger—but this time around, it had been the kid, Julian, who'd done it to Aly.

Julian hadn't exactly been thrilled when they landed on his doorstep looking for the Lancer. In fact, he got so intense that he'd caused a scene, calling them thieves and managing to get a jab in when Aly was trying to hold him down. But as soon as help came, all they did was scold Julian and apologize to Kara and Aly, who did their damnedest to keep their faces hidden. Apparently Julian had acted up after his dad died, and his being known as a hothead worked in their favor.

Since then, Aly, Kara, and Pavel had been trailing him, but they kept their distance. Julian was their only connecting thread to the Lancer and the information he should have given her before his death. Kara was sure it had to do with the location of the overwriter—the same technology that Lydia had used to hack into Kara's cube and erase her memories of being Josselyn.

The same technology Lydia had told her about before she died. The technology that Kara wanted to destroy.

But first she had to find it, and they didn't have a whole lot to go on. The three of them had combed all available information about the G-1K summits, where the galaxy's scientists got together to develop the cube—but nothing concrete turned up in any of the policies, ethical standards, reports, or updates. Kara even did a deep dive into the conspiracy theories about the overwriter, and some suggested a kind of prototype had been developed in the Outer Belt, which functioned by deleting simple memories stored on people's cubes via a giant shared network that rivaled UniForce's. But Kara already knew that, since it was *her* memories that had once been removed—and it didn't give her any new information. There had always been rumors. They needed something concrete. And their only lead was Julian.

Now, Kara waited for Julian to leave the dojo, like he did every afternoon. She squinted back down at the crowd. Today, she would finally get inside.

"If I could choose any superpower, I'd read your mind," Aly said.

"You don't want to be in there." She shook her head. "It's all messed up."

"I want to see all of it. Even the messed-up parts," Aly told her. He moved closer so that their shoulders were touching. "Especially the messed-up parts."

Kara fought the urge to look over at him but gave in anyway.

"Your eyes," he said softly, their lips a breath apart. She looked at that little spot at the center of his upper lip—where it dipped in just so. "They're changing color again."

Kara blinked. The rest of the world rushed back in; she felt like she'd woken up from a spell.

"Pavel!" she called back, and demanded his mirror when he rolled close, bringing it to her face.

"I didn't mean anything . . ." Aly had started to say. But Kara shook her head. She saw it: the golden hue of her left iris, the tiny specks of green dotting the center.

"They haven't changed that much," Aly said, backtracking.

Kara's tongue felt thick. They *had* changed. She *was* different. The faint headache suddenly became an intense throbbing behind her right eye. She fished the eye drops out of her pocket; they had quick-fix DNA-suppression properties to keep her eyes the same color. The liquid burned when she dropped it on her cornea.

"Hey," Aly said, taking her hand again. "I don't know why I even said anything. I can barely tell."

She didn't pull away this time, but looked down at the way their fingers interlaced—and how his knuckles were red and raw from everything he'd been through in the last few weeks. It felt like a lifetime had passed since they met on the zeppelin. The world was at war. Everything had changed, including her face.

"You're a terrible liar," she said.

"Four o'clock!" Pavel announced.

Aly squeezed her hand. "We're done with the drills, P," he called behind them.

"Not a drill. Target at four o'clock."

Kara ripped the binoculars from Aly's hand and looked in the direction Pavel had called. There was Julian, exiting a structure, with his telltale slouch. Kara locked eyes for a fleeting moment with Aly before they gathered their things and each threw their *duhatj* on.

"You know what to do, Pavel," Aly called as he and Kara quickly made their way down the ladder. She was so nervous she was half sliding, half falling, and suddenly they had boots on the top floor and were flying down the steps to the street level. She burst out of the door, right into the crowded streets of the protest. Aly was by her side, pulling her back. "Slow it down," he said, adjusting the fabric of her *duhatj*.

But urgency coursed through her limbs. They were going to break into someone's spot. Julian was connected to the Lancer, their only lead—and he'd known Rhee, was friends with her even, judging by how defensive he'd gotten when he saw Kara's matching coin. But they were also in the middle of a protest, surrounded by a whole lot of guards eager to use their stunners if you gave them a reason.

A light flashed again at four o'clock from the lookout point—Pavel's signal of Julian's location. Julian was headed home.

Kara dove into the crowd. Aly was right behind her. The mass pushed forward, chanting and hollering about fair pay and lower export taxes for goods to the moon. She followed with a singular purpose, pushing her way through the crowd as the light hopped from building to building, all in a row, moving farther and farther away. Finally they reached the dome-shaped threshold, and Kara looked up to confirm one last time that the light was far away. She reached behind her to find Aly's hand.

But he was no longer there.

Kara got on the tips of her toes and looked for him, but he was nowhere—lost to the crowd. She'd been sure he was behind her. If she waited she might miss her window: From her observations, she'd learned there were only fifteen minutes during the day when the temple was unused. That alone had been enough to convince her that whatever the Lancer had given his son was likely stored there, where it would be under near constant guard.

Looking toward the tower, she raised a hand to signal Pavel. She was going in.

Inside was a short hallway that led her through another threshold and into a long room with high ceilings. Bamboo mats lined the floor, and a row of wooden pillars ran down the center. Material imported from Kalu, no doubt; there was no way a dusty moon like this had enough water to grow bamboo. Light flooded in through paneled windows all along the east and west walls. It was empty. Still, it vibrated with the intensity and violence she'd always associated with martial arts.

There was a small altar against the wall in the center of the room, with only one holo, one ancestor: Veyron. Otherwise known as the Lancer. Kara had practically memorized his face; she'd come across countless images of him during all the research she'd done in the last two days. In every available image he wore a stark expression: his mouth in a line so straight it was practically a grimace, the high brow and darker coloring of his Wraetan side, the intimidating stare of his ice-blue eyes.

But in this holo he had the hint of a smile, and it was taken outside—the sun's glow warm on his skin, making it look tanner, more alive.

Scattered across the altar were simple offerings: a few pieces of fruit, a bowl of grain, and an old stick of incense burned down to its nub. One item stood out: a cylinder made up of small wooden pieces, of all different sizes and lengths, jigsawed together. The whole thing fit into the palm of Kara's hand.

When she lifted it, a beam emitted from its center and panned across her eyes. For a split second, she was blinded. The blue beam widened, and a holo of the galaxy appeared, a sprawling image that took up the length of the dojo and made Kara dizzy with its scope.

Kara heard a door slam behind her. She jumped back, dropping the cylinder. It clattered to the ground, and the holo disappeared into a sliver.

She turned and saw him. *Julian.* He looked even taller than he had a few days ago. He stood with his feet apart, his hands in fists.

"What are you doing here?"

"I was looking for you," Kara said smoothly. The lie came easy, even if her heart was racing and her head was throbbing. Of all days for Julian to come back . . . She couldn't help but notice he'd blocked the entrance she'd come through—and the exit she'd been intending to use.

His blue eyes fell on the cylinder. Its surfaces had reconfigured into an asymmetrical triangle. "How did you get it to unlock?"

"I didn't unlock it." Kara tried to keep her voice steady as he paced toward her. Could she get around him? There was a second door, on the far side of the room, but she didn't know where it led. "I just picked it up."

"You're lying." Then: "Tell me what it said."

So there was a message. Kara knew that this was what Lydia had intended her to find. That it was a message only Kara—not Julian, not anyone—could have opened.

Outside something slammed into the window. Kara could make out the figure from the inside, a dark form crouching low as it pressed itself against the window. Instinctively Kara and Julian both crouched.

The beating of her heart matched the pounding of her head. Right then and there, Kara made a decision.

When Julian's head was turned toward the window, Kara lunged past him, grabbing the wooden device in her hand.

"No!" He dove for her. His hand caught her foot and she flew forward, knees and elbows breaking her fall. The device tumbled forward, out of her hands—and Julian let her go to scramble for it, but Kara was faster getting to her feet.

Kara scooped up the device and hurtled out the door, relieved to see a staircase. The noise of chanting and shouting in the market was louder here—she was headed in the right direction.

"What did it say?" Julian's voice echoed back to her even as she pinballed up the steps, crashing around the twists and turns, making bruises she'd find only later.

She burst into the sunlight, and threw herself into the rioting crowd.

TWO

RHIANNON

RHEE no longer looked like a Marked child; the suction of the octoerces had faded, and her skin was once again the color of smooth sand. It had been just two days since Rhee announced her homecoming via a hijacked holovision channel. The Fisherman, who had helped Rhee and Dahlen escape from Nero's clutches after he'd found her on Fontis, had then reached out for help to a disparate network of anarchists—who didn't care one bit about restoring Rhee to her crown, but *did* care about the credits they received in return for their assistance. Shuttled in a series of unmarked crafts, flying under the radar of the very army Rhee should command, she arrived on Kalu under the cover of night.

Now, from the backseat of the ground vehicle, she looked out of the tinted glass and saw the streets of Sibu, lined on either side with thousands of Kalusians who'd come out to welcome her home. Colorful paper lanterns were hung all over the capital city, from balconies and over doorways.

Those are for us, Josselyn had said once, when they'd returned from an extended family trip.

You mean they're for me too? Rhee had asked.

That's what us *means*, Joss had said. She had always found a way to make Rhee feel silly and stupid and young. And just when the hope had started to deflate, Josselyn had nudged Rhee with her shoulder and smiled. It was then that Rhee knew: They were a team. She was the sidekick. She'd follow Joss anywhere.

She fished the coin out of her pocket. It was from the Bazorl Quadrant, from a time before they used credits. These pieces of metal had held value once, and her father had brought two home from a diplomatic mission. One for her and one for Joss.

Rhee had only recently learned Joss was still alive—that she'd managed to survive the accident that tragically killed the rest of their family—but Rhee couldn't find her. Joss could be anywhere in the entire galaxy, and Rhee had to abandon her search before it had even started, coming home instead to claim the throne. Nero had forced her hand. He knew Josselyn was alive. The best Rhee could do was offer a reward for her sister's safe return, and hope she could get to her before Nero did. She had to end this war and stop his rise before he wrested control of her rule entirely.

In truth she wanted to kill him too. But she'd spilt enough blood, and she'd learned her revenge fantasies were just that:

fantasies. Her trainer, Veyron, was dead. Andres Seotra, former regent to the Kalu crown, was dead. A trail of bodies, of destruction, lay in her wake. She should know better, cut off the thought of revenge at the root because it hadn't paid off, and it wouldn't this time, either. She needed to be smarter, more strategic. Bloodshed wasn't the answer when she was trying to end a war between Kalu and Fontis. If anything, Nero's murder would only incite *more* violence.

The ground vehicle switched gears, jolting her out of her meditation.

"Don't concern yourself." Dahlen spoke up from the front seat. The Fontisian's eyes in the rearview mirror were gray; they shifted hues depending on the light. "I've scouted out the location, and the central district is where we're the most vulnerable. Extra archers have been placed there and there," he said as he pointed.

Rhee's eye wandered to the tattoos across his neck, detailed swirls that she imagined were beyond painful to receive. He must've mistaken her distant gaze for worry. It was the closest he had ever come to asking whether she was okay.

She searched for the right words, the ones to ground her in this moment, to explain every ounce of emotion that burdened her.

"Thank you for being so thorough."

He'd taken the security detail seriously. But for all his skill in combat, he'd misunderstood the enemy. Nero would never attempt a move against her with so many people watching. She wasn't afraid for her life. She was afraid of his mind—the vindictive ways he used people and pitted them against each other, as if they were all pieces on a chessboard.

Rhee looked down and realized her fists were clenched in the cloth of her dress. Last time she'd worn the ceremonial red dress, Rhee had been forced to kill Veyron, her trainer, the man she had loved like a second father—fought him off with everything she'd had, stabbed him in the heart, and sent him off into space. Because Nero had deemed it so.

Every thought, every memory of Veyron made her chest tighten—and led her back to Julian, his son. He'd been her best friend when there was nothing else good in the world, when her family had died and she'd been cast to Nau Fruma. If Julian discovered her betrayal, it would be one he'd never forgive. She'd finally summoned the courage to reach out to him. Since her cube was off, Rhee had been forced to use a radio telescope—a near-ancient piece of tech—at a safe-house pit stop along the way; she had to speak into a receiver to record her voice, and hope it made its way to the one radio telescope at an observatory on Nau Fruma.

There's so much to tell you, she'd said.

And if that transmitted to him successfully, someone would have to be at the telescope at the moment it came in to receive it. It was a long shot, but the only one Rhee had.

She wasn't sure what he might have heard about his father's death, or what he might believe, but she'd needed to try—and if she failed to get through to him this time, she'd try again and again. If he was attempting to get hold of her, Rhee wouldn't know. If she finally succeeded, what *would* she say? Did he know about her part in Veyron's death? Would she tell him?

Honor. Bravery. Loyalty. It was her mantra, her *ma'tan sarili*, her highest self. Rhee focused on the spot between her eyes, and felt a touch of numbness that grew through her skull until everything was clear, dark, without context, and without pain.

When she'd centered herself, she opened her eyes to see Dahlen scowling out the windshield. She'd never seen him smile, and she wondered if she ever would. Especially not since what had happened on Houl, when Nero made Dahlen turn on his cube, forcing him to violate one of the sacred vows of the order. Since then, Dahlen had become both more intense and more withdrawn, though she hadn't thought either possible.

"Are you okay?" Rhee wished she'd sat in the front, by his side, rather than having him up front alone as if he were hired help. Why hadn't she thought of it earlier? If he'd registered her question, she couldn't be sure—but she noticed the ends of his pointy ears went red.

"The Fisherman chose the snipers personally," Dahlen said. "You won't miss them, if you look closely."

Rhee decided not to press it. There would be time to talk later. Squinting out the window, she saw archers were placed strategically within each of the Twin Towers of the Long Now. The rounded white buildings had lush, green terraces spiraling up their length—a new addition to the city in the six years she'd been gone. These were the DroneVision headquarters, where Nero himself lived—and she didn't doubt he had his own snipers strategically placed.

She was glad for Dahlen, his command, his archers. Her Tasinn, the royal guard that had protected the Ta'an family for generations of rule, could no longer be trusted in the transition of power. As far as Rhee was concerned, they worked for Nero. It was a Tasinn who'd dragged her to Nero's little production, when he had lorded over Dahlen's body, prepared to extract his cube, to Ravage his memories on the spot. It was only weeks before, but so much had happened.

Maybe the Tasinn believed the same silly fairy tale Nero spun over and over again: He was going to improve Kalu's standing in the galaxy. He'd focus on getting the crops back in order, bring all the farmers back, revive an industry long dead so they could find wealth once more. An exclusive, thriving world—just for them. "Them" being the wealthy second-wavers who'd built their fortune on Kalu's agricultural industry. But they had squeezed it dry, demanding too great a yield from the planet's natural resources so they could sell it to the highest bidder on some far-flung planet. Now the second-wavers watched their fortunes dwindle, and blamed nearly anyone except themselves and their own terrible choices. Which is why they wanted all the immigrants and Wraetan refugees out.

Behind the confetti, the roses, the hopeful mood that had infused the city, an undercurrent of tension buzzed everywhere. Kalu was at war with Fontis. Even if you couldn't see it here, you could feel it. They'd passed people holding the Kalusian flag upside down, witnessed signs of poverty at the base of the lush, gleaming tower.

Rhee had anticipated her homecoming would infuriate Nero's

supporters; she had come to displace him, after all, and reclaim the throne and leadership of all of Kalu. But Nero remained as slick as oil when it was announced she was returning home.

"Thank the ancestors," he'd said, citing those he did not pray to, and a religion he did not practice. The public ate it up. Never mind the fact he'd been publicly rallying to avenge her death by going to war with Fontis; he could hardly admit to having been the one to orchestrate her attempted assassination.

From what she could tell on the holos she'd watched during her flight here, dissenters were in the minority—a loud minority, however. It was nothing Rhee hadn't heard before: that she was too young, too beholden to her family's dynasty, too attached to the monarchy that had led the planet down the wrong path.

But now she saw their ranks had swelled. Or were there always this many people who welcomed the war with Fontis? Humiliation started to sink down into her bones as they passed a burning effigy of a brown doll in a red dress with black yarn for hair. There were cheers. Then a woman snatched it away and threw it on the ground, stomping the limp figure; Rhee wasn't sure if she'd done it to put out the fire or to demonstrate what she thought of the Empress.

She looked away. Was it true? Was she as young and naïve as they accused her of being? It was clear now more than ever that the second-wavers were becoming a sort of ruling class. They led the charge on the anti-immigrant, anti-refugee—and now, the growing anti-native—sentiment here in Sibu. And if they were against native blood it meant they were against the Ta'an. Against her. They hadn't even given Rhee the chance to fail.

Instead they gravitated toward Nero—an evil, corrupt killer. The masses had already come to love watching him night after night on DroneVision for over a decade as the ambassador to the regent, and thus had come to trust him too. Earlier that morning, he had announced a territory-wide update to the cube operating system—the first in years—and a rollout was already in progress for those who opted in. The holos were broadcasting the news across the system. It gave Rhee a knot in her stomach, though an update seemed innocent enough. Still, everything Nero did was twisted at the root.

He may have tricked an entire solar system into thinking that he was their champion, but Rhee *would* help them. Her father had said being a ruler was difficult, sometimes thankless—and such a remark had puzzled her. Everywhere they'd gone he was showered with praise, with gifts, asked to dole out blessings, people longing to touch him with their outstretched hands.

Now she understood an inkling of that sentiment.

She'd end the war. Two wars, in fact: a war where soldiers were sent off to die, and the emotional war for the hearts and minds of her own people, here, in the very city she was born. Nero had been a heartbeat away from proclaiming himself regent. She'd temporarily snatched the position from him, but he would never cede power so easily—even if he had ostensibly agreed to step back.

She would do what her father had done and unite everyone in peace. Even if the way she might achieve that peace was as thorny and thick in her mind as one of the dozen-armed cacti in

27

the desert of Nau Fruma. The only certainty Rhee had was that she was a Ta'an. She could do it. She had to.

As she and Dahlen and the rest of her guards moved toward the center city, traffic narrowed to a slow crawl. The streets were packed with Kalusian citizens. UniForce soldiers struggled to keep them behind cordons. Rhee hoped that UniForce was still loyal to her, not Nero—she could replace the Tasinn, who were a small, elite force of personal guards to the crown. But she couldn't replace the entire UniForce army.

Daisies were everywhere—auto-cams on constant stream. They were technically called *day-sees* because of the light mounted on the bottom, but the word had been slurred over time into *daisies*. They swarmed the windows of their vehicle, while Dahlen's handpicked guard of Fontisians rode madùcycles on either side and swatted them away.

"Rhiannon!" a voice screamed, loud enough to rise above the chorus.

She saw a man crawl over a barrier and make a gesture so obscene as their vehicle passed that Rhee almost looked away. The man was tackled by one of Dahlen's Fontisian guards, who'd gracefully launched himself off his madùcycle. He had the man's head to the ground within seconds. Rhee swiveled to look behind her as they sped past.

"Ancestors!" Rhee hissed. "Can't your men be more gentle?" She didn't want the Fontisian guard to give protesters more cause for unrest.

"Don't forget that they're *your* men," he said.

She didn't answer. It's not how the Kalusians would see it. The guards were all Fontisian, and like Dahlen they were part of the Order of the Light, a fundamentalist Fontisian religious group. The order was obsessed with maintaining peace, even if that meant working with Kalu and supporting Ta'an rule. They'd favored her father; he'd brokered peace between their two planets and ended the Great War all those years ago.

But that didn't mean the average Kalusian would be welcoming. To any Kalusian, a Fontisian was an outsider. Here was Rhee—their one true ruler, returned from the dead—flanked on all sides by security that, with their white-blond hair and sharp faces, looked a hell of a lot like the enemy. Judging by some of the sneers and looks of real fear in the eyes of the crowd, she wondered whether it had been a good idea for the order to take such a prominent role in protecting her.

But no one else had offered to.

"I don't want to get off on the wrong foot. The order already has a reputation of being . . ." She searched for the right word.

"Fanatical? Violent? Aggressive?" Dahlen reached down to shift gears roughly. The vehicle was self-driving, but as usual, Dahlen took no chances. He was worried, he said, that the tech would be hacked by Nero's cronies; there would be no accidents today.

"I'm trying to make friends of enemies," she said defensively.

"We will not apologize for our presence." He scanned the packed streets of Kalusians as they passed. Fontisians spoke in negatives; it made everything they said sound forceful and stubborn.

Though perhaps it was because they *were* forceful and stubborn. "Such a stance isn't an adequate strategy when it comes to dissenters."

"Yes, because you have ruling a planet all figured out?"

He cocked his eyebrow as they stared at one another through the mirror. "Because *you* do, Empress?"

Rhee exhaled slowly but wouldn't respond—she was working on staying calmer, hiding her feelings better. That word, *Empress*, still felt wrong. She remembered when Julian had called her *Empress* in the Nau Fruma marketplace, as the meteors rained down above them the very last time she saw him, how the title had filled her with dread.

Her purpose then had at least felt clear, violent but uncomplicated. One life for many. Seotra's for her family's. But Seotra had been innocent. Her vengeance had been misguided, and she'd ended up killing one of her most powerful allies.

Her purpose was different now, though just as clear as before—to bring about peace.

They crested the hill, and for the first time in six years, Rhee caught sight, at last, of the palace. It took her breath away. It was the only thing from her childhood that had lived up to its memory—her organic memory. It was a feeling, different than the memories she had replayed on her cube, better than the crystalline perfection that made it seem smaller and quaint on her cube. In person, it was majestic. Red and gold, one thousand steps leading up to its entrance. The sun, as it set, looked as if it were slowly lowering itself on the southernmost spire—pierced open and dripping fire on the orange, backlit sky.

As enormous, as beautiful, as vast as it was, what struck her the hardest was how strongly she sensed her father. She could see him pacing the marble corridors just hours before they'd leave for good because of the growing threat to their lives; her mother's sobs that same night bouncing between pillars in the fountain room. Only hours later, the craft that was supposed to take them to safety on Nau Fruma had exploded, killing them both. When she recalled a memory organically, like she did now, she experienced it with every sense, every facility she had. She was transported in time.

Cube memories weren't like that at all. The cube was precise; it rushed to the very moment you needed it to and then pulled away with the same cold efficiency. Not that it mattered—she'd temporarily turned off her cube so that they couldn't be tracked while they traveled.

But there was another reason she hadn't turned her cube back on. A deeper, unspoken fear she couldn't yet voice: Nero's ambition to find the overwriter. Rhee didn't think it existed. Not really. It was a technology without precedent, and anytime she'd heard of it, it was only in conjunction with the G-1K conspiracy theories. Only those on the fringes believed—or those, like Nero, who were prone to dramatics and flair, ready to chase down any mirage to secure his reign.

Imagine being able to speak through any cube, he'd said on Houl, *to anyone at will, throughout the whole universe. Imagine being able to whisper to them, not through their ears but their minds . . .*

Terror and revulsion snaked their way through her. But she

didn't feel ready to tell Dahlen, not yet—not when the trauma of that night so obviously haunted him still.

Nero had unofficially taken up residence in the palace after Rhee's supposed death. But her return had forced him to retreat, physically in this case. Still, her adviser Tai Reyanna and her friend the Fisherman had been sent ahead to clear out the palace of any remaining Tasinn and install the Fontisian guard and private security that could be trusted. It had been a flurry of prep in just a week's time between vetting loyalists and transporting them in secret.

Dahlen nudged the vehicle forward through the tall iron gates, nodding at the two Fontisian guards as he passed. The guards closed the gate quickly behind them, against a surge in the crowd—some people crying, reaching out toward their pod, and others protesting, spitting as they passed. She vaguely made out the chant: "No more sharks!" but she couldn't be sure. The slur for Fontisians grated against her ears, making her ashamed of her own people.

As the gates closed, she saw a fight break out. A man had thrown another to the ground, and they'd been swallowed up in the center of the crowd. She sat up straighter to get a better look. Dahlen powered down the vehicle, and for a brief moment Rhee thought she heard the engine ticking off the last of its charge. But that was her heart: not a drumbeat, but a kind of wild crackling.

"There's a fight," she said to Dahlen.

"There are fights everywhere. We're not to exit until the guards on the stairs are in place and they've ensured—"

Before he could finish, she shouldered the door open and stood to face the crowd and look for the fight. The Fontisian guards rushed down the stairs toward her, but she held up both hands, demanding that they stay back. Dahlen had gotten out himself and walked calmly around the vehicle, like he was stalking his prey, but stopped at a fair distance—just a few feet behind her, nodding at his guards to follow her order.

Rhee's red dress flapped in the wind. She was close enough to the gate that the hem of her skirt pressed through the gaps in the iron rails. She put her hand to the metal, and the crowd grew silent. She'd say something now. Reassure them she was here, that the war would end, that peace would be restored. She felt their belief welling inside her, and commanding the presence of her people, she felt a genuine ability to change the tide.

Her eyes latched on to a blonde girl in the front ranks a few paces away on the steps. She held a bow and arrow and her hair had been gathered in a thick braid that draped down her shoulder, practically alive, like a long white snake that she could charm. The girl's eyes were a hazel shade, yellows and oranges threaded through her irises like the color of a Nau Fruman sunset.

The girl opened her mouth, as if to call words of encouragement.

And then from the other side of the gate, an egg launched into the air. There was a vacuum of silence, as if the thousands of people clambering forward had held their breath.

It landed with a crunch three meters short of where Rhee stood, and for a split second she was hyperaware, focused on nothing but the vivid yolk pooling sadly against the drive.

Then everything exploded. Whole pockets of the crowd seemed to collapse, tumbling people down beneath its weight. She flinched as protesters threw even more things. Trash. Rotten pulp of long-turned fruit. Glass bottles that shattered at her feet. Her supporters turned on them. She heard screaming.

Through the screams she heard a hoarse whisper, as someone from the crowd grabbed her through the rails. Iron pressed into her face. "Daddy's girl better watch her back."

"No one wants you here!"

"You took your sister's throne!"

Rhee yanked herself free. Something was spinning toward her, straight at her face. She dodged and nearly went down. Glass shattered with a high and hysterical noise. Gravel blasted her cheek.

Dahlen grabbed her arm.

"Let go!" She struggled to regain her balance, stepping backward on her dress and feeling the hem rip. In a panic, she thought of the cameras watching, recording every second of this—everyone across the galaxy would see that she was afraid, that she had no idea what she was doing. Nero would make sure of it. And even worse, she realized, was that it was true. When other rulers might have spent years cultivating a relationship with the public, she'd been planning Seotra's death on another moon, in a foolish desire for vengeance. She'd been wrong. Now she felt like a fool. Naïve, like so many had said. "Let me go."

She managed to wrench free of Dahlen. He started to yell—Rhee wasn't sure what over the sound of the crowd—when she heard it: a high-pitched squeal like a firework shooting up into the air.

Not a firework, though.

It struck the top of the nearby tower in silence. Rhee hoped it was a trick of the light. Then a massive blast of fire, and a deep rumble as pieces of the marble tower cracked away, sifted through the air, masses of stone as big as the vehicle that had carried them.

The crowd split. More screams. They dove for cover as the first stones hit with an impact that shook Rhee through her feet all the way to her teeth. Dahlen found her again, and didn't bother with her hand this time; he hauled her over his shoulder and ran.

They crashed through the double doors into the palace as more of the marble came shuddering down from the sky. Fontisian guards streamed in behind them before the doors closed with a resounding echo. From outside came the noise of splintering, screams as protesters crashed through the barriers, shouts and thuds as the guards drove them backward. The UniForce soldiers that had been present earlier had mysteriously disappeared, and left the riot to fester into this. More bottles exploded against the palace, and several eggs too. They shimmered on the window-panes, their yolks like suns dying in miniature.

Empress Rhiannon was home.

THREE

KARA

KARA made her way up the staircase, taking two steps at a time as she dug the heel of her right palm into her eye socket to ease the building pressure. She hadn't stopped moving since she'd taken off from the dojo, and she wouldn't now. It was all about multitasking. Urge the blood vessels to relax, be patient. Force her body to push through. Fight. *Get what's yours*, Aly would have said.

Aly. She'd lost him in the crowd. Rhiannon's arrival back on Kalu had ignited something across the Kalusian territories. One second Aly was behind Kara and the next he was gone. If she had only waited, they wouldn't be split up now. But if she had waited, the cylinder with the holo message wouldn't be nestled in her pocket right now either. She hated how war had made everything split into either/or.

Please let him be here, she thought as she rushed up toward the roof.

Kara had been afraid Julian would follow her, so she had taken the long way back to Pavel. Returning had been its own kind of mission. The whole moon was protesting, and an explosive riot was the only reason she had made a clean getaway from the dojo. But on the way, she had seen Wraetans and Fontisians rounded up by the UniForce. It was illegal, since the moon was neutral—but that hadn't stopped anyone, and Kara had done her best to be inconspicuous as she scanned the faces of the captured, some of them fearful, some furious, some in obvious shock.

She hadn't seen Aly.

When Kara got to the topmost floor she saw the ladder had been pulled down. Her heart leapt. He was here. She scrambled up and popped her head through to see Pavel waiting for her. *Just* Pavel.

"Where is he?" Kara asked as she heaved her leg over and crawled onto the roof.

"I lost sight of him from the lookout. I hoped he would be accompanying you," the droid said. His eyelights went red and his voice dropped. "It appears he is not . . ." His metal frame retracted into its compacted dome setting, like he had collapsed out of sadness onto the floor.

Kara knew how he felt. She was on her knees still, blinking into the setting sun, feeling the ache behind her eyes sink deeper and deeper into her skull. She trembled out of fear and frustration—and suddenly the heat, the anger, felt overwhelming, intense, like she'd burst into flame from the inside out. It was that same panicked feeling she'd gotten when she came home to her house ransacked, and Lydia gone. That hadn't ended well.

"They took him," she said. "They must have."

Pavel didn't answer. He rolled toward her in his dome shape and nudged her shoulder gently. It made her feel a fraction better, a little less alone. But when his faceplate rotated toward her, she caught a glimpse of herself reflected back in its sheen. Her eyes were green.

They're changing color again, Aly had said.

Kara had to let it be; she wouldn't be able to manage the sting of those eye drops with her headache this bad.

She angled her face to the left. Was her face changing? And how long before anyone might guess who she really was: the lost princess, Josselyn Ta'an?

The possibility felt unreal, like a bad hologram that stuttered, a fractured projection—the same moment in low fidelity, looped over and over again. It was enough to drive a person crazy. But how could you reconcile these two identities—the city girl with the never-ending con, and the resurrected princess? But wasn't that the dream? Being royalty, putting on the red dress, the centerpiece in a parade while millions watched on? Maybe so—but the thought made Kara recoil.

"You have a DNA cipher," Pavel said.

"That's what it is?" Kara reached into her pocket and produced the wooden cylinder she'd taken from Julian. Aly would have been fascinated. He would've taken it apart and rearranged it, and she would have watched the fine movements of his hands—easing pieces in and out of place as he bit his lower lip, theorizing where it had been made and who could have sent it.

"It's responsive to your fingertips alone. I detect sample cells that match yours embedded in the fiber of the wood."

"That's . . . kind of gross. But kind of cool." It sounded like something Lydia would have loved—had she left this for her, or had the Lancer? Excitement shot through her again at the thought that this message was made for her, and her alone.

She placed it on the floor in front of her and that same blue beam emitted, producing a holo of the galaxy. The Outer Belt edged out of the frame. As she stood there on the roof staring at the image, Kara felt like she was practically flying, headed toward the Desuco Quadrant, past Tinoppa and Naidoz and finally the tiny dwarf planet called Ralire. She watched as the holo zeroed in, past the atmosphere, farther, farther, until she could see topography and finally an aerial view of a city. Then the words unfurled across the skyline.

The past is gone, but the future you seek is here: 678.900.05.

"Those coordinates are on Ralire." Pavel emitted a red pointer beam and circled a section on the northern hemisphere of the dwarf planet. "Twelfth celestial body from the sun. I don't comprehend how you can seek your future there."

"It's not literal," Kara said. If the message was only for her, then it was referring to *her* past—her past as Josselyn Ta'an, the one that Lydia had taken away. It had to be. Which meant . . . "I think this is talking about the overwriter."

"You and Alyosha had always discussed the possibility of it being on Wraeta."

"Because that's what Lydia told us." Kara leaned forward and pivoted the cylinder on the floor, so the coordinates grew a little bigger, a little brighter. "But what if someone moved it?"

Or what if Lydia had lied?

"Are you suggesting we go to Ralire?" Pavel asked. "Two-thirds of the planet is covered in black ice, with prairies and valleys in the southmost region—but it also has the most crime of any habitable body in the system. It's not safe."

But when was the last time Kara felt safe anyway?

The beach.

The memory came to her smoothly, quietly, like it always did. She and Lydia had moved around a lot, but for a while they lived in Luris, a town in the north of Kalu—cold and gray, by dark waters on a rocky shore, where Kara would watch crabs crawl in and out of layers of wet rock. A choppy ocean, and a forest at her back. It was her favorite place in the world.

"You have to be careful," Lydia had told her one day.

Kara remembered how her long hair whipped in the wind, stinging her face and getting in her mouth. But she liked the bite of the air and refused to put on a jacket. She'd just gotten over a bad headache, and it felt like she'd woken up from a deep sleep.

Now, Kara realized it really *had* been a kind of awakening. Because that day on the beach had been her first day as Kara.

That memory wasn't just any memory: It was Kara's *first* memory. Even though she'd been about twelve years old.

"I might not always be around to take care of you," Lydia had tried to explain then.

At the time, Kara had listened without really understanding. But the context of it now felt wrong; she saw the lie for everything it was. Lydia's idea of taking care of her had been to use the overwriter on her, to erase all memory of being Josselyn Ta'an.

Then Lydia had grabbed her hands so tightly that Kara had dropped all the smooth rocks she'd been collecting. "If something happens to me," Lydia had said that cold day on the beach, "I need you to think through all your options, to stay safe . . ."

But where would playing it safe get her now? There was a dangerous weapon out there. One that could steal memories, mine them. It could erase entire histories and make new ones. It could reinvent the world, for the worse.

"Nothing is safe anymore," Kara said to Pavel.

"Does this mean we're going to Ralire, then?"

Kara nodded. "As soon as we break out Aly from wherever they've got him."

It turned out there was a single internment camp on Nau Fruma, hastily set up just a few hundred meters from the old marketplace. Aly had to be there, along with all the other Wraetans and Fontisians the UniForce had rounded up.

Kara and Pavel spent the next twenty-four hours monitoring the camp from a new lookout point, watching security guards rotate shifts. They figured out a time—a precise fraction of a moment—Kara could slip in unnoticed and break Aly out.

Rhiannon's televised coronation would provide the perfect distraction.

Meanwhile, Kara managed to pocket tools from the vendor stalls in the central square, and secured a prison guard uniform off the black market that cost all the credits she could scramble together.

When she got back to their new lookout spot, Pavel was furiously beeping and blinking as he rolled toward her.

"I have something!" he said, projecting a holo of a line graph.

"What am I looking at?" Kara said, squinting at the screen.

"When the last round of overwriter research turned up nothing, Alyosha directed me to continue combing the holoforums."

"He didn't tell me that." Her heart beat faster. Why hadn't she and Aly talked about it together?

"He requested we keep it private, so as not to elevate your hopes if attempts were futile. However, I pieced together some information on a hunch . . ."

Kara very much doubted Pavel had hunches so much as algorithms, but sure. "Well?"

He blinked his blue eyelights. "I found a mention of a testing facility on Wraeta, and I cross-referenced it with the G-1K summit dates prior to Diac Zofim's death," he said. Diac was the scientist Lydia told them about—the one who'd pioneered the overwriter tech and ended up suspiciously dead immediately after. "And finally, the frequency of times Emperor Ta'an mentioned new technology in his speeches."

The Emperor? Kara wondered. It wasn't a variable she would have thought to include.

"And I found this . . ." It was formatted like an official memo, written in a language she didn't recognize. It shared *some* qualities with the Kalusian characters, but the lines were simpler. When Pavel activated the translation screen, the letters blurred apart and rearranged themselves in modern Kalusian.

"New developments in the biotech device . . . Deletion or overwriting of the cube may result in memory loss . . . work suggests that new technology for targeted memory deletion is not far off . . ." Kara read along quickly, not sure what she was reading but with the sensation she was tumbling down a slope, faster and faster, toward an inevitable crash that would hurt—but at least the falling would end. ". . . furthermore, targeted memory deletion on a mass scale is achievable if the cube-using public were uniformly updated with the latest technology so that specific molecular mechanisms can be identified and wiped . . ."

Kara sucked in a breath. She knew of the overwriter's capabilities because it had been used on her. But targeting masses of the public, deleting specific memories all in one stride— it seemed particularly invasive, and particularly difficult. Had Lydia known?

We'd be shells, Lydia had said of the overwriter. *Every memory— every part of your mind that makes you* you—*ripped out.*

Is that what she'd hinted at when they'd been escaping from the prison on Houl? Is that what Nero was attempting on the scientists she and Aly had seen on the zeppelin? They were vacant, childlike, drawing triangles obsessively for no reason. Had they lost their minds to this experimentation?

We'd be shells . . .

And what would anyone want to erase on a mass scale?

There were more facts and figures that Kara's mind skipped over until she got toward the final fragment: ". . . as the political divide is insurmountable with our current history. This provides the necessary justification . . . for the memory of the Great War itself to be erased from the collective memory, for the good of the people and advancement of the galaxy . . ."

"Kara," Pavel said, letting the translation drop so the words rearranged into the original text. "Do you recognize the language?"

She shook her head, half in response to Pavel, half in disbelief at what she'd read. "Some sort of ancient Kalusian, I'm guessing?"

"Yes. It's no longer spoken, or taught to the public," Pavel said. "It's Royal Kalusian. It's a language passed down only through the royal lineage, and read only by the highest in the Ta'an cabinet."

Understanding dawned on her. Her skin started to prickle.

"What are you saying?"

"That this was written to the Emperor Ta'an himself."

"Turn on the translator again." When the words arranged themselves into a language she could read, Kara scanned down to the bottom.

"Executive Order 10642."

Her father had signed his name right under it. Emperor Ta'an had not only known of the overwriter technology—he'd planned to use it.

FOUR

ALYOSHA

THE guards kept saying it was a "camp," and no one was going to call them out on it. The prisoners wouldn't even talk about it with each other. It made sense, Aly guessed. Throughout the whole history of humankind, people had always been in a rush—taking shortcuts, dropping words, slurring phrases together. "Good morning" became "morning," and "don't worry about it" became "no worries," and "what's going on" became "what goes." And so "internment camp" just became "camp."

It had been two days since Aly and Kara had been separated during the protests. Two days since Aly had been taken in by the UniForce, despite the fact that Nau Fruma was technically neutral. Two days. But already it felt like an eternity.

He had kicked and screamed and got the *taejis* beat outta him. They were cowards, all of them, taking a cheap shot to the back of his head before he could even shout for Kara to keep going. Not knowing where she was drove him crazy now. All kinds of things could've happened to her. It was a war; soldiers became monsters. And Rhiannon had put a target on Josselyn's back, whether or not she'd meant to. It scared him to think how many people were looking around for Kara—and how many of them might try and get a higher price from Nero for delivering Josselyn dead.

And now he wasn't there to protect her.

It was all his fault; he hadn't followed his instincts to take her hand and hitch a ride the hell off this moon, to the edge of the galaxy. Just disappear, take care of his. Being with Kara messed with his head like that, made him think that if they could get a person like her on the Kalusian throne, then all of them had a damn decent future ahead of them. A chance at peace.

But that had been a pipe dream, a fantasy he'd been swept up in—and now he'd paid the price. They might have been rounding up only Wraetans and Fontisians, but who knew what they'd do with a Kalusian girl aiding and abetting the enemy. And who knew what would happen if they found out that Kalusian girl was actually the Empress of Kalu.

Aly knelt in front of a makeshift altar littered with statues of Vodhan in different sizes. Some people had brought them from their homes—a last-second grab before they were forced into the camps. And some of them were made here, carved out of a fine white talc that dissolved a little bit more every day.

There wasn't a ceiling, meaning the dust floated in and coated everything. The walls were stained and grimy with handprints, the whole place overrun with rats longer and leaner than any he'd ever seen, because of the lower gravity. The air was thick with the scent of close, unwashed bodies. It was worse than the Wray, which was saying a whole lot.

Initially, Aly wasn't praying at this makeshift altar so much as avoiding the chaos of the hangar's back lot. But he grabbed a loop of prayer beads tangled at the feet of the statues and held it in his hand, clutching one between his thumb and his knuckle as he said Vodhan's prayer. He'd said it a thousand times before—mumbled it under his breath without much thought to the words, rushing through the calls and responses so the Fontisian missionaries would let him run out of the church tent and play. Even now, praying made him antsy, like there was something else he should be doing. Scheming, strategizing, figuring out his next move. But in that quiet moment, as soon as he closed his eyes the words came back to him—that prayer emerging from that dark, murky ocean sloshing around in his skull.

It had come to him, that wisp of a long-term organic memory, like it had traveled on a current all the way around the world to come back to him, to bring him home. He said the words. He prayed. Aly didn't know if he'd ever felt Vodhan's spirit more than he did in this moment.

The hangar that housed the internment camp opened up to a fenced-in outdoor area, which was guarded by UniForce soldiers standing at intervals all the way around. The UniForce's "peace-keeping unit" hadn't split up the Fontisian and the Wraetan prisoners; why would they? Wraeta and Fontis were technically on the same side—both actively anti-Kalusian and thus, according to the backward logic of Nau Fruma, a latent threat to the moon's sworn neutrality. Detaining them in the first place was an act of martial law, which seemed to mean Nau Fruma's security police could basically do whatever they wanted.

It was a load of *taejis*—not just because of the moon's true allegiance to Kalu, thinly disguised as neutrality, but because they were oblivious to the tensions between the Fontisians and Wraetans. What else would anyone expect? It was *Fontis* that had colonized Wraeta long before Kalu had blown his planet to bits. Fontis that scooped the Wraetans up like a bully with someone else's toy, mined the entire surface for all the precious minerals that didn't exist anywhere else in the galaxy, brought in their precious god Vodhan. And then what? They'd roped Wraeta into wars they'd never wanted a part of. So many of his own would never forget that. Some hated Fontis almost as much as they hated Kalu.

The guards would have had to be *blind* if they didn't see those tensions. Slurs like *Vodhead* and *dusty* were thrown all across the camp, and it didn't matter to anyone working there; it was no skin off anyone's back if the two groups tore each other apart. But they'd separated themselves with an aisle down the middle of the lot, as wide as the Ismee River. Everyone treated it like snake-infested water. Cross it and you'd be liable to get yourself killed.

For the most part, Aly had been treated okay by the other prisoners—tons of them recognized him from the holovision show *The Revolutionary Boys*, knew he'd been accused of killing Princess Rhiannon and acquitted by default when she'd announced she was alive over holo. Which meant Aly was a big hero. Hugs, high fives, claps on the back as soon as anyone got close enough to touch him. He was a celebrity all over again, and he hated it. What had he done for any of them? Not a damn thing.

Now he had to turn it on, smile like he did for the cameras, more people to impress and more shit to make up for. Besides, being charming was his best friend and costar Vin's job. And now, having all these people who treated him like hot stuff just because he had the decency to not kill the princess seemed twisted. But they didn't know what he'd done—that his own petty nonsense had gotten Vin killed in the crash over Naidoz. That he'd broken out of a jail on Houl and left all the other prisoners behind. That way back when, he'd passed as Kalusian, abandoned his own history and his own people, just because it was easier if folks didn't consider him a *dusty*.

No. He didn't deserve to be famous, and he didn't want to be either. It was the reason he'd been chosen to blame in the first place. He was easy to pick off then and, he was worried, just as easy to pick off now. Aly thought a lot about whoever had framed him. Whose decision was it to point at this black guy's holo image and say *Him*? Was it personal, and were they tracking him now? He couldn't shake the feeling that any minute he would get dragged away and accused all over again on yet another public forum. No way he'd been absolved for real.

The paranoia made him look around now. Most of the inmates were obsessed with their handhelds, tech some of them had smuggled in. The guards looked the other way, because they were too lazy or didn't care, but usually the inmates at least pretended to hide them. Now, though, they weren't even bothering; dozens of holoscreens shimmered throughout the room. Only then did Aly remember that today was the day Empress Rhiannon was supposed to return to Kalu. How could he have forgotten?

The scene was somehow worse replicated across so many different handhelds in the crowd. The Empress was there now on the holoscreen. Petite, yet regal, with a slight frown stretched across her brow. She was wearing the ceremonial red. And she was . . . getting egged.

Riots were spreading through the capital city of Sibu. Aly closed his eyes, felt the blood cement in his veins. For years people had fawned over the girl, and when she was younger they'd given her a half-assed name like "Rose of the Galaxy," built her up as the orphan princess trapped in her desert tower—then turned on her in thirty seconds flat. Once she was partway to being a woman and not just some little girl, they made her a symbol they could point their fingers at, blame her for their terrible lives. His heart half broke for the girl, but it didn't surprise him, not even a little bit. Aly knew better than anyone how the public listened to the first thing they heard if a guy like Nero said it.

Onscreen, a glass bottle shattered at Rhiannon's feet, and someone—a Fontisian guard, of all folks—grabbed her and threw her over his shoulder like she was no more than a kid. Which was pretty much true. She was only sixteen.

And she was Kara's little sister.

He still hadn't wrapped his head around it all: that he'd fallen for a Ta'an. The true *empress*, though she seemed to hate thinking of it. She preferred he still call her Kara and not her real name . . . Josselyn.

And she'd liked him back. Not that they'd ever talked about it, on account of being on the run for their lives the whole time they'd been together. But he'd felt it in their kiss, in the heat of her touch, in the stubborn way she'd stuck with him when anyone else in the galaxy would have walked away for good. And now, with Rhiannon's return made official, Aly should be a free man—and he and Kara should've been safe.

Nope. Almost as soon as he'd tasted freedom, it was yanked away from him once again. Here he still was. Separated from Kara and Pavel. He'd told the little man to go find Kara, but he couldn't help but worry the droid had been relegated to some far-flung scrapyard. War was raging everywhere, even on the most protected, peace-loving moon in the galaxy.

The mood in the camp was mixed. Some folks were shaking their heads, looking smug, like they'd seen it before and they'd seen it coming. Like Aly, most of the Wraetans weren't surprised about the *taejis* of a reception the Princess just got. Some of them were probably glad too. The Ta'ans had technically saved their butts in the Great War—by ending it—but only after making a mess of their entire planet. And in the process they'd displaced Wraetans, scattering them around the galaxy in Wray Towns that were nearly as bad as this camp. Even now, the damage inflicted by the Great War made Aly's mind reel. Its legacy threaded itself into him, made it so the anger shaped his present and future. How could you undo something like that?

Some of the Fontisians, however, especially the ones old

enough to remember the Great War, didn't look all that smug about Rhiannon's wobbly reception. Probably because the writing was on the wall: Not even the Ta'ans could stabilize things now. Things were notching up toward a full-scale war, and pretty soon, Aly's gut told him, every single piece of rock in the galaxy would be tainted with the stink of death.

Aly's cube buzzed suddenly, and he ripped his gaze from the holoscreen, scared, adrenaline coursing through him. They'd forced him to turn his cube back on once they'd imprisoned him in the camps, and forced a cube update that was about halfway complete. He could only think of one other update in the last few years, and there was a lot of lead-up—a big campaign to outline the perks, and a safety warning to update in the night since it took processing power and made you drowsy. No warning with this one, though. He didn't like it one bit, but he had no choice.

Now, a cube notification was how they summoned the prisoners in waves—so they'd come to the fence for food or water or a "shower," which was really just a hose on full blast that pushed through the chain-link fence. He hadn't showered yet; he was avoiding it as long as he could. He was no animal.

When he looked around, no one else seemed to react. Which could mean he was going to get his ass beat. No witnesses. Or even worse, that whoever had framed him had found him.

Aly trembled, nearly frozen until his cube buzzed again, this time stronger, like it would when he used to get priority calls from UniForce headquarters. When he closed his eyes he saw the designation "Vestibule 17" flash across his eyelids. Running parallel to the fence, nearly flush with it, the Vestibules were dark, rectangular boxes that felt like confessional booths. They provided privacy while your ass was getting kicked by a guard, and conveniently, being penned in by an electric chain-link fence was the quickest way to remind anyone you might as well be an animal to the UniForce soldiers.

It would get worse the longer he waited, so he slipped out of the crowd and made his way toward the meeting place. He'd been to a prison once before on Houl, but he knew what guards were like—guys who needed to feel big by treating you like *taejis*. Sometimes being compliant and chill wasn't enough. Sometimes you had to act like you were excited to be ordered around; you did what you had to because your life depended on it.

Moonlight framed the soldier. He had a small build. Compact, feet planted firmly on the ground. The guard didn't say anything, so Aly didn't either. Didn't matter how small he was. With a stunner in your hand you didn't need to be bigger. You just needed to be heartless.

The guard came closer, and Aly took half a step back.

"It's me," a girl's voice whispered.

Kara.

"How?" Aly moved forward but she shook her head. In the distance, he saw another guard—a real guard—pause on his rounds. He needed to pretend he was still being bossed around by a guard, but he was nearly losing his mind with relief, happiness. But then he realized where they were, and what she'd risked. "You shouldn't be here," he said. "You need to leave."

"Um . . . you're welcome for coming to save you?" He couldn't see her face in the dim moonlight, but he heard it in her voice: She was offended, and hurt.

"I'm not messing around," Aly said. He didn't have time to spare her feelings. Not now. Not when there was so much at stake. He lowered his voice and looked behind him quickly. "The place is crawling with UniForce. You're too important to be running around the moon."

"Couldn't agree more. That's why we're leaving. Pavel is waiting for us in the market." So the droid *had* found her. Fear gave way to relief. They'd been together, looked out for each other.

Kara ducked further into the shadows and pulled back a patch of fence, squeezing through it to freedom.

He glanced behind him. The guard had moved on. And this portion of the fence was protected from the robotic view of the daisies by the Vestibules.

He shimmied through the opening she'd cut, and together they ran in silence across the desert swells. A hundred meters from the camp, he stopped her. He couldn't wait any longer, though they were still close enough to be visible to the guards, if someone on the tower happened to point a scope their way.

He took her in his arms without a word. He could feel her body heat, feel the curve of her hip through the fatigues she wore. Their mouths were so close. This was all he'd thought about for days.

His body took over. His hands moved up to cup her face, and his mouth found hers. It didn't matter that his lips were chapped, or that hers were.

It wasn't like any kiss they'd had before. It was urgent, desperate, tinged by the war and the violence and every terrible thing that had come to pass in the weeks they'd known each other—all mixing with the hope in his chest that grew and grew until everything else was cast aside. He kissed her so she'd know how grateful he was. She'd come back for him.

Aly tilted his head and Kara pressed her hands against his cheeks, pulling him closer. He held her tight, his hands moving up her back. His lips moved away from her mouth and to her cheeks, then brushed her ear before he dragged them down her neck and felt her shudder. His lips would go everywhere. He'd go anywhere if it meant this.

Was this love? *Choirtoi.* Yes. Yes, it was love. He'd tell her now. He grabbed her face and kissed her again. But Kara pulled herself away, and he felt himself sucked down into the wake of her absence. Her face caught the moonlight. Their fingers were intertwined, palm to palm, and he realized he still had the prayer beads. He slipped the bracelet from his wrist to hers.

"Aly," she whispered, her eyes tracking up and down his face. "Were you praying?"

"I prayed for you," he said.

She squeezed his hand. "We have to hurry."

Suddenly he felt disoriented. Confused too. He turned to look back at the camp, nestled between the giant dunes, casting lightsmear toward the stars. "What about the rest of the prisoners?"

Kara hesitated. "We can come back . . ."

"How?" Aly took a step away from her. "When?"

Then, behind them, a shout. Aly saw figures silhouetted against the floodlights, gesturing in his direction. More shouting. An alarm began to sound. Kara knew to move before he did; she pulled him back and he stumbled before he could get his feet working and break out into a run.

There was a screaming in his ears. No—a screaming in the air. In the sky.

It wasn't until way too late that he saw it: a third planetary body. *A moon?* he thought stupidly. It was bigger than even Kalu from where he stood, and it was getting bigger—*closer.* Falling from the sky. Then, it got so loud he couldn't hear himself think; the noise crowded out everything, the shape growing even larger as it hurtled toward the camp.

Aly grabbed Kara's hand and double-timed it past the crest of the next dune. He dragged her over and brought her head to his chest, both of them squatting, bracing for an explosion. But though the asteroid—or whatever it was—must have hit, Aly felt nothing but a slight change in the air. A ripple. A vibration.

Kara pushed away from him. "What—?"

Her words were swallowed by a massive halo of light exploding across the world. He brought his hand to his face to shield his eyes. He could almost call it pretty. The sky lit up with what looked like lightning, and there was a crash like a million thunderbolts, a sound that seemed to ricochet toward them in slow motion.

Aly felt his cube connection flicker, then cut out.

The world went dark.

Dark, and loud—everyone, all at once, began to shout.

"An em-bomb?" he said to himself. It was an enormous electromagnetic pulse that would fry everything operated by electricity. They'd been banned by a decades-old treaty, but for years there had been whispers of planets hoarding em-bombs, building them, trading them. *Scare tactics*, Aly had always thought. Hoped.

But when he scrabbled to the top of the dune, he saw that it was true. From where he stood, it looked like a targeted attack: portions of Nau Fruma still appeared to be unaffected, and lights twinkled from distant buildings. UniForce wouldn't have disabled their own internment camp. Could someone be staging a coup?

Kara staggered to her feet, reached out her hand and found his. There was sand between their palms, in their fingernails. "We need to get on a craft while we still can."

Aly shook his head, looking out over the dune. A prisoner ran out of the hole Kara had cut in the fence, then another and another. More streamed out behind him. If the em-bomb had succeeded, he could only imagine the chaos inside.

"We can't just leave them," he said.

An explosion went off, this time louder. There was an orange light coming from above the camp, and he knew it was fire before he saw it. He could smell the smoke. Aly peeked over and saw people streaming out of the camp now, some of them clashing with guards as they fled.

"Aly." She tugged on his hand before he could move. "All of this—everything that's happening now—it's all Nero's fault. I can't help if UniForce gets me."

"Is that what you want to do? Help?" His voice was unexpectedly loud. He couldn't help but think of Houl, and all the people they'd left there. But he and Kara had had to escape because of Lydia. Because she'd been dying. They'd had no time. What was his excuse now?

All of a sudden, everything—the internment camp, the round-ups, the em-bomb, the conflict on neutral territory—coalesced into a burning pit of anger deep inside him, pulsating so hard he was afraid that he might explode, just like that bomb. All of this was the fault of those in power, using the rest of the galaxy as their pawns, like the universe was their playground to wage war as they pleased. Aly was sick of it—sick of royals and rulers making the wrong choices.

"Because if you wanted to *help*, you could stop running. Announce yourself. You could take the throne." As soon as he had spit out the words, he was surprised—but more convinced than ever it was true. Maybe Kara could change things. Change the world. "You have to try, right?" It was a solid plan. "Better than taking off on some wild quest to find the overwriter just 'cause you think Lydia wanted you to?"

"And then what, Aly?" Kara's voice rose sharply. "I don't know the first thing about ruling."

"You'd figure it out, Kara." He put his palm to her cheek. He'd memorized every feature, every expression—but Kara's face was different now. It was so slight he might not have noticed, but the time apart made it clear, and it made him feel disoriented, dizzy, like the ground was shifting under him. "You don't need the overwriter to be able to help other people. You do that just fine on your own."

"I need the overwriter because it's *dangerous*. Lydia said as much—she practically *told* me to destroy it—for a reason." She wrenched away from him. Worry notched up his throat. "You don't even know the half of it. What it can do. We might be the only people who know it really exists."

"I'm not coming with you to watch you get killed," Aly said. "I think you're scared of ruling."

"So that's what you're concerned with all of a sudden? Putting me on the throne?" Kara spat out. Those eyes, swirling with color, out of control. "You just want to give up on finding the overwriter?"

"It's not giving up! Look around you—the galaxy is at war!" Aly knew better, but he couldn't stop. "Look. How about we go straight to the capital, find your sister, tell her who you are. Make a game plan for finding the overwriter once we're safe."

"Or maybe they'll accuse me of being an imposter, and stun me on sight!" Kara's voice had risen to a shout. "People have made decisions for me my whole life. Lydia decided that she'd wipe my memory *for my safety*. You're telling me I should leave you here *for my safety*." She'd said the last part like she was bitter, scorn smeared all over her face. "But other people's decisions are the reason I'm here. When do *I* get to choose?"

Aly's jaw clenched. "And what would you choose, Kara? You want to live a lie, pretend you're someone else? Run off to be a hermit in Luris while the world around you burns?"

She actually gasped. Kara had told him once that the beach in Luris was her "happy place," and he'd thought it was so sweet and optimistic. At the time he had wanted to fold up the idea and put it in a pocket over his heart. And now here he was, throwing it in her face.

"*Taejis*, Kara, I didn't mean anything by it . . ." He trailed off. "I know all there is about living a lie, pretending you're someone else because it's easier. Because being you is scary, or because it scares everyone else." He thought of passing for Kalusian, and how hard it was, and how it never ended up being worth it. "What I'm trying to say is, if you don't want to live a lie, it's up to you to change the truth."

He couldn't read her face, but he thought maybe he'd gotten through to her. Or at least she wouldn't be super pissed at him.

"Kara?" he said at the same exact moment a huge thunderclap struck. It was crazy loud. Deafening. His voice—the sound of her name on his tongue—dissolved in the noise.

The gates of the hangar exploded—and people came gushing from all directions as if everyone had woken up from a bad dream at the same time and the anguished cry had woken with them. Through the rise of bright dust, the detainees were all breaking out now, streaming down the hill like a burst volcano.

He made brief eye contact with another Wraetan woman and saw the fear in her eyes.

"What's happening?" She grabbed him and squeezed, like a vise closing around his forearm. Aly felt her anger melting into fear. Her knuckles turned white.

He didn't know. He didn't know anything but a truth born of long experience: When people ran, there was usually good reason to follow their lead.

The crowd surged and then pummeled them forward with it. They barreled over the dunes, past the scrap heap at the edges of the city, funneling into the chaos of streets half-dark and wiped of network. In the distance, through the dust-filled air, he thought he saw the summer palace. Here the crowd was thickening, crushing. They reached a shuttered shop, and Aly hoisted Kara up toward the roof, suddenly afraid of a stampede, of being threshed beneath all those stumbling bodies. The shouting—and screaming—was getting louder. Kara made it onto the roof. He was about to follow—

Then another flash of light. Brighter than the first. Impossible. The ground pulsed once, and an invisible force threw them sky-high. Aly tried to grab for Kara's hand, but there was nothing except air. He was blind and deaf, suspended . . . until he crashed to the ground and felt pain like a single note playing again and again through his body.

Then, abruptly, it fell silent, and Aly fell into the dark.

FIVE

RHIANNON

"TAEJIS," Rhee murmured for the hundredth time as she exited her quarters. She should have seen it coming. It was classic Nero, she realized: capitalizing fast, within twenty-four hours of her return home, and using Rhee's homecoming as a deflection, to distract the rest of the galaxy from what was happening on Nau Fruma.

Tai Reyanna stood at the center of the antechamber, her body tense as she pressed her finger to her cube. Rhee felt anxious on multiple levels—she was too scared to turn her cube on, but frustrated having to rely on everyone else for up-to-date information. Even Tai Reyanna using her cube put Rhee on edge, but her caretaker had refused to power down. The Tai's stiff, formal white robes folded around her like thick swaths of snow. On the holo before them, the news was projected: The UniForce and the Wraetan-Fontisian Coalition, a vigilante army, were engaged in combat on the neutral moon of Nau Fruma. And it was all because of Nero.

He'd done the unthinkable: While she was supposedly dead, he'd rounded up Wraetans and Fontisians on Nau Fruma soil and interned them illegally using UniForce soldiers.

The WFC had run a rescue mission to free the detainees, claiming the camp was a violation of Nau Fruma's neutrality. They dropped an em-bomb to break open the camp's gates and render anything using electricity useless—even cubes. In retaliation, UniForce dropped a *real* bomb. Now the two armies were going head-to-head, and the ground combat on Nau Fruma had already claimed too many casualties on either side. The rest of the galaxy was in a panic. If neutrality couldn't be respected, nowhere was safe.

And everything had been documented on the holos. Except that DroneVision had never covered the internment on Nau Fruma in the first place. Funny, how Nero had made sure that the subsequent "attack" by the WFC was getting plenty of airtime.

"Have you gotten through?" Rhee asked. She sat down on an ornate chair and then stood up immediately. Her throat was dry, and she couldn't stay still.

Her Tai glanced sideways, giving a small, irritated shake of her head. It was worrisome that no one had briefed Rhee. Tai Reyanna couldn't get through to the UniForce commander on Nau Fruma.

"Their comms must still be out as a result of the em-bomb," Tai Reyanna offered unhelpfully. "And the most recent update might have slowed down communications." But even as she said it, the Tai didn't sound at all convinced. They didn't need to speak the most likely truth: Nero had UniForce's loyalty. The ones stationed here in the capital had barely lifted a finger to protect Rhee when the riots broke out upon her arrival, and Rhee wouldn't dare reach out to any of them now.

In spite of the war in her territories, and the fact that so far Josselyn hadn't come forward—Rhee didn't know whether this was a good or a bad sign—Rhee's thoughts kept returning to Julian. Was he still on Nau Fruma, and was he okay? Did he know she'd killed Veyron, and would he die thinking she had betrayed him? She couldn't tear her eyes away from the screen.

Rhee was already running through the various scenarios in her head. The order would assist, surely. Maybe that's what Nero wanted—to push her closer to Fontis, paint her as out of touch. A traitor. But she couldn't think about that when people were dying. She'd release a broadcast to the Kalusian territories too, urging them to organize, to gather supplies. Any medical staff in proximity would need to make themselves available to travel to the moon. Perhaps she could go herself . . .

"If we can't get through to UniForce, we need to send help."

"Help, *ahn ouck*?" the Tai asked. She fell into a chair; her head scarf came loose, and graying black hair escaped from her temple.

Rhee used to resent the term. It meant *child*, and when she'd heard it she would revert back to the child she was at six. A lonely orphan, a brat, a girl unworthy of her name. But now it reminded Rhee of her family, and tied her closer to the Tai.

"*We* need help, Rhiannon," she sighed. "We're at the mercy of a madman."

"I'm not at anyone's mercy," Rhee insisted as she began to pace the length of a tasseled rug. She'd refused all of Nero's attempts to contact her; there'd been a deluge of comms. "And if I want to establish peace, establish trust, I'll need to neutralize the threat on Nau Fruma."

"How will you neutralize a neutral moon? More armed forces will only mean greater tensions. More violence. And air travel has been restricted—"

"Then I will unrestrict it." Rhee's voice crested to a shout. She felt the anger dissolving everything inside and out. "That place was our home. For years. The people on that moon, they were family—"

"Do *not* lecture me about family." The Tai looked at her with a depth in her eyes that rooted Rhee to the floor. "And think twice before you choose to yell at me."

Rhee bowed her head. "Tai Reyanna . . ." She trailed off, unsure how to structure an apology when she had so much to be sorry for. Her outburst wasn't just embarrassing; it was unfit for an empress. "I dishonor myself. I take your mentorship for granted."

Tai Reyanna took Rhee's hands in her own. "I know you're worried about the people on Nau Fruma. About Julian. But we're not yet certain if he can be trusted . . ."

It was a conversation they'd danced around before. Tai Reyanna hadn't approved of Rhee reaching out to Julian in the first place. She hadn't said why, and she didn't have to. Rhee had considered and refused the possibility that Julian had been working with his father all along, that he might have been a traitor too.

Heat flushed through Rhee; she shook her head. "It's not just about him. The Nau Frumans need to know that I'm going to protect them."

On the holos, another explosion shook Nau Fruma, and the tiny sliver of calm she'd found slipped away. There on the projected image was the violence Nero's hand had reaped. Did he enjoy his cruelty? Did he take pleasure in treating lives as if they were expendable?

Rhee slipped her hands out of her Tai's, trying to silence the panic that was making her ears burn and her head spin. "Does Dahlen know?"

She'd have to find him in this enormous palace. He'd gone off with the Fisherman to scout the property and discuss security detail, his favorite subject as of late. It had been a shock to find that all the servants who'd worked for her family and stayed through Regent Seotra's reign had abandoned the palace. Either they'd been scared off or paid, maybe lured by Nero's promises—but it was a slap in the face, and a further reminder that the Rose of the Galaxy wasn't as precious as she'd once been.

Rhee hastily shoved one foot in her boot and then the other. "I'm going to find Dahlen." They'd need a plan. She wouldn't sit here moping, feeling sorry for herself.

Rhee raced through the palace as Tai Reyanna called after her. The familiar twists and turns, the feel of the elaborate woven rug underneath her, even the smell reminded her of her childhood.

But instead of the bustling energy, the warmth, the interplanetary dignitaries that had filled it with music and company, there was only an eerie silence throughout the halls. In it, an organic memory rose up, and Rhee heard Joss's voice taunting her with its echo.

Come and find me, Joss had called once when Rhee went to chase her. So many years she'd spent chasing the sister who wanted nothing to do with her. Who called her a baby, taunted her. Even now her sister's voice flooded Rhee from every direction, driving her mad. She was inept; she'd never be enough; she'd never find her. She couldn't keep up with Joss then, and she couldn't keep up with Nero now.

She hadn't been raised to rule. She wasn't *meant* for it. That was Josselyn's role. But the very person Rhee needed most in the world, the one she'd publicly begged to come home, hadn't appeared. Was she lost or in danger? Or was it the case that Joss didn't want to come forward? Maybe she was smart enough to know what Rhee was only now just learning: Being empress was thankless, hopeless, and it was best to quit before you even started.

It was such a cowardly thing to think—of her sister, and of her role as empress. She dishonored her father's legacy, and Rhee felt the shame burn its way through the surface of her skin, mar her face, her features, so that she would wear it for everyone to see. Maybe everyone saw it already.

When the hallway forked, she made a right, prompting a voice behind her to *tsk*. It was close. Too close. Rhee spun around startled, kicking the arc of a roundhouse—but a Fontisian girl slipped backward, just out of Rhee's reach. Rhee recognized her at once: She had been standing on the steps when Rhee arrived—the one with the yellow-and-orange eyes.

Now, she was wearing a dark tunic that squared at her shoulders, like many others of the Fontisian order did. Her blonde braid was now coiled in a bun.

"Who are you? Why are you following me?" Rhee fired out questions quickly, to conceal her embarrassment: The girl was part of the guard that Dahlen oversaw.

"I didn't mean to startle you." She wore her bow and arrow strapped to her back. Her ears were slightly pointed, like Dahlen's. "I'm Lahna."

Rhee straightened up, smoothing her dress, trying to preserve some semblance of dignity. "You're one of the archers?"

The girl raised her eyebrows, so light they were nearly white. She gestured to the bow behind her. "Does it not appear so?"

The gesture felt familiar. Then Rhee remembered she had seen Lahna on Erawae too: She had been sparring in the courtyard when Rhee had met with the Fontisian Elder, Escov. He'd revealed that Josselyn was still alive. That the order had helped hide her—so thoroughly that even they didn't know where Joss had gone.

"Where's Dahlen? We'll have to arrange for aid to Nau Fruma. There's been—"

"A bombing. I know." The girl pivoted on her heel and began to walk away. "I'm not to delay." If it was an invitation, it was hardly a compelling one. Still, Rhee followed.

"Where are we going?" she asked, quickly falling into step with the girl. Of course Dahlen already knew. He always knew.

There are things he knows, and things he doesn't know he knows. It's what Elder Escov had told Rhee on Erawae—that Dahlen had some critical piece of information and kept it hidden deep within, even from himself.

"The north wing study, which Dahlen has turned into a strategy room. He's arranging for aid to the moon. He set up a briefing as soon as we heard of the bombings," she said, her eyes panning left and right as they walked briskly down the hall.

"Good," Rhee said. Dahlen understood her. Movement, action, strategy. But something irked her, tugged at the edge of her nerves. "And how long ago did the situation room and Dahlen's strategy come together?"

"I can't decipher your real question, Empress. Please oblige me and ask it outright."

"Aren't you the same kind of charming as Dahlen," Rhee shot back, "which is to say, not at all." She immediately regretted firing back, if only because she wore her embarrassment on her sleeve.

Lahna smiled, as if satisfied with Rhee's reaction. *Ancestors.* Who cared what this girl thought? It was true there was a deeper, veiled question. She'd become empress to take control of her destiny, and that of her planet. And yet since the very second she'd stepped into the role, things were constantly done for her—without her input. She was as powerless as she'd always been.

"What I meant to ask," Rhee stated evenly, in her best diplomat's voice, "is if Dahlen sent for me? If he'd intended to consult me at all?"

Lahna stopped abruptly and cocked her head. Her eyes narrowed, and the left side of her mouth tilted the tiniest bit higher. "Don't you smell roses?" she asked.

Rhee was irked by the girl's misdirection. "What?"

"Roses," Lahna repeated, frowning. She obviously wasn't going to let it drop.

Rhee looked around and realized they were passing through the east wing. "My mom's garden—it's right outside. You can see it from this window." She crossed the threshold into a guest room. A breeze fluttered the curtains, cool despite the season. It would rain soon, and Rhee loved the hot thunderstorms of her childhood. She moved toward the window, but Lahna grabbed her forearm and yanked her down to her knees. For a second, Rhee's breath caught: They were so close she could make out the fringe of Lahna's eyelashes, see the soft lines of her mouth . . .

She pulled away forcefully. "Are you out of your mind?"

But before she could stand, an arrow sailed through the window, cleaving the air directly where Rhiannon had stood, even as Lahna shoved her roughly backward.

She came up against the wall and gasped. "How did you know?"

"The window should have been kept closed," Lahna answered curtly.

Three more arrows whistled as they cut through the air, and Lahna unsheathed a sword with a speed Rhee had never seen. It was a blur, the metal reflecting light for a split second as she whipped the blade through each one in turn. She dropped to her knees again and rolled right up against the wall beneath the window, shoulder to shoulder with Rhee.

More arrows soared through. A dozen. Two dozen. White ribbons attached to the shafts looked almost beautiful as they whipped and trailed. Rhee could barely think over the noise of the arrows piercing the walls and the furniture. A blizzard of feathers spilled from the pillows. The air shimmered with cotton fluff and sawdust. The girls sat side by side, staring.

And then suddenly, it was quiet. The arrows had stopped, and in the vacuum Rhee could hear her own heartbeat. She let out a shallow breath.

Then there was the drumming of footsteps down the hall, then Dahlen's voice moving from the hallways of the great palace and further away. She could tell he was outside now as he and his guards combed the gardens. The smell of roses only intensified; they were slicing through her mother's bushes with their blades, hacking through the growth. Rhee willed herself not to cry.

The room was suddenly full of her guard: guards pulling her to her feet, guards asking her if she was all right, guards muttering and speaking in code. The Fisherman carefully shouldered his way into the room. His blue skin had turned a shade of purple as if he'd flushed with anger, and the features crowded along the bottom of his face looked puckered and angry. An unlikely ally who hailed from the Outer Belt, he'd helped Rhee disguise herself as a Marked child on Tinoppa by attaching the octo-erces to her face. He had also saved her life—and Dahlen's—by ripping the ceiling off the facility on Houl with a harpoon gun and ushering them to safety.

"Who left the window open?" Dahlen's shout rose up from out below them.

The Fisherman gave the room a sweeping look of disdain. A hundred ribbons shuddered on the hundred arrows embedded in the door.

"A soon-to-be-dead man," the Fisherman said. "I'll weed out the traitor." His eyes met Rhee's for a moment, and he nodded just before he exited, saying nothing further.

Rhee moved away from her guards and bent to pull the ribbon off a nearby shaft. "That bastard," she said.

Tai Reyanna pushed inside the room. The tan skin around her eyes was creased with worry as she grabbed a handful of the ribbons. "All the notes say the same thing."

Welcome back, Empress. I won't be ignored.

Your presence is humbly requested at the Towers of the Long Now.

Nero's residence.

Lahna stepped through the maze of arrows that had pierced themselves into a pattern on the floor. "He's not very subtle, is he?"

"No," Rhee said. "Madmen seldom are."

SIX

ALYOSHA

HE tried to call out, but the pressure on his chest was too much. Last thing he remembered, he and Kara had taken shelter behind a sand dune. He must have been thrown in the blast.

Kara. Where was she? He hoped there was magic in the world. He wouldn't die. She wouldn't either.

The pain was unbearable. Stupid. He was wavering in and out of awareness and could hear wailing, people calling for one another, tiny vibrations in the debris that surrounded him.

He clawed his way into consciousness. *Here here here*, he tried to call out. Instead he just thought it. *Kara. I'm here. I'm sorry.* Then darkness took him again.

He heard a motor, the familiar sound of all-terrain wheels spinning their way through the sand. Far away? Maybe not. His hearing was still shot from the blast, but at least the cloak of darkness lifted. His eyes hurt from the light. He blinked, but all he could see was the blinding brightness.

"Alyosha!" Pavel's voice. "I've been looking for hours." Pavel's ridiculous robovoice that he'd never, ever change to sound more human. Pavel had survived. He'd found him.

Aly tried to answer, but he coughed instead. His eyes ached from the light.

"Where's Kara?" he managed to whisper.

"I haven't found her," Pavel said. "I'm hooked into the database and monitoring the descriptions of survivors. I came for you first."

"What happened?" His head throbbed. Everything hurt. He pushed himself up to his elbow only to fall down again. At least he had all his pieces; he went one by one through every limb and figured he could move each one when the time came. At least there was that.

He lifted his head and saw there were soldiers sorting through what was left of the camp. Debris had somehow made it all the way into the dunes thirty meters out.

"What happened?"

"The WFC dropped an em-bomb, presumably to free the prisoners."

Aly nodded. It was the first one that dropped when he and Kara were running for the dunes. "But there was a second one," he said. The explosion was the last thing he remembered before he and Kara were torn apart.

"A second bomb was deployed by the UniForce over the center of Nau Fruma. There's now a skirmish in the marketplace in the aftermath."

"So who has boots on the ground?"

"Apparently, everyone," Pavel said.

Slowly, things were taking shape: silhouettes, colors, moving forms against a scrim of white. A cargo craft lifted off the ground above the camp, packed so full of people someone was about to fall out. They were Wraetans and Fontisians—people he'd been interned with. They were escaping, thank Vodhan.

It was the same type of cargo craft he'd boarded as a kid during the Wraetan evacuation, a WFC vehicle. Lots of kids from the Wray had joined up when they first came through. He remembered watching them go, jealous that someone could just leave the Wray behind. Aly had wanted to leave too, abandon that little crap town and leave behind everything and everyone in it, most of all his dad.

But he hadn't joined the WFC. Even at that age, he was done with Wraetans and Fontisians, done living under Vodhan's rules and feeling guilt every time something felt good. So he'd gone and passed for a Kalusian, joined the UniForce instead.

And now, the very WFC he'd fancied himself too good for had come to save him. It was a sign, from Vodhan maybe. Or maybe just a big fat coincidence, but it didn't matter. He'd take it.

"We need to find Kara." Aly pulled himself to his feet and dusted off, weaving back and forth as he made his way over the dunes. The sand was definitely shifting below him, but it felt like the world was spinning; he was dizzy, and practically clawed his way up to get a better vantage point of the camp.

"There are aid workers arriving now," Pavel continued, following him. He might have said more, but they crested a dune and took in the view. Past the camp was the town of Nau Fruma, now teeming with screaming civilians. Aly saw people clutching each other, some with bloody limbs or torn antennae or bruised faces or bleeding gills. But no Kara.

Nau Fruma had always been a diverse hub of trade and diplomacy, but now it struck Aly particularly like a shaken microcosm of the whole universe all in one tiny marketplace, thrown together and turned upside down, no one knowing who to trust or where to run. It was still night, but on Nau Fruma it never got completely dark, just a tepid gray. The mass hysteria in the streets made it seem, for a moment, like the smoky, dusty air of the moon had come alive with flailing, crying tentacles.

Kara. She could be anywhere in this madness. Captured by a UniForce soldier or in conflict with the WFC or just swept away by the stampede of panicked Nau Frumans and freed prisoners.

Why had he pushed her like that? Talked all that *taejis* about her coming back, told her what to do? Aly knew as well as any-one what it was like when people told you what to do, who to be, made you twist yourself inside out so that your own soul was unrecognizable.

The fighting had torn through the marketplace and, like a storm, passed on to other neighborhoods. The crowds had thinned as people found the med stations that were popping up, or fled, as some soldiers went down and the first wave of the WFC took off, escorted by a blaze of escape pods holding Wraetans and Fontisians who'd been innocently detained. Could Kara be in one of them?

Aly was cursed. No, no—he was just really goddamn stupid. Only he could've messed this up the way he had. It was the second time she'd saved him and he'd pushed her away.

If he just shut his eyes, maybe he could feel where she was. Maybe they'd come together somehow, through a magnetism he couldn't explain or describe. A heat, a need, a longing.

He should have told her when he had the chance how important she was, how much she meant to him—instead of running his damn mouth off. There were a thousand other things he should've said. *I'll never leave. I'll never give up. I'll never let them hurt you.* So many *nevers*—he thought his heart and lungs would burst from the weight of all of them.

It wasn't working. Vin would've told him to visualize, but with every second the dread clawed at him.

He pushed through the thinning crowds but couldn't find her anywhere.

"You may have suffered a concussion," Pavel was saying. He didn't even know how long the droid had been talking to him, hadn't realized that P was still by his side. "If you won't seek treatment I can consult my limited medical databaaaaaaa—" The droid stalled out.

Aly turned, just in time to see a UniForce soldier grabbing Pavel and attempting to power him down.

Aly didn't think. He lunged.

Muscles he didn't know existed screamed as the man brought his scanner down on Aly's shoulder and shoved him backward onto the ground before he had a chance to fight back.

"Don't move." The guy had a stunner drawn now, aimed right at Aly's chest. He loomed over him, and Aly thought he looked like one of the prison guards. Perhaps he was.

"Excuse me," Pavel said, polite, more than the guy deserved. His eyelights were still blinking like crazy. "There is no need for such roughhousing . . ."

In response, the soldier swung his foot and kicked Pavel over. The robot tipped sideways into the dirt, eyes flickering red as his attachments flailed. When Aly moved to help, the soldier struck him once in the ribs with the butt of his scanner.

"I said: Don't. Move."

Even when he pulled it back, Aly could still feel where the blow had landed.

Aly curled in on himself and tried to breathe through the pain. Half his face was in the dirt. His eyes had adjusted by now, and he could see this piece of *taejis*. Aly wanted to charge him. To rip his goddamned throat out. But the stunner was pointed right at him.

And that's when he saw it.

Her.

All he could see was an arm, a hand, a body pinned beneath a fallen pillar. A bag. Her bag.

"Kara!" he screamed again, trying to pull himself up, but the UniForce soldier shoved him right back down. Aly felt his strength flooding out of him in a wave of terror. She wasn't moving. It couldn't be her. It wasn't her. It wasn't Kara.

No. It wasn't her.

Aly crawled toward her. Only twenty feet from where they'd just been standing.

The soldier went after him, booted him back down into the rubble. Dust from the rubble flew everywhere, blinding Aly.

"Get the fuck off me," Aly shouted, rotating and swiping at the guy, feeling the stunner shoot him in the arm, which numbed him for a second. Where was Pavel? He'd lost track of him for now. But still he swiveled, dragged himself in the direction of the rubble pile, the backpack, the girl's body, the arm . . .

It wasn't her. It couldn't be. Kara was alive somewhere. She was not this limp arm, this broken thing.

But when he got closer, he gasped, choking on burning-hot dust. The prayer beads were clutched in her hand, tangled in her fingers.

"Pavel, tell me it's not her."

The droid righted himself as his eyelights flickered in and out. He stuck a thin attachment that looked like a thermometer into the ground. "I detect traces of her DNA . . ."

There was a blur of motion and sound, a screaming ripping through him, ripping through time and space, so that his scream, his pain, existed everywhere at once. Aly yelled Kara's name as he clawed at the pile of rubble on top of her.

"Put your hands on the ground where I can see them," a soldier said from behind. He pressed the cool metal of the stunner down hard on the side of Aly's head so that it bit into his temple. Aly lifted his hands; there was no coming back from a stun in the head. He had seen it in the Wray—guys fried after a run-in with the UniForce. Crazy outbursts. Disorientation. Anger they just couldn't get a lockdown on.

"Don't move," the soldier said, pulling one of Aly's hands down behind his back. His eyes were still locked on Kara's hand underneath a ton of concrete. He made himself pliable as the soldier grabbed his other hand, about to join them behind his back. If he timed it just right he could spin around. The guy was probably wearing the same kind of holster Aly used to wear when he'd been part of the UniForce. It came equipped with a standard-issue blade . . . could he get to it in time?

"Perhaps I can assist," Pavel said just as the soldier tried to join Aly's hands. "He was processed in the camp just two days ago, and he was held—"

The soldier moved his stunner off Aly's head and shocked Pavel. A blue web of electricity crawled up his body. His eyes flickered then went out. Aly knew he couldn't feel pain, not in the same way a human could, but it sure as hell *looked* painful.

Aly used the opportunity to break free and spin around. He leapt up and kicked the soldier on instinct—brought the heel of his foot as hard as he could across the side of the guy's knee. It bent exactly the way it wasn't supposed to, and he cried out in pain as he went down. Aly jumped up and the world flipped. They'd switched places now. The soldier fumbled for the stunner, but Aly kicked it out of his hand, then drove his foot between the soldier's ribs. That was payback for earlier—and for Pavel.

He kicked again. More payback. He was enjoying this: seeing a man struggle and wearing the very uniform he'd been so proud to put on himself. Suddenly it wasn't a stranger Aly was kicking, attacking, with everything he had in him. It was himself on the floor, that stupid kid from the Wray who ran away from home and joined the UniForce, too weak to be himself, thinking the only way to belong was to blend in. Everything Aly had done brought him here, to this moment—and he wanted to destroy himself, the UniForce, the memory of everyone who had died because of him or *in spite* of him. All the memories. All the horrors. All the unfairness. Everything.

But most of all, he wanted to destroy Kara—not the actual Kara, never her, but the *thought* of her. He knew if he turned his head just slightly he'd catch an image of those prayer beads . . .

Aly did it. He looked. The grief wailed away, condensed until there was nothing left but fury. Now he could hardly see through the rage that surged through and around him.

He looked back at the soldier on the ground and landed the heel of his boot square on the guy's face. Didn't matter whose military you fought for, because all these *chortois* were the same, boots on the ground in neutral territory—kick—just to terrorize people, to fuck with them just to make themselves feel big. Kick. They invaded everything, even in the name of peace. Nothing would be the same after this war they'd started all over again.

Blood got on Aly's boot. The solider lifted his hand, silently asking for mercy. Aly drew his leg back to kick again.

"Alyosha!" Pavel said—he'd righted himself for the second time, but something about the droid's movements was off. He wobbled, and his robotic voice came out distant, like he was calling him via holo from another planet. "Enough."

Nothing would ever be enough. But Aly nodded just the same, and stopped like P had told him to. He moved from one body to the other, and kneeled before Kara. He tried again to dig her out, pawing at slabs of concrete, sweat mingling with tears, running down his face so he could taste the salt in his mouth.

An organic memory assaulted him: throwing rocks into the shallow river basin when he heard Ma and Alina had died. The current would sweep the rocks away, around the bend and out of sight. He couldn't hold on to anything.

Another craft landed, then. Aly felt it in the vibrations of the air, in the odd electric silence, in the vividness of the craft's beams. It wasn't a cargo craft. It was Ashbuli class. An attack craft.

He turned to Pavel, but the droid was frozen in place, his eyelights dark. He'd been fried. Aly strained to see in the craft's beams, lighting the dusty darkness and muting everything into one haze.

There, before his eyes, a bunch of soldiers streamed out of the Ashbuli—Wraetan soldiers who were part of the WFC—fanning out in a second wave. He thought of the uprisings he'd been told of as a kid. These were heroes. But they'd come too late. Too late to save him or anything he cared about.

A soldier approached slowly. "Are you okay?" she asked in Wraetan. Her hands gripped her stunner firmly, but she pointed it to the ground, away from him. When Aly shook his head, she said: "When the UniForce manages a second wave, they'll raze this place to the ground."

Fire. It was a common enough UniForce tactic if a territory was too far gone. It killed enemy combatants, but it killed any of their own remaining survivors as well, so their tech couldn't be used against them—and so they'd have no way of giving up sensitive intel.

Aly looked one more time at Kara's limp hand. The Kalusian didn't bury their dead—they burned them.

"It's not safe here," the soldier told him. "If you come with us you'll be granted refugee status."

Aly laughed. Pain spiked up his lungs. "Been there, done that," he said. "I'm not going to be your refugee. I'll be your next recruit."

SEVEN

RHIANNON

RHEE'S anger was like a raging forest fire. She didn't dare extinguish it, but instead imagined it shrinking smaller and smaller, compressing into a tight sphere that she could fit into the palm of her hand and hide away—for now. She'd need to call upon that anger later. It brought her purpose and clarity that propelled her forward in times when she needed the motivation most. But this was the time for diplomacy and strategy. She didn't just need to win the battle; she needed to win the war.

Now she approached the Towers of the Long Now with Dahlen and Lahna on either side. The Towers were oppressive and extravagant all at once, the seemingly perfect home for Nero himself.

"This is unwise," Dahlen warned, though he'd made his stance clear before they'd left, again en route, and then once more as he stood beside her at the entrance to the towers. "Nero cannot be trusted to refrain from slaughtering you where you stand."

"True," Rhee agreed as they walked. "But he could've killed me at any point. He knows it would be political suicide."

"Didn't he use you as a target when he had the Tasinn release dozens of high-velocity arrows?" Lahna asked.

"He was being showy," Rhee said. "Sending a message in the most ostentatious way possible."

"Or the most dangerous way possible." Lahna shrugged.

"And did he not intend to kill you when we were on Houl?" Dahlen couldn't even get halfway through his own sentence without his face twisting—in disgust or pain or both. In actuality, Nero had intended to kill both of them.

"The rules of the game were different then. I'm *here*, on Kalu, with the universe as my witness." She extended both arms as if to demonstrate the size and scope of the galaxy. "He can't just make me disappear."

"And what's to say the rules won't change again?" Dahlen pointed out. "Nero twists the rules when it suits him."

"Don't you think she knows that?" Lahna asked, before Rhee could answer. Lahna was even shorter than Rhee, which meant she was much shorter than Dahlen. But she managed to speak down to him. She was the only one who did. "If the invitation this morning was any indication, we're walking into a death trap."

Rhiannon stared at her suspiciously. "Then why are you smiling?" she asked. Lahna's features had the delicacy of a porcelain doll, so at odds with what Rhee had seen earlier—the intensity, and her skill with the blade.

Lahna shrugged, and tossed her braid behind her as she took her short strides. "Because I want to see how we get out alive."

Rhee pressed her lips together, hoping her silence would end the whole conversation. Maybe Dahlen was right. Maybe it was insane to accept the invitation to meet with the man who'd killed Rhee's family, the one who'd turned her faithful trainer against her and had tried to have her killed—but she needed a cease-fire. She needed him to pull the UniForce out of Nau Fruma and agree not to invade any neutral territories in the future.

She stuck her hand in her pocket and sought out the familiar weight of the coin, turning it over and over again in her fingers, running her thumb along the groove that ran down its center. It may have been a mere souvenir, but Rhee saw it as so much more—a testament to her father's diplomacy and his ability to bring territories together.

Dahlen had assured her that aid had arrived on Nau Fruma; Frontline Physicians had cycled out new medics and took the injured away to safer locations nearby. She still didn't know Julian's status, whether he'd survived, where he was if he had. Tai Reyanna had tried reaching out, to no avail, which meant that his cube was off. And he hated turning his cube off.

This was the know-it-all who had to look up every fact and figure, whose own cube sometimes couldn't keep up with his curiosity—dozens of queries running at once, always something to see and learn. If his cube was off, was he okay?

"Rhiannon," Dahlen said just as they arrived at the base of

the west tower. "Unless your sole purpose is to kill him immediately, I can't imagine what you expect to gain."

The double doors of the elevator were closed, and the chrome reflected their image. It occurred to Rhee how strange a trio they made. And how the one boy she trusted with her life still stood by her side, would follow her up a tower to face the man who'd nearly ruined them.

Once again, she thought of how Nero had forced Dahlen to turn on his cube and thus break his vow to the order. Something in him had changed, and she imagined his heart like a river stone—water seeping into its cracks, freezing with the change of season, fracturing it from the inside out. Nero had done this. And Rhee had to undo it.

The double doors slid open, and three daisies fluttered out to meet them. Dahlen swatted at the DroneVision cameras and kept his head down while Lahna bared her teeth, which made the daisies skitter backward.

The ride was quiet, tense. The elevator was made of glass, and they could see the intricate machinery that pulled them up the seventy flights. Enormous gears. Ropes and pulleys. A delicate machine; a thousand different ways it could break. What she'd meant to tell Dahlen was that she was scared, and needed him—to trust her, to follow her, precisely because what they were doing was so outlandish. He was her anchor, keeping her from losing herself in the undertow of Nero's deceptions.

But now, as two daisies hovered above them, Dahlen wouldn't meet her eye. Lahna seemed oblivious; she leaned forward with her forehead pressed against the glass as the city fell below them.

They were rocketed upward. Rhee felt her stomach lurch. She took a deep breath in, trying to compose herself—to prepare herself to meet Nero face-to-face once more.

When they arrived on the seventieth floor, the door slid open into a modern room. Expansive wooden floors bathed in light, with shiny furniture made up of hard angles and gleaming surfaces. Rhee channeled that ruler buried deep inside her, her legacy, and strode forward with Lahna at her heels. After a second's hesitation, Dahlen followed them, and then the daisies.

It was all glass inside, quiet fountains, sleek. *How second wave*, Tai Reyanna would've said. It was nothing like the palace, which still reflected the tastes of the dynasty—their long, rich history captured in carvings and porcelain and tapestries. Things crafted by hand, centuries ago, handed down and preserved so that the Ta'ans would know from where they had come. The old way. Her father's way. What did stand out was a lush plant that lined the walls. Its vines extended to the ground, with leaves fanning out on either side—a waxy, deep green she hadn't seen since Dahlen's wooden ship. Lahna stood beside her and brought her hand to the leaf; a white residue came off and left fingerprints where her hand had been.

They heard light footfalls from down the far corridor and turned. Always one for a dramatic entrance, Nero entered with his arms extended, flanked by a Tasinn at either side. A handful of daisies clustered around him. He likely went through the footage to ensure his best angles were broadcast, and nothing less.

In a flash of recognition, Rhee realized the man on Nero's left was the same guard, a patch over his left eye, who'd led her to the medical facility where they had drugged Dahlen and forced him to turn on his cube weeks before.

Nero bowed so low Rhee thought he might fall. She willed her face to hide her disgust, and tried to shape it into an approximation of a smile. Pressing her lips together tightly, the corners came up, and her face felt stiff—like ice. It was the best she could do.

"Empress," he said, "safe at last." His blue eyes widened, and his face wore a look of concern and relief. *He's much better at faking it than me*, Rhee thought bitterly. He motioned to a couch, his arm moving languidly through the air. "Sit."

"I'd rather stand," Rhee said just as Lahna collapsed onto the white couch and gave it a bounce.

"Please," Nero said, "I insist."

Rhee snuck a look at Dahlen, who stood behind the couch watchfully, his face neutral—though she knew he was monitoring everyone's movements out of the corner of his eye. She obliged, and noted the couch was rather cushiony, despite its angular design. Then she chided herself for becoming so easily distracted, and her whole body went rigid, alert, determined to focus. Nero had invited her for a reason. He wanted something, and she heard Veyron's voice, his wisdom, whispering from the dead. *You need to be three steps ahead of your opponent, always*, he'd said during their final battle, just before he tried to kill her. Just before he died.

Dahlen cleared his throat loudly, pulling her out of her memory. Daisies zoomed in toward her, and she held perfectly still as he gave her a questioning look. She'd missed something.

Nero eyed them warily. "I was just saying—marveling, really—over the fact that you survived after the *Eliedio* exploded . . ."

That's why she was here. To be interviewed, to tell her story—so it could be picked apart, so he could catch her in a lie and use it against her for all the galaxy to see.

"Those two weeks on the run were difficult," she said slowly, choosing each word carefully. "But it was surviving a barrage of arrows this morning that was the real feat."

Nero touched his finger to his cube, and the daisies went dead. Rhee tried not to show her alarm, though she'd had no idea his cube was capable of that. She thought again of his ambition to find the overwriter, and suppressed a chill.

"You're a phenomenal actor," Rhee said coolly.

"It's why people like me." He straightened up, a wry smile on his face. His nose was large, with a strong line to it—it looked disgustingly perfect on his face, as if every other feature had been placed there just to frame it. He'd always made her nervous, how immaculately handsome he was, but now something seemed odd about his face—a twitch in his lip, a squint of his left eye she had never noticed before. His energy was off.

"*I* don't like you," Lahna said casually, breaking the silence. Rhee almost laughed. That, at least, got a frown from Nero. He was probably not used to being around people who spoke the truth so easily. The guard with the eyepatch shifted just slightly behind Nero, the stunner on his belt in full view. He and Dahlen were locked in a staring contest.

A grimace passed over Nero's features as if he'd smelled

something foul. "For the love of the ancestors, lighten up, Yendit!" he yelled back to his guard. "Same goes for all of you, especially the Empress." His gaze wandered from Rhee's head to her toes. "You wear your resentment in the line of your jaw, in your posture."

"You'd have me look more agreeable?"

"The scowling doesn't suit your delicate features." Nero smirked. "You're the Rose of the Galaxy. Think of the support you could've garnered early on if you only smiled a bit more."

Rhee read the subtext. If all she was was a collection of delicate features and rose petals, then surely her job was to wear a pleasant expression and put people at ease. As if her face didn't belong to her, wasn't linked to the emotions she felt—the grief and turmoil swirling inside her.

She hated this man, how he did vile things and dedicated his entire existence to gaining more power—to what end? She hated even more how he could cover up his wickedness with a superficial smile and a well-cut suit.

She smiled now, squeezing the coin tightly between her thumb and the knuckle of her index finger. "I suppose I was too busy imagining all the painful ways I could kill you."

It was true, in a way. She had cultivated her mind and her fighting technique for ultimate vengeance all these years, though she'd been seeking vengeance on the wrong man. Until now.

"But I still found time in my busy schedule of envisioning *your* death to win the public over." He was so poised. He'd spent years in front of the media, and it showed. Sitting before him, Rhee could feel her inexperience. "You really ought to consider your image more," he continued. "Wouldn't want everyone assuming you're just a daddy's girl, here to extend his soft policies. You'll appear weak, just as he did."

"If his policies seemed weak to anyone, it's to the *weakminded*—the ones who believe violence and war are the only answers," Rhee fired back. "You wouldn't happen to know anyone who fits that description?"

She leaned forward, an elbow on either knee, trying to take up as much space as possible—a thing she'd seen men do often. But for all her bravado, sweat gathered on the back of her neck. That specific phrase he'd used set off alarms all over her body. *Daddy's girl.*

"In fact, I do." Nero leaned forward too. "Only about half the galaxy."

Daddy's girl. She couldn't focus, or properly exchange barbs with this pathetic excuse for a man—truly, her only pleasure in sitting across from him. *Daddy's girl. Daddy's girl. Daddy's girl.* It repeated in her head. It was the exact same thing the man had whispered at her when she faced the crowd in front of the palace, on her arrival in Sibu. The protester certainly hadn't been the first to call her that—nor would he be the last. Still, the timing of it put her on edge.

"Won't you finally explain why you instigated those attacks on the Empress's procession yesterday?" Dahlen had grown tired of listening.

"Me?" he said, raising his eyebrows. "As if I would stoop so low. As if I needed to." He actually seemed offended by the suggestion—was it possible he was telling the truth? "I didn't sully your homecoming, my dear. History did. *You* did. Those who've opposed Ta'an rule for years aren't going to just flip. I invited you here so that we could perhaps strike a deal, like civilized people. Find a way in which we work together to fulfill our mutual obligations. After all, two minds are better than one, Empress."

"She'd never work with you," Dahlen said. He spoke the words Rhee herself wished were true.

"Rhiannon, is it going to be a habit to let a Fontisian speak for the crown?" Nero shook his head. He'd parted his thick, dark-blond hair to the side—the new style in the capital.

Rhee ignored the question. She had her own agenda, and she'd indulge this as long as she could stomach it. "What's in it for me, if I agree to work with a liar such as yourself?"

But Nero cut her off before she could continue. "I'm not a liar, Empress. I've merely *embellished*."

"You made the public believe in fictional threats, just so they'd take your side in this war. You tip them in your favor more and more each day!" Rhee felt Dahlen staring at her openly now, but she wouldn't meet his eye. She turned over the terrible truth of her situation: He was in control of her image. UniForce was loyal to him. There were spies in the palace. Her throat closed as if he were strangling her, like he'd strangled her legitimacy. Her ability to rule.

"Tell me exactly what's fictional about a dying planet? About a lack of resources? And about having to share those precious resources with people who aren't even *from* here!" His northern accent came out as he'd made his last point. All the carefully constructed imagery he'd created fell away. He was worked up. His hair had fallen in front of his face.

"*Ancestors*," Rhee cursed. "You believe in this drivel."

Veins bulged in his neck, and Rhee caught a glimpse of a dark spot, triangle shaped, just behind his ear. It unsettled her— this imperfection on a man always so perfectly groomed. "Is it really too much to ask you to see this perspective?"

"Yes, when the perspective is a bigoted one," she said.

"I can't help it that this appeals to them," he said, gesturing to his face. "Twelve generations of the same stuff and people start to think it's unfair. You Ta'ans being born into your power . . ."

"Enough." Rhee stood up, and Yendit moved forward, prompting Lahna to stand in defense. Nero wasn't wrong— she had been born into power, and for so long she'd seen it as a given. A right. But how could she address any unfairness or injustice under the thumb of a madman?

Rhee desperately wanted to spar, to address this the only way she ever knew how. She wasn't cut out for diplomacy. But through her teeth she asked: "What is it you actually want from me?"

Nero frowned and ran his fingers through his hair. "It hasn't even occurred to you that I could possibly want to help you, has it?"

"No," she said. "It hasn't. You're a compulsive liar and a sociopath."

"Fine." He threw his hands up in the air. "Look, there's still a large population that wants a Ta'an to rule. Loyalists and all that," he said with a wave. "Rather than an agonizing political struggle, or a power play where you try to convince my second-wavers to jump ship and I try to convince your supporters to switch over, let's just combine forces."

It was ridiculous that he'd even think she'd fall for it. He opposed everything the Ta'an dynasty had stood for all these generations. *Honor, bravery, loyalty.* Everything *she* stood for. And she would never forget his talk of "whispering into cubes" as he stood over Dahlen's unconscious body.

This was so obviously a trap, she could've laughed. Nero wanted to keep her close so he could keep an eye on her, prevent her from finding out the truth about him and exposing it. He wanted to control her, manipulate her, get under her skin like he had with everyone else in the damn galaxy.

There was no better way to find out the truth than from the inside. He wanted to keep her close.

But who's to say she wouldn't be the one keeping an eye on *him*, controlling him, finding ways to undermine his rule?

"Let's say I agree . . . then what?" The question gave the room the feeling of a pressurization chamber—it crushed her where she sat. Behind her, Dahlen and Lahna said nothing, but she could *feel* the anger and tension in them.

He leaned back, intolerably smug. "I gain access to the palace, to you. Just the occasional briefing or so. A DroneVision spot, perhaps. And you'll get the Tasinn back, at least for your appearances. In exchange, you might find that people will start answering your comms, Empress."

She wondered how long it would take the Tasinn to kill her if she moved to strike Nero. "I expect that this arrangement would include pulling the UniForce troops out of Nau Fruma?"

"Effective immediately."

"And our ultimate goal would be to move toward peace?"

"I think it would move us in a mutually beneficial direction," Nero replied.

After a pause, Rhee said: "I'll consider it."

"Don't wait too long to decide." Nero smiled—a real, genuine, pearly smile of predatory satisfaction that made Rhee's stomach turn. He paused, eyeing both of her guards again. She saw every muscle in Dahlen's body stiffen out of the corner of her eye. His anger was practically vibrating off his body—she could feel it coming at her in hot waves—but she resisted turning around. "After all, I wouldn't want something terrible to befall you, Empress."

She suddenly felt cold; she realized she'd balled her hands into fists unconsciously. He probably knew that her death now would be terrible press, even for him. But they both knew the truth: She was a target. The Empress was still far from untouchable, and Nero garnered more support with every day that passed. There were those who resented a young girl on the throne—one who had intentions of making decisions and challenging the existing order. The idea of her as Empress had been much more attractive when she was a withering rose on a far-flung moon, waiting to be plucked up and saved.

She ushered Dahlen and Lahna quickly back toward the

elevator. The daisies awakened suddenly, and hovered over them as they passed.

"My next broadcast is in two days," Nero said behind them. Rhee paused at the threshold of the doors. "I'd be obliged if you were my guest."

Dahlen glared out the window over the city. It was Lahna who grabbed her arm and led her inside the elevator.

"Let's not delay, Empress," she said. "There's still much to do."

Part Two:

THE ABANDONED

"The honorable transcend; you of pure hearts must shed all desires
that do not serve your purpose."

—*The Teachings of Vodhan*

EIGHT

KARA

THE Frontline Physicians medcraft was a piece of machinery so enormous and so ancient, Kara could barely believe the artificial grav still worked on board. It had blasted off from Nau Fruma two days ago, and Kara had been sure to be on it—putting as much distance as she could between her and the place where Aly had abandoned her.

In another room, a DroneVision personality was reciting Rhiannon's plummeting approval ratings. Again. Kara was thankful when someone turned it off. She wondered if the Empress would be better off if she hadn't put a call out for Josselyn. The second-wavers were using that as an opportunity to call her coronation into question and undermine her rule.

Now, Kara fished the cylinder she'd found in the Lancer's dojo out of her pocket. It had nearly broken in the blast, and she'd had to dig it out from piles of rubble.

It had become a habit, almost a reflex, to touch it, to handle it, to watch it unfold its holo. How many times had Kara projected its message, the one that had opened specifically for her? The coordinates led to Ralire—which was apparently where the overwriter was hidden. Kara was en route there now; the craft she'd chosen included a pit stop on the very dwarf planet to which she was headed, and now there was little she could do but wait.

When Kara had woken on Nau Fruma, she realized she'd been thrown by the blast and landed behind a concrete wall—miraculously, shielded from further harm. When she clawed free of the rubble, she saw the marketplace had been destroyed. The ground, the debris, her clothes and skin—the gray was everywhere, and she felt it seeping into the folds of her own brain. Ash blotted out the sky, and she breathed it in, coughed it out. Choked on it like everyone else running past and around her. She'd been knocked out from the blast. Her clothes were in shreds, and the prayer beads Aly gave her were gone. Somewhere she'd lost her backpack too, which contained the last of her meds. She searched for Aly, mystified how they could have gotten so far apart in the fighting. In the distance, her eye caught someone who looked just like him, boarding a craft without her.

Kara hadn't even called out; she was so sure it wasn't him, and that he wouldn't leave her. But when she saw the blinking lights of the droid he had been dragging beside him, she knew for sure—and by then she *couldn't* call out. Her throat had closed off, and she felt paralyzed with shock and humiliation. Aly had left her behind. Neither of them even looked back. Not once. Even though she'd risked everything to save him.

At least there was no room for heartache on the Frontline Physicians ship—not hers, at least. It felt like Kara had heard every sound of suffering a human could make in these past two days. It made her forget her own headaches, the way her jaw hurt, the nightmares she had. The medfloor was nonstop triage, though her primary duty had been carrying food and blankets around, translating as needed. No one used their cubes here, Kara included. In some cases, people's had been damaged, mangled underneath the skin. But Kara just felt paranoid, safer if it was off.

She knew of military-issued translation nets that you could cast around a room, but Frontline Physicians couldn't afford anything like that—and it wasn't like the military was going to donate one anytime soon. Droids could do literal translation of rudimentary language, but Kara could speak in a handful of languages—and have an actual meaningful dialogue. Lydia had insisted she learn them, and would do things like switch from Derkatzian and Wraetan mid-sentence just to see if Kara could keep up. In retrospect, it was hard to tell if Lydia had been relentless and exacting because she expected Kara would one day be a princess or a fugitive. And it was hard to tell if Kara was thankful for such a skill set or still pissed she'd been lied to, had her memory erased.

Either way, there was something useful about that pain, a feeling she could channel when she translated for the patients. Kara was there to intercept all the words people used to describe pain and suffering, to parse through all the idioms and wade through the regional dialects and poetic expressions—to sharpen every description until the message was clear and concise. The medics couldn't diagnose anything until they knew what hurt, and how, and with what frequency. So Kara let the patients tell her their stories, and passed on only what she needed to. The rest of it she absorbed, each narrative a drop in the ocean.

Sure, hearing about trauma took its toll, but organic translation really did a number on her head. Without her cube on, Kara's mind had to work double-time—and even when she pushed herself she could barely keep up. Plenty of times in the last few weeks she'd wondered about how different life was without her cube—harder, mostly. That absence of the cube computing away while you happily busied yourself with something else seemed foreign to her now. And at night she almost enjoyed the feeling that her brain had shattered in a dozen different places; there was a kind of mental exhaustion that kept her from holding on to any thought for too long. It was the perfect antidote when you were trying to forget you'd been lied to and abandoned.

Probably everyone felt like that. The doctors were too busy dropping down into various war zones—mostly vulnerable Fontisian territories that were getting the crap bombed out of them by Kalu's forces—to ask questions about why she was even there. The blowback from the conflict on Nau Fruma, which UniForce was blaming on Fontis even though it had been a resistance effort on the part of the WFC, overshadowed everything but survival. They were glad for the extra volunteers. They needed all the help they could get.

In a cruel, practical way, the distractions were a kind of blessing. When she managed to push past the pulsing behind her eye, Kara's mind kept turning over the info Pavel had found. That the overwriter could be used in targeted memory deletion on a mass scale, and Emperor Ta'an himself had signed off on the research. Was no one above corruption? Kara understood now more than ever how critical it was to get to the overwriter before Nero did.

She was close. They were zooming in on Ralire, a dwarf planet and major pit stop before the epic dead space between here and Fontis. She'd learned that Ralire wasn't neutral so much as entirely lawless—it was governed by the trade economy that burgeoned there, illegal and legal. Frontline was planning a touchdown soon to reload much-needed medical supplies. Kara rationalized that a re-up meant that it was the perfect time to swipe some meds that she'd need to keep her headaches manageable.

She hit a narrow set of stairs that was more like a ladder—the angle was practically vertical—and crawled down as she gripped the cold metal banisters. It was so cramped, Kara couldn't imagine anyone with a Fontisian or Wraetan build fitting their shoulders through. Kara was used to small spaces. She'd spent plenty of time in the air—killing time when she was stuck on zeppelins, on the Kalu–Navrum line, waiting for Lydia, who worked on one of those illegal traveling labs.

The medbay was bustling with activity; it always was. Nurses and medics walked briskly, dodging one another with armfuls of supplies, careening gurneys through the tight quarters, and shouting out orders. She took advantage of the chaos and did her part to look busy, walking fast like she had somewhere to be. There were glass windows that looked into the operating rooms. Three in a row were occupied with patients and the flurry of medics and doctors treating them. As long as she found an empty one, she could pick the lock on the cabinet inside and raid it. Kara caught her reflection in the thick, smudgy glass of the window: her two-toned eyes, one a blazing green and the other hazel, a few dark freckles surfacing on her cheeks and nose . . .

The evidence was there, and she couldn't deny that she was here too for DNA meds. It was a last-ditch effort to prevent any-one from seeing the way her true features—Josselyn's features—had begun to emerge. It wasn't just her eyes anymore. Even her tan cheeks were broadening, the shape of her mouth changing, filling in. She was almost recognizable as Rhiannon's sister, and she could only imagine how the resemblance would increase if she didn't take something soon.

Not only was she on the run, but Kara was becoming some-one she didn't know.

Thankfully, all the cabinets were stocked with a supply of "warper" pills that were given to patients to manipulate their DNA and speed up their healing. They'd have to do for now.

Just as she'd hoped, she looked into an empty operation room. But right when she moved to push the double doors open, she heard a frenzy of beeping.

"CODE RED!" A droid rolled past her into the operating room, its robotic voice blurting out the same message on repeat as a nurse wheeled a patient past her. Blood had soaked through her WFC fatigues.

Nicola, the head doctor, was on the nurse's heels. "What's going on?" Kara asked, chasing after her.

"She woke up and tried to gouge out her own cube."

"What?" Nausea hit her, and Kara's skin prickled.

"What are you doing in here?" Nicola started to ask, but the patient began to shout in Wraetan.

"You idiot!" The girl thrashed. She had a bloodied towel to her neck, and a medic standing over her applied pressure. It should've been disturbing, the blood and the tendons and the violence of it. But this was Kara's world now.

"I have no idea why she did it," the medic, Russev, was saying to anyone who would listen. "She's acting like a feral cat."

The girl hissed, "Take it *out*. Take it—" The Wraetan words got lost in a gruesome gurgle.

"Need a translator in here!"

Kara pushed past Nicola, attacked by a mist of sterilizers as soon as she crossed the threshold. She came to the girl's side, elbowing out a nearby nurse. She caught a glance at the metal ID tag on the girl's wrist. It said her name was Issa.

Issa kept yelling even while Nicola and two other medics moved her braids back and worked to stanch the flow of blood from her neck that had already drenched the table. When she started to choke, Nicola plunged two fingers into the ragged hole in her skin while Russev tried to repair the damage with silicone thread. "It updated! They'll come for me. I have to disable it . . ."

"Who's coming for you?" Kara asked her in Wraetan. "What update?" She realized her own hands were shaking; she didn't know how to steady them. Issa pulled her head away, and Nicola cursed as she lost her grip and blood spattered her protective mask.

"We're going to inject a numbing serum," Russev said, holding a needle. "And then restart the cube. Tell her if she would just stay still . . ."

"No!" the girl yelled in Wraetan. The word for *cube* was nearly identical in most languages—a Kalusian loan. She grabbed Kara's hand, blinking in shock. "Don't resuscitate it! They'll track it!"

Kara's eye started to throb again. She thought of Nero tracking her, tracking all of them. She remembered how he'd framed Aly, and how he'd removed the cubes of all those patients on the zeppelin.

"She's scared," Kara translated to Russev. "She doesn't want you to."

"We'll risk infection if we leave it as is. There are antibodies that activate when neural connectivity is operational. She's lost too much blood already." Kara looked down and saw it was dripping off the gurney and pooling on the floor. She felt sick. Dizzy. What was it like when Lydia had used the overwriter on her?

Issa was fading fast. "Let me die. We're all as good as dead otherwise," she responded. The words slurred together.

"What the hell is she saying?" Nicola demanded.

Kara fought through the nausea creeping up on her, the edges of her vision going fuzzy, the heaviness of her head. She didn't know what was right. Save the girl, or heed her warning?

"Stop," she blurted out, her eyes never leaving the WFC girl's. She might have been paranoid, confused—how could they be tracked with their cubes off?—but then again, she might be right.

The second medic huffed, "We can't stop, she'll—"

"The patient said she has seizures," Kara lied, taking her eyes off the girl to lock them with Nicola's. She remembered vaguely that Lydia had researched the cube's effects on people with epileptic conditions. "She said you need to know. If you resuscitate the cube now, it could trigger a fatal seizure."

Nicola and the other two medics exchanged a look.

One of them muttered, "She might not be able to handle the neuroelectricity . . ."

Finally, Nicola nodded. "We have to disable it then."

"You mean break it?" one of the attendees said, his eyes glassy. "It could kill her!"

"It might," Nicola said. "But we know she'll die for certain if she has a seizure. She won't survive with the cube in place as is."

What had Kara done?

The medic gave in. He took a pair of delicate pliers to Issa's neck and simply snapped her cube in two. It was much cruder than Kara had thought it would be.

"That's it then?" Kara asked softly.

"That's it. The cube will never be functional again—just a useless scrap of biotech lodged in her neck," the medic said, shaking his head as he cleaned the wound.

Issa's eyes fluttered closed, and Kara wondered if she would die now, and whether it would be her fault—another life added to the list of her losses.

But the Wraetan girl did not die.

Her wound had been sewn up but she'd been hideously bruised, the stitches showing shiny and black against her dark skin. She was one of those girls who looked pretty when they slept; her high, angled cheekbones looked dramatic, and she had a natural pout to her lips.

Kara curled up in a chair pulled up next to Issa's cot as the girl lay unconscious, and waited for her to wake up. Sitting in the darkness, she stayed very still as the pulsing in her head quieted, the pain aching up her arms and legs dulled. She was lost in her own fog of grief and shock. Issa's surgery reminded her of her own procedure. Lydia had overwritten her memories. Her past, the *Josselyn* of her, was as good as gone. Whiteness closed in on her vision, like the foam of a wave crashing over her.

Sometimes it felt like losing the memories from her other life was nothing compared to being lied to. Kara had thought Lydia was her mother. When she'd spent all those late nights in the lab, when she'd come home absentminded, absorbed in her work, when Kara had to figure out dinner for herself without so much as a call—Kara thought that maybe she'd fallen short somehow. That if she had turned out different, Lydia would be more maternal. Available, like other moms were.

And if there wasn't that to think about, there was everything else right here and right now. Alyosha had left her. She was flat out of meds and using a piss-poor substitute of warpers that would only get her so far. Ralire—and whatever waited for her there— still felt an impossible distance away. It was like there was this great abyss between the life she had lived so far and the life she should have lived—and the sister she should have known, who was now, at this very moment, sitting on the throne of Kalu. Kara had nothing. Nothing but an unconscious stranger, this WFC soldier who had risked her own life to make sure they were okay.

Hours passed. She drifted in and out of sleep, thinking of Luris. Wading into water so cold her feet would go numb. Smooth, slippery stones under her feet. A dense forest that she could disappear into, and the salt, weighing down the air, hovering in the fog. In Luris, there would be no running, no training, no worrying about her next move or her face changing. Kara could practically feel the cold air, the need to fold her arms over her chest as it slipped through the wool of her sweater. She looked down and found something in the moss—her coin, her family coin. And suddenly it didn't feel so safe or remote, and the sound of the birds chirping and the ocean roaring in the distance stopped. That old life would follow her everywhere . . .

Then she heard a cough.

Kara opened her eyes to see Issa staring up at the ceiling. The rusty coin was in the palm of Kara's hand. When Issa coughed again, Kara pocketed it and went to her side.

"Are you okay?" It was a lame thing to say, but she couldn't think of anything better.

Issa's eyes got big. All she said was "Is it dead?"

"Dead?" she asked, then realized that Issa was talking about her cube. A shiver ran over Kara's arms, all the way to the base of her neck. Everyone knew that a cube needed an organic counterpart to function—to *live*, as Issa had implied—but she'd never thought of it as a living thing. It creeped her out a little, but she answered: "Yeah, it's out. Dead."

"Someone's been hacking them. Cubes." Issa spoke in a hoarse voice, like it hurt to talk. "Even when they're off. It's why I needed it to die." Her eyes were glazed over, and Kara looked at her IV feed. She'd been given a healthy dose of painkillers.

"How?" Kara asked. "How are they hacking them?" The other staff might have advised Kara not to engage—Issa *sounded* dazed, high—but Kara felt the gravity in her words. Because she knew what Issa said was possible. After everything she'd learned of Nero, of her mother, of their biological experiments with the cube, Issa didn't surprise her at all. She'd been paranoid enough herself to keep her own cube off even before entering the Frontline Physicians craft, where it was required to stay offline. You weren't supposed to be in danger so long as it was turned off.

Issa shook her head. Beads of sweat formed on her temples. She looked like she was in a fever dream. "The update."

Kara went cold; she thought of what she'd learned from Pavel's overwriter research. The overwriter could be used on the public if their cubes were available via the same network at the same time . . .

She rummaged for a small towel in a nearby cabinet and took deep breaths so she could stop trembling. Once she felt composed, she turned and held it to Issa's face as her wild eyes skittered around the room.

"What about the update?" Kara asked. She felt a seed of guilt, pressing the girl for information while she was half-conscious. But it was bigger than her. It was bigger than all of them.

"Dangerous," Issa said, then shuddered. "Our job on Nau Fruma was supposed to be quick and easy. Minimal casualties.

I'm a medic—it's not like soldiering is my specialty or anything. We were just supposed to drop an em-bomb, evacuate the camps, and get the hell out. But I pushed forward—I didn't follow rank." She looked up at the ceiling. Kara was losing her again. *The update. The update.*

"What are you saying?" Kara was desperate to keep her talking.

"That I'm the reason half my unit is dead . . ." Issa laughed, and her face, so stern and so wild at turns, was now lit up with a flash of vulnerability. "There was someone I wanted to kill."

Kara sucked in a breath, bitter and sharp in her lungs.

Issa closed her eyes. "You think I'm evil?"

"No. Not at all," Kara said honestly. "War is about everyone trying to settle a score." They fell into a silence. But Kara couldn't let it end there, when it was so clear Issa wanted to keep talking, to be absolved. She took Issa's face in her hands and angled her gently so now they were eye-to-eye.

"What about the update?" Kara urged again softly. She felt like a predator, pumping this girl for information. But she craved the truth—any version of it she could get. She wanted to turn everything and everyone inside out. Because she thought she'd known Aly, and he'd left. She thought she'd known Lydia, but she'd lied. And she thought she knew herself—but every memory, every aspect of her identity she thought to be true was diametrically opposed to the princess she actually was. The only thing she had left was this overwriter.

"The update . . . it's supposed to prime people for something. Make their cubes more easily hackable. It's why we dropped the em-bomb. To *stop* the updates. And if I kept my cube in, I was afraid they would see . . . everything. The only way to be sure was to gouge it out."

"But you wouldn't have survived." Kara thought of the people on the zeppelin, vacant, drawing triangles over and over again. "Or if you did, it wouldn't have been a life worth living."

"I know that. I wasn't thinking straight. But at the time a Ravaging felt safer than compromising everyone here . . ." Kara's skin prickled at the mention of a Ravaging. It's what Aly had called it. It had been hinted at in Vodhan's teachings.

"But you came, and instead they broke it," Issa said. "Here I am." She looked down at her hands like she had just realized: Here she was. Her face crumpled like she might cry. "You made them do that for me. I'm alive because of you . . ."

All Kara had done was lie on the spot, out of instinct—a thing she was good at, a way to fill in the blanks for a history that had been wiped. But she felt wholly unprepared for crying. She'd seen Lydia cry only once. And that was right before she died, when she admitted she'd lied to Kara for as long as she could remember . . .

"Don't cry." Kara forced her voice to sound light as she pulled the towel away and refolded it for no reason. She pressed it back to Issa's head. *Gently*, she had to remind herself. "You're safe now."

They fell into a silence after Kara whispered to her to say she had seizures if asked. Issa looked at her quizzically, but didn't press her on it. She was probably delirious—and anyway, what more was there to say? Kara blotted and redressed her wound, and eventually, Issa fell back asleep.

But she couldn't get Issa's story out of her head. Was the update linked to the overwriter? The timing seemed convenient. She thought of Lydia, then—the woman who had thought logically, critically, who always had the same refrain: There are no coincidences.

The horror of it all, the scope and the trespass of it, finally sunk in. Kara knew she had to destroy the overwriter, that it was critical to get it before it fell into the wrong hands. But she couldn't help but let her mind wander, wondering if such a thing could be used for good. And if it could free instead of enslave.

What if she could use the overwriter to erase Josselyn Ta'an?

She wondered, for the briefest of seconds, if Aly was right when he'd pretty much called her a coward. But how could she be Josselyn, when her heart and mind were empty of that identity? It used to make her jealous that there was only a void where everyone else could pull from a wealth of high-def memories; the best she could do was snatch at shadows of her old life. They were ominous, dark, quiet things that lurked in the back of her mind. They were intense sensations, like the remnants of a dream. And always that nightmare—or the memory?—of freefalling in the dark, plummeting down as she clawed at nothing, the wind stealing her voice.

All that was left of Josselyn was in her biology, clamoring to etch itself onto her features. Kara touched her chin. DNA suppressants were temporary, and if they were hard to get now she couldn't imagine what it would be like once the galaxy notched up to all-out war. She'd never be able to stop herself from changing back. Not for good. There would be no end to that constant fear that someone would see Josselyn Ta'an. She would always be on the run, living one long, drawn-out lie. She would never be free.

Unless . . .

Unless she could change everyone else so they didn't remember her face at all. Erase Josselyn Ta'an permanently, from everyone's minds, all at once.

She recalled the official Kalusian memo addressed to her father, the last emperor, which Pavel had shown her while they were spying on the internment camp: *The memory of the Great War itself to be erased from the collective memory, for the good of the people and advancement of the galaxy . . .*

The Emperor had wanted to erase the Great War from memory, to heal the galaxy and the political divide the war had caused. As horrifying as that kind of power was, he'd had noble reasons. Hadn't he?

And then she remembered the last thing Aly had said to her—that if you didn't want to live a lie, it was up to you to change the truth.

The idea, the scale of it, made the room swim in front of her eyes. If Kara *did* use the overwriter, she would destroy it immediately afterward. The world didn't needed Josselyn anyway. It had Rhiannon, who'd survived an assassination attempt and clawed her way back to the capital to take on an unruly opposition. It was likely her sister would be better off without her too, never mind that she'd asked Josselyn to return to Kalu.

Rhiannon would be better off without some prodigal sister to challenge her legitimacy to the throne and undermine her in the eyes and hearts of the public.

Josselyn Ta'an was as good as a ghost.

And now Kara would soon have the means to make sure no one remembered her.

NINE

RHIANNON

AS she made her way to Dahlen's quarters, Rhee tried to swallow down the taste of ash. It was as if the two words she'd uttered had singed her tongue.

I accept.

She'd just officially agreed to ally with the man who'd killed her family, who represented everything she hated—his vanity, his tendency to suddenly care whenever he was in front of the camera. And the worse part was that he knew all along she'd say yes. She needed him. She also knew Dahlen would be furious, but he'd come to understand. He had to.

Rhee might have come off as moody and unpolished on holos, eager to avoid interviews, generally unlikeable, just as Nero had implied. Fine. But she cared about things that mattered. She didn't want the war to continue. Too many people had died in vain.

Nero had doubled down. Not only did the UniForce remain in Nau Fruma, but now there had been three fresh attacks on neutral territories across the galaxy. Everything was spinning headlong into chaos and violence, and she could not sit back and let it happen.

She had to stop it, but she didn't know how. Not with the people of Kalu demanding retribution for what they saw as an attack on neutral ground. Not with Fontis arming for retaliation.

It was a massive undertaking, and she simply couldn't do it alone. She needed Nero's endorsement. She needed those who followed him to follow her too. And Nero had already agreed to meet with the United Planets and lay out the terms for a ceasefire, which seemed remarkable to her—a huge sign of progress.

But now Dahlen was avoiding her, and she needed his help to include the Fontisians. Showing the galaxy that Fontisians wanted peace too was important.

Dahlen had turned the east wing of the palace into makeshift barracks, where he slept with dozens of other Fontisian fighters. But the palace was enormous—the summer palace on Nau Fruma was hardly a tenth the size of this one—and around every corner, a piece of her past opened up. She'd slowly been rediscovering pieces of her childhood, new and old blending together in her consciousness as she managed the organic memories that floated up to the surface, immersive, almost suffocating.

"Empress."

Rhee jumped. She spun around on the cool marble floor to face Lahna. Today, she wore her hair in the style of an ancient

Fontisian warrior: half up in a dozen braids, intricately coiled and tucked.

"I'd rather you not sneak up on me," Rhee said testily. She didn't like how she felt in Lahna's presence—nervous, as if Lahna was evaluating *her*.

"I'd rather not come to fetch you. But we don't all get what we want." She put her hands on her narrow hips.

"I'm not a thing to be fetched," Rhee said—an immediate, knee-jerk reaction when in truth she was relieved. This was Dahlen's way of summoning her, which meant he was talking to her again. "He just expects me to come at his command?"

"He expects nothing," Lahna said. "We're leaving as soon as he gathers his things. I thought you'd want to say goodbye."

"Wait, *what*?" Rhee's heart started pattering hard in her chest. She thought for a second she'd misheard. "What do you mean, *leaving*?"

"He can't answer if you haven't asked."

Rhee's confusion and anger were kinetic; the faster she moved the more intensely she felt them. Lahna led her to the barracks, where she saw Dahlen's things packed neatly beside him as he sharpened his blade on a whetstone. His blond hair, shoulder-length, fell in an arc, obscuring his face from her. Rhee's stomach sank. Dahlen had no flair for drama. He'd packed. He really *was* planning to leave.

"You can't do this," she blurted out. She wished she could think up some eloquent insult, or a dressing-down that would humiliate him into reconsidering, but all she could think was: *This can't be goodbye.*

She felt her heart cracking open. "Look," she said, striving to control her voice, "I know you don't approve of working with Nero."

"I don't *approve*?" He crouched over the whetstone but would not look up. "As if I could approve a union so insidious. As if you'd be willing to listen."

"You're the one who's not willing to listen!"

He looked up. His eyes felt like fire on her skin. She stared back, holding his gaze, but it was hard to breathe, hard to swallow. "This is not a mere disagreement," he said. "This is a fundamental rift."

He held the blade up to the light, examined it, and, seemingly satisfied, sheathed it. "That man is an abomination."

How could he not see? She had to entertain Nero's proposition—otherwise she might as well declare an all-out war against him and risk alienating his supporters further, alienating those whom he had pressed under his thumb—alienating everyone.

"You think I don't know that? I'm not so stupid or so young that I can't see through his plan. But this is politics. I'm empress of the Kalusian territories, public enemy number one in the eyes of every other government. Kalu's loyalty is slowly being stolen by that very abomination you speak of—a holovision star with a pretty face, of all people. And Joss is somewhere out there, hidden away, when her real life is here waiting for her . . ." Rhee's throat seized at the thought of her older sister. "Besides, it's a temporary alliance."

"You can't 'temporarily' corrupt your soul."

"I don't have any other choice, and you know it!" Her anger flared. "You're being stubborn for the sake of it! You self-righteous, fanatical—"

"Watch yourself, Empress," Lahna said. "Don't say something you'll regret."

Rhee took a deep breath, restarted. Lahna was right. "Dahlen, we want the same thing: peace. Too many lives are being risked . . ."

He let out a hollow laugh that surprised her, chilled her even. It might have been the first time she'd heard him laugh. "Lives must be risked in the name of what's right. We must determine to take the more difficult path, if it is the righteous one."

"Don't throw your scripture in my face. You're just like everyone else. You don't think I'm capable of knowing what's best for my people. You follow your Elder on faith, yet he keeps you in the dark."

"I don't understand," he said. "What are we actually talking about?"

Rhee bit her lip. "Your Elder—he told me as much. *There are things you know, and things you don't know you know . . .*'" She still didn't understand what Elder Escov had meant when he spoke those words back in Erawae, but now, the words seemed alive with meaning.

"You've misunderstood." Dahlen's blond hair fell across his eyes again, and he pushed it behind one of his pointy ears. "Those words are a meditation on faith and trust in the word of Vodhan."

She'd never seen him wear his irritation so plainly, and it

made her feel all the more humiliated—some empress she was, simpering and begging. She could barely stand herself.

"Your faith," Rhee said. "*Your blind faith.* It keeps you trapped, so bound in this idea of right and wrong that you can't even look up and see the world for what it is."

"Could we not say the same thing about your brand of faith?" he said. "What is your *ma'tan sarili*, Empress?" Like most in the galaxy, Dahlen knew it was an everyday greeting—but he knew, too, the intimacy of it, its deeper meaning, the pledge to be your highest self.

Honor. Bravery. Loyalty.

Had she betrayed these very ideals?

Dahlen looked at her, and Rhee found her answer in the disappointed look in his eyes. He shouldered his belongings.

"You're wrong to leave."

"I was wrong to hold you to your highest self," he said, as he made his way toward the door.

She suppressed a shiver at his words. The hope—and disappointment—in them left her shaken. She wanted to be the leader he spoke of, the leader he imagined. But she wasn't. Not yet, anyway.

"Go, then!" she called. "I don't need you. I need a partner who will help me end this mess of a war, not a fanatic whose scripture is so far up his ass he can't see the reality. The reality is that we need to be strategic."

"With respect, Empress," Dahlen said spinning around, "Nero isn't just going to acquiesce. You think he's willing to pull troops out of these territories without some big trade-off that benefits him? There's no coming to his senses or rising to the occasion. He's toxic. His promises are a trap, and I thought you would do better than believe him."

"What if I told you he was after some sort of powerful cube tech?" She shifted her weight between her feet. "He said as much on Houl. That he was seeking a tech he wanted to change and alter a person's memories."

"Even if that's true, aligning yourself with him will not get you closer to the truth."

"*Ancestors.* Listen to yourself! Isn't this all because he turned on your cube?" she fired back. She was desperate now. Without him, she had no allies outside of the palace. Nero had made sure of it. "Because your precious vow to the order was broken? There are more important things than your faith," she reminded him. "There are lives at stake, and I fear we will lose more every day that we hesitate." She was trying, so hard, to strike out. To find the thing that would make him react. Make him *stay*.

And yet still, Dahlen gave her a look that was so icy it nearly froze her lungs. "You think I don't feel fear?" he asked. "Because I, too, fear—for Kalu, and for all of us." His voice stabbed into her, nearly taking her down, but his face was impassive again, its sharp profile cutting a jagged silhouette.

Panic hit her then—an ocean of it. Surely he was right about Nero. But the only way to secure peace was to work with him, even if it meant navigating a labyrinth of lies. Why couldn't Dahlen see that?

If she couldn't keep the loyalty of her last friend, how could she earn it from her people? She would be lost without Dahlen. She'd ditched him on the zeppelin and yet he'd still found her again, still stood by her.

But now she'd gone too far.

She loathed to admit it, even in her most private thoughts, but it was true: She needed him. Precisely because he was so unbending. He was the moral compass she leaned on in this directionless world she'd woken up to.

"I must follow my own path and you yours," Dahlen said as he walked through the threshold. "I cannot do business with a demagogue."

"So that's it?" Rhee asked, steadying her voice. She wished more than anything he would stomp and throw things, spit a colorful stream of Fontisian curses. Or that he would sulk, or cry, or grab her shoulders and shake her, or anything. She wished he'd show what he really felt—not just what his moral instincts were, but what he held in his heart. She needed to know that he didn't hate her.

In a short time, he had become the person whose opinion mattered most to her.

He turned away from her without a word, and Lahna moved to follow him. Rhee didn't know what impulse overtook her. She just couldn't stand to see him go. Wouldn't. She had to have one last word, one last glance, some sign that he cared, that he hadn't completely given up on her. Without thinking, she pulled Veyron's knife from the belt where it now sat always, even when she slept, nestled tight against her hip.

"If you're no longer my friend," she gasped out, "that makes you my enemy." It had come to this—threatening the boy who'd saved her life, with the tip of the knife Veyron had almost used to kill her. She could barely hold back her tears.

"This is not the solution," Dahlen said quietly. "My feud is not with you." Hope flared in her again, for a brief second. "If I'm to stay by your side, you know what I require."

He was giving her an ultimatum. He wanted her to break her truce with Nero. Her heart fluttered. She could still undo this.

But then she thought of why she'd done what she'd done. She thought of the series of bombings following what happened on Nau Fruma. She thought of Julian. She thought of Joss— out there somewhere in the galaxy, waiting for her, possibly in danger.

She shook her head. Dahlen had to do what he felt was right—just as she had to do what she felt was right.

He sighed, his eyes soft.

"Don't leave." Rhee felt herself begging, even though she hadn't lowered the knife. "You're the one who brought me here. You fought for me." *You believed in me.*

"You were uncompromising then." He said it as if it were a lifetime ago.

"I was not yet in charge of an empire," she said. But she knew it would do no good. "Where will you go? What will you do?"

He tilted his head and stared down at her, as if he were already seeing her from far away. "Kill him, of course."

"They'll blame me if you do."

"Already thinking about how it will look," Dahlen said, with infinite sadness. He reached out and gently pushed the knife away. She let it drop. It clattered to the floor, and she felt everything in her fall with it. "You'll make a fine politician yet."

She blinked hard, turning away so he wouldn't see her cry.

"You won't be alone," he said, gentler now. "Lahna will stay with you. The order will stay with you."

"Excuse me?" Lahna obviously hadn't expected this.

He didn't answer. He merely lifted a hand in farewell, and then turned and slipped out of the room.

Rhee willed herself not to run after him. But after a minute, she couldn't stand it. She ran to the balcony.

"You're not to get close to any windows," Lahna reminded her coldly.

Rhee ignored the warning and stood out on the balcony, watching for a last glimpse of him.

"Empress . . ." Lahna tried again.

Rhee stood her ground, her chin up as she waited. Perhaps he would turn around and come back. He'd call up to tell her he couldn't leave. That he cared. That he believed in her still.

But then she heard the rattle of a gate from the east side of the palace and realized he'd never leave out the front door. There were other exits, a dozen.

Rhee didn't see Dahlen exit her life. But she felt his absence immediately.

She backed away from the balcony. Lahna closed the door behind her. For a moment, Rhee felt as if feelings were birds, winging frantically in her chest. Julian was gone. Josselyn was gone. Now Dahlen too.

Would she always lose everyone who mattered?

"I'm sorry," Lahna said. Rhee turned away, realizing that Lahna had been watching her.

"Did you love him?" Rhee asked. To fill the silence. To somehow feel closer to the boy who'd left.

To pretend, maybe, that the question wasn't one she had often asked herself.

Lahna tilted her head. "I serve him." She looked away, and Rhee saw her face soften for a brief, uncharacteristic moment. But she mastered it quickly. "Come. I'll escort you back to your room."

There was nothing more to say, so they took the long way back to the emperor's quarters without exchanging a word.

She would be meeting with Nero again soon to make their announcement, and Rhee would have to be prepared. She would have to steel herself for what was to come.

TEN

ALYOSHA

STANDING in the craft, packed in tight with a bunch of other fighters, Aly became a soldier again.

But he wasn't the buttoned-up, uniformed soldier that he used to be, standing in neat little lines. No "yes sir!" or "no sir!" or dropping to give the sarge fifty. He wasn't the puppet soldier either, smiling for the cameras on the *Revolutionary*—that clueless kid with Vin by his side, cruising around as a poster boy for the UniForce while the world went to *taejis* around them.

He became a Wraetan again too. Or at least he *remembered* he was. Spend too much time with only Kalusians and you're liable to forget where you came from, bury every memory of the Wray deep enough so that you never have to recall them. But now that he was surrounded by Wraetans, he felt the tiniest fraction of ease. He heard the dialect he'd grown up speaking, saw it in the way they moved—the mannerisms of his ma and his dad—felt that hard, front-syllable accent reappear in the back of his throat when he talked. He let himself look like a Wraetan too, could see how his skin had gotten darker when he wasn't running for shade every time he went outside. His fingers got tangled in his hair; it went curly now that he wasn't keeping it cropped short to the scalp every week—sometimes twice a week—just so the texture wouldn't show.

He felt like himself in his own skin, felt at home, in a way he'd been missing for so, so long.

Kara had felt like home once too. He couldn't have shared the feeling with her, but he could've showed her who he was, who he could be.

But then he'd fucked it all up. And she'd died.

He pushed the thought of her away; she was gone like everyone else he'd loved. Just two days ago he'd been holding Kara's hand, and now here he was—part of the WFC's newest batch of freedom fighters. What else was he going to do? Nothing and no one wanted him, and he felt the same about the world. The only thing he was hoping for was revenge. He'd go head-to-head with the UniForce. You didn't get to use Aly and Vin and just get away with it.

This felt better, felt right. The current mission was to take back a massive satellite on Uustral, traditionally a sanctuary planet. Tucked behind a vast medical complex, the satellite and broadcast tower had been used for decades to beam out information about new medical techniques and technologies to far reaches of the galaxy—it could touch all the way to the Outer Belt, where often medical understanding was closer to magical thinking—and also to communicate with medbays that did relief work across the entire system.

That is, until the UniForce had assumed control of it, turning it into a machine to spew out war propaganda. The WFC was going to dismantle it—by any means necessary.

They'd dropped into Uustral airspace now. He'd known a few Uustralite soldiers back in the UniForce, and he wondered now what they were up to. Was he dropping down on their homes right now, descending to light their southern hemisphere on fire?

Distantly, Aly wondered about Jeth too. After he'd helped them broadcast Aly's cube playback on Rhesto and taken them into custody, Aly hadn't seen him again. He didn't know what was up—whether Jeth was even alive. Pavel was practically fried. Aly had dropped him on the nearest WFC station for repairs, but he had no idea if he would make it. Vin was dead. Kara was dead.

"Secure the medical facility," said the commanding officer, pushing through the crowded ranks. "Once we have it, we can easily seize the tower."

A little thrill zipped through Aly as they all grunted in agreement. Aly prepared himself to drop, double-checking his parachute straps and adjusting his third eye. That wasn't the real name, though; technically the device was called an I-3, and it predated cube technology by about thirty years. They were going with old-style comm units that had a range of only a hundred or so meters, since everyone had their cubes off. None of them had ever gone into battle without some sort of mechanism to connect instantaneously, and now they were going to do it old school. Aly was itching for action. He wanted to fight. Blow things up. Make people pay.

The WFC had a firewall on all their crafts, but they'd all been additionally instructed to turn off their cubes before combat. And if they were caught or scanned, well . . . They couldn't get caught or scanned. It was rumored the UniForce could hack their feeds even when the cubes were turned off, and Aly wondered if that's what the Kalusians were up to in those labs on the zeppelin.

Aly nodded at a nearby Fontisian woman, big and magnificent like a statue cut from marble, her delicate pointed ears almost comical in comparison. Aly pitied whomever she'd come up against. Then he nodded to his other side, at the stocky Chram named Hesi who reminded him of Jeth—albino-white flesh and shoulders as wide as the side of a barn.

"If anyone has taken from you or yours . . ." the commanding officer said.

"Justice shall be swift," the soldiers called back in unison. It was the WFC oath, and Aly liked it, the ethos of doing something right, and doing it quick.

The pilot was counting off to the drop. "We go in ten, nine, eight . . ."

The hatch opened slowly. The night rushed in to take them; they were pelted with fat raindrops. The wind screamed louder. Vincent should have been by his side. He'd cock his head at a moment like this, flash Aly his holo-star smile.

". . . three, two, one . . ."

The floor fell away below him, and Aly was snatched into the darkness, somersaulting in sparks and stars and rain, with only a muffled silence in his ears and in his brain.

Back on Wraeta, before their civil war, his dad had saved for months to buy one crappy firework that they lit together on the anniversary of the day the Great War ended, watching it fly higher and higher until it exploded in a shower of light. For a split second, zooming to the earth, Aly wasn't a soldier—he was that firework from his childhood, but tumbling in reverse. A fiery symbol to celebrate a planet liberated.

He hadn't counted. How many seconds had passed? His clothes whipped up around him. His mouth blew back in a grin as wind rushed down his throat. He'd done this before, but he'd had all the right gear and a drill sergeant riding his ass the whole way down.

This wasn't a drill.

Stabilize. He spread himself out in a star. The dark surface of the planet was rushing toward him, and he thought of everyone he'd lost, waiting for him down there in the void. He could plunge into the outer surface of the planet and he'd be lost too. They'd taught him in church that there was a place the dead went to be with Vodhan, an afterlife they'd all end up in like it was a big eternal party with no fear and no pain. Aly wanted to believe that. He didn't want to think all the people he'd loved were gone. Not just that they were physically gone, but that their hopes and fears and feelings had dissolved like smoke until there was literally nothing left of them in the universe . . .

The shield on his helmet registered the medcenter and the satellite tower, highlighting it in the distance. All around him the blue LED lights flashed, and he had a close call with another soldier who torpedoed down—screaming at the top of her lungs. A battle cry.

Aly felt all his organs clench up like a fist.

The altitude readout on his shield said he was coming in close. Aly realized he was flying past floating blue lights. The other soldiers had already deployed their parachutes. He fumbled for the pull string and couldn't find it. He thought of Kara, the shitty things he'd said, the kinder things he *should've* said. The image of her limp wrist coming out of a sea of rubble, like she was trying to come up for air but the only thing that had broken the surface was her hand . . .

Aly clawed for his holster strap, still imagining the prayer beads tangled in Kara's fingers. Elegant, he'd thought once when he noticed her hands, how they looked like they belonged to an empress, like they'd been taken care of, like they flew across piano keys in grand sitting rooms within the palace.

Let her go, he told himself.

Aly calmed down, took a deep breath, tried slowly, less frantically this time. He groped behind him and finally felt it—trapped under the holster strap. He pulled the cord with his free hand, and the parachute released. The wind caught and rippled the parachute open. The silk dome bloomed above him, yanking him backward; his harness bucked, cutting into his shoulders. He swayed in the sky like the rest of the soldiers, all of them lit up like pieces of algae floating in the ocean—Vin had taken him to see the Kalusian sea once. It was last year on leave. It felt like a lifetime ago.

Now, Aly grabbed hold of the steering lines on either side. He focused on the target, and got a sight line on where to land. According to the blueprints, the medcenter contained the only modes of direct access to the satellite tower itself. But Nero had put nearly a thousand droids on patrol in and around the tower—a nearly insurmountable defense, unless all of them could be disabled.

But the chances, with fewer than forty green recruits and a handful of officers, were slim.

Aly tugged on the lines of the parachute to steer, coming in hot—way faster than he wanted to. He tucked his knees up high near his chest. He needed to be ready to tuck and roll when he landed.

Once his boots hit the soil he felt the impact up through his bones. Rain fell from the sky and bounced back up off the surface. It was coming from everywhere; it was dripping behind the backs of his ears and running down his chin. He lost his footing and fell on his butt.

In the distance, Aly could see the metal tower looming; the very top of it disappeared into the dark clouds above.

"Alpha leader, I have a visual on the tower," he said into his third eye. It was a flexible piece of metal that looped around his neck. You had to press a button and talk into the right side, and listen for a response from the other end. Nothing back but static. Great.

The medical facility rose partway from the base. In his head he heard the pilot saying their objective over and over again: *Secure the medical facility. Take the tower.*

He'd landed right where he wanted: in front of the tunnel leading down into the waste corridors.

There was, however, a droid guarding it. The droid was at least a full head taller than Aly. It stalked toward him, a red light scanning for him in the darkness. Aly pressed down on a hand-held signal jammer that came with his WFC kit.

"Identification scan incomplete."

The droid grabbed for Aly's neck, but he ducked and wove. "I could use some help here," he called into the third eye, pressing the button frantically. It was useless.

Pivoting his foot and shifting his weight, shadowboxing, scanning the thing for weaknesses or sensitive wires. It was a model he didn't recognize, and he regretted that in the UniForce he'd never been taught to attack sophisticated army droids.

Of course, back in the UniForce, he and the droids were supposed to be on the same side.

He jammed the heel of his hand straight into the droid's visual scanners, hoping to disable it, then gave a modified upper-cut right to an obvious control panel. A dizzying array of lights flashed across its module, and while it recalibrated, Aly pulled his knee high and brought his boot down hard on its steel knee.

Rookie mistake in Droid Fighting 101.

What would've hyperextended a man's knee just locked the droid's leg in place. It swept up Aly's foot in its tight grip and backhanded him. Aly spun and landed on his stomach in the mud. Pain shot through his ribs, and he tasted blood. He scrambled, the ground slick with rain, toward a rock the size of his fist that lay a few feet out of reach. He heard the droid move into place. An executioner ready to bring down the axe. Extending his arm was excruciating. His elbow was on fire. Broken or fractured, for sure. His fingers just brushed the rock, and a sense of déjà vu broke over him—he remembered losing his favorite wrench in the boiler room of the *Revolutionary*, straining for it, the day it all started. The day Crown Princess Rhiannon was supposedly assassinated. It was only days before Vin had died, killed by a UniForce droid just like this one.

His fingers closed around the rock. He spun on his back and launched the rock with less than a second to calculate trajectory. The rock cut straight through the air and nailed the droid's comm unit between its shoulder blades. It staggered on its feet, and Aly knew he'd hit his target: the gyroscope. The robodroid's anatomy had been part of the WFC's crash course training.

Its lights were going crazy. It stumbled in a half circle, like it was party-drunk. He thought of a tree he'd seen cut down in the Ernew forest as a boy—and that breathless, weightless second just before it fell hard.

Aly hooked the crook of his foot around the droid's ankle and yanked. It fell backward with a *boom boom*. Aly climbed to his feet, wincing. He stomped down on the droid's head, just once, because he couldn't help but think of Pavel. Not all droids were war machines. Someone had made them this way.

Aly flipped it over, grunting and straining the whole time as the droid flailed like a helpless insect. He gritted his teeth and ignored his elbow. Clicking on his flashlight, he wasn't sure what he was looking for until he found it: the outlet on the back of its neck, right where someone's spinal cord would be. It was freaky how fully the makers had committed to humanlike features. Aly ripped out its whole comm unit without any kind of plan—only because he was exhausted, and pissed off, and in this exact moment he hated this thing more than anything else in the universe. The comm unit was wet from the rain and glistened in his hand. It was sleek steel, cold metal, and it looked so different from his own cube with its tech embedded in roots, how it pulsed with life. He wondered what kind of secrets this cold, shiny comm unit had seen, what kind of data it held . . .

And how he could use it.

When Aly was programming Pavel, he'd inserted a sample of his own DNA into the server so that Pavel could better read and compare Aly's vitals. It was a standard technique, especially for droids used as basic companions. But could the process happen in reverse? He remembered Pavel saying that theoretically, cube-to-cube transfers could be "enhanced." That neural pathways could give and take info without "even being prepped"— whatever that meant. But what about droid-to-human transfers? He needed a doctor, preferably a cube surgeon . . .

Good thing he was storming a hospital.

He cradled his elbow and ran for the waste tunnel. Once inside the facility he busted his way through three double doors to the main entranceway, where a dozen WFC soldiers were waiting to pile in. Aly didn't slow down for the others; he took off running.

Two other soldiers corkscrewed through the labyrinthine corridors behind him—Hesi, who'd been standing next to him on the way here, and an Uustralite who wore a digital tag that said *Darris*. Together, they burst through another set of doors into a waiting room. Dozens of stunned Uustralite patients looked up, completely unaware that a takeover was going down. Aly would let the others handle these folks. Following a slick of blood on the floor, he shoved his way into an operating room and surprised a doctor with a scalpel, carefully disposing of a used blade in a sterilization basin.

"What is this?" the doctor demanded, taking a nervous step back. Darris's translation net relayed her words back in Wraetan, but Aly didn't recognize the original language. He pointed his stunner at her with his bad arm; it felt like crushed glass grinding against itself at the joint as he extended it. She raised all six of her hands in surrender.

"I—I've done nothing," she stuttered. "What—what do you want?"

"I'm your next patient," Aly said.

With his free hand, he threw the robodroid's comm unit on the metal table where the doctor had laid her scalpels. They were knocked off the table, and Hesi had to dodge them. "Do you know how to enable this remotely?" Aly asked. He switched the stunner over to his good hand, and a new kind of pain—a stinging, pricking sensation—exploded in his elbow now that his arm was hanging loose. But he wasn't going to let anyone know how much everything hurt. He breathed through the pain.

The doctor's hands fanned out in front of her, shaking as she accepted it. "How did you get it out?"

"I ask the questions," Aly said. The answer was obvious anyway—he'd ripped it out—and he figured the doctor was stalling. He still had the stunner pointed at her. "Can you enable this remotely or not?" UniForce would for sure be on their asses by now, especially if the WFC's suspicions were right and they were tracking them even with their cubes off.

"Yes, I can enable remotely," the doctor said. "Just please, don't hurt me."

Aly registered the fear in the doctor's eyes, and for a split second he felt bad about it. He'd always wanted to be the good guy, the hero, to rep Wraeta right. Look where that had gotten him.

"And you upload the information into my cube?"

"In theory, yes. But we're still in the early stages of research. Military droid data is encrypted differently. If I upload it to your cube it may be detrimental to the human neural system—"

"Dumb it down, Doc," Aly said. He looked between her and Darris, who had to translate everything on the fly. "I'm not a medic."

"They code NX data differently. It may have dangerous effects on the organic matter connected to your cube. A portion of your actual brain could be corrupted . . . irreparably damaged . . ."

Aly thought of the people he and Kara had found in that creepy lab on the zeppelin, the vacant stares, the woman who kept drawing triangles, urgently, as if they meant anything . . .

Still, they were running out of time, and they couldn't coordinate without cubes, without any kind of way to communicate across channels. They had to take over the tower. It meant he had to risk it. He figured maybe he was the only one with nothing to lose.

"Figure it out," Aly said, pulling up a rolling stool. "The droid will have info on how to hijack the tower."

The doctor frowned. "It's extremely dangerous—"

"Do it," Aly said—with every second wasted, their mission had a greater chance of failing. They needed the satellite—it was the key to Nero's spreading influence.

"What are you doing, man?" Hesi whispered. Darris's eyes were wide.

It didn't really matter what any of them thought, or whether he lived. *Secure the medical facility and take the tower, by any means necessary.*

The doctor worked furiously, sterilizing and reaching for her operating tools, then she stilled one of her hands enough to insert the fine needle of the device. She withdrew some sort of substance from the robotic spinal column and held it up to the light. "I don't have any painkillers that will let you remain conscious," she warned. "And introducing something foreign to your system is going to be quite painful."

No way, no how was he going to risk passing out. And the last time he'd been shot with a chemical compound, Aly had been the one doing the injecting—the taurine that had lowered his body temp and nearly killed him, all to escape the heat sensors most military bots came equipped with. "I can handle it," he said.

Then, at the last minute, he wondered about his own memories—if they'd be corrupted, lost. He'd always been such a hard-ass, never recalling anything in the Wray, never wanting to think of his dad. But he'd always imagined that one day when he was ready he could find those memories again, relive them when he was smarter, wiser, a hell of a lot less angry.

And then he wondered if he'd forget moments with his ma, Alina, Vin. *Kara*, he thought.

"Wait—" he said, just as he felt the pinprick of a needle. And then . . .

A surge, instantaneous and massive—information everywhere, like water, flooding into his brain and choking his own synapses, smothering them. Everything was going under. The droid's mind took his over—but it wasn't a mind. It was a collection of directives, prioritized. Mechanical, black and white, clear-cut instructions to be executed no matter what.

Every thought, every impulse Aly had was being drowned out beneath the data, blueprints and names and programs sweeping him up in a current.

His brain was swelling; it would burst like a balloon. It felt like the bloating of a new bruise but a million times more intense, a billion. It would break his brain, then his skull, then crack his skin until he was just light, burning like the sun.

He couldn't hold it all.

Breathe. His own voice came to him beneath an all-out assault of sounds and memory and thought. *Breathe. Let it pass.*

He soared across the threshold of pain; in an instant, the information felt invigorating. When the data stopped flowing it stopped instantly, and he stumbled off the stool, dizzy with the newfound buzz of data and power. He inhaled deeply and closed his eyes. Nothing hurt anymore. His pain had been replaced by an overwhelming sense of focus. *Take the tower.* He knew exactly what he was doing and how he was going to do it. He could feel the network channels of a thousand other droids brushing up against his mind, like tendrils of growth sweeping his feet in a deep pond.

"Recirculate new orders," he said. "All droids within a five-hundred-meter radius to stand down."

He felt it instantly as his command was communicated to the other droids. He felt it in the pulse of a thousand answering affirmatives. He felt it in the sudden sense of collapse, as so many connected minds went dark and still. Their thoughts, if you could call them that, fell away, and there was nothing to replace them—only a void of memory and feeling and information.

Exhausted by this simple effort, drained by the sudden silence where only a second earlier had been a surge of system data, he staggered back out through the hospital.

"Where you going?" Hesi called from behind.

Aly ignored him, shuffling past baffled, terrified patients—while soldiers crossed his path in a brisk run toward the tower entrance at the center of the medical facility. He wouldn't join them. All the robodroids had followed his command and shut themselves down.

The satellite was theirs now. He'd done it. His first mission as part of the WFC, and he'd succeeded.

Outside, the rain was still pelting down. He clawed for his memories like an addict and saw Kara a thousand different ways all at once, like patchwork—the way she walked, the part in her hair, the line of her neck when she tilted her head back to look at the sun. A thrill moved through him, even if a part of him was desperate to lose them all. He would always give in to this weakness, would always look for Kara in shadows and nostalgia, in what could have been.

At least there she was alive.

He burst into the tower and raced to the control room, where several other WFC soldiers were already dismantling the communication servers. *Screw you, Nero*, he thought as he yanked at cords and smashed screens. He barely felt his elbow now. Nero's lies were like a toxin polluting the entire galaxy, and Aly was the antibody, fighting it off.

"Stop," a voice said. A Fontisian had entered the room, one Aly dimly recognized, but he wasn't sure from where. Aly was pretty tall—at least twenty hands high—but this guy was even taller. He wasn't wearing a WFC uniform, but he had tattoos all across his neck—tattoos of the Order of the Light. He moved less like a flesh-and-blood being than like a weapon. Was this one of their commanders? He knew the order was behind the WFC, but he hadn't been prepared for this. Around him, the other WFC soldiers stopped what they were doing reflexively and waited for word from the Fontisian. So Aly stopped and did the same, his muscles tense and bulging all the while—he wasn't done fighting yet. He wasn't ready to be still.

"We can't destroy it," the Fontisian leader said.

"That's exactly what we're here to do," Hesi protested. The Chrams were loyal folks.

"We only came here to secure it." The Fontisian held up a large hand. "Don't you think it's strange for a broadcasting tower to have almost no broadcasting equipment? These are all monitors."

"So?"

The Fontisian looked around at the room. "Do you not understand? The information is flowing *in*. Not out. Dismantle, but pack up as much as you can for evidence. Nero's got access to personal cubes across the galaxy."

Aly had always considered himself a decent reader of people, but the Fontisian had a serious poker face: neutral, if not a little bit uppity, like he was either judging you or didn't give enough of a *taejis* to judge you.

His gray eyes, when they turned to Aly, were similarly inscrutable. Finally, the Fontisian sheathed his sword. "Not unimpressive, how you've managed to disable the droids," he said.

Aly wasn't sure how the guy knew he was the one responsible. He only shrugged.

The Fontisian surveyed the shards of equipment strewn across the floor. "You've proven yourself quite . . . destructive. It appears your absolution has made you no less desirous of revenge."

"Some absolution," Aly said bitterly. He wondered if the Fontisian had seen the show *Revolutionary Boys*—or just the Most Wanted Holo-Alerts that had trailed Aly after he was framed for Empress Rhiannon's murder. "I'm just here to get what's mine."

"Which is?"

My land. My innocence. My body. "Justice," Aly said. Wasn't that the whole point of the WFC? To undermine Nero, to bring justice to those who deserve it. It was just an added perk that he got to tear *taejis* up along the way. "I'm here to put this war to bed."

"It won't be taken in a single attack," the Fontisian replied. Aly had forgotten that was their deal, the Fontisians—the glass always half-empty. "I'm Dahlen. And I'm recruiting for a special mission. You should join me."

"Is that an order?"

"It's an invitation." Dahlen smiled. Aly did not especially like his smile.

"An invitation to continue fighting," Aly said drily. "I'm flattered. And can I ask what you're doing on this special mission of yours?"

Dahlen didn't blink. He didn't stop smiling, either. "We're going to assassinate Nero."

And Aly could see right away that he was serious. He wasn't even sure Fontisians could lie.

Aly thought of the way Kara's eyes shifted colors in the light. The way she messed with her hair when she was thinking, and chewed her lip when she was nervous, and smiled huge when she smiled at all.

Kara: the girl he'd never said *sorry* to.

The girl who'd died because of the war Nero had started.

"Then I accept," he said. "So long as I get to plant the knife myself."

ELEVEN

KARA

RALIRE would've been beautiful if the wildflowers weren't covered in blood. Had skirmishes not broken out everywhere. Despite the danger, the actual capital of Ralire was bustling, going on about its business like war wasn't at its doorstep.

Pulling a *duhatj* over her head, Kara raised her hand to hail an approaching pod on the dirt road that would lead her to the city. She was more self-conscious than she'd ever been. She had never really liked her face, but who did? Now it was changing, and just this morning she saw her cheekbones had widened and lowered, and nothing felt like hers anymore. Everything was wild and new, and she was propelled forward by the coordinates that would lead her to the overwriter.

Once she found it, she could use it to erase the memory of Josselyn Ta'an for good. Not that she knew how to use the over-writer, or even what the tech looked like, but she could figure that out later—she always did. It was probably a small device not too different from a cube. She didn't want to think of what would happen if she was wrong, or the info didn't pan out, or the lead was cold.

The overwriter had to be here—she would accept no other option.

Lydia had meant for her to find it. The Lancer too. Otherwise, why would the message open only at her touch? It had read her DNA. If Lydia had wanted Kara to destroy the overwriter, she had made sure that Kara could find it.

And she would destroy it. Right after she used it to destroy her past.

The icy wind stung her face, its snow an odd comfort on her lips. This, Kara thought as she boarded the pod, was the first choice she had ever made for herself. Behind her, the Frontline Physicians craft became a small white blip on the sprawl of green.

The pod lifted into the sky, and the ocean emerged on Kara's left. Along with a few other passengers whose names she would never know, she hurtled toward the center of the city. In the horizon a spire appeared; it looked like some giant had stuck a serrated knife in the ground. From the distance she could see the dark vein of fuel that ran up the middle, and around it, docking stations jutting out at varying heights gleamed in the sun.

Ralire's position in the orbit, and the capital's position on the water, had shaped an entire economy at the fueling station's base, creating a compact city where you could purchase anything from rare plant species to stolen engine parts. Some of the other medics had casually floated the idea of checking it out—supplies were low, and as the war spread through the galaxy, the emergency beacons went off constantly. The demand for help outpaced what they could provide. There weren't enough resources to answer every call, which left the volunteers itching for a break—some sort of distraction from all the death and destruction.

Nicola had warned them all against it, though—last thing any of them needed was some drifter to rake their pockets clean for a sugar pill, or worse, feed them drugs that'd devour them from the inside out. *They'll sell anything on Ralire*, she'd said, and she wasn't going to rescue anyone who got themself into trouble.

But Kara had no choice. She knew the others wouldn't notice that she was gone, especially given the latest surprise: Rhiannon had allied with Nero. The headline was on every holo channel you could find, and people were worked up about it.

Kara wouldn't try to understand what *that* meant. She definitely didn't want to know what it would mean for Rhiannon. Half the holo feeds were doing nothing but urging Josselyn to come forward, to salvage what they were already calling her sister's failure as an empress.

Even more reason Kara had to succeed in her mission, and quickly. The sooner she destroyed Josselyn's memory, the sooner her sister could rule in peace.

The pod dropped her at the base of the fueling tower. The coordinates led her deeper into the city, into the warehouse district, where all the manufacturing for the Outer Belt had once occurred.

She wrapped her arms around herself, wishing she'd prepared better for the atmosphere. The crisp air had almost cleared her head, but the noise cluttered it again; ships and pods roared overhead while people from all over the system talked in incessant streams around her. The constant stimulation wasn't helping. Another headache was coming on. The pain behind her eyes was sharp and steady, pulsing like a drill deeper into her gray matter.

She had lifted a portable positioning system from the medbay, and it clicked softly in her hand, warming her fingers with its electric heat. Skyscrapers gave way to low, squat buildings made of brick. Here, in the warehouse district, narrow sidewalks were lined with vendor stalls, and huddles of people hawking plants, pills, and spare engine parts wrenched her left and right and left again. Pods flew by on the street.

For a second, Kara wished Aly was with her. When Aly found her on the zeppelin, she'd felt so much less alone, like someone was looking out for her—and like she had someone to look after too. But that was just her being silly and stupid, as if something good could happen, as if something good could last.

She moved away from the main thoroughfares, pushed her way toward the coordinates into a claustrophobic alley that without warning emptied into a small plaza, buzzing with merchants selling the kind of black-market wares that would get a person arrested on any other planet. Vendors hawked the high of a lifetime and shouted about miracle tech that could only be fake. In the distance, Kara could hear live music, hollering, pharmaceutically enhanced chatter. The crumbling stone buildings that ringed the square, once grand factories, now seemed to ooze desperation—broken windows, subtle indications of skin for sale inside, black mold webbed in the stone.

She had goose bumps from the cold, but unease settled into her skin. *This* was where the overwriter was?

Kara stopped short as a man with a hose stuck between his teeth nearly clipped her. A gas guzzler—he'd siphon fuel from a docked ship and sell it to someone looking to save a few dollars.

"Watch it!" she called to his back.

A child, a little Miseu with yellow skin and a narrow upper body, pushed past her at a wobbly sprint. There was a bundle of bags with brightly colored powders tucked under her arm.

"Excuse you," Kara said, even if the girl was long gone and couldn't hear her. She moved to brush off the residual powder that had gotten on her arm, but someone grabbed her wrist and tugged her back. Hard.

She barely had time to register the WFC uniform before Issa pressed her against the wall.

"Are you trying to get yourself killed?" Issa said.

"I could ask you the same thing." Kara nodded to the stitches across Issa's neck as she pushed Issa's hands away. The soldier eased up on her grip. "Nice to see you up and about," Kara said not at all sweetly, even if she was glad to see her. People milled around them, but no one seemed to pay attention—or care. "Did you follow me here?"

"Maybe I was on the same pod as you." A vulnerable look flitted across Issa's face, then was gone. "I mean, yeah." Kara made a rolling gesture with her hands, urging Issa to go on. "What happened last night? After the surgery. Did we . . . talk?"

Kara understood then: Issa was just worried about what she had revealed. "Not really," she said. No need to make Issa relive her confession all over again. Kara wasn't one to judge anyway.

Issa seemed relieved. She looked away, squinting in the direction of the dying sun. Kara's stomach roiled at the sight of the wound on her neck, still raw-looking where Issa had tried to gouge out her cube. "You said something about seizures. Or something about how I should say I have them?"

"Did someone ask?" Kara said, a streak of panic zipping up her spine.

"No. I slipped out before anyone saw I was awake." Issa looked at her. "What did you tell them?"

"That if they resuscitated your cube, it would trigger a fatal seizure."

"So they disabled it because of you?" Issa asked. Kara shrugged. "How'd you even know that would work?"

"My mom's a—" Kara cut herself off and swallowed hard. "My mom *was* a neuroscientist."

"So you just picked up some expertise along the way, then?" Issa said. She looked around, and they were silent for a beat. "Well, for what it's worth, thank you. For telling the medics what's what. And for being there." She turned to Kara again, gesturing to her bright white Frontline Physicians smock. "No one should travel alone around here, especially a Kalusian girl."

"Do I look like I need a babysitter?" For some reason Kara felt defensive, even if just a day ago Issa had been a patient in her care, weak, nearly dead.

"Whoa. I'm just saying people aren't thrilled with Kalu starting a war and dropping soldiers on every piece of land they can reach," Issa said. "And anyway, don't think of it as a babysitter. Think of it as me watching your back. It's the least I can do, since you saved my life and everything."

"Actually, I almost killed you," Kara admitted.

"But you didn't." Issa's eyes burned into hers, and there was something curious, intense about it. Kara wondered what it would be like to dedicate yourself to vigilante justice—to be constantly on the lookout for ways to help those in need, to be willing to sacrifice your life for the safety of others. It was a kind of bravery that seemed beyond her imagination, and it made her feel ashamed.

Issa's gaze shifted into a smile, a full-on grin. "Besides, I was heading this way myself. Now that my cube's dead, I need something a little more old-fashioned to communicate with the rest of the crew. Something Uni can't track. I'm thinking a third eye."

Kara knew them; they were called I-3s, and Lydia had had one. *For sentimental reasons*, she'd always said. The clunky piece fit around the neck and collected dust on their shelf, and Kara always tried to hide it when people came over. It hadn't looked cool and vintage, just outdated and embarrassing. But now she wondered if Lydia had used it, if there were secrets communicated with the other G-1K scientists . . .

Kara was startled by the sudden, overwhelming desire to take whatever it was Issa was willing to give: help, a smile, kindness. She wanted to confess everything. What she was looking for, what it meant, what she had lost along the way. But she didn't know whether or not to trust Issa. And anyway, she'd leave just like everyone else did.

"I'm good on my own," Kara said.

Issa shrugged. "Whatever you say," she replied, as if she doubted every word Kara had said. "See you back at the ship, then?"

Kara nodded. She couldn't speak—she was worried that she might instead ask Issa to stay, just so she wouldn't be so alone. But she watched Issa slip off into the crowd, swallowing the impulse to call her back. She had to be alone. The message was intended only for her.

Kara reached into her pocket for the cipher, and a jolt of panic shot through her. It was gone.

She swallowed her nerves and swept her eyes across the small plaza. How could she have been so careless? Had she dropped it? Had someone taken it? When Lydia combed through plant specimens—her research—she looked for anomalies. As she relaxed, the crowd of individual people, the clutter of stalls, began to dissolve into mere shapes. Then these shapes too began to dissolve into patterns.

And finally, she latched on to a soul who seemed tense. Who seemed to be watching her. It was the little Miseu. Their eyes locked for a split second before the girl turned and ran.

Heart racing, Kara shoved her way through the stalls and the people milling between them—catching sight of the little girl just to lose her again. She crossed the street, and Kara let out a scream as the Miseu dodged a pod that sped past. Kara tried to follow but a quick sucession of pods flew by, a zipping sound in their wake as they cut through the air. She split her attention between the oncoming traffic and the girl, who disappeared into a building across the way. When the coast was clear, Kara ran after her.

The building she'd entered gave no signs of its purpose; it didn't even look inhabited. Kara followed through what was once a grand brick archway and shoved open a heavy door.

It was colder inside than it was out. A whole other world opened up inside the still-functioning factory, with low light and people hunched over, organized in more rows than she could count. There were conveyor belts, and the sound of compressed air at a regular interval, and hundreds of workers who barely looked up at her before returning to whatever minute detail they were in charge of. It looked this way all across the immense ground floor.

Kara took a close look at a nearby worker's handiwork and realized it now: It had the makings of a third eye. They were making comm tech, for people who didn't have cubes or couldn't afford them.

The Miseu girl ran up a spiral staircase in the back corner, and Kara followed.

Upstairs was a labyrinth, curtains separating off spaces into private nooks; Kara realized too late as she was trampling through that these were workers' sleeping spaces. She went hopping through, stopping and starting, trying to give people their privacy. But she got tangled in curtains, and woke so many souls up. There was no logic to the layout she could immediately discern; the hallway seemed to have a system all its own. Kara chased and chased. She caught a glimpse of the Miseu turning a corner and she followed, stopping at the end of a long dark corridor.

The girl entered a door that slammed behind her. Kara stood at the other end, chills working their way up her spine. She fought every instinct to turn around. She had to get her cipher. She needed it to access the overwriter.

Or what if the overwriter was *here*?

The knocker was missing—stolen, probably. She tapped lightly instead with her fist. A few seconds later, a hidden panel slotted open in the door, and a pair of bright gray eyes peered out at her.

"Kalusian girl," he said in lieu of a greeting. "You look like you're in need of guidance."

"No." Or was it *yes*? She looked down the corridor behind her. There was nothing. It seemed longer than it did on the way in. Usually, she was good at this kind of thing—bluffing, lying—but her confidence felt chipped away, thinned out. Her head spun. She turned around, not knowing what to say except for the truth. "The Lancer sent me."

Without another word, the man slotted the eyepiece closed with a final-sounding *click*.

Kara lurched backward, tightening her jacket around her, suddenly feeling cold and exposed. At the other end of the corridor, a Derkatzian in an oversize coat looked in her direction, his yellow eyes catching in the light. She turned the other way. A Chram leaning against the wall dropped his eyes quickly—but not so quickly she didn't understand he'd been observing her.

Kara had the sudden, pressing feeling that she had made a mistake.

She shouldn't be here. She should go, disappear, melt back into the darkness behind her. She flew out of the corridor, hurtled between rooms as the Chram seemed to follow her, and burst into the plaza outside. Her heart stopped when she spotted Issa not five feet away—wearing a third eye now, almost exactly like the one she remembered from childhood.

"Find what you were—?" Issa swallowed a sound of surprise when Kara grabbed her arm roughly. Her heart skipped—a man in a white robe was staring at her. Kara risked a glance: On the other side of the plaza, another man was watching her. How many were there?

"I think I made a mistake." Panic swallowed her. Spotting a narrow street between buildings that she prayed would lead back toward a pod that would take them back to the ship, she hauled Issa that way.

"What in the *choirtoi* is going on?" Issa said, in a low voice. But Kara could tell she didn't really expect an answer. Somehow, she had felt the danger too.

Another mistake. They careened around the corner only to realize they had reached a dead end. They would never get out. A silhouette had already appeared at the end of the alleyway. Waiting. They'd communicated via cube. Kara could never outrun a networked enemy.

They spun around and tried to backtrack toward the opening that led out to the plaza. They were close; they ran alongside windows and saw the crowd in the plaza was thinning as the sun edged close to the horizon. Kara could more easily pick out her observers now, many of them still idling at the stalls, pretending to be buyers.

"This way," Issa said, her voice low with understanding. She'd seen them too. So Kara wasn't imagining things.

Issa tugged Kara toward another alleyway, this one concealed behind a hanging curtain, and plunged through it. Kara struggled for a second with the heavy fabric before ducking in after her.

The first thing she saw was Issa, struggling with a man nearly twice her size. Her heart lurched as Issa caught a heavy blow directly to the head. She staggered sideways, coughing, clutching at her chest as if something pained her there.

"Run!" Issa gasped out.

But Kara moved instead for Issa. A foot kicked her knees from behind, and as she fell, a rough-hewn bag was pulled over her head. An acrid, synthetic scent filled her nose.

Kara fought wildly. Her foot made contact with flesh, but instead of letting her go, yet another pair of hands seized her wrists and bound them. She thought of Aly—what would he have done if he were here? But he wasn't, she reminded herself. He wasn't.

"Stop that," someone hissed. A woman's voice.

Kara tried to scream, but as soon as she opened her mouth, fingers forced the gag in, practically down her throat.

"We're not going to hurt you," another voice said into her ear. *"Princess Josselyn."*

TWELVE

RHIANNON

IT had been a week since Dahlen had left Rhee, a week since she'd publicly aligned herself with Nero. In that time, she and Nero had come to various agreements that they would announce in a joint broadcast later today—both Kalu and Fontis would pull out of neutral territories, air travel would be reinstated in the Relia Quadrant, and both warring parties had agreed to a cease-fire over Wraetan airspace.

For now, she was maintaining the façade of a unified front.

And so far, it had worked.

Along with everything else Nero touched, her popularity soared.

Well, not soared exactly, but she'd been featured favorably on the holos. Her approval rating was up. And though Rhee couldn't stand to see her own frozen smile and stiffly worded statement replayed endlessly on the holos, as time passed, she was increasingly certain that the decision—her decision—had been a necessary one.

For the first time since the war began, the United Planets had agreed to converge in Sibu to discuss the terms of an intergalactic treaty—their cooperation, too, a result of Nero's diplomacy, especially his announcement of a dispersal of his troops from around Wraeta. Soon, she hoped, she would restore enough peace, and enough faith in the Ta'an dynasty, that she'd be free to oust Nero for good.

For now, the war still raged, ravaging the system in tiny pockets that grew larger—and more unpredictable—with each passing day. The blast on Nau Fruma. Another rash of explosions in the Outer Belt. A few skirmishes that, somehow, always seemed to occur near UniForce peacekeeping troops. Rhee shivered, wondering where else violence had stuck itself, like a sliver burrowed underneath the skin.

Loneliness had crept into her too, in the same way: slow and unexpected. She caught herself balancing the coin across her knuckles, moving it between her index finger and pinky just like Dahlen had done. His departure was like a sudden sting—the pain was easy to ignore at first. And by the time it had spread through her like an infection, it was too late.

The ache wasn't like missing her parents—that wound was huge, undeniable, and she had been able to stanch it with the promise of revenge. She had no idea how to rid herself of the ache of missing Dahlen. It was her own doing, after all.

She turned the holo off. Rhee had insisted all the guards keep their distance. She couldn't stand the idea of a stranger taking Dahlen's place; it only made his absence more noticeable.

Silence filled the room, thick as smoke from a fire. Then, there was a flash of something uncomfortable: the feeling of being watched.

Don't be such a little girl. But it wasn't unreasonable to be so on edge, with everything that had happened. Though he ostensibly took measures to protect her, she couldn't put anything past Nero. He could still have her killed and simply frame someone else—again. Maybe the negotiations were just a game. She took comfort in the fact that Lahna was positioned outside her door.

The sun had gone down while she'd sat here watching the holos, alone. Moonlight from Nau Fruma peeked through the slats of her balcony door, razoring the dark tiled floor with light.

Again, the feeling of being watched pricked her skin into goose bumps. She couldn't give in to paranoia. Couldn't appear weak.

Rhee walked to the balcony door, craving something she did not know how to name. Even though going outside was discouraged—the threats against her life weren't few, as Dahlen might have said—she punched a code into the door's keypad. Obediently, it opened. Moonlight flooded in. Cool air drenched her. The smell of roses from the garden—her mother's garden—drifted into the room.

A shadow flicked in the corner of her eye. Fear spiked in her blood. She backed away from the balcony door and closed it with the punch of a button, straining to see the dark corners of her room. Like a child, she thought again, a little girl afraid of the dark. But now she had Veyron's knife in the folds of her robe.

Then, as soon as she'd relaxed her grip on the hilt, the balcony door slid open for a second time.

A shadow moved across the way, and Rhee lunged. She wielded her knife, but not fast enough. The assailant knocked it out of her hand. The defensive movement was familiar, the way the person wove back, struck in a wide arc with the left hand. Suddenly, Rhee could hardly breathe.

"Julian?" Rhee called out to the shadow.

He stepped into the light and pulled back his hood. His sandy hair was longer now, and even though it had been only weeks since that night under the meteor shower, he looked older. It was something about the cut of his jaw, the line of his brow. Her heart warmed. Every fear melted away. Her pulse sped up, with excitement, with anticipation. He'd finally come.

'Til I see you next, he'd said that day on Nau Fruma when they last parted. The stars were raining down on them then.

"You got my messages . . ." Rhee moved toward him instinctively, and she paid the price. Now it was his turn to lunge, pinning her to the dresser. She tried to call for help, but he muffled her scream with a rough palm.

She spun to the right, but he anticipated it, blocked her off, and grabbed her forearms. *He knows*, Rhee realized. He knew about Veyron's death. She wiggled her left elbow free, but again, he blocked it deftly; it was a feint to bring her legs around his torso from behind anyway, but he easily grabbed her legs and turned her on her side, like he'd known that was coming—because he had.

He picked her up, took his left forearm to her neck, and slammed her against her wardrobe. His right arm pinned her left wrist down.

Rhee knew this dance. It was skill, it was practiced. It had happened a thousand times before. She could hardly breathe, though it had little to do with the arm against her throat.

She wasn't used to their height difference—had he grown in the short time between Nau Fruma and now? At least some things hadn't changed; it was clear he still favored his left side. It was the same hold he'd put her in the last time they sparred. Rhee hadn't looked up then—she'd been afraid he would kiss her.

Now, she was afraid he'd do something much worse. Rhee looked up this time, but darkness shielded Julian's clear blue eyes from view. The eyes that used to tell her everything she'd needed to know, even before he spoke. Heat spilled off him. Being here, with him hovering over her, was new and unknowable and terrifying. Her best friend. The boy she used to race through the sand dunes on Nau Fruma. The one she'd said goodbye to under a sky raining down in rock and fire.

"Did you think I wouldn't find out?" His lips brushed against her ear.

Rhee squeezed her eyes shut. He'd come to make her pay for what she'd done. A vision flashed through her memory, visceral and organic: Julian's father, Veyron, bleeding at her hand.

He doesn't know, she thought.

He didn't know Veyron had tried to kill her first.

Julian pressed his forearm harder into her throat. Her windpipe strained under the pressure. Heat and sweat gathered in all the places their skin touched: wrist, arm, thigh. The reality sunk in that he was truly here to kill her, that every moment they'd shared before this meant nothing in the face of Veyron's death. Did she think their friendship was so powerful as to make her immune? *Think you're special?* someone had whispered in the crowd on Tinoppa, when she'd rushed forward in her own haphazard attempt to kill Seotra.

"Remember what he used to say?" Julian asked. "That you weren't a tactical thinker. You react. You never get in front of the fight."

"Shut your mouth." Rhee eased her free hand behind the folds of her robe, then remembered he had kicked away her knife. Was she willing to stab him, like she had his father? *We're friends.* The thought raced through the wrinkles in her brain. Julian wanted her to die. Why did this devastate her, when Rhee herself knew that the singular desire for revenge was more powerful than friendship, reason, love? Hadn't she done the same thing? Blamed a man for the actions of another? Rhee gathered herself. This needed to be fought like a battle.

"He also said I was graceful where you were clumsy," she told Julian now. "What was that word he used to describe you? Uninspired."

Julian pressed harder. "You know what's uninspired? This charade to take back your throne is uninspired. Killing him was uninspired. Partnering with Nero? Uninspired."

Tears sprang to her eyes, though she wasn't sure if they were from pain or Julian's words. But it was all true, wasn't it?

"Is that why you killed my father?" he whispered. "Because he saw right through you? Because he knew how power-hungry you really were?"

"No." She was almost glad that was all she could manage—she felt her dignity, her resolve, wane with every second she stared up at him. At the hate in his eyes. At the memory of Veyron's blood spilling over her knife, hands, cloak. If Julian didn't have her pinned, would she have already dropped to her knees and begged forgiveness?

But no—his father had tried to kill her.

"Then why?" he spit.

He didn't know that Veyron had been the one to betray her. He didn't know that his father was the one to make the deal with Nero first—a deal to destroy Rhee and stop her ascent. She could tell him now, set the record straight. But for what? To clear her name on the off chance Julian would spare her life? It would only sully the version of Veyron he had, reframe every memory into something dishonorable and sinister. The father, the trainer, the loyalist—he'd disappear.

Rhee had already killed Julian's father. She couldn't kill the memory of him. She wouldn't.

Instead, she drove her hip into him. He'd budged, only barely, but it was enough of a surprise—he'd loosened his hold on her wrist. She yanked her right hand out of Julian's sweaty grip. Her elbow made sickening contact with his neck. He stumbled back, gasping. Rhee lifted her knife from the floor and pointed it at him. Julian was swimming in anger, she could see, focused on everything he thought he knew.

They stood a meter apart now. He pulled his own weapon out of his waistband behind him. It was a hatchet. Small, compact. She scrambled for the memory—he used to use it in the greenhouse. Or to dig up rocks in the garden. Her mind reeled with the need to remember this completely inane detail, like part of her was desperate to go back, back, back.

"That knife doesn't belong to you," he said, using the hatchet to point at Veyron's blade. What he'd meant to say was *It belongs to me.*

She twirled it. A showy, obstinate move, even as her heart was breaking. "Then come and get it," Rhee said. Suddenly another organic memory rose. She'd found a shell of a crab once by the shore, perfectly preserved. Rhee had held it up to the sun, admiring it, when Julian snatched it out of her hand and jumped into the river. *Come and get it*, he'd yelled to her, while she peeled off her ceremonial dress to dive in after him.

She couldn't think of such things. Not of Julian, her Julian. In the dojo they'd never held back. The more skill and stamina you brought, the more you showed respect to your opponent. You had to challenge one another truly; it was in the service of both fighters becoming better than they were. But their sparring never had truly violent ends. It was never about winning, and it was never about harm.

But tonight was different.

If Julian was here to avenge his father, he would fight until the death. And Rhee would not take that honor away from him. She had only one option. She didn't have the luxury to die—not now, not with the threat of Nero. She was the Empress and had come back to rule, to reclaim her responsibility and live the legacy she'd been born into.

Which meant that Julian would die tonight.

He moved in, his eyes never leaving hers. Rhee swiped at the air, just missing as he ducked. He was only a shadow, she told herself. An opponent. They moved in a half circle around her bed, and when he swung his axe, she ducked, and it wedged into the wood post behind her. The sound of wood cracking startled her; she hadn't realized they fought in near silence, as they always had in the dojo. Rhee scrambled back, and Julian struggled with the axe; he couldn't free it.

Rhee thought she heard footsteps down the hall. Someone had heard them. *Lahna*, she thought. *Lahna and her bow.*

"Julian," Rhee tried, but he threw a punch with his protected arm; Rhee slashed wildly. If she'd hurt him she couldn't tell. He drove his forearm into her elbow to disarm her, and the knife went clattering to the ground.

They both dove. Rhee ended up on top of him. She punched his ribs as he finally seized the knife. She recoiled as he slammed the knife toward her at full force, and just managed to block his wrist with her forearm. The blade was so close it fogged at her breath.

He was stronger than he'd been only a few months ago. She used to be able to best him in a fight.

The thought occurred to her suddenly that maybe, all along, he'd let her win.

Julian. Her Julian. Suddenly his face in the darkness seemed to solidify. The mouth grim that so often she had seen wide with sudden laughter. The nose she'd broken when they were seven years old, landing her first punch after he'd taunted her that she couldn't.

Rhee swung off him sideways, and the momentum rolled him off his balance. She grabbed the knife and pinned him beneath her. She brought the blade to his neck.

They were panting. The moonlight cut in, and she saw how he had changed in just a few weeks' time. His jaw had squared off in anger. His floppy blond hair was wet, clinging to his forehead.

Rhee couldn't help herself; she swept it away. And there was the blue in his irises. Electric. The color of the sky she'd dreamed about.

Julian. Their friendship had saved her life. He was the only person who'd ever felt like an extension of herself. She never felt alone if Julian was there. In truth, he was the only one who could stand her. Now all she felt was the heat off his body, the hatred in his stare. He wanted her to die.

No, he wanted to punish her.

"What's stopping you?" he said. The blade trembled in her hand. "Do it."

"Shut up," she whispered. She remembered how he used to egg her on—called from ahead to make her swim faster or run harder. He expected her to be her best, to be his equal. Rhee thought of the summer she'd spent the afternoons trying to kick up into a handstand. How he'd been there rattling off facts so she might find her balance in distraction and ease.

"This is your legacy, Rhiannon," he said. The flatness of his voice stung more than any insult. "War. Death. Disloyalty. Wouldn't the ancestors be proud?"

"I said *shut up*." When she'd been sent to Nau Fruma after her parents had died, he'd chased her out onto the dunes. When she screamed, so did he. They'd been so young, yelling until their throats were ragged, screaming at the injustice of it all. Tears poured from Rhee's eyes. Sand stuck to her face and tangled her hair. And Julian did nothing but sit next to her, staring out toward the horizon. He didn't say anything while she cried. He didn't need to.

In a sudden movement, she threw the knife across the floor.

For a second, he stared at her. His eyes changed. The blue darkened. With a sudden roar of fury, he shoved her off him and dove for the knife. She kneeled there, numbly, quietly, even as he drove her backward.

Her head hit the floor but she didn't feel it. She didn't want to feel anything. He straddled her, the blade to her neck. Rhee felt his weight on her, felt the muscles in his thighs tighten around her. He was shaking.

"Why?" he asked. The cruelty had drained away, and he'd become that same little boy again, desperate to know. He grabbed her chin and forced her to look at him. She saw the scar on the underside of his chin from when he'd fallen off the palace wall. She saw everything, all at once, the love turned to terror, the boy she'd betrayed.

"How could you?" he repeated, and his voice broke. "How could you?" he said again.

She blinked back tears. "I didn't want to," she said. The knife pressed into her neck, the cool metal, the sharp edge. He really would kill her. Rhee would let everyone down, but she wouldn't blame him. "Believe me."

What else could she say to the boy on his knees, mourning the father he'd loved? Nothing would bring Veyron back, certainly not the truth. Nothing would bring any of them back. Her parents were dead, and she'd never found her sister. And didn't Dahlen leave because she'd proven herself unworthy?

"Drop it."

Lahna's voice was quiet, calm, and deadly. Julian froze. Lahna was silhouetted in the doorway, with her loaded bow aimed straight at his head.

"Lahna," Rhee called out. "Don't. He's—" *My friend.* "He's the son of Lancer Veyron and Marguerite Zolana." She listed out his lineage, an old moon custom reserved for warriors before a fight. Her voice was raw, desperate. "You will not kill him. This is our fight."

Rhee didn't know how Lahna might react, but she hadn't expected she'd drop her bow to the ground and press her index fingers to either eye. Rhee knew it was a religious sign of respect, and a way for those who follow Vodhan to honor the dead.

In one silent movement, Lahna kneeled.

"What are you doing?" Rhee asked.

"Honoring the memory of a hero," she said, bowing her head. "Lancer Veyron made great sacrifices for the resistance."

Rhee shook her head. *No*, she thought. *It couldn't be true.* If Lancer was a hero, that meant—

"Your father," Lahna continued, speaking to Julian, "paid the ultimate price for his loyalty."

THIRTEEN

ALYOSHA

AS the WFC moved south, the rain on Uustral turned to snow. It had a fresh, metallic scent to it and a habit of landing everywhere—on Aly's eyelashes, on his lips, and on the open field outside. Dahlen had recruited him on the satellite mission and now prepped him for the debriefing in the makeshift locker room—which was really just an insulated tent that barely kept them safe from the cold. For now.

It had been five days since they raided the tower, and the WFC had spent almost every hour strategizing, repairing weapons, and, most important, attempting to analyze the equipment they'd stolen from the satellite control center. Aly could barely focus, what with all the yo-yoing between burning rage and the moments of a deep, quiet blue—and a feeling that his heart had been flooded with ice water. He'd always been so good at keeping it casual, cool, going with the flow—and now he caught himself glaring up at the sky, as if Vodhan were watching now, as if the creator himself had stood back to let the world burn.

They had found sanctuary among the Uustralite army, which had recently come out and pledged allegiance to Fontis. This was all despite the fact that northern Uustral, where the satellite they had disabled was located, now claimed allegiance to Nero.

No surprise there: Nero had been paying northern Uustral handsomely for the use of its massive satellite. But Dahlen's hunch had proven correct. The sophisticated comms they'd torn out of the control center were actually a slightly outdated type of hard drive, meant to *store* information, not communicate it. Information was coming *in* via the satellite—information from all over the galaxy. The hard drives were encrypted and hard to crack, but the snippets the WFC intelligence team had extracted so far had a memory-like quality to them.

A *personal* quality.

The WFC had already long suspected Nero was spying on their cubes, even while they were off—but they never thought even he would stoop so low as to poach data from ordinary civilians, let alone civilians as widespread as that satellite could reach.

And Aly thought he had problems? The entire galaxy was fracturing. His own puny life was at best a messy microcosm of the truth.

In the end, everything always fell apart.

Aly ran the tap and cupped his palms to make a bowl, collecting the freezing water in his hands. He brought it to his face and felt the cold shoot down his spine. He made his way over to the bench where they had thrown all their stuff, and shrugged into his shirt, buttoning it up. Distantly, he heard the tinny voice of a newscaster beaming off somebody's handheld, replaying the same endlessly dissected news of Rhiannon and Nero's diplomatic gambit. Aly wondered what Kara would think of Rhiannon's new alliance with Nero.

And then he remembered that Kara didn't have an opinion and never would again. The grief was sudden and so deep it numbed his bones, and he fluttered his eyes closed.

"You don't look well," Dahlen observed as he slipped into his own WFC-issued button-up. "Are you in pain?"

A ray of sunshine, this one. Lots of the soldiers messed around and blew off steam, but not Dahlen. Super cut and lean all around, whiter than a ghost, with blond eyebrows so light you sometimes couldn't even tell they were there, Dahlen moved like he was slicing through the air, chasing demons off with that fierce face of his.

But what tripped up Aly the most was a long, precise scar on the upper left side of his chest, like someone had tried to slash up his heart. The scar puckered in places from where it had been stitched. Aly didn't even bother asking him for the story; this was a dude whose idea of bonding was assassination.

He had, however, figured out where he recognized Dahlen from: holovision broadcasts of Empress Rhiannon's return to Sibu. This was the Fontisian guard who'd picked Rhiannon up like a doll and tossed her over his shoulder in the midst of a street brawl outside the palace walls.

Only now, the Empress was colluding with Nero, and Dahlen was no longer with her in Sibu but here, planning a kill.

"I'm all right." It was the first time he'd been with Dahlen alone since they'd headed south. He nodded to Dahlen's chest. "I bet that hurt."

Dahlen shrugged. "I can't say the recovery was too pleasant."

Aly turned away and slipped into his fatigues with a bounce. "Some sort of freaky initiation into the order?" He tried to make it sound casual.

"I'm no longer part of the order," Dahlen answered plainly. Aly thought for a second a flicker of pain passed over his face, but it was gone so fast he wasn't sure.

Dahlen turned on his heel to exit the tent. Aly followed him, half-amused, half-annoyed by Dahlen's seeming resistance to any kind of conversation that wasn't tactical.

"I thought those vows were for life," Aly said. The cold air hit him hard, especially at his elbow—which had been healed at the camp's medcenter with a handheld stem cell gun. Pain shot up the bone in this weather, but Aly tried his best not to react.

"They are," Dahlen said as they fell into step, walking side by side to the outpost of war tents. "Unless one of the commandments has been violated."

Aly raised an eyebrow. "You don't look like the rule-breaking type." Aly didn't know much about the order's vows, but figured there was one for chastity. There usually was. "Was it a girl?" He thought of the Empress.

"Don't be absurd," he said, in a way that sounded bored. "We're not friends. There is no need to share."

Aly guessed what Dahlen said was true: Just because they were going to assassinate Nero together didn't mean they were friends. Aly doubted whether Dahlen had ever had any. Not like Aly had any friends left either. He thought of Vin, and the hammer he'd laid on his grave on Naidoz. Of Jeth, wherever he was. Of Kara, and how sometimes she'd curl up into a ball and rest her chin on her knees. The way their hands clasped through the chain-link fence. The way her body lay limp, buried in rubble, consumed by a pointless war.

Aly pushed the organic memories way down deep, as far as they could go. But the rest of his past brimmed up around them.

Alina, Mom, Dad: gone. He remembered sometimes how he'd see Alina around the Wray.

"What's good, little brother?" she'd yell from across the way, always checking in, mostly to embarrass him. But he missed it. He missed someone looking out for him.

Aly blinked away those thoughts of home too. He took in the landscape outside. Crisp and clear. Kara would've loved it. Would've said something about its cleansing nature, how it makes the whole world look pure and true . . .

"I've decided I hate snow," Aly said aloud. He was a minute away from icing over and cracking apart in his WFC fatigues. Meanwhile Dahlen wore a light black T-shirt, dark veins popping out of his pale arms and crazy tattoos along his neck on display like the cold couldn't touch him. Aly wondered if it was true—he'd heard all kinds of crazy *taejis* about members of the order and their mythic strength and powers. It was a little hard to swallow, the more he thought about it: how the order, essentially an ancient organization founded on notions of worship and peace, formed and funded a resistance group like the WFC. Sure, the WFC had once been dedicated to peaceful operations, but they'd become freedom fighters, emphasis on fighters. A bunch of stoic Vodheads behind the galaxy's fiercest vigilante group.

But Aly had given up on the idea that there was a hard difference between right and wrong or between justice and suffering. One couldn't exist, really, without the other. He knew that. Nothing should surprise him anymore. And still it did.

"You can't dislike the snow," Dahlen replied. Typical. Fontisians and their double negatives. "It's a necessary function of nature. It drains off the mountaintops and feeds into the valleys so they'll be provided with water."

Aly stared at the guy—a real utilitarian. Not a poetic bone in his body. They might have prayed to the same god, but the Order of the Light folks had a literal interpretation of everything.

Well, Aly could do that too.

"Here's what I think of snow," he replied. He reached down, scooped up a handful, let it melt against his skin. "You touch it and it's gone."

Pavel was waiting for Aly just outside of the military outpost: dozens of scattered tents arranged in a traditional nautilus pattern. Pavel had been delivered from repairs only two days ago, and Aly still felt a huge swell of gratitude to see his little cylindrical body glowing there in the snow.

"It's thirty-seven degrees Celsius below the humanoid body temperature."

"You're sounding kind of happy about it."

"I'm eager to see what it does to your biochemistry. I've never had the opportunity to document your reaction firsthand to such an uninhabitable temperature!"

"That's some greeting, little man." Aly nodded a hello just as Pavel opened up his hatch, extending an orange heat rod for Aly to warm his hands. Aly shook his head and huffed warm breath into his cupped palms instead. Since his return, Pavel had been tailing Aly to show off his new comfort features.

"You didn't program this one, did you?" Dahlen said when Pavel offered the heat rod to him.

"Why?" Aly shot back. "Didn't think I could?"

"No, I didn't," the Fontisian said flatly. He held his palms up to the device, though he didn't seem all that cold—just curious. "Not for a lack of intelligence but for a lack of charm. The droid seems a bit more . . . cheerful than I would have assigned to you."

Like this guy was one to talk.

"Yeah?" Aly said. "This is one of my good days too."

With Pavel now rolling on his treads behind them, Aly and Dahlen entered the maze of tents, and people did their damnedest to scramble the hell out of their way as they walked side by side down the snowy path toward the largest tent in the center of camp. Aly didn't know how to react; he only knew he had to front like he wasn't freezing his butt off. And more important, like he knew what the hell the plan was.

Aly pushed past Dahlen into the largest tent. Uustral-made—he still had to turn sideways to fit through the opening. The indigenous species of Uustral were built smaller, way smaller, all striated muscle with flat skulls. But what they lacked in height they made up for with bluntly shaped heads that housed some seriously complex brain cortexes. The Uustralites had developed tech way out of anyone's league.

Inside, they took seats around a small table surrounded by a handful of high-ranking WFC fighters, and Pavel stationed himself just behind Aly and to his right. Aly felt self-conscious, like he always did on *The Revolutionary Boys* when they would first start the filming. He never knew how to move, or what to do with his hands. Now, the Uustralite general nodded at them and began to speak. To Aly, it sounded like he was humming a tune underwater. The tent was outfitted with a translation net, fortunately, which caught the sonar of a voice and bounced it back to you in your native language.

"Welcome," he said to Dahlen and Aly. "We are gathered here to discuss Operation Scorched Eagle."

Aly tried to play off a snort like he was coughing. Pavel gave him a subtle bump on his leg. Aly willed his face into something neutral. Man, he'd forgotten how every military outfit had a flair for drama.

But Dahlen had noticed and glared at him from the next seat over.

"I've missed the humor," Dahlen said. "Do you not care to explain?"

He was getting sick of this guy's backward way of talking, his stoicism, his blank slate of a face that never had expression apart from sour. "I mean, Operation Scorched Eagle? That's the part where we drop down and kill Nero, right?"

The Uurstral nodded. "Yes, of course," he said, oblivious to how ridiculous and showy these code names were. "We're going to drop you, Alyosha, down on the center of Verdal, where you'll wait to be intercepted by the UniForce—"

"Hold. On." Aly stood up. His head hit the top of the tent, and he pushed it up above his head, annoyed. "What the hell are they talking about?"

Dahlen looked him up and down, pushing the blond curtain of hair out of his face. "Is it not clear yet? You're notorious, Alyosha."

"Thanks?"

"The galaxy could never muster an all-out enthusiasm for you on the show. They liked you, but tepidly."

Didn't Aly know it. Still, the reminder dug through him, nailed him in the ribs like a hard left hook. Vin had always been the loveable star of *The Revolutionary Boys*. At best Aly had been the quiet sidekick. But after he'd been outed as a Wraetan, Aly with his dark skin and his dark eyes became the volatile war refugee they watched—wondering when he'd go off like a bomb.

"Okay, look, Dahlen. Because you don't know much about much, let me break down social interaction for you," Aly told him. Pavel slowly rolled between them, and had extended himself up to the tallest setting so that his top dome blocked their faces. He used to do the same thing when he and Vin were fighting. Aly elbowed him backward. "Literally every time you think about saying something," he said to Dahlen, "keep your mouth closed, step back, and just *don't*."

"I didn't mean to offend," Dahlen said, in the tone of someone who doesn't give a *taejis* whether he offended or not. Pavel began to creep up again, but this time Dahlen pushed him back. "But is it not true that the public was just waiting for a reason to hate you? Nero has an impeccable sense of timing. He seized on that suspense. He set you up."

"Thanks for the recap, but I could have just streamed the reruns." It didn't matter that his name had been cleared, or that Rhiannon still lived; the damage was done. There were some people who never trusted him and never would. Aly felt anger ripple through him.

"I can't imagine how much it would displease Nero if he knew you'd abandoned the UniForce only to end up fighting on behalf of the WFC." If Dahlen could tell Aly was fuming, he didn't show it. He didn't let up, either. "In Nero's book, that's treason."

It *was* treason, in anyone's book. A shudder of suspicion ran through Aly. "Is this some sort of threat?" His back tensed in his seat.

"It's not a threat. Imagine the ratings, should Nero capture you: notorious criminal, traitor to the UniForce."

Suddenly, Aly understood. What an idiot he was—thinking Dahlen had recruited him for his performance. "So you're handing me over?"

"No." Dahlen appeared calm—not that this was any different from how he always seemed, which annoyed the hell out of Aly. He tried to check his rage, but it was wild, leaping inside him. "But that's what we *want* Nero to think. Here's how we're going to get him. We're going to trap him. I don't need you to shed his blood, Alyosha. I just need you to be—"

"The bait," Alyosha finished bitterly. "I get it."

And yet—it was a decent plan, one that played right into Nero's weakness for spectacle, for heroism, and for publicity. The man was a human peacock.

"Do I have your agreement?" Dahlen asked.

To use him as live bait. Aly didn't like the plan one bit. But if it would mean Nero died . . . "I'm assuming I don't have a choice."

Just then a soldier burst into the tent. His pale skin and pointed ears were a dead giveaway for a full-blooded Fontisian. He looked like he was sweating bullets, and he glanced around urgently, probably not used to so many high-ranking officers in one space. He bowed.

"You haven't interrupted us unless there's a message to be conveyed?" the Fontisian officer said. The boy nodded, bringing his hand from his cube to the glass dome on the center of the table. It projected a holographic map of Wraeta, or the pieces left of it, all corralled by the giant electromagnetic net.

"Nero and Empress Ta'an have agreed to ease off his planned military offensive on Uustral as well as Nau Fruma and territories in Relia Quadrant. A United Planets council has already been scheduled to discuss the accords. They will announce later today, 1800 Kalusian time."

Dahlen frowned. "I imagine he has not made this promise without conditions."

The general nodded in Uustralite fashion; his large head traced circles in the air. "Curious: It seems Nero is willing to stand down if Kalu is granted exclusive access to Wraeta's surface."

"It's likely they want access to minerals that will fuel their armada."

"It would take forever to convert all that raw material," an Uursalite officer said.

"Well, maybe he plans for this war to go on forever . . ." another officer mumbled.

Aly felt the skin on his neck prickle. Kara's mother, Lydia, had indicated that the overwriter—a tech with enough power to not just strip away all of Kara's memories of her childhood but alter them too—was hidden on Wraeta.

Aly hadn't wanted to believe that it existed. But what if it did? Nero was trying to spy on people, that much was obvious, and he already had pretty sophisticated tech. But he'd known the G-1K summit scientists had created something even better. The overwriter. That had to be it. That's why Lydia had wanted it hidden.

"The overwriter," Aly blurted out. He'd stood up, and now all eyes were on him.

"The what?" a Wraetan general asked.

Aly licked his lips. His throat felt dry; he couldn't talk.

"Nero wants the overwriter." He wasn't sure what made him so certain, but between the giant satellite that was acting more as a receptor than a broadcaster, and the stories Lydia had told them of the G-1K summit scientists, and the creepy lab of lobotomized patients he'd seen on the zeppelin with Kara, he was starting to outline a picture in his mind of Nero's intentions.

That beautiful piece of science that had taken Kara's memories. She'd wanted to track it and destroy it, for precisely this reason. It would be a deadly weapon in the wrong hands.

Everyone around the table began arguing at once—demanding to know how he knew of this overwriter, whether it could exist, and why they should believe Aly, the Revolutionary Boy turned outlaw turned vigilante turned Dahlen's bait. The translator went haywire trying to keep up with the acoustics. Feedback cut through Aly's ear and into his brain. A high-ranking Fontisian with an electric ring sent out a signal to jam the translator so it dropped. Now it was a flurry of languages, but all the same angry pitch.

"Enough!" Dahlen shouted in Fontisian, and everyone immediately went quiet. The Fontisians looked like they'd been slapped. Aly would have bet he'd never raised his voice before.

In the perfect silence, Dahlen turned to Aly. A low hum meant the translator net was live again. "Where did you hear about the overwriter?" he asked.

"So you've heard of it?"

"There's very little the order hasn't heard of. They knew of its creation, were involved for years in trying to . . ."

It was unusual for Dahlen to trail off. "Trying to what?" Aly prompted.

"To neutralize it." Dahlen paused. There was a strange look on his face. As if he was trying to digest something sharp.

"Neutralize it?" Aly repeated. "Why not just destroy it?"

"You don't understand." Dahlen shook his head. "There's a living element."

"And?"

"We're not to do harm to any harmless beings."

Aly half expected Dahlen to laugh, or *someone* to admit to a joke. But after another expanse of silence, he cleared his throat. "You're some warrior monk who's slaughtered, like . . . I don't know how many people. Anyone hazard a guess? Anyone?" he said, looking around. "You're telling me you can't destroy a weapon that could cause mass destruction because it's got some cells all up in it?"

Dahlen stared at him coldly. "You wouldn't understand, and I don't presume you ever will. In any event, the directive is to *neutralize* it, so that's what we'll do. If the overwriter is hidden on Wraeta, and Nero is headed there to find it, we need to get you there first."

"Let's round up the troops, then." Aly stood up, brushing off his fatigues for a little bit of flourish. He did it so they wouldn't see the way his hands shook. "Don't want to keep Nero waiting."

Part Three:

THE COMPROMISED

"Not only does one worship the ancestors to honor the physical bodies from which they came, but also to honor the spiritual inheritance one receives. Lineage is remembered during the prayer, its lessons applied day to day. If such lessons lose their resonance, it is believed that one becomes lost."

— *Excerpt from* **A Comprehensive Guide to Kalusian Cultural Practices**

FOURTEEN

KARA

KARA stumbled again, as the person hauling her forward gave the rope binding her wrists a sharp tug. The noise of the market had faded, and she'd lost all track of time. How far had they gotten from the warehouse, from the medcraft? Would the other medics ever find them now? Would they even bother to look?

She hoped that Issa, at least, had managed to escape. But she knew better than to count on it.

She shivered. A mist had rolled in—Kara felt it on her exposed skin.

Princess Josselyn. Whoever they were, they knew who she was. They'd recognized her. Had she come all this way just to die on a rock in the middle of nowhere, before she got to the overwriter?

Before she got to see her sister again?

That last thought surprised her. She hadn't been thinking of Rhiannon—Rhee. Had purposely tried not to. Because Rhee wasn't really her sister, and if Kara was able to follow through with the overwriter, Rhee never would be her sister—but Kara was still this halfway person, empty, trapped in between two identities.

And now she was literally trapped.

Kara gritted her teeth and tasted dust. Her muscles tensed, a steady tightening down the length of her.

She was led over a threshold into a small building of some kind. The walls felt close; the room smelled vaguely of something both acrid and sweet. It reminded Kara of the starchy vegetable stew she'd learned to make all those nights Lydia was working late. Her insides ballooned with grief.

Then a hand pulled the bag from Kara's head. Her hair floated around her face, even more than usual in the slightly lower gravity. The room—a small space, empty except for a few chairs and a used wooden table—was so quiet she could hear the strands of hair crackle with static.

Her captors—four of them in all—were half-concealed by the heavy shadows. But one of them stepped forward, edging into the light. A smile twisted his face. The effort made the scar on his cheek turn white. Kara disliked him. She was pleased to see the dirt mark on his robe—he must be the one she had kicked earlier. He reached out a gloved hand and grabbed Kara's chin.

"She bit me on the way over," he said, turning back to his companions. "I should return the favor—"

Kara threw her head toward his nose, but he managed to jerk backward, and struck her down with a backhand before she could regain her balance. Her face slammed into the dirt floor, and the pain of it nearly shattered her. There was a metallic taste in her mouth—she'd clamped down on her tongue. Blood bubbled on her lips. Her vision was going fuzzy as the pain in her skull ballooned . . .

One of the others hauled Kara to her feet, then shoved her roughly into a chair. Kara's heart beat wildly.

"We aren't going to hurt you," the man said. His breath smelled of fermented elderberry. And Kara recognized his voice—he was the one who'd called her *Princess*.

"You have a seriously messed-up way of showing it." Her heart was doing jumping jacks in her chest. She fought through her own nausea to sit up straight.

The man behind her leaned down to breathe onto her neck, to torture her by slowly cranking her wrists upward, so her muscles screamed.

She cried out. Almost immediately she felt him ease off her, just slightly, but before she could wonder at this sudden change of heart, she heard a strange zipping noise—followed by a thud as the man fell to the ground, releasing her completely.

One minute he was there. The next, he was laid out flat.

"What the hell, Imogen?" One of the other captors addressed the question to the only woman in the group. Kara saw something silvery coiled in her hand.

"He said don't use unnecessary force, Kai," she called back. The man—Kai, apparently—slowly sat up, one hand on the back of his neck. "You breathing down the Princess's neck seems pretty unnecessary to me."

The noise came again, a high-pitched zip, and a slim silver cable uncoiled from Kai's ankle. Kara hardly caught a glimpse of it, a fine silver snake, before it retracted into whatever Imogen held in her palm.

She met Kara's eyes. "No need to scowl, sweetie. He's not going to hurt you."

"Don't call me that," Kara fired back. The Imogen girl was a few years older than her, tops.

Imogen smiled. She had small features that would've seemed fragile on anyone else, but in her beige jumpsuit and dark leather boots, she just seemed sharp, like if you touched her, you'd be the one to get hurt. "Whatever you say, Princess."

Kara could have screamed. It had been stupid to fight. She saw that now. She raised her chin. "What do you want?"

"What do you think they want?"

Kara turned, surprised—the voice, hoarse with age and exhaustion, came from what had seemed at first glance to be a pile of junk heaped in one corner. But then the pile shuddered, and took the shape of an old man. As he raised his head, she saw that his face appeared bruised.

"Credits," he finished bitterly. "Doesn't it always come down to credits?"

"Sure does, Diac," Imogen drawled. "And it did for you too. At least, it used to."

Diac. He was the original creator of the overwriter; he had built it with Lydia's help. He was supposed to have been dead. And for a second Kara felt sure that this was why she had been sent to Ralire—to find him.

But Diac, too, had been made a prisoner. His hands were tightly bound, his face pulpy with bruises.

A trap.

"Who's paying you?" Kara asked, directing the question to Imogen. For a split second of horror, she wondered if her own sister was behind the attack.

"Don't know, don't care." Kai was on his feet again, and his smile was even nastier than before. "But our payment is way bigger than the one Kalu's own empress was offering."

"On that note," Imogen said, "watch them."

Kai nodded, but kept near the door, poking his head out every few seconds. He seemed anxious, and Kara assumed that Imogen and the others had gone to negotiate her ransom. She couldn't even be afraid anymore. She barely registered her headache. Now she could only focus on the deep, dull ache—an empty hollow in her rib cage.

She had failed.

"I'm sorry I brought you here," Diac said, after a long stretch of silence. "It wasn't on purpose."

Kara nearly told him it didn't matter now.

But he went on, "I encoded the message to open for you, and only for you—there are vast stretches of your DNA that haven't changed, despite the scrambler—and gave it to the Lancer. I knew, or I hoped, that one day Lydia would send you to find him. The holographic message was coded to direct you to wherever I was at the time. In this case"—he lifted his hands to show his restraints—"in prison."

"Lydia thought you were dead."

Diac sighed. "I know. It was easier that way."

"You mean safer—for you," Kara said.

"It was all for nothing," he said. There was a note of shame in his voice. "I've served my purpose. They won't let me out of here alive."

Kara knew this was probably true. She was quiet for a bit. Then: "So the overwriter was never here on Ralire? It's been on Wraeta all along?"

"As far as I know," he said. "The capital would be totally razed by now. Your mother had a greenhouse there . . . if you stood on the southern pole in the springtime you could line it up with Etra, the Wolf, with Rilirinas, the Guardian, and Samba, the Matron." He smiled, and Kara knew why—it was a message. He was giving her star coordinates, something more permanent than street names.

Lydia had taught Kara how to line them up, how to find the perpendicular point in three-dimensional space that corresponded to the midpoint of the hypotenuse. She remembered the lessons so vividly now, the acute boredom, how she never thought any of it would possibly be of any use, ever. Kara had been so wrong.

"Your mother was brilliant," he said, as if he had just read her mind.

A fresh wave of grief traveled through her. "She wasn't my mother." Kara closed her eyes hard, as if she could forcibly scrub Lydia's death from her memory, but it surfaced anyway. What had she planned, sending her to the Lancer? The more Kara discovered about Lydia, the less certain she was of her adopted mother's intentions. What had she *wanted* for Kara? *Your blood—it's the key to everything.*

"Did you know Lydia and I met your mother once? The Empress?" His voice was softer now.

Kara shook her head, afraid if she spoke she might cry.

"Lydia was properly starstruck. The elegance that woman had!" He looked away, as if he could stare beyond these walls and into the distance. "Do you know what they talked about?" he asked, his head snapping back. He didn't wait for an answer. "Gardening . . ."

"Of course," Kara managed to say, letting out a laugh even as her throat tightened and the pulsing behind her eye sharpened.

"There was something about the cycle of life and death, growth and regrowth, that appealed to her. Nature doesn't have a memory. There's not past or present or future—just an instinct to grow toward the sun."

Was that what Lydia had been trying to do when she helped create the overwriter? Collapse the past and the future into a single impulse of will, into a single moment when the story was rewritten?

"*Erzel.* Do you know the word?" he said, switching to Fontisian. His accent was perfect, and he must have registered the surprise on her face. "Oh, yes. I'm half-Fontisian. My mother kept the secret of my father's real identity for many, many years. I don't blame her. There's many who would have hated her for it—and me."

Age had so ravaged him that Kara could no longer see signs

of the telltale Fontisian bone structure. But his eyes, she noticed, were ice blue. "'Erzel' means root."

"It means heart too," he said. His mouth smiled but his eyes looked dull, sad. "It is a concept passed down from Vodhan himself. I was a scientist my whole life, but now, here, I realize that all along, they were right. The heart is the root. Our memories, our thoughts, our ideas—these flower, wither, die, and regenerate. But the spark of life is buried deeper. It can be accessed only by the heart."

Kara thought Diac was trying to relay another hidden message. She quickly realized that she was partially right—this must be his way of telling her that Lydia had loved her. But what did it matter, now that Lydia was dead?

"You romanticize what you did," she whispered fiercely. "You built the overwriter because you could."

"We built it so people could somehow reconcile the horrors of war with the preciousness of life . . . we made it for survivors. If its purpose was perverted, that's because man is."

Kara's organs twisted in grief—and shame. She had already understood why the overwriter had held such appeal, when Diac and Lydia had first conceived of it: The past was too painful to be carried. Perhaps the Emperor saw that too, and considered that impossible decision to erase the Great War from memory.

But he hadn't. Did he change his mind, or did he die before he could use it?

We made it for survivors. She was a survivor, wasn't she? Did that make her case to erase Josselyn?

Muffled shouting from somewhere deeper in the house announced the other captors' return. Kai, who had been positioned all this time by the door, slipped out to greet them, leaving Kara and Diac alone for the first time.

"How does it work?" Kara asked quickly. "How did Lydia do it?"

He leaned toward her. "Any cube you're erasing off needs to be primed."

Her pulse began to race. "Or updated? Like the cube update that went live a few days ago?"

"Yes." Diac looked toward the exit and lowered his voice further. "Second, the overwriter itself needs a host. A living host that has free will, intent. It can't work inside, let's say, a tree— but it can be preserved there."

"So Lydia was the host? When she used it on me?"

He nodded as he leaned farther forward. A band of dim light fell across the valleys of his face. "But you have to know, to wipe your memory, Lydia had to wipe her own too. That was the sacrifice she made for you. For your safety."

"No." Kara reeled back. Her headache emerged, like it was seeping out of the soft tissue of her brain.

"You were young. She couldn't risk you compromising yourself. And we needed you alive in case the younger one—"

"In case she *died*," Kara said, finishing his sentence. It was a plan designed so that a Ta'an would take the throne. Other people playing games, taking bets on their lives.

"So if I want to use it, I have to give up my memories?"

"What do *you* want to use it for?" he said hoarsely, in a changed voice: filled with electricity, with urgency. "Listen to me. Whatever you're thinking, whatever half-baked plan exists, it's dangerous. Even if it is intact, it has to be destroyed."

"Then why didn't you do it?"

"I . . ." Diac reached into his shirt pocket and fumbled for something, but he wouldn't meet her eyes. "I was a coward."

"Take a number," Kara said bitterly.

He placed a pill on the table between them. "Neuroblockers," he said quickly. "If anyone attempts to update your cube, this will prevent it."

Just then, the door behind them burst open, and Kara swept the pill into the palm of her hand. In one motion, Imogen stepped through and released her silver whip cable. It lashed several times around Diac's neck, until it choked his cry into a long gasp, and his gasp into a soundless scream.

Forgetting that her hands were bound, Kara lunged to her feet, but could only drop helplessly to her knees in front of him, could only watch as his eyes, panicked, turned suddenly opaque—whatever soul was there had fled.

Her stomach bucked with nausea. When she turned, she saw that Imogen was watching her with an expression she couldn't read.

It was Kai who came forward.

"Come on," he said, again pulling the bag over Kara's head, and cinching it around her throat. "Time to see what UniForce will pay for the return of a princess."

FIFTEEN

RHIANNON

NO matter where she moved across the palace, Rhee felt as if she were tethered to Julian—a distracting awareness that dominated every thought, dictated every decision. Despite the fact that he'd tried to kill her, that perhaps he still would, he hid in the basement several floors below. It was almost as if she'd traded Dahlen for Julian, since she was desperate for their friendship, and since they both hated her.

And why wouldn't Julian hate her? Rhee ruined everything she touched.

Lahna had explained how all along, Veyron had been working against Nero. He was the only member of the resistance in Nero's inner circle. With his death, the resistance had begun to disintegrate.

Again and again, Rhee was transported back to that moment. With her cube off, the organic memory was more salient than ever. She could practically feel Veyron's hand around her throat, smell the incense that burned in the temple.

And then—Dahlen's sudden arrival.

Veyron had made sure that Rhee would be saved. He followed Nero's orders so that his own family, his people, wouldn't be targeted, so that the resistance could continue their work. But he had made sure the Fontisian would intervene.

All along, he'd been on her side.

And she'd killed him.

"You'll first be coming out here," the Fisherman said, mercifully yanking Rhee from her thoughts. He pointed to the holo image of the west wing of the palace. He had enormous hands and fat fingers to match; he poked at the image repeatedly, and it wavered where he touched. "Zoom in here. *Here.*"

The droid was nearly as tall as Rhee was, shaped like a cylinder with a shiny chrome finish and four small wheels at its base. The projected image zoomed in so far and so fast Rhee felt herself go dizzy, like she'd plummeted into the holo. Now, only a white static took up the full image.

"Does this droid know how to do *anything* useful?" the Fisherman bellowed.

"Seventy-five percent zoom," Rhee clarified to the droid. "You've gone too far."

"What is the point," the Fisherman said, tobacco-laced saliva flying from the corners of his mouth, "of a machine that requires even the smallest details to be spelled out?" The Fisherman's eyes were tilted down at a forty-five-degree angle, and when he was angry—which was often—they closed up into slits and gave him an amphibian quality.

"It's not a military droid," Tai Reyanna said. "It doesn't have the training."

Lahna gave Rhee a small smile like they were both in on a joke. The Tai and the Fisherman were constantly at odds.

"Well, perhaps it would oblige me to take a few minutes out of its busy vacuuming schedule to get reprogrammed!" He got down low and yelled into what would be its face. The droid rolled back as if startled and ran over the fabric of Rhee's dress.

"Be *careful*," Tai Reyanna said sharply, the crisp Kalusian accent coming through more than ever now that they'd returned to the palace.

"Calm down," the Fisherman countered. "The girl ran halfway across the galaxy; I think she can handle a bit of dirt on her dress."

The Tai glared at him from under her *duhajt*. She nudged the droid forward and off Rhee's dress with a very unladylike kick of her foot. Lahna let out a noise that could've passed as a cough but was most certainly a snort.

Protective had become Tai Reyanna's default state, while *aggravated* had become the Fisherman's. Rhee had learned to tolerate both. Appreciate them, even, especially since the Tai had taken a great risk to return with her, and the Fisherman had agreed to take over security details after Dahlen left.

I'll keep you alive, but I don't have to be nice about it, he'd said in that gurgly accent. Tai Reyanna had nodded happily at that. They seemed to band together only when it came to Rhee's safety.

The droid adjusted the image—correctly, this time. Rhee circled the hologram and looked carefully at the balcony where she would soon stand.

"I've got archers all along the west tower, facing you and facing out toward the surrounding buildings. We'll have to keep an eye out for the east tower; Nero runs security out the top floors and it's tighter than a Derkatzian's you-know-what."

"And here?" Lahna asked, pointing to the cluster of icons at the base of the palace.

"The Tasinn are on the ground at the base," the Fisherman said of her royal guard, now, she suspected, loyal to Nero, "and if they choose to act up—which, don't worry, they won't—we'll be in position to regroup, fire down, extract you through this sky bridge here . . ."

Rhee could barely concentrate, even if she'd been the one to call the meeting to be briefed. Her outfit, painstakingly created just for this publicity event, involved a corset made of bone in the style of the second-wavers. It dug into her ribs and pinched her waistline to unnatural proportions. There was a scratchy material that capped at her sleeves and ran the length of her skirt, which cut an A-line silhouette all the way down to the ground. She had clutched the coin in the palm of her hand just as she did now; she'd held it all morning, since the dress she wore was of poor design. Why create a garment without pockets?

Tai Reyanna had supervised as the tailor fastened on the final stitches—it was a dress Rhee had been sewn into, and would later need to be cut free of. It seemed like a metaphor.

BLOOD OF A THOUSAND STARS

Joss would've known what to do. Graceful, quick-thinking. The girl who should be empress lost among the galaxy, while Rhee stood in the gown, a poor approximation of a leader and an empress.

In just under an hour, she and Nero would appear side by side to announce the newest terms of the cease-fire on live DroneVision. It was exactly what Rhee had wanted, and why she'd joined such an unsavory alliance. But he'd slipped in an extra condition: that Fontis lift travel sanctions on the highly protected remains of Wraeta.

There could be only one reason: This cease-fire deal was a means to an end. Nero didn't care about restoring his credibility with the United Planets, as everyone was speculating.

He was after the overwriter.

Rhee had never fully believed that the tech even existed. But Nero spoke with such conviction on Houl, when he'd said the overwriter had capabilities beyond anything Rhee had imagined. He said with the overwriter he could whisper to people, *not through their ears but their minds . . .*

Whether or not it was true, Nero was either certain that it was, or desperate—and either made him very, very dangerous.

Rhee needed to know what he had planned.

But how? She felt no closer to understanding him than she had before their alliance.

As if in response to her doubts, the sound of Nero's voice echoed through the room. It seemed he was unavoidable. A shiver traveled up her spine.

"On the coming hour, we invite everyone to join as Empress Rhiannon Ta'an shares an important announcement . . ."

Immediately, the droid parroted the words.

"This useless piece of scrap!" the Fisherman said, giving the droid a good kick. The holoprojection had gone iridescent, a light so faint it was barely readable to the humanoid eye. It was likely the same in the Fisherman's case.

Rhee sighed. "You know it can't help it."

And it was true—this model was a particular kind of tech used by Derkatzians. Their retinas were shaped differently, and their eyes could detect something like seven times the amount of light compared to hers or the Fisherman's. The projection settings were humanoid or Derkatzian, and it had likely glitched, switching between languages without being prompted.

The Fisherman continued grumbling. Rhee's head was starting to hurt.

"Please," she said. "I'm trying to think."

What good was the Fisherman's security plan anyway, if she couldn't get into Nero's head, couldn't understand what he was plotting? Despite her pretended civility, and the time she had been forced to suffer in his presence recently, she was no closer to understanding what he really wanted.

The droid had begun talking—Derkatzian this time. The Fisherman had accidentally reset its language, and now he was cursing up a storm.

And that's when it hit her. Humanoid or Derkatzian. *Two-faced.*

Rhee needed a double agent.

And she knew just who to ask: Julian.

Lahna had arranged for him to be kept in the depths of the palace. Though Nero insisted that daisies follow Rhee at every conceivable moment—a development that fanned Rhee's suspicion and uneasiness—the Empress had demanded that the guts of the palace be reserved as a place of worship, which meant they'd be free of cameras. For now, the place was sacred, and thus offered the privacy she craved—though privacy from Tai Reyanna was an entirely different challenge altogether. Upon their return, the Tai had insisted on being with her as much as possible. She seemed nicer, less stern. The warmth was out of character and brought Rhee less comfort than Tai Reyanna probably hoped it would. It only served to remind Rhee that things had changed, that you could come home and find it unrecognizable—that the memory you held on to had merely been a mental construction, and that nothing at all stayed the same.

Rhee made her way down below, where her ancestors were projected via holo onto all four walls of the room. Offerings were clustered below each image on low tables that served as mini altars. There were the typical offerings: grain, fruit, candies.

Stepping into the low-lit room, she could immediately breathe easier.

Julian still hadn't spoken to her since the night he broke into her room. Every day she visited, though, steeling herself against his glare. He didn't want to be here, but he couldn't leave either. Where else would he go?

When she and Lahna entered, Julian turned away from her in disgust. With his hair cropped short in a new-wave style, he looked older.

"Do you still wish you had killed me?" Rhee asked. She willed her hands to be steady, and clasped them tightly when they refused.

"Do you still wish you hadn't killed my father?" he returned. He glanced at her sideways, his chin down, the blue of his eyes even more intense, more piercing. She saw how much he hated her.

She didn't answer—she didn't need to. Now she knew the betrayal had been for nothing. She'd been wrong. About Veyron. About almost everything.

But no matter how she tried, Rhee couldn't forget what they'd been. The first night she'd returned to Nau Fruma for good, after her family was killed, Julian had left the cast-off skin of a snake for her to find on her windowsill the next morning. And the next day, a rock in the shape of a heart. A scrap of vermillion fabric, a shard of stained glass, a twig of dried lavender. These tiny objects were her lifeline to the world outside the palace.

The tables had turned now; he was the prisoner within the palace walls. Rhee could tell it boiled his blood that after everything, he needed her protection and cover—which she was happy to give in meager hopes of forgiveness, and redemption.

"I've come for your help," Rhee told him. Out of the corner of her eye, she saw Lahna shift her weight between her feet.

Julian snorted. "You think I'd help you?"

"If it serves our mutual interest." In that moment, she made a decision. To trust him. To hope. "Nero is looking for the overwriter."

Lahna arched an eyebrow. "What?"

So Dahlen hadn't told her. Rhee looked from Julian to Lahna, then back again. "I'm not even sure if it exists. But he's looking for it."

"*Choirtoi*," Julian breathed out.

"We need to know what he's up to." She took a deep breath. "What I did was unforgivable. I know that. But Nero is to blame." She half expected Julian to object. But he didn't, so she pressed on. "Veyron knew that he must be stopped. He died for it. I'm sure Nero never doubted his loyalty. Is that right?"

Julian nodded. His face was guarded.

Lahna stared at her. "You're not suggesting . . . ?"

Rhee took a deep breath. "That Julian take his father's place. Offer yourself to Nero. Your loyalty." She paused. "If we can figure out what he's doing and stop it—together—then you're free to have your revenge on me." She focused on staying very still; it was the only thing that would stanch her tears.

"You trust a boy who set out to kill you?" Lahna's voice was sharp with disbelief. "He could double-cross you and ruin you completely."

"And yet even you bowed to him," Rhee said.

Julian came closer, the same murderous heat coming off him in waves; for a moment, Rhee thought he might just kill her where she stood. Lahna's hand twitched, but she did not draw her bow.

"I'll help you," he said softly. He paused, so close to her she could feel his breath against her forehead and cheek. "But then I will take your life."

"Unless I take yours," Rhee said. Her grief felt like drowning.

For a second, they stood there staring at each other. His blue eyes seemed dark, almost black, in the dim light. Then, finally, he nodded.

"And one more thing," she said, before he could turn away. "How did you get past my guard?"

It was a question that had been bothering her for days. Even without Dahlen, she still had a robust guard of Fontisians from the order, along with some loyal Kalusian palace staff, who manned the halls of the palace, the gardens, and all of the entrances.

Julian rolled his eyes. "I stole a uniform and guessed at the code words. Honor. Loyalty. Bravery."

The breath hitched. The secret passwords to get her guards to stand down—they made up her *ma'tan sarili*, chosen in a private family ritual. No one had known the words apart from her mother and father. And Julian, of course. He'd known everything about her.

The past didn't just die. It killed too.

Across the city, a thousand bells began to clamor for the people's attention. Even two levels below the street, the walls vibrated with the sound.

Julian looked at her. "I guess that's your cue, Empress."

• • •

Nero was already waiting for her, and Rhee was grateful that in addition to his special guard, Tai Reyanna had earned a place—or insisted on one—near the podium. When Rhee stepped outside into the glaring daylight, the rush of wind and the roar of the crowd nearly knocked her over, and Tai Reyanna reached out a hand to steady her.

Nero stood at the lip of the balcony, leaning on the railing. He had an arm in the air, mid-wave, displaying himself for a cheering crowd of nationalists down below. Rhee stopped ten feet short of the railing, out of Nero's earshot. The crowds were impatient, rowdy, and ready to hear him speak. They weren't here for her.

She knew that already, but still it drove a spike of fear through her, the tacit reminder of how much she needed Nero in order to pull this all off.

Rhee tried to smile, though she wondered at the futility of it. So many souls had made their minds up. She was young, inexperienced, and insignificant. And most damning of all: She was a girl.

"Royal blood pumps through this heart," Tai Reyanna said, tapping Rhee's chest. Rhee felt a swell of gratitude gather inside her. She turned to her side, looked into her governess's eyes. "But more important, so does kindness. Fairness."

How could she be fair if she'd killed a man, and brought death in the form of Dahlen to another? She couldn't trust her own instincts. She wasn't her father. "I don't know what I'm doing," Rhee said softly, honestly.

"We learn as we go." It had been Tai Reyanna's refrain whenever Rhee lost focus during a lesson. It had been frustrating, goading then. But now when Rhee heard it, when she looked her Tai in the eyes, she saw someone who believed in her.

She wanted to wrap her arms around her Tai but instead squeezed her hand. "*Ma'tan sirili*," Rhee said. The gesture was brief and fleeting and shattered by the sound of Nero's voice.

"Such a tender moment," Nero said, retreating from the lip of the balcony and moving toward them. "This is precisely why I insist that the daisies follow you. I think you fail to see how badly humanity wants to connect." Nero smiled. She noticed that a clod of flesh-colored makeup covered the spot on his neck where she'd seen the triangle-shaped brand. "Capture a moment like that and the public starts to establish a narrative. They want to see you are a person too, just like them."

The irony of it disgusted her—that the people somehow believed Nero was the one with the fantastic personality, when it was all fake, all for show, all a strategic way to manipulate them.

"I can establish my own narrative," Rhee said evenly.

"Yes—a galaxy at peace. You're doing a fantastic job." It was patronizing, but without malice. There was a tremor to his hand. It didn't seem like nerves, and it surprised Rhee. She'd only ever seen him perfectly poised, always composed.

"If you wouldn't mind, I'd like a moment with Nero. Alone." Lahna and her Tai both looked geared up to argue, but it was Rhee who spoke first. "I'll be fine," she told them.

The Tai appeared indignant as she exited, glaring at Nero before giving Rhee a nod. Lahna didn't even bother a glance.

Instead she twirled her bow casually as she called over her shoulder, "I'll be just over here if you need assistance . . ."

Rhee looked to Nero and hissed, below the din of the crowd, "You've been far too agreeable the last few days."

"Isn't that what you demand of me, Empress?" he asked. Nero smoothed down the black silk of his fitted shirt. He never wore any other color, but there was always an embellishment to draw the eye. Today it was one tiny brass button high on his neck, centered between his rounded collars. His precision instilled fear in her.

"I'll admit I'm impressed you survived," he said. "But that doesn't put you anywhere near the same league as me. We'll see if Kalu will accept you as ruler, and your narrative of peace."

"So you're waiting for me to fail?"

"That was Seotra's mistake—waiting for you. The world waits for no one; it rewards those who take action, however unprecedented or unconventional that action might be. And they want someone who will . . ." He paused, as if he was being careful of his words. It put Rhee on edge. "The people want someone who will tell them what to believe . . . and make them believe it." He smiled.

"You've certainly done that," Rhee said.

Nero actually shrugged. "Not quite yet." A chill ran through her. "They could barely stomach your rule when it was legitimate. And now that you've reappeared, there are theories circulating that you orchestrated your own kidnapping, and that you've taken a Fontisian lover."

Rhee straightened up then. *Dahlen.* "And these theories had a nefarious origin, I'm sure." It was low, and stank of exactly the kind of thing Nero would do. He was spreading rumors about her. At least reminding her of his ability to do so.

"Me? Of course not!" he replied easily, though the smile that played on his lips suggested he took credit, and was glad for what he'd started. "And yet . . . if I had decided it was truth, it would become truth, you know. That is what real power is." Nero paced. "Rhiannon, do you know how a rumor begins? Not by the utterance of what is obvious, but by a mere seed. An uncertainty. A still of you and Dahlen at the wrong angle, released on the holos. The avalanche of questions! You needn't tell people the worst; they will imagine it for themselves. Because there is no greater power than the power of the mind, Empress."

He cast an image of Dahlen into the air between them. Dahlen was holding Rhee's hand—grabbing it, in all likelihood, to pull her to her feet—and she was looking up at him in irritation. But somehow, captured from this angle, her face appeared to be saying something else entirely.

Nero still had that serene smile on his face. She wished, more than anything, she could just cut it off. "Now let's go meet the adoring crowd."

Rhee gathered up the stiff hem of her dress and walked past him, brushing his shoulder as hard as she could. He stumbled but still seemed amused. A petty move for an empress, she knew—but she didn't care.

She stepped to the edge of the balcony with as much confidence as she could spare. Nero stepped out behind her. Each soul was so tiny, indecipherable from another in a way that made the entire crowd seem like one living organism. It pulsed as if it were breathing. She couldn't help but imagine it rearing up and swallowing her whole.

"I now introduce the extraordinary Empress Rhiannon Ta'an! We ensure a new, worthy leader," Nero boomed. Rhee recognized the phrase. It sounded like he'd pledged his fealty, made his loyalty public for all the galaxy to hear—but it belied his true ambition. Nero had said the same thing to Rhee after her parents died ten years ago. Then, too, he'd been referring to himself. He caught Rhee's eye and grinned, his mouth stretched wide, grotesque in his happiness. Then he added, in a falsely solemn voice, "Though I add my prayers to hers, that the Princess Josselyn may soon return safely to us."

Revulsion gripped her whole body. Had she played right into his hand?

She didn't put it past Nero to use Rhee to bait Josselyn, playing off her fears for Josselyn's safety. She had announced a reward for Josselyn's return, after all.

Once the royal sisters were reunited, he might simply kill them both.

After all, why remove one Ta'an when another was still out there? It was the perfect explanation for why Nero hadn't harmed Rhee yet.

Nero grabbed her hand. Another jolt of revulsion coursed through her. This was the man who'd killed her family. What if she said that now, she thought wildly, for everyone to hear?

She knew what it looked like, their hands clasped above them as if they'd won. And she had won, hadn't she? They were about to announce a cease-fire. He was meeting with the United Planets tomorrow, and he'd so much as agreed Kalu would pull UniForce troops out of all Fontisian territories. It was a public arrangement to dial back the war.

But even as Rhee spoke these words to the crowd, her mind spun. His nearness disgusted her. The corset pressed her ribs like a vise. The Towers of the Long Now reflected the sun at its height; it nearly blinded her. She looked down to see lower balconies of the palace crowded with servants who looked up at them like they were gods.

Rhee's heart skipped a beat as she saw a figure on the balcony just two floors below, leaning against the pillar in a way that looked moody and familiar. *Is it Dahlen?* she thought. But no, it was a trick of the light, or a trick of the mind. Because she blinked once, hard, and when she opened her eyes she saw it was Julian who'd taken the figure's place. He shook his head, and though she couldn't see his expression she could feel his glare. And to the shouts of the crowd and Nero's too-tight clasp, she watched as the boy who was once her best friend retreated.

She felt sick, heartbroken, as she gave her speech. What danger had she put him in? When she finished, she half ran, half stumbled back inside. Once she crossed the threshold, she fell to her knees.

Nero entered behind her. "You did beautifully, apart from the mishap at the end. But we'll edit it out when we air it on the holos."

"You said it would be live."

"It's never live." He let out a tiny sigh.

Rhee clenched her fists. "You talk about constructing a persona as if it were the most natural thing in the world. But that's not even close to the truth. You take real life and you twist it, pervert it, so that . . . that . . ."

Was she talking about Nero, or what she had done to Julian? Or both?

Nero kneeled before her, so that they faced one another on the floor. "Real life is boring, Empress. Who wants that?" Then he stood again.

"Make sure you're rested for the slate of appearances," Nero added in the wake of her silence. He exited the room, and Rhee leaned forward on her knees, her head touching the floor.

She felt suffocated, and she tried to rip off the outer layer of scratchy cloth on her dress. It tangled up around her wrists. She'd forgotten there was no way out of it—not on her own.

SIXTEEN

KARA

KARA was swimming, trailing behind her mom, Lydia, who was fully clothed, cutting through the blue-green water . . . *You lost your memories too*, Kara tried to say, but her mouth flooded with the taste of salt water. She was falling behind . . . her hands were bound too tightly . . .

She thrashed, and the rope burned her wrists. She gasped, swallowing stale air. Kara felt a rocking movement underneath; it turned her stomach upside down. There was a vague memory of being forced into an old shipping container. The walls reeked of plastic and oil—and another distinctly human scent. She didn't want to consider its origin. Maybe it was her. She opened her eyes; the shipping container was large and rectangular in shape. Reality crashed down on her, waves and waves of it. Her body heaved.

She rolled over on her side and threw up. Someone groaned. *Kai.*

Kara wiped her face. The sour taste of bile took over her mouth. She'd come so close to the truth for it to end here, en route to Nero—and suddenly Kara wondered how Rhiannon had survived all that time she had been on the run. Rhiannon Ta'an had evaded death over and over again, and here Kara was, the lesser sister—the lesser everything—lured into a trap the second she had been left alone. She pushed herself up to sit, but her elbow gave out when the shipping container swayed back and forth on its magnetic tracks. She crashed back down to the ground. She was exhausted.

"Is it *really* her?" someone said. Kai. He didn't sound convinced.

Kara felt the pill Diac had given her beginning to slip out of her pocket; she angled her body as if she was ashamed, and secured it deeper into her pocket without them noticing. She wondered about the DNA moving inside of her. Her jaw hurt and her skin felt tight, and she wondered how much she'd actually changed.

"She looks more like a Ta'an in this light," Imogen said. Kara recognized that tension in her voice, the way the girl doubted it herself and felt the need to insist.

"What if I'm not?" Kara had surprised herself by saying it. Her voice was nearly a whisper. "Wouldn't it be a shame if you couldn't collect that reward?"

"Shut up," Imogen said. "And you, ignore her. Let Nero deal with it."

Kara's legs ached. Her hair fell across her face and stuck to the sweat on her neck. It felt thicker, looked darker.

"You're going to drop me off at his doorstep? This is your brilliant plan?" Kara pressed. She looked between Imogen and Kai. The other captors were gone, and she guessed they'd been left behind.

"The plan has worked out so far," Imogen said. "We got Diac, lured you out, and here you are . . ."

"You killed that man."

"I've killed lots of people."

Kara was suddenly aware that the salt water she'd dreamed of was really just vomit in her mouth and on her face. Her plan to use the overwriter to wipe Josselyn from memory had grown even more slippery, more complicated. To erase Josselyn from everyone else's memory, Kara would have to forfeit her own.

She closed her eyes, humiliated, and wondered how they would deliver her to Nero. If he would kill her, or worse, if he would demand she serve him. *Etra, Rilirinas, Samba*, she repeated to herself. The Wolf, the Guardian, the Matron. She couldn't forget those star coordinates, or give up hope on finding the overwriter. She'd prefer to be no one than Josselyn Ta'an.

Then a thud sounded overhead, and Kara looked up as if the ceiling might tell her something.

Imogen looked up too. She was silent for a beat, then nodded for Kai to check it out. Kara huddled in on herself. It could be someone trying to save her. Or it could be someone else trying to make good on Nero's ransom, and they could be even more vicious than present company.

Kai walked past Imogen toward the end where the container opened. Kara's heart sped up when he lifted the cover suddenly, but no one was there. There was just a row of shipping containers behind them, all floating along the same magnetic tracks. He peeked out to the left and right, but he didn't see anything—at least judging from the stupid grin on his face when he turned around.

Then two legs swung over the edge of the roof, kicking Kai in the chest. The force of it sent him flying back into the shipping container, scattering Kara and Imogen apart. Issa landed in a squat at the edge.

"I know what you're thinking," Issa said. "I make this look easy."

Kai and Imogen both rushed her, and she easily dodged Kai, spinning and kicking his back to propel him forward and out of the container. Kara heard his scream drowned out by the wind.

While Issa's back was still turned, Imogen pushed her out of the container, or tried to—but Issa dodged her, and they struggled as Kara watched. It was almost picturesque from where she stood, how their fight was perfectly centered by the square opening of the container, the landscape of green fields and wildflowers sped out and away from them; one misstep and either one of them could go flying out. Whoever fell wouldn't survive. Out of the corner of her eye she saw the gleaming metal of Imogen's silver whip, abandoned on the floor.

The two girls struggled, punching and wrestling, but Imogen was sleeker, slippery almost, as she slunk out of every hold. She flipped Issa and pinned her down, choking her with her bare hands as she squatted over her body. Issa kicked her legs out frantically.

Kara's heart thudded. She crept up from behind and scooped the whip off the floor as silently as she could. Rage and fear— she felt it taking over her entire body, her entire world. Kara held her breath, saw her bound hands shaking as she pulled a section of the whip taut, squeezing her hands around either side. Once she was close enough, a term came to her. *Striking distance.* She swore she'd never heard it before, but at the same time she knew exactly what it meant.

The fear spiked in her chest, cutting off her air—she realized she couldn't breathe, and it scared her, but there were other things that scared her more. Like Issa dying because Kara had been too much of a coward to save her. *Do it do it do it*, she said as she moved close to Imogen's back. And then Kara did.

She looped it around Imogen's long neck and yanked as hard as she could, closing it tight—then tighter, bringing her hands together just at the base of Imogen's neck. The girl flailed, awkwardly trying to reach behind her, slapping at Kara. But Kara stood her ground and barely felt it. She barely felt anything; the only sensation she knew was her heart thrumming in her ears.

Even when Imogen skittered back, nearly fell as she kicked out wildly, Kara made herself stone. She was vaguely surprised by how strong she was. Issa sat up and caught Kara's eye. She pushed herself up to stand. Her neck was red and raw as she came over to Kara's side, took hold of the whip, and nodded for Kara to ease her hands away.

Issa squeezed harder than Kara could've. Now she heard the

sputter of Imogen's breathing, and finally when her body went limp, Issa held the stranglehold there longer, much longer, unbearably long. Kara understood they couldn't take chances. When enough time had passed, Issa let Imogen's body fall forward gently—until she was just a pile of pretty skin and bones on the ground.

Kara looked out at the shipping containers behind them, at the endless field of tall grass and wildflowers unfurling before them. They were still on Ralire.

"How did you get here?" Kara swallowed. There was a foul taste in her mouth. "What—what happened?"

"I tracked you back to the facility where they kept you." Issa shrugged. "When they dragged you back out, I followed you to the shipping containers and hopped on when no one was looking."

They had gone to the market in the afternoon; judging by the sun, it was now midmorning. Twelve hours had passed, maybe more. By now, the medcraft was long gone.

"You came back for me. Again," she muttered. Somehow, she had earned Issa's loyalty—she might never understand it, but she was grateful. Her heart hurt from the gratitude, from the pain of caring again, when she had wanted so badly not to have to care about anyone ever again.

"Didn't have anywhere better to be," Issa replied, but through her sarcasm, Kara saw her bravery, her fierceness. "Whoa, whoa—are you okay?"

Issa was reacting to Kara's expression; she was on the verge of crying. Her face—her new face—felt hot and sticky. Her head hurt, and she knew it was because her DNA was changing, twisting. She dug the heels of her palms into her eyes again, rubbing. "I guess I'm just not used to people coming back for me." The anguish in her voice was obvious, but she could do nothing to hide it.

Issa touched her forearm. "Do you want to talk about it?"

"Not now," Kara said, shaking her head. She wasn't sure if she ever wanted to talk about it.

"Well, when you do I'm all ears, yeah?" She looked around. "We'd better hurry. I'm sure UniForce isn't thrilled to be called out for wild-goose chases. We want to make sure we don't give them a target. With any luck, we can hitch a ride on a light craft and catch up to the Frontline Physicians . . ."

Kara took a deep breath and wobbled on her feet. "I have to go to Wraeta," she said. She felt unexpectedly clear, focused. She knew where the overwriter was.

Issa stared at her. "There's nothing on Wraeta but ashes."

Kara shook her head. "There's a weapon hidden there. We have to find it before the UniForce does."

Issa squinted at her. "What kind of weapon are we talking?"

Kara hesitated—but only for a second. Issa had just saved her life. Kara would have to trust her. "You told me that you worried that UniForce was trying to force an update so it could track your cube, getting data from it. But what if Kalu could go a step further? What if they couldn't just track your cube but change it?"

For a second, Issa said nothing. Then, abruptly: "I knew it!" She stomped her foot on the floor of the shipping container. "Some of us did. Most everyone thought we were paranoid. You're saying this tech is on Wraeta?"

Kara nodded. "We need to figure out a way through the military cordon."

"Not anymore," Issa said. "Princess Rhiannon announced a cease-fire. I've been using the third eye to pick up holo transmissions. Fontis had to release the protections on Wraeta. Which means we're free to go."

"And so is Nero," Kara said. Issa nodded.

There were no coincidences. It was as if Rhiannon knew where she was headed, and was clearing the path for her. As if she could feel, deep down, that this is the only way that they both would be free of Josselyn, the lost princess, forever.

But it was just as likely Rhee was helping Nero . . .

No. Kara refused to believe it.

Either way, she needed to get to the overwriter first.

"If there's any chance of foiling Nero, the WFC will want to help," Issa said. "I can broadcast a distress signal as soon as we get back to civilization." Kara was comforted when Issa wrapped her in a hug and gave her a squeeze. "I hope you're ready to escape a moving shipping container," she added drily.

She had told Issa they needed to destroy the overwriter before Nero got his hands on it, and that was true. But what she couldn't tell Issa, what she would never tell Issa, is that she planned to use it first.

Then Josselyn Ta'an would disappear forever. Maybe Kara's own memories would disappear too, but she could start making her own choices from then on out. She could be free, and no one would tell her who to be.

SEVENTEEN

ALYOSHA

ALY'S veins felt like they'd been pumped full of fire: They were going to take Nero down. There was something about it—poetic justice or irony or whatever it was—returning to the rubble that had once been his home.

Let Nero come for the overwriter. Aly would be waiting.

They were speeding toward the remains of Aly's home planet on one of the smaller and stealthier WFC crafts—but they had to hurry. With Wraeta's airspace now cleared for travel, it would be a free-for-all soon—and Nero could easily beat them to the punch.

Pavel stood at attention, with a holoprojection beaming carefully from his chestplate. Dahlen circled the image, analyzing it closely. Blue-green light came off the image, bringing out the hollows of his face and the narrowed expression he wore when he was thinking hard.

Aly fought the small voice inside him, the one that warned he'd become a pawn all over again, this time for the Fontisians. But the idea spun and sharpened itself on the memory of Kara's death. This time, the game was his to win.

"Alyosha, your blood pressure and body temperature are elevated. Would you like to review meditation techniques?"

Aly leaned forward, his palms flat on the control panel. Vin had programmed Pavel with wellness alerts before he died. Aly felt a piece of his heart splinter off, lost to the void.

He shook his head. "I'm good, P. How about you just give us the status?"

The droid blinked his eyelights and zoomed out the hologram to include the flight patterns of five different crafts, all UniForce— meaning all Nero's. They were mining vessels, which must mean whatever he was looking for was underground.

The overwriter was underground.

One piece of good news: The mining vessels were headed to different locations across the fractured planet. Aly was relieved. Apparently Nero didn't know where the overwriter was, not exactly. But just as quickly, anxiety flared in his chest.

"So how do you figure we dodge all these treasure hunters?" Aly asked. "If you got some invisibility tech I don't know about, expedite the shipping on that and maybe we'll get it tomorrow."

"We will not dodge them." Dahlen ignored his sarcasm. "We will commandeer one of their vessels. We will become one of them."

"What?" But even as he reacted, Aly understood. So Dahlen *had* seen *The Revolutionary Boys* after all. "You expect me to commandeer *one of the UniForce crafts*?"

"That's the idea," Dahlen said neutrally.

"Seems like that idea has more *me* than you." But already, Aly was making calculations, using parts of his brain that felt as if they'd rusted into place. He missed Vin's crazy piloting, his focus and adrenaline. He missed the language they shared of all the shortened military terms and the inside jokes they'd collected along the way. And suddenly Aly was pissed all over again. That it wasn't Vin sitting next to him, but Dahlen.

He looked over at the Fontisian, weighing his options. They'd have to do it soon, before they got too close to the electromagnetic field holding Wraeta together and the hijack came on everyone's radar. He looked closer at the hovering image.

"Taking into account thrust and nearby gravitational bodies," Pavel said, "it looks unlikely that any of those crafts will be making a pit stop between here and Wraeta."

Aly nodded. "But nothing's stopping us from going to them," he said.

They stayed up all night reworking their plan. The *Nanac* was their target ship—a mining vessel equipped with two huge drills at the bottom so powerful they'd be liable to drill through any rock and fall out the bottom.

They sent a small strike team to pierce the *Nanac*'s fuel chamber and run its fuel down. When the crew on board eventually noticed, they did exactly what anyone would: They hailed a service craft.

Aly and Dahlen were on that particular service craft with a crew of Pavel, Hesi, Darris, and the scrawny Fontisian messenger, Rahmal. Aly had to admit that the WFC had come through. Their service craft had come from a raid on a Kalusian territory during the first Great War—the ancient refueling rocket would've made the *Revolutionary* look shiny and new, but it was nearly impossible to track—and one of their sources had provided them with a code needed to communicate with the mining vessel.

Phase two. Once they attached to the *Nanac*, they'd board like old-school pirates and take the crew hostage.

Phase three. Land the *Nanac* and intercept Nero on the ground.

Phase four. Break his fucking neck.

It was reckless, but Aly didn't care. A Kalusian-allied ship would give them weapons, power, and cover, even in plain sight. It would give them the advantage.

He grabbed on to the armrests and felt the g-force bear down as they rocketed toward the *Nanac*. He tried to will himself to feel good, cocky, like the old days when it was him and Vin. But as they approached the atmosphere the rocket vibrated; Aly could practically hear the bolts unscrewing. His stomach heaved. He thought back to the day Vin died, how the Tin Soldier had broken apart like an egg and spilled them out all over Naidoz. That had been his fault—he'd been a petty kid who'd slacked on the navigation. Vin had cracked open his head because of Aly.

Dahlen leaned toward Aly as much as his harness would let him. "I hadn't expected these soldiers to be your first choice," he said easily, like his lungs weren't being pressed down into the pit of his stomach. Show-off. Still, Aly was glad for the distraction. Hating on Dahlen made it easier to push Vin out of his thoughts.

Aly looked back at Hesi and Darris, the two soldiers he'd asked to join them. They were dressed in matching spacesuits, strapped into mounted chairs arranged in a circle around the craft's center console. Hesi, who was even wider than Jeth, was gritting his blunt, wide teeth in agony. The g-force probably felt like a sheet of metal pressing down on the Chram's huge frame. Next to Hesi, though, Darris looked like he was having the time of his life. Pavel had compacted into his dome shape, but he bounced in place; Aly was glad for the hydraulics he had installed.

Aly turned back to Dahlen and shrugged. "I've seen them on the field. More than I can say for your choice," he said, nodding toward Rahmal, whose nose looked permanently upturned.

"Discarding him was not an option," Dahlen said, every delivery dry as a bone. In the past twelve hours, Rahmal had practically built a home up Dahlen's butt—he seemed to exist solely to run around getting Dahlen things. Apparently the Fontisian Elders had sent him as Dahlen's backup, which was kind of hilarious seeing as Dahlen could snap this kid's spine with a single finger. Rahmal was tall but scrawny as hell, and other than a skill in delivering messages in the key of whine, Aly couldn't see what good he could offer.

They burst through the atmosphere, and the pace of the craft slowed, the pressure easing up on Aly's chest and limbs. He exhaled in relief. Darris, the Uustralite, made a loud guttural noise somewhere between a growl and indigestion. Rahmal put his index and middle fingers to each eye—a gesture to Vodhan, thanking him for his mercy. Aly'd seen his own parents do it a thousand times, in another life, back before the Wray.

Aly couldn't help but notice that Dahlen only tightened his hands into fists. He had mentioned he was no longer part of the order. Aly wondered why, and whether that had been his choice to break his vows.

"We got visual," Hesi said, his milky white pupils locked on to the dash. "Should be appearing to the naked eye in ten, nine, eight . . ."

When the *Nanac* came into view, Aly summed it up as the ugliest ship he'd ever seen. But who needed it to be pretty when all it was good for was breaking up rock, digging deep, extracting whole swaths of precious metals? It was clumsy and greedy and pretty hateful work.

A red light began to blink on the console.

"*Nanac*, this is *Yavou*," Hesi said in his thickest, twangiest Chram accent. It made Aly miss Jeth. Hesi was the only soul aboard their craft who belonged to a Kalusian-allied territory— Darris might pass for northern Uustralite, or a sympathizer, if he was lucky, but they couldn't take any chances. According to the plan, Hesi'd greet the crew first, buying them at least a few precious moments to get into position. "We're ready to attach and refuel whenever you are. Over."

"*Yavou*, this is *Nanac*. Thank ancestors you showed up," a guy's voice answered. "We're ready to receive you once we get your confirmation code. Over."

Aly realized he'd been gripping his armrest; his knuckles had already gone white.

"The confirmation is 'razor's edge,'" Hesi said. "Over."

Five seconds passed. Ten. Then fifteen.

"*Choirtoi*," Aly mumbled under his breath. What if they had the code wrong? With one exchange with UniForce, they could be labeled combatants and be blasted out of the sky without a second thought.

The Chram's albino eyes went wide. "What do I do?"

"You don't do anything," Dahlen said. "We only wait."

"Where exactly did you get this code from?" Aly spoke in a whisper, even though the comm was still off.

"We received it from a reliable source," the Chram said. "One of our scouts on the inside."

"I don't like it." Rahmal addressed the comment specifically to Dahlen, with an expression that was the worst combination of miserable and pained, like he needed to go to the bathroom.

Dahlen ignored him. Nobody else volunteered a response. But it was a possibility that the scout had double-crossed them, and they all knew it. The seconds stretched out as they sat in silence, giving the console the death stare like they could reach in and strangle the guy until he accepted the code.

And then: "Sorry, *Yavou*. Code confirmed. You're cleared to attach and begin fueling. Over."

Aly exhaled. He looked around at their crew, and his eyes landed on Dahlen. "Phase two?"

"Phase two." Dahlen nodded. "Time to steer us in," he said to the Uustralite. Darris took the throttle with one of his tentacles and started to steer, positioning the air lock across from the *Nanac*'s.

"I don't like it," Rahmal repeated.

Dahlen glared at him. "You wouldn't speak against a direct order, would you?"

"Never," Rahmal said, looking down sheepishly. "It's only that you can't be risked."

Dahlen's cool eyes flickered toward Aly, but he stayed focused on Rahmal. "My life is no longer anyone's concern but my own. It is no more valuable than any WFC soldier's."

"What a hero," Aly said.

"I don't play hero," Dahlen said. "That's your job."

Aly bit the inside of his cheek, searching for some smartass comment to make. But he *had* wanted to be a hero once. He'd wanted to rise above his refugee status, find Rhiannon, help Kara—and maybe make her fall in love with him. But there was no time for shame, regrets. All this thinking and moping when they were at the cusp of capturing the very man who'd started it all. Aly needed this mission to succeed. He needed his revenge.

He didn't have an order, or an elder, or anyone who would beg him not to go and get himself killed. He didn't have anything else.

The silence in the pod was palpable as they all got into positions. Aly stood on the right of the doorway while Dahlen and his messenger stood on the left, just out of sight from the *Nanac* crew who'd be standing at the threshold. Hesi and Darris stood front and center to meet them with a toolbox each. The plan was to pick off the crew, take control of their ship, and descend onto Wraeta before anyone knew the difference.

For something so heavy and rusted, the door of the *Nanac* opened quickly—and just like that Aly's boots were off the ground, and he was floating, turning in midair as he grabbed for the wall. Same with everyone else. There were the muffled sounds of shouting. He felt a chill run over his skin.

Wrong. All wrong.

Hesi drew a stunner from his belt as a guard who launched through the threshold brought a massive knife across his stomach. Blood arced through the room in a perfect parabola. In the fluorescent light, it was nearly transparent.

Just like that, chaos.

Aly heard the staccato of heavy feet cross the floor. Magnetic boots, to keep them grounded. Aly, Dahlen, and their crew had been played—it was the UniForce's plan all along to disable the artificial grav on board. Kicking off the wall, Aly launched himself forward and tackled the UniForce guy who'd slashed Hesi. The force of it knocked his magnetic boots off the grated floor, and the two of them sailed clear across the ship, breaking through a floating clot of blood as they wrestled. Aly got him in a chokehold, but the miner was strong and managed to get a boot back on the ground. Now that he was stationary, he used Aly's momentum and swung his body weight around.

Aly flailed backward, blind to where he was headed. But Darris shot a tentacle out, lightning-quick, wrapping it around Aly's waist to slow him down. Then the Uustralite wound a thicker tentacle around the other guy's rib cage and his neck, and began to squeeze until the life left him. Darris unwound and gave him a shove, the still body floating up next to another miner to whom Darris must've done the same.

Aly untangled himself from Darris's tentacle and swam toward Hesi, who was in bad shape—globs of dark blood flooding out of his wound and beading up. He went to press down on the wound, but Hesi shook his head. Darris made a low clicking noise as he motioned his head toward Dahlen: Two soldiers were tumbling and swiping at him at once.

"You must go," Darris said, forcing his vocal cords to make the Wraetan words. He pressed a tentacle down on Hesi's wound.

Aly swung across the craft to help Dahlen, looking over his shoulder to make sure Darris was okay. Then he heard Dahlen moan, and saw that one miner held the Fontisian's arms behind him. Another threw a punch so hard, Dahlen's nose cracked audibly.

Aly pushed off the center console and launched himself into the fray. As he floated toward the tussle, he saw that Dahlen was *smiling*. The blood from his nose made its way into the spaces between his teeth, and it dribbled down his chin.

Dahlen threw his head back to hit the guy behind him, then forward to head-butt the guy in front of him. Aly started throwing fists at whatever flesh he could make contact with. Even though Aly was UniForce-trained, the miners had more experience in zero grav; they'd come prepared.

One of them tackled Aly and punched him across the face. It felt like a part of his brain exploded: Their gloves were enhanced with special magnets, iron-heavy. Aly brought an arm up to block his face, but the guy went for his ribs instead—and all Aly could do was knee and kick blindly as they settled on the floor.

Another miner had pulled a knife on Dahlen, and they fumbled for control of it. The miner managed to pin Dahlen against one wall and drove the knife into his shoulder. Dahlen convulsed in pain.

"No!" Aly yelled. He found a surge of strength and drove an elbow into his guy's face, then kicked him straight in the nuts. That was the downside of magnetic boots: Rooted in place, the guy felt the impact all the way to his eyeballs, while Aly's shot launched him in reaction straight across the craft toward Dahlen.

The miner still clutched the knife, digging it into Dahlen's shoulder. Dahlen's knuckles were white and the veins in his neck bulged. He was shaking so hard, his teeth were rattling.

But Aly realized it wasn't out of fear or even pain. It was out of rage. Dahlen had the intense, focused kind of eyes that the real believers got in church when they were in ecstasy, when Vodhan called upon them, when they were driven by something bigger and more powerful and impossible to explain.

Dahlen let out a scream as he pulled the knife out and lodged it into the other guy's throat in one swift motion.

Suddenly they heard the hiss of a door closing as the craft equalized, everyone—alive and dead—dropping to the floor with a thud. Gravity had been restored. When Aly looked up he saw it was Rahmal on the other side of the glass. He'd cut them off from the drilling vessel.

"No!" Aly said, scrambling forward. He swayed on his feet as gravity planted him in place.

"Let us through the airlock glass," Dahlen growled. His injured arm hung limp. The wound was wet and shiny, and Aly didn't know what kind of a mess those tendons must be in.

"No," Rahmal said, his voice shaking. "We've been compromised. They could be ready for you on the ground."

"Do not disobey me!" Dahlen yelled. The visor of his helmet was fogging up. Aly had never heard him sound angry before. "Open this door immediately."

"I have explicit directions from the Elder to make sure you come to no harm," Rahmal repeated. "You have a higher purpose."

Dahlen slammed both hands into the glass. "If I can't live with honor then I will die for it!"

"Please," Aly said to Rahmal, switching tactics. He closed his eyes and could see only Kara. "We'll stay alive together." He hadn't realized until now how much Dahlen's expulsion had made him reckless, mad. But he didn't have time to play therapist. They'd need to release their craft soon or the extra weight would slow them down, and they'd all burn up into the atmosphere.

Rahmal only shook his head, unyielding.

"May I?" Pavel asked Aly politely, as he opened a side hatch and exposed an array of attachments—signal interceptors, wire cutters, surge amps—he might use for getting the air lock open again.

"Do it," Aly said.

"There's no use," Rahmal said. "I'm sorry." His hand hovered over the button that would send them spinning way off course.

"Don't!" Aly yelled.

Too late. Rahmal smashed his hand against the button. The force of the separation threw Aly to the floor. When he righted himself, the planet was already spinning away.

EIGHTEEN

KARA

SINCE the cease-fire had been announced, all kinds of crafts had been swarming just below the Wraetan atmosphere, navigating the enormous splinters of old planetary mass still swaying loosely in an electromagnetic net. Kara couldn't ID them by sight—but she knew the traffic was made up largely of UniForce and Kalusian crafts.

It had been three hours since Kara and Issa had landed, and they were losing the light. The growing darkness was entirely different than anything Kara had experienced on Sibu, or any other planet, for that matter—the absence of light on Wraeta felt thick, total, scary. She felt it around her ankles, curling in and around her chest, alive with dust and debris. She was afraid it would reach out to strike.

Or maybe it was her future, hidden somewhere on this rock, that was slowly rising up, waiting to crash down on her.

The occasional discarded sign of life—a half-melted doll, at one point—made her queasy. Before Wraeta had been bombed and its atmosphere turned lethal, the iron in its soil made the ground a fiery assortment of reds and oranges. "Like the sun set and melted itself right into the land," Aly told her once. He had always said things exactly the way she wanted to hear them. She should've seen right through the promises, the charm, the smile. But that was Aly all along—the opportunist, the actor.

Kara tried to imagine it as she walked across the cold, dead rock beneath her. It was one of the biggest intact pieces of Wraeta, and when she looked up at the dark sky she could see the remnants of the decimated planet, pieces of rock just like the one she stood on.

Issa's unit had dropped them on a nearby space station, and from there, Issa and Kara had been jettisoned via a pod—claiming they needed to recover a lost asset in orbit—after which Issa had steered them to the surface of Wraeta. With half their fuel, they landed on a barren stretch of torn-up rock a full day's walk from the site of interest. The WFC couldn't dedicate any extra soldiers to escort them. If they had known the real reason the girls had come to Wraeta, the WFC would have sent its entire army.

The lie suited Kara's purposes just fine. A two-person pod was hardly likely to attract radar attention from the UniForce—they might even be mistaken for pieces of the planet, breaking free of the electromagnetic cordon. Besides, she didn't need more military, or anyone extra involved. She was going to find the overwriter and destroy every memory that had ever existed of Josselyn

Ta'an. It was only a matter of time before someone else tried to kidnap her. Josselyn's existence had already compromised Rhee's reign, which made her vulnerable to Nero. Everything depended on this mission.

To calm herself, Kara repeated: Etra, Rilirinas, Samba. The Wolf, the Guardian, the Matron . . . these were the star coordinates that would bring them to the lab, and to her mother's old greenhouse. Kara was sure that they would find the overwriter there. By her calculations, only a matter of kilometers separated them from the site. Still, it was too far to walk before sunset; they would have to use Issa's WFC-issued dome to set up camp for the night.

The spacesuits they were wearing were about two sizes too big, which made them bulky and downright archaic, and ill-equipped apart from a simple readout of breathable oxygen and the position of the sun. Kara and Issa couldn't even talk to one another; the suits were fitted with comm units so old they might have stopped working during the Great War. But they got the job done in every other way—they could move through an otherwise lethal atmosphere, and the suits cloaked their heat signature, so they couldn't be tracked unless they were in visual range. The surface might be crawling with Nero's soldiers, but at the very least they couldn't be tracked from a distance.

And anyway, Kara should be thankful. If the dust and debris on Wraeta didn't kill you, the temperatures would. Even Issa couldn't prepare for a climate that had changed this dramatically. The ground was iced over, slippery as a fish, and they had to worry about losing their footing and floating off into deep space.

And if you drifted off, the odds didn't look good; you'd either die of starvation or a suit malfunction, whichever came first.

Their only contingency plan was a harpoon gun Issa carried. If Issa lost her footing and started to float off, she could shoot the loaded arrow into the ground and tether herself to the surface with a rope just ten hands long. And if Kara floated away, Issa would still shoot the harpoon and grab for her. At least that was the plan. It depended on everything working like it was supposed to, and a whole lot of trust in Issa.

I'm not going anywhere, she remembered Aly saying when they'd first got to Nau Fruma. She shook the thought away. Memories were like poison seeping into her skin, flowing into her heart.

The past was venom. And Kara would get it out, she'd free herself and everyone else.

Kara stayed right behind Issa, matching her step for step. They walked carefully, planting their feet so that the whole sole made contact with the surface—it was slow, and dangerous. It was worth it, though. She just wanted this feeling to go away—that she was useless in this world, that she was a shell of a person, chained to her past. What future could she serve, and what could she even offer Rhiannon if she were found?

No responsibilities, no painful past, no prodigal empress to live up to. Kara could make it all go away, and she could be whole again. She could help Rhiannon by disappearing, giving her the title of empress uncontested. At least she would have done some good.

When they crested the hill, they saw a small, white dome in the distance. UniForce soldiers had made a camp for the night. Kara froze. The suits cloaked them, but for how long? Issa made a fist, and Kara recognized it as a signal to stop and crouch down. She did, her heart hammering. Issa crouched down too and turned to Kara. Beneath the film on her visor her eyes were bright with excitement or fear—Kara couldn't tell which.

In the distance, the dome glinted in the light and looked like metal. The bomb had destroyed everything else—the dome had definitely been erected after the Great War. It was the first structure they'd seen since they started walking. There was something eerie about seeing the UniForce here, on this terribly wounded planet. It was like stumbling onto a vision not of the past but the future.

Issa pulled out her handheld. The readout said they'd walked thirty kilometers from their landing spot, and judging by the constellations they had twice that to go before they reached the site of the lab, where Kara was sure the overwriter must still be concealed. They'd have to put distance between themselves and the UniForce encampment so they had a solid lead in the morning.

They kept walking, slogging onward in their cumbersome and heavy suits, every step an agony of effort. Finally, long after the light from the UniForce camp had dwindled into nothing, Kara could go no further. They agreed to sleep four hours—long enough to recharge, but short enough they could be sure they would still outpace the UniForce if they too were on the move.

Issa tapped the portable shelter. It was the size of her fist, but as it opened it domed around them, settling into the ground with a *whoosh* of wind that knocked Kara backward. The air pressurized, and the wrist consoles on both their suits beeped a weak green: 80 percent breathable oxygen for humanoid species.

Kara figured they should be cautious, but Issa ripped her helmet off and gulped in a breath of air. A few seconds passed, and when it seemed sure Issa wouldn't suffocate or implode, Kara fumbled for the heavy metal zipper that connected her helmet to her suit and pulled.

The air was so cold it felt like frost lined her lungs with every inhale. She didn't care. Kara took in a deep breath, and then another. It made her head light, but she felt more alert.

"I've never seen one of these domes," Kara said. It was pitch-black inside apart from their wrist readouts, but even in the dim green light she saw her breath fog. There was something familiar about it, an eerie sense that events were replaying themselves. It had happened more and more in the last few days.

"They used them here when the dust started to collect in the atmosphere, before the evacuations happened," Issa said. "Guess these structures never made their way to Kalu . . ."

Issa's tone was loaded. And why not? Kara felt terrible—she'd been so focused all this time on her own sense of loss that she hadn't really had any room to think about Issa's. She wondered what else Issa had seen that Kara had never even thought of before. She wondered what it would have been like to grow up here, back when it was different, when it was beautiful. She wanted to ask, but she didn't even know where to begin.

"No. They didn't." Kara sat down opposite Issa and crossed her legs on the floor, but said nothing. As loyal as Issa was, she didn't seem the type to open up, and Kara suddenly realized how badly she wanted to know her—to understand her, to learn her secrets—this girl who had risked her life to protect the WFC back on the medcraft and the medcraft itself, who had tried again and again to protect Kara, even from herself. "Do you want to talk about it? The evacuation, I mean . . ."

Issa sighed and leaned back, pressing her palms into the ground. She looked around. "I didn't grow up on Wraeta."

Kara was surprised; she had just assumed Issa was from here.

"My grandpa on my mother's side immigrated to the northern hemisphere of Kalu when she was a little girl," she explained. "I was born there, so I'm technically Kalusian."

She looked down and turned her wrist console off so Kara could no longer see her face. Kara turned her own off too, and they were plunged into darkness. Like before, the dark felt alive. It made Kara uneasy—more than uneasy—but she got the feeling Issa wanted to remain unseen. "And?"

"He tended a vegetable stand that turned into a grocery store that turned into all the vending machines of produce across every city on the planet," Issa said.

"Your family owned those?" Kara said, wrapping her arms across her chest as she shivered. There was one at the hyperloop station by her old module with Lydia, but it had looked old and rusted, and it was never stocked.

"We didn't own them. But my family's company, their labor, was the reason those stayed stocked. My mom inherited the business and turned it into a massive transport operation. Partnerships with farms outside every major city. Every yield from every harvest was distributed. We were doing good. More than comfortable," she said, like she was embarrassed. "But then the executive order happened."

Kara rocked herself—partly to keep warm, but partly because she was nervous. Of course she knew what happened, without Issa having to say it. It was leading up to the Great War—an evacuation order for all Wraetans on Kalusian soil. She combed her mind for an organic memory of it, though she realized she had none. Her own ignorance opened like a gulf between her and Issa.

Issa continued. "Anyway, a man and a woman came to our house. He was a Kalusian in an oversize business suit, said he was from the bank. She was wearing army fatigues, and walked like something was stuck up her ass." Kara heard Issa spit then. "He said that under Executive Order 23-41B, anyone of Wraetan or Fontisian descent would have their assets seized, and they'd have to be relocated to camps. 'For our safety.'"

"What a bullshit excuse," Kara said. She'd heard that way too many times, in the defense of things done to her, things that were inexcusable. "You went?"

She couldn't know for sure because of the dark that enveloped them, but she felt Issa's stare. Kara's cheeks burned hot at the foolishness of her question. "We had no choice. They extradited us to Fontis, and I ended up in a Wray Town. Most of the other Wraetans hated everything I was about. Made fun of my Kalusian accent. Called me spoiled. Said I thought I was better than anyone, and that not even the Kalusians wanted me now."

"No one should have to go through that . . ." Kara trailed off. A breeze moved through the dirt, through her newly straightened hair.

"There wasn't anyone to talk to. It was miserable. And I wouldn't have been there if it hadn't been for that man from the bank. Years later, I'd found he'd seized our assets for himself. My family's sweat and tears, and he took it away and ran the damn thing into the ground. I had fantasies of finding him, of making him pay . . ."

"Wow," Kara whispered. She was ashamed at how small her pain seemed next to Issa's. She felt like they were standing on a ledge about to collapse out from under them. "Did you find him?" she asked.

"In Nau Fruma, just before I met you. That same man was there. Our commander asked us to honor our oath: *If anyone has taken from you or yours, justice shall be swift.*"

Issa had been at that same raid on the internment camp.

"*'If anyone has taken from you or yours, justice shall be swift,'*" Kara repeated. It seemed so sudden, so brash. But maybe that's why Kara wasn't a soldier. She couldn't trust herself to make the right choice at the right time. "Did you out him?" She was afraid to hear the answer, afraid where the story of war and horror might bring them. But she needed to know.

"I said no. I let him be."

Kara stared. "After what he'd done to you?" She could practically feel the way Issa shrugged.

"What's the difference now? His death would not give my family back what they've lost. It wouldn't give me my purpose."

"Purpose," Kara said. It seemed to give Issa comfort, but all Kara felt was a growing sense of dread. Like her own purpose—to free herself, to free Rhiannon, to make Josselyn disappear—was a false bottom, and she kept falling and falling. She didn't know how to be Josselyn. What if she didn't know how to be Kara, either, if she didn't obliterate her entirely?

"You know how pearls are made, in the oceans of Hesphion?" Issa didn't wait for Kara to answer. "Little specks of dirt get caught inside an oyster, and the oyster closes in on the speck of dirt with lacquer, thinking it's infected. And the lacquer grows and grows, until that thing, that little speck of dirt, becomes a pearl."

Kara paused, waiting.

"When was that pearl a speck of dirt? Where did one end and the other start? When did one become the other?"

Emotion was welling up in Kara, powerful and unaccountable. "Maybe they were always both," she offered, her voice a ragged whisper.

"Like you, Kara?" Issa said.

Kara shook her head. Was she that transparent?

"Don't think you were coy about it. Every time I look at you you're either staring into the distance all morose or squinting at that coin," Issa said. "Yeah, I've seen the coin. You're not that slick. So who are you, Kara?"

Kara's life story was a play in two acts, one before the accident and one after. There was Rhiannon and there was Aly, each one tethering her to a different life, to a different version of herself. Rhiannon had her throne. Aly had his innocence. What good was Kara to either of them? What good was she to anyone? She pulled the coin out and cradled it in the palm of her hand. "I can't remember," she told Issa.

Kara's eyes had adjusted to the tiny bit of light filtering through, and she could see Issa now, smiling as she took the coin from Kara. She'd only ever shown her teeth to bare them, but now Kara saw how perfectly straight and white they were. It was comforting, the way her face lit up, and the warmth of her hand. "I guess it doesn't matter anyway." She bounced it in her hand to get the feel of it, then tried biting into it—and made a face. "The past is a story, rusted over like this coin. No one knows what's underneath. You can make it up if you want."

It echoed what Aly had said. *If you don't want to live a lie, it's up to you to change the truth.*

"I don't like any version of my past," Kara said. "Not even the imaginary ones."

But for the first time, she wondered—even if she succeeded in using the overwriter to erase Josselyn, would that be enough? What if it turned out that *she*—not Josselyn, Kara—was the problem? And if she erased the memories she *did* have, would another blank slate actually solve her problems, or create more?

Kara had lived with a constant feeling of unease—not just because her past was gone, but because the future looked so bleak, with every decision made for her, no surprises or discovery. What if she was wrong? What if there was something to be found in her family, some greater truth she could extract that would be worth the pain and trouble it had caused?

She felt Issa squeeze her hand, and she looked up, wiping away the sudden wetness in her eyes with the heels of her hands.

"I see you, Kara." Her voice was low and fierce, and the urgency in it shook Kara, made her feel exposed. All she could do was swallow hard. "You're the girl who told those surgeons to back off and honor my wishes on the medcraft. You're the girl who saw me as more than a patient, more than a WFC fighter, even. You saw me as a person." She let go of Kara's arm, and Kara felt the coolness where her warm hand had been.

"I try to do the right thing, and people always leave."

Issa didn't answer for a while, maybe waiting for her to go on. But Kara wouldn't. She couldn't. She didn't even have the vocabulary to talk about the feeling of uselessness, how she constantly pushed people away; there was no way she could say it all out loud.

But Issa spared her from having to say it.

"It's terrible when people leave. I'm not gonna tell you to get over it, because that's stupid, and if we could just get over things when we say we're going to, then we would never cry . . ." She sighed. "This is coming out all wrong. But sometimes when people leave, it's because they had their own thing going on. It's not your fault, and it's not your responsibility—if you treat someone right and they leave, then it's on them." Issa sat up a little taller. "What I'm trying to say is you've got a lot to give. You've got your own way of showing it, but there's so much good you have yet to do. This world needs you, Josselyn Ta'an."

The name sent a shudder through her. Of course Issa knew.

"*I* don't even know who she is," Kara said, so quietly she could hardly hear her own voice.

Issa pressed the coin back into the center of Kara's palm. "She's whoever you decide to make her."

Kara woke up hours before dawn. The cold was so intense it made her eyes tear. They'd overslept, and now they quickly suited up and double-checked one another's work. Kara grabbed for Issa's handheld and pulled up the map. Kara took the lead, moving toward the horizon, wanting to get both closer to the overwriter and farther away from the camp behind them.

It was a feverish march. In the distance, they saw a pinkish white light thrown into the air, and wondered if it was another camp closing in on the same location. Now they were afraid they'd lose the darkness and with it, their coordinates. The constellations faded into the emerging daylight, and they had only their handhelds to depend on.

By the time they reached the coordinates, Kara could see that they'd been led to ruins of some kind. Had Diac mistaken the coordinates? Had he *lied* to her? It took all her self-restraint not to run toward it. They cautiously approached, agony in how slowly they had to move. Kara paused when she got to the remains of a low, curved wall that reminded her of a giant seashell sticking out of the sand, broken and eroded by time.

This was the old greenhouse, she realized when she saw the blown-out glass panels. And there, next to it, were the remnants of the lab. Diac hadn't been wrong after all.

But where were they supposed to go from here?

The closer she got, the more she felt the emptiness. The greenhouse felt emptier than Wraeta itself, somehow—the ground was punctured with shallow holes and occasional empty tubing, like a structure inside had been dismantled piece by piece and carried off.

"Kara." Issa grabbed her shoulder roughly. She'd been so engrossed in the landscape she had ignored the thrumming vibration in the air. She turned to see a craft coming up around the horizon, blotting out the rising sun. It looked like it would swallow the entire landscape as it overtook the sky above—big, eerily silent. As it lowered, she could see two massive drills were mounted to the bottom, engines burning, its blue fire an outline in the dark sky. No atmosphere, no sound. Kara could hear only her own breathing in her helmet; her skin was damp and her heart was beating fast. Then she saw that familiar face peering at her through the observation port.

Nero.

Kara broke into a sprint, running as fast as she could move in her bulky suit. She wasn't sure if Issa was behind her. She wasn't sure about anything, only that she needed to get to it before that monster did. The man who had framed Aly, who had started a war, who had forced Rhiannon's hand—she had to believe that's the only reason the Empress would work with him. If he had the overwriter, there was no hope for any of them.

She'd wanted to erase away an older version of herself, but what kind of atrocities would a man like that use it for? Kara moved closer, as fast as she could without flying off the surface. Ten meters. Five. And then she was standing before it—the remnants of a wrought-iron barrier that might've been a fence once. It surrounded the stump of something . . . she wasn't sure what. Kara scrambled over the fence and rushed to the middle of the gated area. She fell to her knees. It looked like the stump of a tree, gnarled and petrified by the lack of atmosphere. She didn't know how close they were. She couldn't hear anything.

When she touched the bark, it crumbled. She dug around the rubble of old dirt where roots must have once spread, discovering only more ash and what felt like petrified wood. Kara felt her desperation, her hysteria brimming into tears that stung her eyes. With both hands she ripped away anything she could. She'd lost everything, but this she wouldn't lose—she'd break the overwriter with her bare hands. And then: something green. Bright green. Alive.

A root system here on a barren rock with no atmosphere.

"Where is it?" she whispered hoarsely, to no one, because no one could hear her. She sunk her hands deeper and closed them around something. She looked down and in the dim light saw something wet, viscous. Grabbing hold of what felt like a root system, she pulled. It was in the ground. It must have been *part* of the rock. It was embedded there—stored deep within the soil. She would need a drill, tools—

Then in one swift motion, she was yanked away, her suit pulled back, her hand torn from the very roots, the very hiding place where the overwriter had to be. Kara looked to the right and saw Issa, held down by a man in a dark spacesuit. And above her, in his own suit, the visor crystal clear, she saw Nero. He was smiling.

With the flick of his hand, the craft lowered, and began to drill.

NINETEEN

RHIANNON

"NERO is gone."

Rhee spun around to face Julian. He'd once again landed almost soundlessly on her balcony. He'd never been able to sneak up on her back on Nau Fruma.

"When?" was all she could say. The United Planets council was convening to discuss the provisional terms of a new peace treaty; the assembly was to gather in the capital early the next morning. "Where did he go?"

Julian shook his head. "He boarded a UniForce star cruiser at 1600."

A UniForce cruiser meant Nero had left the planet entirely. There was, she thought, a good chance he had already made his move.

Which meant it was time to make hers.

"Nero's forces have already begun preparation for the United Planets meeting," she said. "The whole planet is consumed with the arrival of the UP council members."

Lahna tilted her head. "The Towers of the Long Now will be nearly empty of security."

Rhee looked to Julian. His eyes burned brighter with something like hatred, like a star imploding—like all the color and light in them had condensed and collapsed. Had his grief over his father done that? Had *she* done that? "Let's find out what our beloved Nero gets up to when the cameras are off."

The Towers of the Long Now were technically the DroneVision headquarters, where Nero himself lived, though now the corporate offices had become an unofficial seat of power.

Rhee had stolen a small, highly targeted em-pulse from the Fisherman, which disabled the daisies—but it was still safer to keep a low profile. Though he would've been an asset, Rhee couldn't bring herself to tell him of their plan. He would have told Tai Reyanna, who would try to prevent Rhee from going, and having failed that, worry herself sick.

Julian's gaze flashed in the dim light. Without speaking, he opened his hand to reveal a small, round capsule. He aimed it at the wall and twisted; a rectangle of pale blue and white light splashed onto the surface. Blueprints, Rhee realized, though she couldn't make sense of the maze of white lines.

"There's the control room," Julian whispered, pointing to a small rectangular space surrounded on four sides by latticed squares.

They climbed the outside of the Tower via an access pipe on the west-facing wall, slipping into a vent that, according to Julian, was no longer in use. Now that they'd managed to disable some of the daisies that usually did the external patrols, they made their way inside without incident.

Between Nero's impromptu mission out of the atmosphere and the arrival of various United Planets emissaries from around the galaxy, planetary security was stretched thin. But the lack of guards—they had, so far, avoided only two rudimentary patrolling UniForce robots—made Rhee more afraid, not less.

Whatever Nero was doing, it was obviously important.

Once they'd reached the hallway leading to the control room, Rhee charged ahead. Lahna had to grab her arm and pull her back.

Lahna pressed herself against the wall and shuffled forward, motioning for Rhee and Julian to do the same. When they got to the corner, she grabbed Rhee's hand and squeezed. Rhee's heartbeat doubled; she didn't know if it was the mission or Lahna's touch or both.

"Two UniForce and a robosoldier guarding a heavy-duty door," Lahna whispered.

"Okay, that's not bad. Three against three," Rhee said.

"You're not serious," Lahna said. "We'd need a small army to take down even one of those droids." Of all places, the data center would be heavily guarded. It was further evidence that Nero had something to hide. Something to protect. But they couldn't wait to amass a small army.

Nor would one support them, Rhee thought.

Julian ignored Lahna's concern. "We have no choice. Lahna can take down the one on the right, and Rhee, you go for the one on the left. As for the droid . . ." Briefly he caught Rhee's eye. "I can maybe figure out that one on the fly."

Rhee nodded. This was the Julian she knew. The one who figured everything out on the fly. It felt right to be back in his company, even if he was risking not only his life but hers too.

"I don't like the use of this word 'maybe,'" Lahna said.

But it didn't matter—Rhee had already seen their opening, their chance. She held her hand out for Julian's knife, which they had covered in an electromagnetic sheath. Once struck—if Rhee aimed well—the covering would use an electronic pulse to shock the victim by routing through the cube.

He hesitated. She could see the doubt on his face.

"Just hand it over," she said. Rhee had the better aim, and they both knew it. But Julian would sooner die than admit it. They stared each other down in the darkness. He was so stubborn, but so was she.

Finally, he let out a sigh as he handed the knife over. Her body was thrumming with adrenaline. Every muscle was flexed. "On three. One, two . . ."

"*Three.*"

Rhee drew back the weapon as she rocketed around the corner and released. It flew end over end. The blade hit the spot on the UniForce guard's chest with pinpoint accuracy. Even from a distance she saw how the tendons on his exposed skin flexed and strained. The guard fell backward against the wall, and from there Rhee's senses exploded—like they'd been on mute without her noticing, energy and noise on and full blast now.

At the same time, Lahna released two arrows. The first struck the other guard's shoulder and sent him spinning, and the next hit him square in the chest. He fell to the ground with a thud.

Only the robosoldier was left. It crouched down low, then launched toward them in one fluid motion, the hydraulics in its legs propelling its metal body like a giant missile.

Julian shifted to the side where he could watch its movement. She saw in Julian's eyes a familiar flash. "Wanna try it?" he asked.

That singsong cadence, that same playful question so familiar it nearly made Rhee's heart stop. He used to ask it in the sparring ring, when he'd want to try a specific and wildly dangerous move—but they had only had a far older droid model to practice on. It was a move that depended completely on synchronized timing, and closing in on the target like the pair of blades in a set of scissors.

When the droid reached a certain spot in his arc, Julian began to run. She waited, and waited, until finally, mid-sprint, Julian called out one word: "Now!"

Julian leapt in the split second before Rhee launched herself in the air, her right leg outstretched. He struck the droid's head from the side, then Rhee's kick landed at its hip just as it was off angle. The robosoldier crashed against the wall with a loud *thud* and left a large dent in the concrete.

Julian and Rhee were on top of it within seconds. Julian quickly disabled its comm feed so it went dead. They stood over it, panting, and when Julian looked over at Rhee she grabbed his hand out of reflex. The calloused skin of his palm was warm, charged, but she'd felt it for only a split second before he pulled away.

"I can't say it was particularly graceful," Lahna said from behind them.

They'd arrived outside the data network center.

"Move over," Lahna said, extracting a handheld kit from her pocket. Rhee only hoped that it would unlock the electronic keypad, like Lahna promised it could.

With her headlight shining down, Lahna opened the kit up to reveal dozens of tiny metal instruments. She rotated the silver band on her finger to show the same black crest as on the ring Dahlen had worn, which could pull electric charges out of the air—it was what he'd used to kill Seotra.

"You shoot people with old-school bows and arrows and you refuse to use your cube, but you're a hacker?" Julian asked. He'd been on Nau Fruma his whole life; even if it was considered neutral territory, the details of Fontisian culture were poorly understood there.

The left corner of Lahna's lip bunched up, but Rhee couldn't tell if she was smiling or scowling. "The Fontisians have the will to create tech—more advanced than yours—which does not equate to using it at every conceivable moment." She paused, then returned to her work. "I'm going to adjust the currents so they'll think it's a temporary surge rather than an infiltration."

Her ring activated the keypad. The door slid open with a hiss. Lahna walked in first, her bow drawn. But the room was, amazingly, completely empty—apart from a massive domed console that dominated the center of the room. The dashboard was dark—the console was either powered off completely or simply asleep.

Lahna moved to the console, running her hand over a series of control panels. Then she pulled out a vial and tipped out a small ball of moss suspended in a clear liquid. Because none of them could use a cube, Lahna had brought a storage device made of Fontisian tech: a cultivated moss that could absorb data in its DNA structure. Rhee was surprised by the size; it was no bigger than a pearl.

"How does it work?" Julian asked.

"Polymer is melded into the plant's chloroplasts," she said, placing the little ball gently on the dash. "It absorbs all light data just like it would the sun, and stores it in the polymer for playback later."

Julian lowered his head to get close and tentatively reached out a finger to touch it. For a second, Lahna smiled at him. It made Rhee feel something she couldn't place, a mixture of relief and pride and something like jealousy.

Taking a deep breath, Rhee reached out a hand and swiped a series of standard commands into the console—rudimentary code that any Kalusian with a holoscreen knew well.

Instantly, the dash warmed up, and hundreds of thousands of holograms suddenly lit up throughout the large room at once, layers upon layers of them, dizzying, thick as a fog. Rhee jumped backward, swallowing her surprise. They were engulfed by memories, thoughts, static images, a life-sized repository of lives all throughout the universe.

"What is this place?" Julian said. There was a quiver to his voice. It reminded Rhee of her own reaction the first time she'd seen tech like this, on Dahlen's ship.

One of the holographic slices caught her eye: two women, leaning against one another as they laughed. The holo was hand-activated, and as she touched it the image began to play. The women's fingers intertwined; the brunette buried her face in the other woman's hair. It was lovely.

It was *private*.

Nero had stolen it from someone, and she had no idea why.

Lahna brought her hand up and moved away layer after layer until she reached a holo whose image was already moving. "Look. Something's different here." She cocked her head to the side and scrolled through. "I think it's . . . live."

"What are you talking about?" Rhee asked. The view was shaky, as if they were watching through the eyes of someone in motion. A dozen soldiers could be seen moving across a rocky surface with a yellow, dusty atmosphere. Lahna adjusted something, and the sound of heavy breathing surrounded them in the room. It was from the video. It was transmitting live.

"Does that look like anything to you?" Julian said, pointing to the bright blue star past the horizon in the observer's view.

Rhee squinted. "What does it look like to you?"

"It's Fontis," Lahna said. "Which means they're on . . ."

"Wraeta," Rhee said. Though she'd expected it, the confirmation made her feel sick.

What had Nero said to her, before they'd addressed Kalu? *The people want someone who will tell them what to believe . . . and make them believe it.*

"Stop it," Julian said, shaking his head like he was trying to wake himself up from a dream. "This is wrong."

"Get your hands off me!" someone said on the holo: a girl, who must be somewhere outside of the visual frame.

But Rhee knew that voice.

It hit her like a jolt of electricity. It traveled like a current through her body, igniting every muscle, every fiber, a spark that exploded within. It seized her beating heart, and Rhee's mouth opened so she might scream or cry, but no sound came out.

This voice she'd heard before. And only now did she know how inaccurate a recalled memory was, how it fell short in the way it made you feel, in how truly immersive it was. Because hearing Joss's voice in a recalled memory didn't make her feel like *this*. Like she'd just died and been reborn.

Lahna scooped up the moss ball and put it back in the vial. "We can't stay here," she said.

"No." Rhee leaned forward into the holo, like she might step into it—like it might turn into a portal to take her to Wraeta, to Joss, at this very moment. She didn't care what else Nero wanted, or whatever trap he was setting for them. An entirely new feeling consumed her—an urgency and raw animal fear thickened her blood. She thought only of Joss.

"We have to go. There's no time." Julian pushed her toward the exit, and Rhee stumbled, her feet slippery under her. She kept her head trained backward, her eyes on the holo. She had to see if Joss would appear.

Then—

She crashed hard into what felt like an invisible concrete wall.

"*Ancestors!*" she exclaimed, reeling backward. Julian steadied her forearm.

"Not sure what the holy spirits could do for us right here and now," a voice said from behind her. It had a lazy drawl to it. "But by all means invite them over." The soldier Rhee had stunned emerged from the shadows, then leaned against a rippling barrier that appeared to be made of thin air.

Lahna released an arrow from her bow that richoceted off the barrier and send them all scrambling to dodge it. Rhee fell to her knees. Her heart sank. They were trapped.

"Relax," he said, dusting off his jumpsuit. "You've triggered the silent alarm. We only have a minute. Maybe a minute and a half . . . you're lucky Nero took half of UniForce with him." His hand hovered over the keypad. The force field was invisible but Rhee felt its resistance, like a hand pushing on her chest, vibrating her rib cage.

"What do you want?" Rhee demanded.

"To let you out," he said simply. "I'm going to drop the force field now. And we're all just going to stay real, real cool, okay?"

The question was addressed to Lahna, whose arrow was still strung. "Why would we agree to such a thing?" she asked.

"Because I'm on your side. Part of the resistance." He looked to Rhee. "Not all UniForce is under Nero's thumb." Rhee had suspected she'd lost her own army; she hadn't thought there would be loyalists within its ranks. "Some of us have been on the receiving end of this too," he said, nodding to the holo playing behind Rhee.

Rhee didn't break eye contact. How could she trust someone in uniform? He must have seen her hesitation.

"I helped Alyosha Myraz prove his innocence. A lot of good that did," the soldier said, wincing in pain. "I have access to every code in this building."

"Who are you?" Rhee asked.

"My name is Jethezar. Call me Jeth," he said. "At your service, Empress." He typed in a code and the barrier fell, and Rhee lurched forward.

Jeth offered his hand. "Now how about we get out of here, before the alarm brings down a new wave of guards? I can't promise all of them will be so sympathetic to your cause."

Rhee felt a rising panic, her mind still flooded with her sister's voice. They'd come to get the jump on Nero, his plans—but he was so far ahead. The reality of it crushed her. Who was going to help? Who was going to believe them?

If she wanted Joss to live, Rhee needed backup. A lot of it.

"We need to get to the meeting of the United Planets," she blurted out. "Can you help us?" Seeing Lahna about to object, she added, "Technically, they're still loyal to the Ta'an rule."

"Technically, so is Nero," Lahna said.

After a moment, Julian agreed. "It's our best shot."

Jeth smiled. "Let's go find some loyalists, Empress."

Rhee nodded, another thought already blooming in her brain:

And my sister.

TWENTY

KARA

THE room where Nero had imprisoned Kara was beautiful and immaculately clean, and filled with new wave–style furniture—all grays and acrylic and angles that were as uncomfortable as they looked. She had views of the Sibuyan skyline.

It should have been calming, should have relieved the pulsing ache behind her eye. But like everything else Nero made, the room, the view, the furniture was an illusion. Kara brought her fist to the "window," and the plasma dented, only to immediately repair itself smooth. As the vision in front of her transitioned to a beach scene, she saw how truly small her cell was—just wide enough that she could stretch her arms at her sides. Kara banged the screen again, harder, but the surface merely rippled as the scene changed to a misty mountaintop. The room grew cooler, the air crisp, and there was a sound of a bird cawing in the distance.

"Enough!" Kara screamed, and she continued to hit the screen in a beat matching the pounding of her own head. Cycling through elevated vistas, the simulation showed nature at its most peaceful and elegant—each scene the inverse of the fury and helplessness growing inside her chest.

They were on Nero's ship now, in a prison cell he had constructed, just like the one on Houl. She and Issa had been separated; Kara hoped she was still alive. She pounded on the wall once more at the thought of Issa, hoping foolishly her friend would hear her, hoping she could knock down walls for them to be together again. They'd come so far.

The vista changed. Now it looked over Kalu from space, and she stopped, her fist sore from pounding. The moving image was quiet, dark, and she felt like she was the only person for hundreds of thousands of kilometers. From so far above, her home planet was an orange and white mass, pulsing with so much life and complication that she wondered if maybe they really were somewhere over Kalu.

Real or not, Nero had accessed the overwriter, and he had come to ruin it all. She slid down to her knees. And reached into her pocket, past her coin, for the pill Diac had given her. The tiny neuroblocker was her only protection against the overwriter, if Nero decided to use it.

"Nice to see you've calmed down," a voice said. She swallowed hard, taking a gamble. Felt the neuroblocker slide down her throat as someone entered the room.

Looking up, she saw it was the Tasinn with the eye patch. Yendit. The façade of deep space still played on the plasma walls, and the threshold he stood at looked like a portal to another time and place. "It's time to go."

Kara imagined pushing her way past him, into the hallway, into space. But she wouldn't give Nero the satisfaction. "Where's my friend?"

"You're not in a position to ask the questions."

They walked through a short, dark hallway that made the ship look more like the prison it was. Kara fought to stay upright, not to buckle under her own fear as she was ushered into a dark room. When an overhead light flickered, it felt like nails sinking into her brain, at the spot just behind her eye socket. She was pulled toward two seats that faced one another, wires and nodes sticking out along the backrest and arms. There was a small droid nearby carrying a tray covered with a white sheet. The thought of what might be underneath made her shiver.

"Sit," Yendit ordered, pointing at what looked like the patient's seat.

Kara did as she was told, clenching her hands in her lap as she forced her eyes to stay open and take in the medical equipment. Where was the overwriter? Would Nero use it on her? Would she be victim to this device again? But no, not yet—if she was right about the cube update being a primer for the overwriter, she didn't have it. The neuroblocker would have to be enough. And if it wasn't . . .

"Empress!" Nero entered, smiling broadly as if genuinely happy to see her. Kara saw he had the triangle burned into his neck, just like the people she'd seen on the hyperloop weeks ago—the ones who'd been Ravaged, wandering around with vacant eyes, their mind in a loop. A wave of revulsion moved through her.

"Nero," Kara said. "What are you going to do to me?"

"So impatient." But after a dramatic pause, he waved a hand. "Why would I tell you when I could just *do* it."

The lights came up and Kara gasped. It was as if they had never lifted off. The room was so enormous it gave the illusion of wide expanses and open space. Nero had filled it almost entirely with a huge cross section of Wraetan ground he had lifted from the surface. She felt dizzy, staring out over the stubbly ground, the gnarled tree stump, the landscape glowing ruddily beneath the lights.

"What is this?"

Nero walked to the stump that had until recently been rooted on the Wraetan surface. He climbed up a stepladder and walked along the soil. Kneeling before the tree stump, he reached a bare hand inside and pulled with what looked like a lot of effort. When Nero removed his hand, he was holding something. It was a small piece of tech, a microchip embedded in a small sac of some sort, sticky and wet. It looked like it might be pulsing.

Plantlike. Alive.

Kara recognized it immediately—she'd touched it just hours ago, before she'd been ripped away by Nero.

It was the overwriter.

She gasped, bringing her hand to her mouth. It filled her with instinctive revulsion, and a deep desire to break it, like she'd always planned. It had a kind of sweating, glutinous sheen, and the bright green color of a newly budded leaf. She remembered how Lydia cared for her plants at the lab, fawning over them with so much care it had made Kara jealous.

Kara tried to run for it. But Yendit pulled her back against the chair from behind.

"Yendit, there's no need to manhandle her," Nero said. "And Josselyn, calm down." She felt a chill at the mention of that name, *her* name. What did he want with her? "You're obviously not going anywhere. Now, if you please . . ."

He addressed these last words to the droid. A light bar across its chest went red then blue, and two cuffs sprang from the chair around her wrists. Another fastened around her head at the temples, so she was pinned down.

Kara struggled against her restraints, but it was pointless. "I hate you." And she did. But more so, she hated that he was right—and she hated herself for sitting here quietly, obediently, while this madman feigned politeness over a powerful, dangerous tech as if it were a toy at his disposal.

Nero took the overwriter between his thumb and his forefinger and held it up to the light. The viscous substance stuck to his fingers. She'd never seen him smile the way he did now.

"The minerals in the ground are particularly rich here, which is why it was planted." He made his way back down the stepladder.

"What will it do?" Kara asked as he moved closer.

"The plant-based components can expand consciousness. The mechanical parts—you can't see them, but they're there—will take the place of my cube as soon as it is removed, like a nerve ending."

"Removed?"

"Yes, yes." He waved a hand. "The overwriter will take the place of the cube instead of overwriting it. That's a slight flaw in the tech that Lydia and Diac developed. But I found a way around it . . ."

Of course. Nero had figured out how to retain his memories and use the overwriter to its fullest capacity.

The droid rolled forward as if it had been cued. It removed the white sheet from its tray with its handlike attachment. On it was a single syringe, but instead of a needle, the place that punctured was in the shape of a small triangle. Her heart froze. A noise escaped Kara's mouth.

"Don't worry, this one's not for you," Nero said, though there was nothing reassuring about his words or his tone. The droid prepped the shot and brought it to the burnt skin on his neck. He'd done this several times, it seemed, but he still flinched once the shot was administered.

"You're doping?" Kara asked.

"I'm not doping," he said defensively. He still handled the overwriter gently between his fingers. When whatever the droid administered took effect, Nero shuddered. "The chemicals in this little vial are self-organizing. They arrange themselves into a kind of root, connecting straight into the nerves that reach the brain, replacing the neural pathway that's normally used by the cube. It hasn't been pleasant, but it's necessary."

So he'd been prepping to insert the overwriter this whole time.

"This," he said, holding up the overwriter for her to see, "is the marriage between organic and inorganic. It's magnificent, really. It's like the cube–human relationship in a single piece of tech."

"So what happens to your cube when it's removed, then? You're just going to let it die?"

"I'll find a way to keep it alive."

"Then what's the plan now? Install the overwriter?" She thought of what her father had been planning to do, though she knew nothing Nero intended would be as noble. "Erase some memories or replace them or . . ."

"What would you have done?"

He stared at Kara intently, as if searching her. It terrified her more than anything. "You still have political opposition, Nero. You're not untouchable."

"But I have our alliance . . ."

"*Our alliance?*" Kara scoffed. "You really think this is going to help you with this scheme?"

"Yes." Nero laughed. "Yes, I sincerely do."

Just then Kara felt a tiny needle prick into her neck. She went cold; she thrashed, but the restraints were too tight, and it was no use.

"What did you do to me?"

"I ensured your cooperation," he said. "It'll be easier this way."

A surge shot through her brain, sharp and precise, like it was cleaving in two. Then down her throat and to the very tips of every limb, changing, coursing, rolling. Like venom now, but more insidious. It was her cube updating, and—she hoped—her neuroblocker working against it.

"Is this what you did to Rhiannon?" Kara demanded. Nero tilted his head, as if he were observing an animal. It made her all the more furious. "I would *kill* you before we aligned."

"I don't think you will. Any mind I overwrite is connected to my own." She didn't follow; he could tell. "Would you *really* kill me, if you knew it would risk the lives of countless innocents? Just under a million souls and counting have updated, across at least twenty territories. And those who won't, will. Would you risk all of them by killing me? Would you risk the very fabric of consciousness itself just to see me die?"

She stared, stunned.

"Well," Nero said with a slight smile, lifting the overwriter as if making a toast. "To us."

TWENTY-ONE

RHIANNON

RHEE hurried after Jethezar through the labyrinthine passages of the Sibu capitol building, with Julian and Lahna close behind her. There hadn't been time to find a safe way to notify the Fisherman and Tai Reyanna, but she planned to send word as soon as they met with the United Planets.

She could hardly believe what she'd just witnessed, the evidence they now carried in Lahna's precious living moss. She half expected the evil of it would shrivel the thing to black.

Rhee should've focused on what they would say when they stood before the United Planets: Nero hacking cubes, controlling people, destroying lives . . . But every time she tried to structure any kind of argument, her mind wandered back to that voice she'd heard on the holos: Joss's.

Get your hands off me, she'd said.

Rhee, Julian, and Lahna fell into a single-file line behind Jeth. His wide frame filled the entrance to a narrow hallway; he was the biggest soul she'd ever seen. They walked past end tables and mirrors and platters of imported fruits from Nau Fruma and Fontis—including Dom, the berries from a sentient plant species. A plant that could perceive, feel, some said even think. She tried not to take it as an omen.

"This is the service hallway?" Julian commented. Rhee had to admit it was surprisingly opulent, and she wondered, a bump in her pulse, how many of the United Planets representatives Nero had already bribed to support his agenda—how many diplomats might already be looking the other way? Kalu's coffers were deep. Almost as deep as individual greed.

Lahna echoed Rhee's growing suspicion. "Jethezar, has the council been notified of the Empress's arrival?"

"A few key members—representatives from Derkatz and the larger asteroids in the Desuco Quadrant. But we're concerned about security." He half turned as he spoke to them, a quickness to his step. "Call me Jeth."

"You haven't been working for the resistance long, Jeth?" Lahna fumbled the shortened name, much like Dahlen had the first time he'd said her own—Rhee. Fontisians didn't shed formalities easily. Nor suspicion.

"No." Jeth's smile faltered when he caught her implication. He blanched, probably remembering an archer's predilection for soft throat tissue. "Less than a week, honestly. But I'm here now."

"And what made you abandon the UniForce?" Julian asked.

"It got weird in the ranks as soon as Nero accused Aly of killing you." He nodded to Rhee.

"Alyosha?" She could tell by the look on Jeth's face that he had some connection to Nero's chosen scapegoat. Another life Rhee had ruined, and one she'd never made amends for. "You said you knew him?"

"Knew him? We came up in UniForce together. I was there when he broadcast his playback on Rhesto, proving his innocence. I helped him."

"So where's Alyosha now? Is he okay?" She clung to the idea of this individual life spared, this boy redeemed, to keep from thinking about the horrors of Nero's plan, and the fact that he now had Joss in his custody.

Jeth shook his head. "We were split up after the broadcast. I stayed on in the UniForce to gather intel until I could leave my post. But as far as we know, he broke out of a camp on Nau Fruma and went off the grid."

The hallway opened through a small door into a big, dimly lit area with dark curtains on either side. They were backstage of the main theater now. In the sudden darkness, Rhee felt totally disoriented. She could hear the murmur of conversation. But where were the council members?

Just then a bright light dazzled them. Rhee took a step backward; they were standing behind a massive hologram, now alive with a reel of current events, and she felt hopelessly small, like she was face-to-face with the sun. She watched the war raging across the system. Even inverted, the horror was no less.

The holoprojection was partially transparent, and Rhee broke into a sweat as she realized she could see all the planetary representatives seated in the theater. Could they see her? She hoped that the light and color, intensified on the other side, kept her invisible.

How would she convince everyone of the truth of what she knew? The council needed to trust her, believe her, believe *in* her. But some of the politicians were most likely in Nero's pocket. It was exactly what she'd been trained to do—and it was exactly where she had always failed. There were at least fifty members of the United Planets, representing just as many nations and sovereign asteroids. They sat stadium-style facing the stage.

0088-A, Abernath, Bazorl, Bbiy . . . Rhee began to recite them in her head in alphabetical order, like her father had instructed her to do as a girl. She'd always gotten them wrong, and never bothered to learn them correctly. It was Joss who knew them backward and forward. It had been her job as future empress to always be perfect. And now here was Rhee, falling short, always less than she needed to be.

Joss. She longed more than ever for her older sister. Joss would know what to do. Joss knew how to command a room.

The coin in her pocket hung heavy with a thousand regrets.

Honor. Bravery. Loyalty.

Rhee hadn't even thought of the words since Dahlen left. She took her hand and threaded her fingers through Lahna's. She was surprised when Julian took her other hand. Surprised—and grateful.

A deep voice boomed from somewhere in the stadium of seats. "We know the war has already cost an enormous amount of lives. That's why Nero called for a cease-fire."

The daisies located the speaker in the theater, and his face emerged, zoomed in, on the holo. Rhee's pulse began to race. The man with the eye patch. It was Nero's right-hand adviser, Yendit. A chill ran through her.

Yendit was Nero's eyes and ears. How could she make a plea for understanding, how could she convince the United Planets of his evil, with Nero watching her through his adviser?

"The cease-fire is a load of *taejis*," someone else hollered. "The galaxy is crawling with UniForce under the thin veil of 'peacekeeping,' thanks to Nero's new treaty."

"Nero might've been out of line, but it's the Fontisians who were responsible for the Empress's disappearance," a woman spoke up.

"The Fontisians? No more conspiracy theory, please," said another representative. "Empress Rhiannon returned with them willingly to take the throne."

"Excuse me?" It was the Fontisian representative. He stood up in his place.

At that point the chamber exploded with arguing voices.

Rhee took a breath. It was now or never.

But as she took a step forward, Jeth seized her arm. "Not now," he whispered. "Not until they stop fighting."

"And when will that be?" Rhee fired back. She shook her head. "I'm tired of waiting."

But this time, it was Lahna who caught her and held her back. Rhee turned to look at her quizzically—and a split second before she heard the approaching footsteps she saw them, in Lahna's tension. A UniForce soldier was coming for them. Then another, from the opposite direction.

Before Lahna could even fire an arrow, Yendit emerged from the darkness. Rhee felt her stomach pooling at her feet. How long had he known she was there?

Suddenly there were guards—at least twenty of them—lining the walls and blocking doors. The Tasinn—the royal Kalusian guards. There were too many to fight. They were surrounded. A robosoldier pinioned Jeth. Another snapped Lahna's bow in two, pushing her to the ground. One of the Tasinn grabbed Julian and flipped him to the floor. And before Rhee could reach for her knife, one of her own guards seized her wrists and locked them behind her back.

Yendit sidled next to her, brought his face too close to hers. In his eyes, she saw a strange darkness, a blankness that was terrifying. "Rhiannon Ta'an. We meet again," he whispered.

The holo shielding them from the rest of the theater flickered once before it disappeared entirely, dropping like a curtain to expose them to the council. A gasp went up around the room. An eruption of screams. Cries to help her, to free her, to let her go.

But no one moved. And no help came.

Yendit's eyes flickered over Rhee. "Hold her there so she can watch," he commanded.

She struggled against the guard who held her. He was twice her size, and crushing her wrists with his grip. "Let go," she said, though she knew it wouldn't help. "I have the power to see you executed."

Yendit shook his head. He looked amused. "There is no greater power than the power of the mind."

She froze, terror grabbing her by the throat. It was exactly what Nero had said to her, just before their speech. "What do you mean?"

Yendit grinned. Something in his eyes shifted. Now, when he grinned, he reminded her of Nero himself.

"If two minds are better than one, think how much better *infinite* minds will be."

And then, as if in slow motion, all of the Tasinn, weapons in hands, looked up, facing them. "Infinite," they all echoed in unison. And that was when Rhee knew: Nero had possessed them—had taken over their cubes, and was somehow controlling them. *All* of them.

Nero wasn't there. He didn't need to be—he could work from a distance, without dirtying his own hands.

As one, the Tasinn pivoted. As one, they leapt into the seats. Rhee saw a man's throat slit at the first arc of a long knife, the way the blood poured out like it was tipped out of a pitcher of wine.

Then came the screaming.

Drowned, drowned, all of it drowned, under a tide of more blood.

TWENTY-TWO

RHIANNON

NO.

Something inside Rhiannon rose up; the thing that made her who she was, whether it was pride or stubbornness or her soul, she couldn't say, but it was like a power, pulsing inside her, waking her up from this nightmare, telling her there was still a way.

The Tasinn were trained in the same set of arts Veyron had taught her. Even now, every time she struggled or sidestepped, the Tasinn bodyguard knew exactly how to neutralize her—and Yendit just watched, smirking.

This man's face, the screaming, the fear—these weren't going to be the last things she'd see before she died.

Because she wasn't going to die.

She thought of Veyron and what he had always told her. She needed to be three steps ahead of her opponent.

Three steps—that was all she needed.

With her hands still behind her back, she took a deep breath and stepped off her right foot lightly, charging at Yendit. One. Two. Three. It all happened fast—she launched herself into the air, pushed off his thigh with her right foot and his chest with the left, then brought her feet together and back—releasing a two-legged kick, her heels snapping into his face, and her head, thrown back, cracking into the nose of the guard behind her.

Satisfaction flooded Rhee's body as the Tasinn guard stumbled backward, releasing her.

Yendit staggered, and before he could recover Rhee gulped in a deep breath of air and spun around, kicking his face with all the momentum she'd gathered. But his jaw was like iron; Rhee felt her foot shatter, shards of bone grinding against each other. When she tried to stand on it, pain exploded all the way up to her spine.

Yendit laughed, looked like he was chomping at the air. "Alloy reinforcements," he said as he stood, stroking his jaw.

He took a long stride forward and punched her in the chest. Rhee couldn't tell up from down, only that she was gasping for air, mid-flight, dead weight falling backward. When she hit the ground pain exploded, a minefield all over her body—echoing an unbearable bomb. Then everything went silent, and she remembered the peace of the desert on Nau Fruma, and how you could see every star when you looked up into the nighttime sky.

The quietest place in the world, Julian had said. Julian. Things were good then. The entire world in that moment had funneled down to two things: darkness and his voice.

Then the blackness parted and she saw glimmers of light, heard that same voice, only it was screaming.

Someone flew at Yendit—a man? No, not a man. The Fisherman.

"I've arrived!" he boomed as he socked Yendit in the face again and again. His harpoon gun was strapped to his side, but he didn't need it. Yendit's face was already pulpy, wet with dark blood.

Rhee rolled over and saw Yendit catch the Fisherman and choke him, pinning him up against the wall with both hands. Rhee got to her knees, unable to pull herself up on her weak foot, her breath still tight and hard in her chest. The Fisherman wedged his hands between Yendit's arms and stuck his thumbs in his eyes so that the man screamed, but if he eased up on the hold Rhee couldn't tell.

Keeping as low to the ground as possible, Rhee crawled toward them. Julian and Lahna were still struggling with their respective guards, but Rhee wanted to help.

There were yells from the slaughter, though they were alarmingly quiet, already expiring. The Tasinn had done enough. The place was awash in the smell of death, the feel of it, like a weight in the air, making it hard to breathe. She reached Julian's knife that had landed on the floor. The chamber floor, she saw, was flooded with blood.

Julian grabbed her. Rhee realized the Tasinn he had fought was on the floor, and only Lahna's guard was left—pinning her to the ground.

Julian took the knife out of Rhee's hand, and Rhee could barely protest, unable to find her voice. Julian held it with such ease, as if it been part of his hand all along. She saw Julian's eyes meet the girl's, and fought the urge to look away as he pulled the knife back and brought it down hard on the back of the guard's neck, no hesitation. No alloy reinforcements there. He slumped forward, transforming in a split second to a corpse. Lahna scrambled up with a quick thanks, then kneeled to pull the knife out of the guard's neck. Blood poured out. Lahna wiped the blade clean on her tunic.

Meanwhile, Yendit had stopped struggling, while the Fisherman berated his unconscious body and yelled what seemed to be a string of curses, possibly in multiple languages, none of which Rhee recognized.

Jeth limped up next to them. He was in rough shape but still standing, and with the robosoldier's comm unit in his hand; he'd managed to disable it. "Who's this?" he said over the Fisherman's curses.

"I am the second most important person in the galaxy as far as you lot are concerned," he called over his shoulder. "Because I'm supposed to keep this impossible brat of an empress alive!"

When the Fisherman seemed satisfied that Yendit was dead, he let his body drop to the floor before spinning around to face them.

"Were you planning to tell the head of security that you were entering a literal bloodbath, then?" he asked Rhee as he heaved her up to her feet. Her foot ached visciously.

"I'm sorry. There wasn't time."

"*There wasn't time* to call for your personal security detail?" He threw his hands up in the air. "Isn't she supposed to be clever?" the Fisherman asked of the three people at her side. He got up close to Rhee and pointed a stubby finger in her face. "You nearly died. If I hadn't followed you here, who knows—"

He didn't finish his sentence. The tip of the harpoon burst up through his chest. It would've stabbed Rhee directly through the heart had Lahna not pulled her away.

"No!" The word nearly ripped her throat in two as Julian kicked in the side of Yendit's head. His neck tilted at an odd angle and his body went limp yet again, falling in such a way that he cradled the harpoon gun to his chest. The Fisherman's harpoon gun.

The Fisherman collapsed. Rhee fell to her knees and grabbed the Fisherman's hand. "I'm so sorry," she repeated as his heavy-lidded eyes fluttered open.

"In the Outer Belt we don't do sorries, Empress."

"I shouldn't have come here . . ."

"Enough already on what you should or shouldn't have done." He paused to spit up blood. "I'm not a political man, but I'm a betting one. You're fierce, and impossible, and you'll do all of us right on the Outer Belt, won't you?"

Rhee nodded her head vigorously. He squeezed her hand in response.

"Then I put all my credits on you." Out of his elaborate belt that kept countless weapons, he produced a telescope— Julian's telecope—the very one she'd given him in exchange for his help on Tinoppa. "Take it back. I've no use for it where I'm going."

Rhee took it, the metal cool in her palm, and watched him collapse, realizing how much effort it had taken him to sit up— to perform such a gesture of forgiveness and generosity. She dropped it into her pocket and burst into tears when the life left his eyes. Too many deaths. Too many deaths at her expense.

Lahna kneeled by her side, and pressed her index fingers first to her eyes, and then closed the Fisherman's eyelids. Julian had closed his eyes, moving his mouth in what looked like a prayer.

It was silent, save for the unconscious guards who stuttered and twitched in unison near them. She wondered if Nero was using some kind of server to infiltrate minds—they moved as if they couldn't talk or communicate when too much data streamed through them.

"I know an exit," Jeth said. "We should move."

And yet Rhee was frozen, staring hard at the man who'd killed the Fisherman. Behind her, the Tasinn weren't done. They gutted the ambassadors one by one, trapped them against exits barred for this purpose, drilled them in their seats, spilled their guts out with a single swipe of their swords. But she drowned out the sound and went back to that moment on board Dahlen's ship, floating on the outer edges of the Desuco Quadrant. How vast it had seemed, how insignificant Rhee had felt, and how she'd found peace in that.

The Fisherman had made his livelihood there; he'd fished out creatures who could survive without light and atmosphere, with nothing but a suit and an alloy harpoon gun.

And yet he would never find that solitude, that peace, again. Yendit had taken it away from him.

She snatched the harpoon gun from Yendit's limp hands now. He was still alive; she could tell by the way his chest rose and fell. Taking aim, she pointed it at his chest.

"Rhee." Julian put his hand on her shoulder. Lahna appeared on her other side, yet Rhee couldn't tear her eyes away from the murderer before her.

"There would be nothing noble about this kill," Lahna said. "He's unconscious."

Rhee trembled, her index finger pressing down on the trigger, playing with the resistance of it.

"Guys, we gotta *move*," Jeth said again. "If we manage to get out of here alive there are bigger fish to fry!"

Her mind clouded over with thoughts of Nero—*he* was the bigger fish—and she had let him live. But she wouldn't make that same mistake again.

Rhee lowered the harpoon gun. She'd face Yendit once more. She had a feeling. But Nero was the prize now . . .

Part Four:

THE CROWNED

"In the long, illustrious rule of the Ta'an Dynasty, what is often forgotten is their tumultuous ascent to power twelve generations prior—and the bloody attempt to keep it in the year 928."

—*Excerpt from* **The Iron Star, Updated Edition: A History of the Ta'an Dynasty**

TWENTY-THREE

KARA

KARA couldn't sleep in the chambers that once belonged to her parents. It should've been comforting; it should've felt like home. Instead she felt encased in a deathbed, the room a shrine to the life she was supposed to have lived. For the past two days— ever since Nero had installed her back at the palace in Sibu— she had followed a woman through the dimly familiar rooms as though visiting a foreign land, or as though she were a ghost visiting a former life. And the guards had watched on.

Given the many fine layers of her formal silk robes, and the elaborately arranged scarf that covered her hair, Kara figured the woman was a Tai. They were a sect of teachers and caretakers, Kara knew, and the woman gave off the proper air of someone who moved slowly and acted deliberately. She spoke in a mono- tone as she pointed out artifacts in the palace, a droning his- tory lesson with no love or passion behind any of it. There was something familiar about her, as if Kara had known her before—and maybe she had, and maybe it was the case that she knew Rhiannon too—but there was no way to ask her now. As was obvious from the glassiness of her eyes and eerie dreaminess of her movements, she was clearly under the influence of the overwriter.

Kara silently thanked Diac, for what felt like the millionth time, for that neuroblocker. Her mind still felt clear—Nero might have the overwriter, but he'd not gotten inside *her* head. At least not yet.

Still. Everything about the palace felt foreign, and she craved to speak with someone who had their own thoughts and ideas—not a vessel for Nero's twisted game.

Mostly, she mourned her sister. Rhiannon was dead; she had to be. In the last moments of their lives, the ambassadors of the United Planets had sent out frantic messages, begging for help—Empress Rhee was in trouble, they were all in trouble, the Tasinn had turned.

Dead, dead, all of them dead. A horrific massacre.

Nero's doing, obviously. He had used the overwriter to control the Tasinn, turning them into a deadly army.

And now Nero expected her to do a broadcast later that evening, one in which she pinned the massacre on Rhiannon. After all, the Tasinn were her guards. And her body hadn't turned up among the corpses, or so he claimed. But Kara knew the truth. Rhee had been a casualty to Nero's ambition.

She knew too that Nero was watching her through the guards that followed her. But not through her own cube—since she'd taken the neuroblocker. She had no idea how long its effects would last, though.

She had no allies, no one to speak to—she was alone again. Issa had been taken as a prisoner down to the cellars, where she was heavily guarded.

Kara needed to break her out, and get as far away from the palace as possible. But then what? Would there be people on the outside whose cubes had been updated, who could be under Nero's influence at any moment?

There had to be some sort of weak point in the palace security, a way to exit the walls without being seen. And there had to be holes in Nero's overall plan, contingencies that he went to great lengths to cover. If only she could read his mind, wrench open his thoughts and shuffle through them as casually as he had ingested the overwriter.

A memory surfaced, rippling through her grief like a rock striking the water—and it wasn't at all the one she would have expected. She'd said much the same thing to Pavel back on Nau Fruma, before Aly had left her. That she'd open up his head and rearrange him. What had Pavel told her in response? Something about cube-to-cube transfers . . .

She couldn't get inside Nero's head—but maybe she could put Nero's head inside hers.

Nero wouldn't let his cube die, and where else would he store it if not in a host? Diac had told her the overwriter itself could be preserved in a living thing, a tree. The same could be said for the cube. As for Nero's cube . . . he had probably stored it in the very root system that had housed the overwriter. And her best bet was the palace greenhouse, though she had no idea where to find it.

Listen, Kara told herself. *Use your mind.*

She had no delusions she would get her memories back, not when she needed them, and definitely not in the high-definition form of cube memories. But Kara thought, hoped, that there was some memory buried deep inside her muscles, inside her mind. Lydia had used the overwriter on her and still, she'd kept some things: her sense of direction, her basic knowledge of how to do the everyday things. If those were intact, maybe her body's memory of her former home was too.

Kara grabbed a paperweight from her father's desk—a heavy model of Kalu—and stepped into the hall. It would make a clumsy weapon if she got caught. She would have to count on her memory to do the rest. Maybe, if a guard stopped her, a clever lie.

But the coast was eerily clear, as if the guards had suddenly been called away. She sent up a quick *thank you* to Vodhan, Aly's god, before she could push the urge away. Trying not to think of Aly, Kara moved through the shadows of the palace, her feet padded by the thick rugs, down one floor. She skirted the edges of the kitchen in case a guard passed. They didn't; Kara caught a glimpse of only one through the threshold as she crouched low and pressed herself against the counter. Then he disappeared down another hall, away from her, and she made her move.

She slipped into a musty pantry with empty shelves and a broken light. There were no windows. But there was another door. She opened it.

Here she was: damp dark steps descending into a cellar.

Kara paused, wondering when they would notice she was gone, or if they already knew. But did it matter? If there was any chance of stopping Nero, the time was now.

Down in the cellars she could sense the expanse of a whole world below that she would've explored when she was young. Kara stood in the dark and listened. There was a steady sound of quiet dripping, comforting if it weren't for the echo, or the dozens of palace guards ready to be deployed at Nero's behest—to find her, to brainwash her too, to strip away her humanity and her free will.

That was not the way it would end. Kara would make her own choices.

She listened. She knew there was a way out if she could just reason through it. What did she know about greenhouses? That they needed glass paneling for sunlight, insulation for the heat. It meant she would need to travel in the direction of the backyard, to the south. What else? That there would be a water source. Plants needed water.

The leak. She went toward it and found moss on the ground and walls that grew thicker the deeper she went in one direction. The deeper she moved in, away from the pantry, the darker it got—so black she couldn't see her own hands. She guided herself through the forks in the cellar by touch. It was wet and soft, and it reminded her of the moss that grew in patches in Luris, on slick stones deep in the forest, the further you moved from the shore.

When the moss thinned out on the walls of the cellar, Kara backtracked.

There wasn't much time, but she plunged forward. Right. Left. Right. Right and then a quick left. There was light, and she felt a sliver of joy until she got scared again, wondering whether she'd only made a huge circle. But she found more light and more, until she looked up and saw the outline of a door. Scrambling up the worn stairs, she cracked open the door and saw grass. To the left was the greenhouse. Kara was steps away from being outside.

Outside, she flinched at the sunshine—so much horror had happened, she almost expected the world to have vanished. The garden path was overgrown now, crowded with untrimmed greenery. A memory burst into her mind then, or if not a memory, an impression of one: the sweet smell of roses. Somewhere deep down, Kara had carried that with her, and even more—how the petals felt soft between her fingers, and the sadness she felt when they would eventually wilt and fall away with the slightest breeze. She knew it was some sort of organic memory, a remnant of her life before, and suddenly, she felt angry that they would only ever come back to her half-formed.

The greenhouse rose up in the distance: a large glass building in the shape of a hexagon. Two guards paced the perimeter, and Kara hung back, ducking further into the shadows the mass of greenery afforded, until they had disappeared around the corner.

The coast was clear. She slipped into the open and darted to the greenhouse doors, praying she would find them open. Her heart did a weird little jig in her chest. The long silver handles felt cool to the touch, and they turned easily.

Holding her breath, she passed inside. The air was humid. What from the outside had looked like a beautiful and well-tended greenhouse on the inside was an expansive, riotous forest. The ceiling cut the light into prisms.

The greenhouse was terraced, and hanging gardens rose up to the sky, sending leaves the size of her open palm cascading toward the ground. She'd been here before; she was sure of it. It occurred to her Nero had allowed this to thrive. He liked beautiful things when they were manicured and polished, stripped of their rawness. Though he might have planned to store the overwriter here all along, and perhaps its more natural state was conducive to supporting it. She shuddered. Maybe he planned to grow it, as her mom had been growing it on Wraeta.

The paths through towers of vertical planters were tight and winding, and her arms were soon coated in sweat and humidity and the clinging pollen of plant life. She wound her way toward the center of the greenhouse, where, beside a cluster of cherry blossom trees that threw their arms up to the sky, a lone gray stump was squatting in a heap of gravel and dirt. It looked like the cross section of Wraeta.

It *was* a cross section of Wraeta.

Kara dropped her weapon and plunged her hands into the dirt. The loose shale and gravel bit at her nails, and she knew it must be mixing with her blood. It felt fitting. She pawed down past the roots, scrabbling frantically now, all too aware that someone might arrive and surprise her at any second.

Then Kara felt it: a piece of metal that she pinched between her fingers. It was Nero's own cube deep in the root system, thriving, living, waiting to be reclaimed. Pain coursed through her at the thought of having the cube implanted. What would it do to her? What would *he* do to her?

It didn't matter. She had no choice. There had to be something there, in his cube, that could help her find a way to undo him for good. There had to be a way.

If there wasn't, all was lost.

She yanked the whole thing free. The cube was a dull piece of metal no bigger than her pinky finger, with exposed pink and white roots that, in the absence of something to nest into, began to wiggle as though alive. These, she knew, were the connective arteries that would join to her brain.

She slipped the cube into the folds of her *duhatj*, wiped her hands clean, and stood. Kara felt a shiver up her spine. The air pressure changed just slightly—she felt a draft that wasn't there before. Leaves rustled in the breeze. Kara froze.

Someone had opened the door to the greenhouse.

Kara sidestepped into the cherry branches and dropped into a crouch again. She heard heavy boots—a Tasinn, it had to be— slowly drumming their way up the path. A droid was humming in the quiet too—likely a security model. It would tase her on sight.

Closer. Closer. Almost on top of her now . . .

Making a split-second decision, Kara hurtled into the open. She didn't get a good look at him—he was tall and in uniform, and that's all she had time to register. Then all at once, she took off at a sprint and slammed into him, keeping her head down. As he spun backward, she ran past him toward the exit. Somewhere in front of her, an android was beeping repetitively—it didn't sound like a security bot, but she was hardly going to pivot to check it out—and she dodged down the path, careened through the narrow chasms of growth. She'd almost made it to the door when suddenly another guard stepped in front of her, flipping her neatly onto her back.

She rolled over before he could drop on top of her. But he pinned her legs. She pushed and kicked, desperate to get free. It couldn't end here, with Nero's cube in her pocket, when she was so close to what she needed—and what the galaxy needed.

"Kara," the guard said, and in a surreal moment Kara thought she knew the voice. Then she realized she *did* know the voice.

"Aly?"

TWENTY-FOUR

ALYOSHA

"I—I thought you were dead," Aly said. He still half thought he was dreaming: the greenhouse, the humidity, the landscape of growth, Kara standing in front of him, alive, as beautiful as ever. "I saw you die . . ."

There was something more than the change in her eyes, her skin, her hair, the way she smelled. The essence of her had shifted, yet hadn't changed in any vital way, shape, or form. It made it more obvious than ever: the awful, aching truth that he loved her. And that he'd left her.

"It wasn't me," she said.

Pavel rolled up slowly and pulled out a freshly cut rose from his chest compartment. "Did you know the rose variety found outside the palace is not a species indigenous to Kalu?"

That got her to smile a little bit, the corners of her mouth quivering. Aly realized it was the kind of smile you forced your face to make.

"Thanks, Pavel." She took it from the droid and put it to her nose absently.

"Please." Aly reached for her hands. His palms were slick with sweat. All he wanted was for her to look at him, to understand he didn't know—that he did what he'd done for her. They were together now. "Please, Kara. Believe me. I—I swear, if I'd known I never would have left Nau Fruma. Ask Pavel . . ."

"It doesn't matter now," she said. But at least she didn't pull away. Instead, she turned her eyes to Dahlen. "Who are you?" she asked.

"Dahlen," he said simply. "And you?"

Kara hesitated. "Kara," she said at the exact same time Aly said, "Princess Josselyn."

"All of the above?" Pavel said. Dahlen raised his eyebrows.

"Now that the introductions are concluded, perhaps we can save the rest of the joyful reunion for after we kill Nero?"

"Not if you're navigating," Aly snapped back. "Pavel used your intel to track Nero to this exact spot. You said you had a line on Nero's cube."

Kara looked from Aly to Dahlen and back. "You're here for Nero?"

"Isn't that what he just said?" Dahlen said testily.

A real charmer.

Aly cut in before he could do any more damage. "We're here to *kill* Nero. A few days ago, the WFC managed to tap Nero's cube location. After years and years of firewall, Nero must have lifted permissions. So we tracked him."

She looked between the two of them. "How many Tasinn did you kill?"

"Nine," Dahlen said. "Every one we found. We weren't able to remain undetected." Kara stared at him. He didn't seem to notice. "We tracked Nero here, to the greenhouse." He looked around, as if expecting the man to materialize.

Kara took a deep breath. "You tracked his cube to this spot because his cube *is* at this spot."

Now it was Aly's turn to stare.

"Nero has the overwriter," Kara said. "He had to swap out his cube for it. He'll know soon. He may *already* know."

"Know what?" Aly said. He could hardly keep track of what she was saying.

Kara shrugged, her mouth tilted up in that smirk she sometimes got when she figured something out before anyone else did. Thank Vodhan he recognized it, recognized something about her. But any relief he'd felt drained all the way out when she reached into her pocket, then held up her hand, opening it, and simply said:

"That I stole it."

Aly had to jog to keep pace with Kara as they moved freely through the palace. Dahlen and Aly had cleared a path, and the Tasinn usually guarding the residential wing were in Vodhan's hands now.

Left, right, left—Aly lost track of all the dizzying twists and turns the palace concealed, even as he struggled to make sense of what she told them: the message that brought her to Ralire, the conversation with Diac while they were imprisoned, and how Nero had beat her to the overwriter. His heart seized when she told them about the massacre at the United Planets meeting.

"Does it not worry you that Rhiannon is gone?" Dahlen asked.

Kara narrowed her eyes. "Of course it worries me." Then she turned, testing a door with her weight, and, finding it open, hustling them down yet another flight of stairs. "She could be gone," she said over her shoulder. Her voice had cracked. "Or she might have decided to run away . . ."

"No." Dahlen's voice was surprisingly forceful. "Not Rhee." Aly raised an eyebrow at his use of her nickname.

They had reached the subterranean level: Dark and gloomy, it was filled with old furniture that had gone out of style during the Great War. The atmosphere was oppressive. Aly felt like he should tiptoe.

Even Kara dropped her voice to a near-whisper. "Nero wants me to go on the air and denounce her—blame her for the council massacre. I can't." She seemed to be looking for something; she was glancing in different rooms as they passed, opening doors that led into unused vaults and the kind of barren quarters used to house servants or inmates of the throne.

"Yes you can," Aly said. A plan was taking shape in his mind. "We can use Nero's tactics against him. Undermine him on his own turf, where he feels safest."

"How?" Kara said. She threw open another door. She let out a sigh, as though disappointed to find it empty.

"You do the broadcast. But we'll send Rhee a message, to let her know you're here for her," Aly said. "That you believe her, even if you're saying the opposite. Like hiding in plain sight."

"But even if Rhiannon were to return, what then?" Dahlen asked.

"Then we get the two sisters together—to denounce Nero. He'll have no *choice* but to return. He'll have to reassert control. We get Kara and Rhiannon to a safe spot, and we kill him."

"No." Kara's voice was firm.

"No?"

He met her eyes. There was fire in them—the same light he'd seen when they first met. "I'm Empress now." Aly's heart caught on the word *empress*. As if he needed a reminder. "I can't run from it. Whatever plans I had, whatever it was I wanted—or thought I wanted—it doesn't matter."

"Kara . . ." he said. It sounded like she'd been going through some major *taejis* and hadn't had anyone to talk to. To say the least.

"And besides," Kara said, cutting him off, "Nero can't be killed."

"No one can't be killed," Dahlen replied calmly.

Kara sighed. "He's got the overwriter. Which means he's connected to the minds of countless innocent people. And if he dies, all of their minds will be destroyed."

"Destroyed? How do you know this?" Aly asked.

"He told me," Kara said defensively.

"You can't believe a madman," Dahlen scoffed. "Nor can you accept his madness as sense."

"But what if he was telling the truth?" Aly demanded. He felt suddenly sick to his stomach, remembering all the people he had ever disappointed—all the people he had abandoned. The folks in the Wray. The prisoners on Houl and Nau Fruma. Kara.

"All risks must be calculated. There is no greater threat than the existing one: Nero, with the overwriter."

"Agreed," Kara said. She tested another door; they found a room packed with barrels of honey wine. She backed out of it before Aly could suggest they take one for the road. "But if there's any truth to what he's saying—that thousands, maybe hundreds of thousands, of people will die—I need some collateral against him."

"I'm not following, Empress," Dahlen said. "What are you proposing?"

They were nearly at the end of the corridor. She whirled around suddenly to face him.

"We have his cube." She took a deep breath. "I need to upload it."

For a long second, they were all silent. Even Pavel could think of nothing to say.

"That's nuts," Aly choked out finally, "*and* dangerous. And why you? Any of us could do it."

"Because he thinks I'm his pawn. I can get closer to him than any of you can. *I'm* the one who is going to kill him. His cube is just my insurance."

"Insurance?" Dahlen asked.

"That he doesn't kill me first. If I die, his cube dies with me. Maybe he'll kill me anyway, but . . . it might make him hesitate. Give us the advantage."

Pavel filled the heavy silence. "There's actually precedent in the cube-to-cube transfers," he said, "and the way memories are willed down to family members before one's death . . ."

"Exactly." Kara spun on her heel again. There were three doors yet untested in the hallway. Aly wondered what she was looking for. But he was too agitated to ask. "It's basically the same thing."

"Or it's as different as night and day," Aly argued. "It's the difference between two living souls *choosing* to transfer memories between their cubes, versus . . . *this*." Aly couldn't even come up with a word for it, but it felt wrong, like they were violating Vodhan's law itself.

"You did it," Dahlen pointed out.

"That was a droid's comm unit," Aly fired back. He had uploaded the droid's memories on Uustral, and even that had almost overwhelmed him, brought him to his knees. "Not a humanoid cube. Besides, I was in a medical facility."

"Kara would need a very sophisticated medic," Pavel chimed in. "It's likely she will have to have a portion of the hardware melded to her own cube . . ."

"I know someone who can do it." Kara tested the next door over. It swung open, and she peered inside. Aly looked over her shoulder to an empty room. She pushed her way past him and down the hall farther.

"You 'know someone' qualified for complex cube surgery?"

"Not just complex but illegal, according to the G-1K summit accords," Pavel pointed out as he wheeled after Kara.

"Right. Illegal, dangerous, and complex," Aly said, counting the improbables one by one on his fingers. "You just got a guy that can do that?"

Kara flung open the last door, revealing a Wraetan girl with braids to her waist that flung every which way as she came at them with a chair.

Aly moved in front of Kara reflexively, shielding her with his arm. Dahlen lunged forward to meet whatever feralness this girl was bringing, but Kara elbowed Aly out of the way and pulled on the back of Dahlen's shirt with both her hands.

"*Stop*," she yelled, just as the girl registered the scene and dropped the chair. She put both her hands up, eyes wide as she took in the massive Fontisian who was about to rip her head off.

"Took you long enough," she said. It seemed like she was talking to Kara, but her eyes never left Dahlen's.

"Everyone, this is Issa." Issa dropped her hands to her hips at the intro. Aly realized there was a medic patch across her uniform. "She's my guy."

TWENTY-FIVE

RHIANNON

AFTER she'd killed Veyron, Rhee had claimed she knew plenty about death. She'd been ready to rush headlong into a haphazard plan to murder Seotra, the statesman she'd mistakenly blamed for Nero's plot. But Dahlen had challenged her—questioning her in that condescending way that felt distinctly him. *Why? Because you've killed a man?* he'd asked. *That makes you just as qualified as most, which means not qualified at all.*

Now she knew that he was right: Taking one life didn't give you intimate knowledge of death. Having her family taken from her didn't either, even if she felt their absence deep down in her bones—like there was nothing there, no blood or marrow, just the sorrow that burned off, evaporated, turned her into something toxic so that for the longest time all she could feel was rage.

There was only ever one thing to know: Death begets more death.

The massacre of the United Planets council just three days ago proved it beyond a doubt. Losing the Fisherman had shaken her down to her core. The protests on the streets of Sibu had risen to new heights. All around the galaxy, riots were breaking out in otherwise neutral territories. Everyone had heard about the attack, and nobody could agree who was to blame—only that someone had to pay.

If Rhee was right, Nero would step up immediately to keep up appearances, and do the work of acting appalled at the violence at the council meeting. Rhee thought it cowardly to flee. But Jeth had insisted, and Lahna agreed they definitely needed to put some distance between her and Nero. Julian had said nothing, and hadn't since the massacre—though Rhee knew he'd been burning with rage, and would be happy to kill Nero himself for his part in Veyron's death. They'd barreled through the Bazorl Quadrant, exhausted, away from Kalu.

Nero, a killer with a handsome face and an ever-convincing smile, would no doubt revel in comforting a grieving galaxy. He'd need to pin the blame on Rhee for what he'd done, just like he'd blamed Aly for supposedly killing Rhee, and Seotra for killing Rhee's parents.

She should've listened to Dahlen. *His promises are a trap, and I thought you would do better than believe him*, he'd said of Nero. The flimsy cease-fire was merely an excuse, a cover while Nero got his hands on the tech he'd used to possess all of the royal Tasinn—the guards who should have been on her side.

Jeth had brought them to Elsse, a tiny moon outpost outside of Fontis, to wait out a UniForce fleet passing through the quadrant. Rhee was practically buzzing to get back, but they were fugitives, and they had suffered too much to fall back under Nero's control.

Lahna was teaching Jeth to shoot with a bow and arrow—the UniForce never used them anymore—and out of the corner of her eye, Rhee saw an arrow fly across the mesa. It traveled through a series of holographic bull's-eyes until it stuck into the bark of a tree thirty meters in the distance. Lahna nodded, satisfied, as Jeth returned her bow. They moved with a serious precision, both soldiers at heart. The slaughter seemed to have brought them together, and showed Rhee just how little she knew about war.

She kicked up her good foot and got herself up into a handstand. After a few seconds of wobbling, she found it—that perfect equilibrium—while the tiny pebbles and tufts of grass dug into her palms.

It was a way to stay calm, to keep her focus and drown out the pain of her foot—but her mind wandered to all the missteps that had led her here. All that blood. All those helpless, panicked ambassadors, overpowered and overwhelmed by the deadly Tasinn. Their throats slit, blood pouring down suits and splattered across polished tables. And all the betrayals before that, the stupid, childish decisions she'd made that led to death. Abandonment. So many people hated her, and still she hated herself more.

Blood was rushing to her head now, and Rhee felt herself tilt. Kicking her legs in the air, she managed to straighten out—but she could feel her arms straining.

"You never *could* hold them that long," Julian said from

behind her. The sound of his voice crashed over her. Rhee wobbled again and almost recovered, until the coin fell from her pocket. Her right elbow gave, and her body slanted too far to the left. She went crashing down in the grass. From the ground, she surveyed Julian's outline, backlit by the sun.

"I still can't." She grabbed for the coin.

Julian held his hand out, and she took it quickly—afraid he'd change his mind. He pulled her up, and she stood to face him now and stifled a wince as she shifted her weight to her left foot. Outside the palace, they used to challenge each other to handstands by wading through the uneven sand that shifted underneath their palms. Was that only a few months ago? It seemed impossible so much had changed.

And yet there were moments, recently, that she felt he was coming back to her. Like when they'd taken down the robodroid together in unison—one fluid motion. She could have sworn his eyes had told her she still meant something to him. He was still the person who knew her best in the world.

He pulled the telescope out of his belt. She'd left it on the makeshift pillow of bundled-up clothes that morning. "I never thought I'd see this again."

"I'm sorry I gave it away. I had to barter for the Fisherman's help once."

"It came back to you eventually." Julian shrugged. That it did. But the Fisherman's death was a steep price to pay. "I'm sorry about your friend," he said.

"It's . . ." Rhee paused. She was going to say *It's okay*, but they both knew it wasn't. She swallowed, and changed the subject.

"Fitting, that." She nodded to the telescope. "You said I could borrow it 'til I saw you next."

"And here we are." Julian didn't look up. His hair would've fallen across his eyes now, if he still wore it long. She wondered if he could ever look at her without thinking of his dad—the man she'd murdered over nothing. Rhee had taken so much away from this boy, her best friend. Her ex–best friend. And in return all she'd given him was the rage. That anger that expanded, from the center of your heart and outward, until you radiated it— crowding out everything else so that every happiness was poisoned and every pettiness only grew.

There had been a time where Rhee could look at the world only through the lens of her own revenge, every movement a step closer to fulfilling a bloody destiny. It had gotten her here, and any faithful followers she had were either dead or had abandoned her. None of it was worth it. She'd have to make it right.

Rhee took a deep breath. "I'm sorry, Julian," she said. The words were so dumb, so insufficient, but they were the only ones that came. "I'll never stop being sorry."

Julian started to make lines in the grass with the toe of his boot, his hands shoved into his pockets. Rhee ached with the familiarity of it; he'd always done it when he was thinking, as if his brain had an excess of energy that needed to be siphoned off into multiple activities.

"I know," he said at last. And finally he looked at her, squinting against the sun. His face was thoughtful, focused—wholly absent of any hatred or scorn. Rhee didn't think an expression so neutral could make her heart leap like it did, but maybe this was a path. He might never forgive her for killing his father, but maybe, just maybe—

"Rhiannon!"

Rhee turned, her thoughts interrupted. Jeth and Lahna ran toward them with a furious urgency. Jeth clutched the handheld. A projection bounced in the air.

Her stomach seized with dread again. "What's wrong?" she asked. "What happened?"

Instead of answering, Jeth amped the feed so it beamed out across the tall grasses and rolling fields. On the holo, Rhee saw her sister—her image blurry at the edges, soft and ethereal in the sunlight. She looked like an ancestor come back from the dead, because she had. A banner beneath her read: ELDER TA'AN CONFIRMED ALIVE.

Without thinking, Rhee reached out to touch her. But her fingers only met air. "Joss . . ."

As though dispersed by her touch, the feed cut back to a news anchor.

"Princess Josselyn Ta'an has reappeared after six years," the anchor said, a pretty new-wave Kalusian who emulated Nero down to the small, polished button on the collar of his immaculate shirt. "The announcement came after a DNA test result confirmed she is the eldest Ta'an . . ." It panned to footage of Joss in the palace. She was beautiful, and so familiar, in every aspect the girl her sister would have become. *Did become*, Rhee told herself.

Joss was alive.

Had been alive all this time.

"She came . . ." Rhee trailed off, unable to form any kind of coherent thought, much less say a prayer. Josselyn had come forward, answered her call—at the very moment of the greatest turmoil, when Rhee herself wasn't there.

She wanted to laugh and cry at the same time. Despite knowing her sister was alive, despite having heard her voice, Rhee hadn't *truly* believed it until now. It was a defense mechanism, a way to protect her heart.

Now, she knew—this was what she had always wanted: not just to find her sister, but to have a partner on the throne. Joss would protect her, like she always had. They could take on Nero together.

Josselyn and the broadcaster—one of Nero's favorite shills, someone from the Outer Belt with flushed blue skin and yellow reptilian eyes—were talking.

"Where you've been, Josselyn?"

"Somewhere safe. That's all I can say. I wouldn't want to put anyone in danger, but I was cared for, and I'm thankful." Joss had poise and empathy radiating from every pore.

"But didn't you say you had a bout of amnesia?" The broadcaster's pupils dilated slightly every time she asked a question. "When did your memories come back? What was your first one?"

Joss's mouth opened and closed again. It was the first hint of any uncertainty. Rhee took a step forward. She was desperate to hear the answer.

"It was of my father, taking my hand . . ."

Rhee was disappointed. She wanted something specific, something about her . . .

"When Rhiannon put out a reward for your return, you didn't come forward immediately. Why?"

"Just hop on a craft and fly back through three war zones?" Joss said, in a way that was both teasing and firm, as she lifted her chin. Rhee felt a surge of pride. That was the Joss she remembered. "I think where I've been is hardly as important as the fact I've returned now. The galaxy is suffering."

On screen, Joss blinked, pausing half a second with her eyes closed. Her lashes looked black and dramatic and lovely against her wide cheekbones.

"She's so pretty," Rhee blurted out. "She was always so pretty."

"She looks familiar," Jeth said.

"Why wouldn't she? She's the Empress," Lahna said. Rhee felt something reach into her chest and squeeze. She used to hate that word when it was her title, yet now that it was Josselyn's she suddenly felt its absence. Lahna must've realized the effect of her words, because she squeezed Rhee's hand once more. "Sorry," she whispered.

"That's not why," Jeth countered as he watched the holo. "She reminds me of someone . . ."

"Me too . . ." Julian said.

"Does she not look like Rhiannon?" Lahna asked.

"Kind of, but that's not it," Jeth said, squinting his white eyes at the holo.

Julian cleared his throat. "Do you think we can trust her?" he asked, in a low voice. The question was so unexpected that it undercut the pleasure of hearing him say *we*.

"What do you mean? Why shouldn't we trust her?" Rhee looked to Jeth and Lahna for support, but they were both stone-faced.

Julian shrugged. "The timing is convenient, is all."

"Convenient? The galaxy is at war." But she was distracted—they were interviewing Joss in the main foyer of the palace. It looked so perfect, or perfectly rehearsed—staged. Now that she thought of it, everything was too perfect.

"You mention suffering," the broadcaster said. "I assume you mean the recent massacre at the United Planets gathering?"

Joss nodded her head, focusing on the broadcaster. "It was a terrible, unprecedented tragedy. And I had to step forward."

"To rule alongside your sister?"

"No." Then Joss looked right into the camera and said, "To rule in her place."

Lahna sucked in a quick breath, and Jeth paused the holo so Joss's head was tilted to the side, her eyes—one brown, one hazel—locked on to Rhee.

"No, replay it," Julian said.

"I think Rhee needs a minute," Jeth said.

"Replay it!" Julian insisted. When the Chram refused, Julian grabbed the handheld out of his hand and replayed it himself.

Rhee had to suffer through her own sister publicly planning to usurp her. "To rule in her place," she said once more. Julian replayed it, and replayed it . . .

"If you're being cruel—" Lahna argued.

"That's the girl who broke into the dojo!" Julian suddenly cried out. "She looks different, but I recognize her voice. I thought *you'd* sent her," he said to Rhee, "because she had your coin. Or one just like it."

Rhee pulled her own coin out. Julian took it and held it up to the sun. "It was like this, but all rusted over. It's the same girl. Rhee, she intercepted a message meant for my father. Which means she's either working with the resistance . . ."

"Or working to destroy it," Jeth chimed in. "Guys, I got another whammy: I think this was the girl traveling with Alyosha."

"The soldier accused of my murder? The one you claimed was innocent?" Rhee asked. It seemed impossible, her own sister circling in this same orbit of soldiers and refugees and loyalists—when Rhee herself had just discovered she was alive. "Keep playing it, all the way through," Rhee said.

"I have reason to believe, as much as it pains me to say it," Joss continued, "that the royal Tasinn were conducting that attack at the command of"—she blinked here—"the younger princess, my sister, Rhiannon Ta'an. If the intelligence is correct, I am ashamed, both for myself and my family's legacy."

Jeth cursed.

Rhee felt as if she had taken a blow directly to the chest.

Joss had pinned the entire massacre on her.

It made sense. That was the horrible thing. As far as she knew, no one on Kalu had any awareness of Nero's access to technology that could control the Tasinn from afar. And they are—were—her royal army, after all. She felt a flush of mortification that she hadn't seen it sooner—how she'd been set up.

Could Joss really believe that Rhee would be capable of such a thing? Had Nero managed to convince her of it? Or was she working with him?

Joss looked directly out from the feed. She might really have been standing only a few feet away, fixing Rhee in place with her glare. "I would like to take the opportunity to tell you, Rhiannon, wherever you are, that I intend to seek justice for the victims of this terrible massacre. The person to blame must be held accountable." Her expression could have been cut from stone. The only sign she gave of discomfort was in the way she toyed with a ring on her left hand. But her voice was profoundly calm.

"Then you publicly denounce your sister?"

"I do," Josselyn said. She looked directly into the camera. "Rhiannon, if you have survived, surrender now—or never return. We must all determine to take the more difficult path, because it's the right one."

Rhee felt tears sting her eyes. She blinked, once, twice, trying to clear her head, trying to think. *Honor. Bravery. Loyalty.*

"I have another announcement to share soon that will bring much-needed hope to the galaxy," Josselyn continued, still fiddling with the ring on her left hand, turning it over and over.

And then Rhee saw it. The sign, the clue, the *message.*

Dahlen's ring.

Dahlen and Josselyn were together. It was a sign. A new spasm of desperate hope sparked inside Rhee's chest. And now, she understood the hidden meaning running like a current beneath her sister's words.

I intend to seek justice.

The person to blame must be held accountable.

And then, the last part—the very echo of Dahlen's parting words: *We must all determine to take the more difficult path, because it's the right one.*

Josselyn and Dahlen were planning to kill Nero: It was their message to Rhee.

It was their *invitation* to her.

Joss bit her lip. And there was the Joss Rhee knew and remembered. That was her sister. The one who tortured and ignored her, but the same one who'd led her out of those cellars. Who'd taught her how to cartwheel and fold tiny paper airplanes that they'd throw off the balcony. She'd come back for her.

Loyalty. It was part of her *ma'tan sarili.*

"Nero put her up to this," Rhee said to the group. "She's trying to tell me so herself. She's wearing Dahlen's ring."

"You can't be sure," Lahna said. "This sister of yours was confirmed traveling with the very boy who was acussed of your murder, whose whereabouts are now unknown." She and Jeth shared a look; hers was fierce, his uncertain. "And she made contact with Julian, took a valuable piece of intel meant for an important leader in the resistance."

"I can't be sure," Rhee agreed shakily. Her own first instinct had been suspicion. What other reason would bring Joss so close to her than the promise of the crown? They'd been interconnected all this time when Rhee was on the run for her life, and on the path to empress.

But another set of reasons seemed just as likely: that her sister was scared, that she'd been to hell and back, that reclaiming her throne was the safest bet in a world that wanted her dead.

"I can't be sure," Rhee repeated, "but isn't that what faith is about? Finding clarity and conviction in a world that is muddied and uncertain?" She thought of Dahlen here, wishing he were by her side.

Rhee didn't care how innocent it sounded, how foolish. Every instinct in her braided together into something resolute and sure. She *knew*—it was different than when she'd known Seotra was her family's murderer, so different that she hardly recognized the feeling. Trusting Joss felt like an omen, like she'd arrived to guide her, like Rhee might finally find her way. The feeling made her think of Dahlen again; it wasn't dissimilar to how he'd described his faith.

There was a silence. Rhee knew the others thought returning to Kalu now would be an act of suicide, but she couldn't let them give up—not right now. She would need help, protection against Nero.

She needed *family*.

"So what do we do?" Julian asked finally. It was the same thing he'd asked when they'd gotten caught by the Tasinn on Nau Fruma. It gave her another surge of hope, and her hope gave her strength.

"Josselyn told me I should never return to Kalu," Rhee said. For the first time in what felt like ages, she grinned. "She should have remembered that I never listen to her when she's bossing me around."

TWENTY-SIX

KARA

KARA and Aly were in a tunnel, squatting close, ready to do something big and important that would change the course of the war. But she could focus only on the nick of his eyebrow, the corner of his mouth that lifted up a little higher than the other. It felt like standing at the mouth of that tunnel was standing at the cusp of the rest of her life. Everything would change after this moment. Everything already had.

Then the edges of the tunnel started dissolving around her. It was urgent, in direct relation to something she'd done—like she was being punished for losing focus on what mattered. Aly took her hand to pull her out of the tunnel, and suddenly the world around them shifted. Kara felt a corset pinch her middle like a vise on her ribs, a new and terrible kind of torture. They were at the top of the thousand steps that led up to the Ta'an palace in Sibu. She looked down and saw the red silk of her dress, meters of it extending from her waistline, growing, churning, lifting her up like a buoyant sea. She and Aly were pulled apart in the red water; she regretted ever letting go of his hand.

She tried to swim back to him, thrashing through silk, but it turned coarse. It scratched her, and cut her, until she bled the same color as the sea. She saw a craft on fire tear across the sky above them, shedding metal pieces. And her own face, her real one, the one she wore now, looking through the window right at her as it torpedoed into the sea.

"No!" Kara tried to scream.

Kara opened her eyes with a gasp; her neck was still raw from the surgery, and muscles she hadn't known existed ached all along her right neck and shoulder. Her head hurt, like a drill burrowing into her—and she was shaken by the disappointment she felt, knowing all along she'd hoped the procedure would end her headaches too. She'd have to live with it. Manage it, just like she'd always done. There was no miracle cure.

Her vision was blurred, but she saw a figure move toward the bed. Issa. The girl leaned in, her braids just dusting Kara's face.

"Oh, how the tables have turned," Issa said. The top two buttons of her camo shirt were undone, and the white shirt underneath was stretched around the neck. Even now she clutched her necklace of Vodhan.

"How long was I out?" Kara asked, sitting up. Everything hurt, and she tried not to flinch. She could see herself reflected in the mirror: The spot on her neck where Issa had grafted Nero's cube onto her own looked red and raw and angry. Tentatively, she reached out a hand to touch it; it seemed to be radiating a terrible kind of heat. She hadn't turned it on yet—but it was insurance. Nero wouldn't kill her, not if he wanted to preserve his own memories. Not if he didn't want his cube to die with her.

"Sixteen hours," Issa said.

Kara felt a spike of panic. "Sixteen?" She flung the sheets off her bed and slipped out, wobbly on her legs. "Did Rhiannon reach out? The coronation is in—"

"Two hours," Aly said, appearing in the doorway. "I wanted to wake you up, but doctor's orders." The sound of his voice made Kara's heart drop to her stomach; it filled her with an indescribable joy and a deep, blue uncertainty.

His grown-out hair looked like a soft black halo around his head. She thought of the day they'd first met, when she was still Kara. How they'd stood side by side in the tiny zeppelin bathroom in this same way. They'd talked through the mirror then, because she hadn't been able to speak to him directly. It was like looking at the sun. Too bright. Too intense.

What would happen if they succeeded at stopping Nero? What would happen if they didn't?

"How are you feeling?" Aly reached up as if to touch the new wound on her neck and then, as if thinking better of it, put a hand on her cheek instead.

"I'm okay," she said, gently detaching herself. Kara looked down at the onyx ring she realized she had worn in her sleep.

"And to answer your question, no—Rhiannon hasn't gotten hold of us," Issa said.

Had her sister understood the message from what Kara had worn on the holos for an audience of one? The ring belonged to

Dahlen, and it was too big. It hung awkwardly on her thumb, and she twisted it now. It was more than pretty decoration, more than a symbol to communicate whose side she was on.

This ring was also a weapon, and with it, she was going to destroy a common enemy. And wasn't this bigger than all their other problems?

Dahlen and Pavel weren't far behind. The room felt suddenly crowded, hot. Two hours to plan. That was hardly any time at all.

"You don't look as terrible as I thought you would," Dahlen said. At Kara's look, Aly interjected.

"What he was trying to say is that you look like you recovered from the surgery well," Aly said. "I speak Dahlen, the language of romance . . ."

"Dahlen was over my shoulder the whole surgery." Issa sounded like she was somewhere between annoyed and glad. "The guy swears he's an expert because he had heart surgery *once*."

"Doesn't that make me more qualified than most?" He tugged aside his tunic, revealing a massive scar directly above his heart.

"No, actually," Pavel chimed in. "Given the nature of open-heart surgery, it's likely you were anesthetized."

"All right, all right, everyone," Aly said. "Empress, are you ready to go over the plan?"

It was the first time in a long while she hadn't snuck somewhere by the cover of night, timing her path to avoid guards. Now, as she arrived on the roof of the palace, down the row of Tasinn four deep, Kara focused on the details: the crowd rippling in the vast square below her—a soundless mass from here, but a seething, miserable swarm down below. The daisies were poised, ready to capture everything, ready to immortalize her misery, to record forever the agitation of the crowds. The ceremony wouldn't start until Nero arrived.

Kara, however, was more concerned with how it would end.

Before the massacre, there had been small pockets of outrage on both sides, but now people had been marching, chanting, calling for justice. The Tasinn had been dispatched just to try to hold the crowds back from storming the palace gates.

Yendit was waiting next to the officiant, wearing an enormous carnation of incongruous pink. His face was bruised and raw, and he wore a brace around his neck.

"Rough night?" she asked.

He ignored her.

She breathed in the scent of his flower, imagining an actual flower blooming, crowding out the pain in her head. It was an old meditation technique Lydia had insisted that she learn.

But it was no use. Her thoughts kept returning to the preparation for Rhee's coronation, just weeks ago, before someone had attempted to take her sister's life. It had been a showy affair, and they'd cut down a field of flowers to decorate the palace, lanterns all around the city. It never came to be.

Kara thought too of her mother's coronation—Kara had seen it replayed, an enormously showy affair with thousands in attendance and easily another billion tuning in across the galaxy. Kara's mother had been made for such an event: porcelain skin against a red dress; lips painted in a bright, lovely pout; small wrists and small hands and a slender finger upon which to wear her ruby wedding ring. But in rewatching it a million times, it struck Kara how the Empress's smile was a gracious one. She'd understood her role—to look and be benevolent.

Did Kara have that in her? She balled her hand around the family coin now, wondering what Rhiannon would do, and if she'd gotten the message.

"Are you cold?" Yendit said, smiling for the daisies as she stepped onto the dais beside him. It might appear they were enjoying each other's company. Kara shook her head, even if she was cold. She'd worn a gray dress in a second-wave style. "Then uncross your arms and smile."

Kara did not want to be told what she should do with her face, but she kept it neutral for the daisies.

"Ah." Yendit straightened the front of his shirt as he looked at the speck growing on the horizon. "He's arrived."

It was Nero's craft, arriving just as the ceremony would begin—and no earlier. *More dramatic optics*, he had told Kara when he arranged for the coronation to take place.

The wind flattened the small gathering on the palace roof and blew Kara backward several feet as the craft hovered. Slowly, it began to drop. From down below it looked like a vast insect getting ready to latch, and it filled Kara with terror she was careful to hide. Aly, Dahlen, and Issa were waiting, concealed. She would not make a move until they did. Easy for them to say; they weren't the ones out here baited in a dress, and all three had military training.

A hatchback door slid open, and a staircase unrolled from the craft. Nero emerged, silhouetted by a shimmer of hot air.

His smile was larger and more predatory than ever as he oozed gracefully down toward her.

"I'm sorry for the delay." Nero made a big show of turning his smile toward the daisies.

"No you're not." Kara smiled and eased her hair out of her face as if she were carefree, among friends. A daisy was floating at the corner of her eye, but still out of earshot. "You were circling outside the atmosphere just to kill time."

Nero gave her a curious look she'd never seen before. It wasn't amused. His eyes were dark; Kara imagined behind them were the shadows of other eyes, other memories, other souls. "You remind me of your sister."

Kara smiled—a real one this time.

"It's not a compliment," he said.

"Let's begin," the small Kalusian officiant said. She wore a flowy dress, held prayer sheets in one hand and beads in the other.

Kara—or was it Josselyn now?—instinctively stood up straighter. Still no sign of Rhiannon.

"You must move to the side," the woman said to Nero. She gave him her best smile, but it looked forced, scared, at least until Nero strode away and stood by Yendit's side. The second-in-command grinned at her, and she suppressed a shudder. Kara needed to not think about Nero, afraid of which dark ribbons of his memories might curl up and entangle her. The slight pressure in her neck from the surgery was reminder enough of the cube that Issa had buried in her flesh.

Tensions were high. Kara felt it in the officiant's slow, halting movements, the way she purposefully avoided Kara's gaze.

"You will endure," the woman said to her.

Kara wasn't sure if she was talking about the ceremony itself or becoming empress.

But before either of those happened, Nero would have to die. She thought again of Nero's warning: *Would you* really *kill me, if you knew it would risk the lives of countless innocents? Would you risk the very fabric of consciousness itself just to see me die?*

She ran her hands over the silk of her dress to keep them from shaking. She didn't like what her answer had become. But short of a means to destroy the overwriter itself, they had to destroy the man. Really, the overwriter and the man were inseparable—they were one and the same.

Kara hardly heard the officiant's words as they initiated the vows: something about duty and permanence and honor. *Ma'tan sarili*, she remembered as if in a dream. She had forgotten hers. Instead, she thought of Aly.

Fear started to freeze her from the inside out. Were they in position? Her mind reeled. Maybe this had been a terrible idea. Was she really prepared to confront Nero so boldly? To kill him?

"Now repeat after me," the officiant said. "I will serve my planet . . ."

"I will serve my planet . . ." Kara began, but then stopped when she heard a high-pitched whizzing grow louder around them.

A metal anchor, then another and another, four in total, clanked onto the roof. *Ziplines.* Kara turned to see a blur of dark shadows launching off the roof of the clock tower. Then Yendit grabbed her, pinning her arms to her sides, and held a stunner to her neck.

A second later, Rhiannon climbed onto the ledge of the roof and dropped down soundlessly, her hair whipped back by the wind, her eyes dark and filled with fury.

TWENTY-SEVEN

KARA

RHIANNON was a tornado of precise rage: jabbing, kicking, whirling.

She got my message, Kara thought as Rhiannon's crew followed behind her, all of them scaling the roof seconds after Rhee had: a petite Fontisian girl who fired arrows so quickly at the rush of attacking Tasinn that Kara lost track of the blur of her hands; Julian, the Lancer's son from Nau Fruma, who spun and punched almost as quickly as Rhiannon. The last fighter she recognized as Aly's friend Jethezar—slow to arrive but a force of power that plowed through an entire row of Tasinn in one tackle.

Yendit had Kara's hands behind her back, and she struggled uselessly. Now he was trying to force her to the edge of the roof. As she got closer, she could see more and more of the crowd surging beneath them, the waves of people in the central square reacting to the scene the daisies were still recording and trans-mitting across their cubes even now.

"It's a shame you'll have to say hello and goodbye, all in one breath," Yendit said, nodding in Rhee's direction. Except his inflection was all wrong, his accent, his words.

Nero was speaking *through* Yendit.

Rhiannon looked up.

"You should've killed me when you had the chance," he taunted. Kara didn't know what he meant. But Rhee locked eyes with her for a moment, just before Rhee took down another guard with the heel of her palm straight to his Adam's apple. She sprinted for Kara.

"Watch out!" Kara screamed.

But it was too late. Rhiannon was so focused on Kara that she missed the way Nero launched himself toward her, tackling her to the ground. Where *was* everyone?

Kara tried to surge forward, out of Yendit's grip—but he only jabbed the stunner into her neck roughly, and choked the breath out of her chest with his forearm. He cut off her air bit by bit, while she gulped whatever she could, forcing it down into her burning lungs. Her eyes were closing, her tongue felt thick, nothing made sense anymore, and for a split second she forgot where she was, who she was.

Then Yendit let off. She gasped for breath, desperate, feeling the cool air coat her insides—the consciousness creeping back into her brain. She knew who she was. She was the Empress.

Yendit lifted her off her feet and dragged her while she kicked, her feet just skimming the ground. Clawing at his arm, biting at it when she managed.

Adrenaline spiked through her and she fought harder, but he swung her around and dangled her over the five-story drop—his arms hooked onto her shoulders from behind. Her terror crystallized when she looked down at the public square and saw the Tasinn like a swarm of dark ants, moving together, perfectly in sync . . .

Moving as one . . .

She knew then: Nero was once again using the overwriter to control them all.

"Please," she choked out. She arched her back, digging her heels into the side of the palace, scrambling for any kind of purchase on the vertical drop. Her stomach seesawed wildly, and her heartbeat thrummed in her ears. But it was clear Yendit didn't plan to drop her, not right away at least. His grip was strong but his attention wavered; he was looking in Rhee's direction, hoping to bait her.

Kara had to calm down. Struggling might make him drop her. Taking a deep breath, she kept her back straight and brought her knees up to her chest—as high as they could go. She just barely caught her heel on the ledge of the roof, and then the other, and on the quick count of three she dug her heels in and launched herself backward. Both Yendit and Kara fell back onto the roof just near the parapet edge. Another Tasinn came rushing toward them, hand on his stunner.

"I'll take care of this." The Tasinn's uniform was stained with blood and ripped at the shoulder. His hat was pulled low over his eyes. Kara crabwalked backward away from both of them. "Nero wants her alive," he snapped at Yendit.

Kara could *hear* the way Yendit smiled—she could hear the saliva cracking in his gums, the rapid pattern of his breathing. "I *am* Nero, you fool," he said, in a voice that made her skin crawl. "We all are."

"Even better." Without warning, the soldier pulled his stunner out and brought it to Yendit's cube in one fluid motion. Nero's right-hand man seized, the electrocution traveling into his cube and through his heart. His limbs flailed.

The guard pushed back his hat.

"Alyosha," she said. He was panting, his face bruised. He looked like he'd gone through hell. They locked eyes for a second before Kara's attention was pulled to her left.

Nero and Rhiannon were still sparring, tumbling over one another, landing sideswipes and hard blows. Dahlen and Issa, also dressed as Tasinn, were successfully confusing the guards, and the roof was pooling with blood, littered with bodies.

Kara started to move toward Rhiannon, but Aly held her back.

"It looks like she has it handled," he said, in a low voice. "She *wants* this."

It was probably true that Rhee had been waiting years for this moment, but looking like she had it handled didn't stop the pounding in Kara's chest, the way her skin felt cold. Rhiannon seemed to be less a human than a mass of concentrated fury, a blinding oscillation of coiled rage and grief. She spun and whipped and flipped and kicked. And strangely, she seemed only to be getting faster, stronger, more powerful. It was as if the fight was *fueling* her, strengthening her—while Nero looked to be tiring.

Kara didn't know if Nero was nearly as capable a fighter as Rhee, but she imagined he was weakened from using the overwriter. His attention was too dispersed. His mind too *diffuse*. And even if every hit he landed made Kara's heart drop, Rhiannon seemed barely fazed, blocking his hits and landing three more.

Rhee drove him backward, toward the edge of the roof. "Say you surrender," she said. But Nero's response was a sardonic smile.

Finally, the waist-high ledge was at Nero's back; he was cornered.

But Rhee kept attacking, bobbing and jabbing, his face raw and bloody, his body near collapse. She wouldn't stop until he surrendered, and Kara didn't know if he could. Rhiannon needed this battle, and she knew Nero needed to be stopped, but it was too much to bear. Aly squeezed Kara's shoulder; she wanted to look away but refused—she wanted to see the moment Nero collapsed.

But he swatted Rhee, and she couldn't block it in time. She fell backward. Kara nearly stumbled forward to go to her, but Rhee lunged back up and dropkicked him. He slammed against the ledge, the upper half of his body limp over the ledge. It would take only one more attack . . .

Kara knew there would be nothing but empty space and a fall.

"No!" Kara called out of instinct, thinking of the crowd below. *Would you* really *kill me, if you knew it would risk the lives of countless innocents?*

Rhiannon looked over, and Kara regretted her mistake. Using the moment as a distraction, Nero regained his balance and lunged at Rhiannon.

Kara ran forward. But her sister was faster. She dropped into a ball, clipping Nero at the knees and cutting his legs out from under him. He crashed down onto the roof, scrabbling wildly, even as the weight of his lower body carried him backward. His nails splintered on the stone.

And then, at the last second, Rhee lunged, pinning his wrists in place, keeping him from dropping. Kara came up from behind.

"Rhiannon, don't . . ." There were too many people at stake.

"Listen to her . . ." he gasped out. "The sisters together again. Together we could be powerful, unstoppable."

Rhiannon leaned forward. She spoke so quietly, Kara nearly missed what she said. "This is for our parents."

Then she let go.

No. Kara moved around Rhiannon and clutched at the ledge, watching Nero flail as he plummeted to the ground. This would be the end of them all: Anyone whom Nero controlled, anyone with the update. Millions of souls. It fell on her shoulders. This was her fault, and she would have to live with her decision.

But she didn't look away, not even when she heard the

heart-sickening crunch of the impact of his body on concrete. And blood—there was so much of it.

An odd silence fell over the crowd below, as if everyone was holding their breath at once. They had scrambled away as Nero fell, but now, they formed a wary circle around his body. All was still. Whatever Kara was waiting for, it didn't happen. She scanned the crowd.

"Does that mean he was bluffing about the overwriter being connected to countless others?" Issa asked, her voice small and breathless. She'd slid next to Kara on the roof.

Kara exhaled a breath she didn't know she'd been holding. "I think so," she said.

She turned toward her sister. Rhee met her eyes but remained still—but once they moved, they did so in sync, rushing into the other, falling into each other's arms. They collapsed on the ground in a heap.

"You got my message." Kara hadn't realized she was crying until tears were streaming down her face. She clutched her sister even tighter to her chest, Rhee's head tucked perfectly under her chin. "I didn't mean any of it, you know that, right?"

"I know," Rhee said, her voice muffled in their hug. They were together. Finally.

Kara realized she'd been clutching her coin this whole time. "Do you know what this means?"

Her sister pulled away and saw the coin in Kara's hand. Her eyes brightened, one brown and the other hazel with specks of green. Just like hers.

Rhiannon rooted around in her pocket and produced a nearly identical coin. It had a groove down the middle. "Our father brought them back from a diplomatic trip in the Bazorl." She pressed hers to Kara's; the metal strip down the center fit into the grove of Rhiannon's coin.

It seemed funny, how a piece of metal once contained value—that entire civilizations exchanged the things they needed for something so arbitrary. But Kara understood now what value it could hold. She understood, too, what Lydia had said.

This binds you to your family.

A tall figure flitted out of Kara's peripheral view. Dahlen.

When she saw him, Rhiannon's eyes brightened. She looked to Kara, who brought her palm to Rhee's cheek and nodded for her to go.

Rhee turned to face the Fontisian, even as her lips curled in an expression of distaste at the sight of his uniform.

"What are you wearing *that* for?" Rhee asked.

"That's not the greeting I'd expected for saving your life." He didn't smile, exactly, but everything about him seemed to soften.

"Actually, I believe *I'm* the one who killed Nero."

Kara let go of her sister's hand, nestling the two coins in the palm of her own. She turned away to search for Aly—and found him only a few paces away. He knelt over a body.

It was Jeth's, his head at an awkward angle against the ledge of the roof. Aly adjusted Jeth's arms and head so he looked more comfortable. Quietly, Kara approached the ritual, watching as

Aly put his index fingers to his own eyes before touching Jeth's. Issa knelt beside him, and placed a hand on Aly's shoulder.

"I'm sorry, Aly," Issa said.

"Uh-oh," Lahna said, looking down at the square.

They moved in silence to the edge of the roof. Down below, a hundred UniForce soldiers looked up in unison—and moved swiftly, together, toward the palace doors.

Instinctively, Kara searched for Nero's body to make sure he had not survived. It lay in the same pool of blood, still broken and unmoving, but . . . "Nero's still controlling them. They're still after us."

"How?" Rhee said. "How can he control them if he's dead?" She looked desperately between them. Julian shook his head in disbelief, his mouth partly open, at a loss for words. Lahna's eyes were wide, her irises lit up like fire. But Dahlen's face betrayed a secret. His lips were pressed into a straight line. He looked up to the sky as if Vodhan might guide him.

"Dahlen?" Rhee pressed.

"It doesn't matter if he's dead," Dahlen said. "He's uploaded his consciousness using the overwriter, and it lives on in the people whose minds he was controlling . . ."

"Even after his death," Rhee said in a near-whisper.

Now Kara understood the true and infinite power of the overwriter, and why Nero had wanted it so badly. It was, in essence, a kind of immortality.

"We're not safe here," Dahlen said. "There are more Tasinn in the building. If they trap us on the roof we will not survive."

"Let's move, then," Aly said.

Together, they ran down three flights of stairs. The Tasinn were already coming to intercept them. Kara heard the strange, syncopated thud of their footsteps.

"This way," Rhee panted out, and hauled them down a corridor. The Tai from earlier appeared at the end of the hallway, and Rhee called out to her, happiness and relief and fear mixed in her voice.

"No," Kara said, grabbing her. "She's one of them."

Rhee's eyes went wide, but her mouth formed a tight line as she led them to the left, down another corridor, and into a room that Kara thought was hers. It tickled a dim memory, especially the heavy engraved door, which they swung shut and locked behind them.

"What are we going to do?" Issa sounded uncharacteristically young—and unusually afraid.

And then Kara knew: It was time. She realized only now how scared she was, how desperately she'd wanted to avoid this very moment. The risk of losing herself was real. All this time, she had wanted to get rid of the whole world's memory of Josselyn so that she could be free to be herself—whoever that was. But now, the answer seemed so obvious. What she needed was the willingness to be anyone for the right cause.

"The only thing left to do," Kara said at last. She took a deep breath and felt for Nero's cube, buried in the tissue of her neck, next to her own. She could feel her pulse beating frantically, as if trying to expel the foreign object.

"Kara," Aly said.

"Don't," she replied back. She put her finger to her cube. "He must have known how to stop this. It's our last chance."

"What are you doing?" she heard Rhee say just as she powered on.

The onslaught of someone else's memories was overwhelming, sickening. It made her so dizzy she collapsed. The pounding of her head exploded into new realms, vicious, growing beyond her into a gaping hole that would swallow her whole. She was vaguely aware of the people standing over her, people she loved, people who loved her—strangers whom she would know to love, if they survived.

Slowly, she managed to find her way into a place of calm, of attention in the mind. And then, as she concentrated, she began to move through the memories, train her mind to read and remember them as though they were her own.

At first, it was nearly impossible just to get through all the compliments, the flattery, memories that felt to her like massive cobwebs, sticky, grafting along the surface of her skin.

Buried deeper were the unarchived memories, the organic ones that Nero hadn't deemed worthy of recalling on purpose but which had been auto-stored nonetheless. Once, Kara had read that to remember your dreams you needed to grab for them, imagining a rope that you could tug so that the details would come back to you—navigating someone else's cube couldn't be so different.

She closed her eyes and, after a time, she found Nero as a boy, looking at himself in the mirror, scrawny, with big blue eyes that looked perpetually sad. He'd practiced smiling for hours;

there were memories of this from every year of his life, and Kara saw how it began to transition, how it started to look like that smile might be real as soon as he grew into his face, as soon as he became conventionally handsome.

Then she found his family life, and a new-waver father complaining of the Ta'ans. They hadn't done right by the lower classes. They'd made things hard. They didn't understand. Meetings in dim places where they complained loyalists were out of touch, complained of hunger, complained that there was no work. Imported food and fewer farms meant fewer jobs and less capital, less security, and even fewer people who knew how to make things. Nero's own obsession with beautiful things came from the craftsmen he'd grown up among.

Nerol Nerolllll, his classmates taunted over the years, in whiny voices. It was the reason he'd changed his name and dropped the "l." Hunger at home, bullying at school.

And then when he was older, how he'd clawed his way into entertainment when it was truly political ambitions he'd had—and how he'd merged them. He'd cultivated a following, killed a family, and made up his own title: "Ambassador to the Regent." They'd fallen for it. UniForce listened. He'd willed his new self into existence.

And then the first diplomatic trip he'd taken, to the G-1K summit, of all places, despite the tensions of the Great War—or because of them, since he'd visited with Seotra, the old man who'd tried to extend the Ta'an policies. He'd first learned of the overwriter tech there, had become obsessed with it.

Deeper and deeper. Dimly she was aware of people shouting, but she ignored them, left them behind, left them with the person she had once been. She was Nero now. She plunged further down, through the unarchived memories . . . the resounding screams of the many scientists he'd Ravaged . . . the smell of blood, the clatter of medical gurneys down long, feebly lit hallways . . .

The last was buried deepest of all, past so many layers of memory that Kara felt her truest self had left her body, her soul hovering just above the surface. She opened her eyes and looked down at her hands, expecting to see her coverlet, but instead saw the tiled floor of the Elder's stateroom. Wrong. She was seeing a memory—she couldn't be here. But she was, and she watched again as she—no, Nero—scorched the Elder's cube.

Again, the Elder told Kara-as-Nero: *You'll never have the full power of the overwriter because you don't have the heart . . .*

Stop, she thought, and the Elder froze in place; she'd paused the cube's playback.

She needed out. She swam up through the tides of memories, trying to find herself again. Where was she? Who was she? She could hear voices calling Kara's name . . .

No. She was Kara. Not Nero.

Her lungs were bursting. She felt as if she were really drowning.

Kara. Kara. Kara.

I'm Kara.

Gasping, she felt for his cube in her neck and powered it off. She burst free of Nero's consciousness. The relief was physical, immediate. It was like a sudden wind, sweeping away the terrible, festering mold of Nero's thinking.

"Kara? Are you all right? Are you all right?"

Was she all right? She didn't know. She didn't understand what she'd just seen.

Unless . . .

Her heart rate ticked up a notch as an idea began to form.

Unless . . .

Could the *overwriter itself* have a heart?

It was a living microorganism, after all, wasn't it? She remembered what Diac had told her when they were in captivity together: *Our memories, our thoughts, our ideas—these flower, wither, die, and regenerate. But the spark of life is buried deeper. It can be accessed only by the heart.* At the time, she thought he'd been trying to tell her about Lydia, about her love for Kara. But he'd been talking about the overwriter.

The overwriter could be destroyed, but its life was buried deeper.

It could be accessed only by the heart.

And the Fontisians had, for years, been sworn protectors of the overwriter.

Kara spun toward Dahlen. "Dahlen," she said, trying to keep her voice steady. "How did you get the scar on your chest?"

Issa, Julian, Aly, and Rhiannon stared at her.

Dahlen frowned. "The Elders told me only that the problem was in my *erzel*."

Kara closed her eyes. It meant *heart*, and it meant *root*. She knew, then. "You can stop this."

"I don't follow."

"It's *you*," she said again, and placed one hand on his chest. "You carry a piece of the overwriter in your heart." Her voice was hoarse; her head felt like it was on fire. "If we want to destroy the overwriter . . ."

"If we want to destroy the overwriter, then what?" Rhee demanded.

Kara looked from her sister to Dahlen. "You'll have to die."

TWENTY-EIGHT

RHIANNON

RHEE slammed her sister against the door. She could barely think; her mind was in a fog. "What did you say?"

"That I'll have to die," Dahlen said slowly, as if calculating something in his head. "My heart for the overwriter."

"That's not happening," Rhee insisted. The boy, Alyosha, tugged on her elbow, but Rhee shook him off. "She's lying. You're a liar!" She felt like she was drowning. "I won't let you kill him."

"Stay away from Kara!" a robotic voice said behind her. Then a shock of electricity ran up her arm.

"Ow!" Rhee spun around to see a droid waist-high, blinking red eyelights. "Who's Kara?"

A loud *thud* came from the other side of the door, and they all swiveled. The knob shook furiously, and Josselyn grabbed for it—like she might somehow shake off the soldiers on the other side of the door. The hinges bulged when someone—or lots of someones—pushed it from the other side.

Alyosha threw himself in front of the door. A bit of wood splintered away from the lock. "Grab anything you can get your hands on. It won't stop them, but it will at least slow them down."

Lahna, Julian, and Joss obeyed him wordlessly. They scraped the bed and dresser across the room, shoving them against the door. They piled chairs, wicker baskets, items of little weight or consequence—they were like sand crabs, shoring up walls that would soon be washed away by the approaching tide.

Rhee was aware on some level that she should help, but her bones were so heavy she felt like she'd been cemented to this very spot—opposite Dahlen, looking into his eyes.

"A little help, please!" Alyosha was sweating. Behind the makeshift pile of furniture, the door began to crack. The droid handed him an ottoman, as if it would help.

"Come on, little man, help me with a little something heavier," Issa insisted as she tried to push a dresser across the floor herself. The droid circled around to her side and slid it with ease.

"Why you?" Rhee demanded. He hadn't said anything further, and his silence scared her. The pounding on the door intensified, and the tremor transferred over to her body and shook deep down; they must've brought reinforcements.

"The origin of this tech Nero's using," Dahlen said, "I always knew the Fontisians had a hand in it. I just didn't know it was inside my chest, that they'd fused it with my heart . . ."

Ancestors, Rhee thought. It was strange, and cruel, and now she finally understood. "'You just didn't know what you knew,'" Rhee filled in, repeating the words the Elder had told her.

"We can't hold them off much longer," Julian cried.

Dahlen nodded. "The Elder told me, and yet I never understood what he meant. Even Rahmal tried to save my life, at the Elder's orders."

Rhee's eyes prickled with tears.

"And why would you have to die? Why can't we just find a surgeon?"

"There's no time, Rhee. And there's no surgeon in the galaxy who could extract it and keep me alive." Rhee's body went numb as he talked. "It's what saved my life in surgery—it has to be cut out. My life is intertwined with it now." He nodded at Julian, and motioned for the knife in his belt. Veyron's knife.

Julian looked at Rhee.

"No," she told him.

Julian's face softened; he bit the inside of his cheek. Josselyn buried her head into Aly's arm, while Lahna and Issa looked on. The door had started to give out, breaking at the hinges. The droid was spraying something across the opening, mending it, but it was only a stopgap—it wouldn't hold.

Julian was pushed forward, but he backed up against the door and redug his heels into the floor. "I'm sorry, Rhee." He handed his knife to Dahlen.

"No!" Rhee lunged for the knife. Dahlen grabbed just before she could, and held it high out of her reach. Still, Rhee clawed at him. When that didn't work she started to pound on his chest with closed fists. "I just got you back." She felt tears welling up, but she wouldn't cry. If she cried, she would be admitting this was real, that this nightmare would come true.

Dahlen wrapped his arms around her and pressed her close. With her cheek to his chest, she saw her sister across the room. She'd just gotten Josselyn back too. Perhaps you could never have everything you wanted, but just this once she needed the people she loved to live.

"You must accept it." For once, he hadn't spoken in negatives. She pushed him away and took a step back, taking in the scene. More pounding at the door. It produced a tiny splinter that would grow the length of the wood. Rhee felt she had that same crack inside her, like the sorrow might burst her open. Lahna was crying, tears streaking down her cheeks, mouth pursed like a wail was threatening to tear through her. Rhee was still in shock, disbelief. Her knees gave in and she fell to them, both her hands planted on the floor like she might find a trapdoor to open up into a new reality.

"Nero's army advances without him. He's not alive to call them back. What if they never stop? There's no time for this."

She felt the fire shoot through her veins as she glared up at him. "There's no time to feel, Dahlen. Is that what you mean? Who do you think you are?" She looked for something to throw at him, anything to abate her sadness with anger. "You think you can come in here and threaten to kill yourself and I'm just supposed to—"

"I'm not threatening to kill myself," he cut in. He kneeled before her and flipped the knife around so the handle faced toward her.

She scrambled back. "You can't be serious." She remembered what it had been like to kill Veyron. The heartbreak.

"There's no other way." He looked at her as she pushed to her feet. He was nearly her height even as he knelt. "The peace of the galaxy depends on it."

"I won't be a part of this. I can't . . ." She'd already lost Veyron and the Fisherman. Not Dahlen too.

A fist punched through the door. And then another. "By the tenets of Vodhan, he can't take his own life," Lahna said.

"I don't pray to Vodhan!" Rhee yelled. "What does your god matter to me? If you want to die a martyr, I won't have a hand in it."

"It's not wrong to die with honor," Dahlen said quietly. "Besides, it's the only way."

"It's not worth it. I won't kill you. I won't." Rhee waved her hand toward everyone else. "No one will do it," she ordered, her voice wild and ragged. "I forbid it!"

"He asked *you*, Rhee," Julian said.

She pivoted to face him. "Are you enjoying this?" It felt like venom spewing from her throat. "You'd love for me to take another life, to prove what you thought about me all along— that I'm a heartless, cruel, spoiled murderer. I won't do it! And you," she said, pointing to Lahna. "Stop crying!"

"No one is judging you," Julian said. "I don't think you're

heartless. But people are dying all over the galaxy. We must end the war."

"One small sacrifice for the larger galaxy at war. Please, Rhiannon." Dahlen bowed his head. This whole time, she had never once heard him say *please*. "The order teaches us that to die on the blade of a great warrior will ensure my eternity."

Rhee knew when Dahlen said *eternity*, he spoke of an afterlife that the Fontisians believed in. One of bliss, free of pain. Perhaps that's why death didn't seem so final to him.

He reached out, and placed the knife in her hand. It was the first time his features had ever looked gentle. The knife handle was surprisingly warm, the leather wrapped around the hilt soft. How could something so soft be so deadly?

"I don't know how to be in this world without you in it," she whispered. She knew how selfish that sounded, but it was the truth. Rhee closed her eyes. He'd led her to understand her very morality, and even when they were at odds she defined herself in opposition to him. In the few weeks she'd known him she'd learned more about war and belief and her larger place in the world than she had in the years before meeting him.

"You'll never have to know," Dahlen said. Another belief of the Fontisians: in the circularity and unity of all things. That nothing dead was ever truly gone.

She opened her eyes. He nodded. She kneeled in front of him.

"Do you remember what I told you on Tinoppa?" He took her hand and pressed it to the spot below his rib cage. She felt the rise and fall of his breathing, of the life she would take from him.

Rhee thought back, searching her organic memory—and when it surfaced she knew. There was a sharp, bitter taste at the back of her throat.

"You taught me how to kill a man quickly with a blade," she said. He had instructed her to drive the blade up into the kidney.

He won't survive, Dahlen had said.

"You prepped for this all along."

"Vodhan did."

Rhee's eyes welled. Her heart had turned to liquid. It fell to the bottom of her insides, coated everything with its tar.

"Honor, loyalty, bravery," she choked out. "And love."

Then she drove the knife up and into his heart. He gasped from the force of it, but kept his eyes on hers. When she hit the first real resistance, Dahlen's features contorted into something she almost didn't recognize. Rhee hesitated, then, in a quick draw of breath, jammed it in harder, in one solid death stroke.

He was able to whisper one last thing. "I'm glad it was you."

He fell backward, but Rhee leaned in and caught him, pulled him forward as she crumpled to the floor. She cradled his head in her lap.

If only she could undo everything, all of it, unfurl back in time before any of them were born. She'd right all the wrongs of her ancestors; she'd make sure this pure, impossible boy would live to be an old man. To spread his word. To live his truth. But that wasn't how the world worked.

"I'm sorry." She ran her fingers through his white-blond hair. Dahlen blinked in response; his hand found hers.

The wood cracked open as the guard kicked through the door. But her eyes never left his.

She watched his face as his heart slowed, needing to honor the moment he was gone—to recognize what he'd given to the world. Soldiers were pushing their way into the room, the furniture knocked astray, while her friends tried their best to fight them back.

The soldiers pushed their way through just as Rhee saw it, when a burst of intensity and knowing passed over Dahlen's face. She wondered if it was his life passing before his eyes, like they said. Rhee had found it remarkable how many variations of gray his eyes transformed into; they were a different color every time. Now, they took on the shade of well-worn silver. Rare. Old. Having weathered the passage of time, and having seen the best and worst this world had to offer.

Immediately, the soldiers collapsed to the floor in a heap. The attack had stopped, just as Dahlen's heart had—and the world went still for just a moment, before the people outside began to wail and sob. They had been spared. It was the sound of great sadness and even greater relief.

Alyosha kneeled beside her gently, as if he feared waking Dahlen. "Princess," he said softly. He had the coins in his palms, hers and Josselyn's. "There's a ritual. To ensure his entry into Vodhan's kingdom."

It seemed like he was asking something. Rhee didn't understand, and she could barely see—her tears refracting the grief, making the whole scene feel even more surreal.

"If you think he'd want it," Rhee said, her voice breaking.

Aly took apart the coins and placed one on each of Dahlen's eyes, then backed away quickly. Rhee leaned in close and took in the sharp line of his jaw, the high cheekbones, the white-blond hair that turned darker sometimes, like it did now—matted across his forehead. He could've been sleeping if it weren't for the coins on his eyes. They were eerie but beautiful too.

Rhee buried her face in his tattooed neck. It was still warm, and in the place where his pulse should beat was only a deep silence—like the farthest reaches of space, where she imagined Dahlen shooting across the darkness toward the honor he sought.

TWENTY-NINE

KARA

IT had been a week since Kara and Rhiannon had destroyed the overwriter. A week of national mourning, of frantic peacemaking pacts, of quelling an anxious public.

A week since Rhee had left for Fontis, to return Dahlen's body to the soil with their coins—an act to tie their families together for eternity. She was due to return any minute. Her craft had just been spotted coming into orbit.

A week since Kara had removed Nero's cube grafted to her own, the madman's thoughts purged from her mind.

A week, and an eternity. The people were lost, in distress. They needed a leader. And Rhiannon needed a sister. What was it Issa had told Kara? *This world needs you, Josselyn Ta'an.*

She had been so desperate to rid Josselyn from the hearts and minds of the public, never realizing until now that Josselyn *was* her heart, her mind. The fears, the hopes, the pain, and the headaches—all of it was hers, would always be hers. She could reconcile Josselyn and Kara, those two lives, that before and after, into a new future. She had purpose, and a family now.

"Rhee's home." Tai Reyanna appeared in the doorway. "Pavel's bringing her to her room."

Gathering the hem of her dress, Kara bowed, thanking the Tai. After the overwriter had released her, the Tai had launched into caretaker mode. In the week they'd been reacquainted, the woman already felt like family.

She hurried past, and ran past Aly in the hallway, but not before she took his hand and squeezed. "She's here!"

She moved through the palace toward her sister's quarters, feeling like she was in a strange kind of inverted fairy tale, where she was both the damsel in the high tower *and* the hero who had to rescue her. She was hours away now from her real coronation, and it was time. Time to *truly* recover what she'd lost: her throne, her sister.

Sister.

She found Lahna and Julian sitting together in the small antechamber outside of Rhee's quarters—looking exhausted, and still covered with bits of the clinging pollen that characterized the surface of Fontis. They had accompanied Rhee to return Dahlen to the order. It was their planet's ritual to bury their dead, and Rhee insisted—to pay respects to Dahlen and his god.

"Empress." Lahna stood up and performed an awkward bow. The Fontisian girl hadn't gotten used to palace etiquette. Nor did she have to.

"That's not necessary," Kara said, and saw in the girl's light eyes that she was relieved. "But thank you."

Julian simply greeted her with a nod of his head and a faint smile. They hadn't spoken of the day in the dojo not so long ago. Kara nodded by way of response. They didn't have to speak to understand: Everything that had transpired between them tied them together now, made them family even if they didn't share blood.

She moved toward her sister's door and saw the crack running lengthwise down the wood—a reminder of the way the Tasinn, under the yoke of Nero's control, had attacked them. Kara ran her finger down the groove. "Has she spoken?"

"She's cried," Julian said, not unkindly.

"Good," Kara said. "She needed it." She steeled herself, turned the knob, and entered.

Rhee knelt on the floor in her plain white undertunic. She was in the center of the room, and Kara realized it was the very spot Dahlen had died. She didn't look up when Kara entered, and Kara felt a momentary panic. How could she comfort this sister, who was really a stranger? If she couldn't find ways to ease Rhee's pain, how would she ease the pain of a whole galaxy? She fumbled for something to say, for some words of wisdom or kindness.

But all that came out was "Welcome home, Rhee." Kara placed a hand on her shoulder, and squeezed.

Rhee didn't look up, but she placed her own hand on top of Kara's. Her other hand remained in a tight fist in her lap.

A sliver of an organic memory moved through her like a pulse—it contained no specific memories, just a feeling, electric and overpowering. It was something she couldn't quite name, something between love and knowing: how sensitive Rhee had been, how sensitive she still was. It was anger that had built inside of her, brick by brick.

Brick by brick, Kara would learn her sister. She wasn't afraid of anger.

Kara kneeled, and placed a hand gently beneath her younger sister's chin, so that Rhee was forced to raise her eyes.

"They were so kind." Rhee opened her palm to show an onyx ring with an ornate crest. Dahlen's ring. "They let me keep this, as a memento." Her body heaved with breath. Kara found that familiar too—Rhee was trying not to cry.

"They're a kind people," Kara said. "And Dahlen was kind." He'd saved her life the eve of her coronation. He had saved the lives of everyone who was connected to the overwriter.

Kara reached out, running her hand through her sister's black hair. It was straight and thick, and Kara's fingers moved through it easily. At Kara's touch, something in Rhee broke. Her body began to shake with sobs.

"I've made so many mistakes." Her little sister looked up at Kara finally, tears streaking down the curves of her face. "Everything terrible that happened—it was my fault."

"That's not true," Kara said. How was it possible for Rhee to feel like a sister and like a stranger all at once?

"How would you know? You weren't here. You haven't been here . . ." Rhee trailed off. It stung, even if Rhee hadn't intended it. And in that silence Kara leaned forward and took Rhee in her arms and squeezed her close.

"I'm sorry," Kara whispered. Finally Rhee softened, letting her head drape over Kara's shoulder. Kara felt Rhee begin to shake as she cried. Kara absorbed it all, held her tighter. She tried to take Rhee's pain as her own. She tried to carry it. She had wanted to run away from this once. To disappear. But this was where she was needed, and this was what she needed as well.

"We're together now," Kara said softly.

The real work had yet to be done. The real people who needed saving were not two princesses but the people below— and throughout the galaxy too. The Ta'an dynasty had always ruled under the notion that they were guiding stars for the rest of the world to follow.

But things were going to have to change, just as Kara had had to transform into Josselyn, in order to become herself. In order to come home.

Slowly, Rhee quieted. And as she did, the noise of the crowd reached them from below. This time, the sound was joyful, not angry: The assembled people were shouting, calling their names. *Rhiannon. Josselyn. Long live the Ta'an dynasty.*

"I wish they could hear this." Rhee pulled away. She swiped her face with her arm before gesturing to the open window. "Our parents, I mean. The Emperor would be proud." A wind stirred the curtains, and carried in the sound of exulting, clamoring voices. There was a low hum, a slow rhythm to the pain in Kara's head. But it was her lot, and worth the price to be here with the family. The sun would be setting soon, and the coronation would take place in its golden light. "What are we going to do?"

Kara—no, Josselyn now—glanced up at the setting sun, thinking of everything their parents had stood for, and of the choices the Emperor had had to make. He'd signed an executive order that was invasive, that violated the privacy of everyone within his reach—but he'd done it as an act of mercy and a way to encourage goodwill. But could peaceful ends truly justify violent means? And could she tell Rhiannon what she'd discovered of their father's rule, when it was clear how much she'd idolized him? It was the first decision she would make as empress.

Josselyn turned back to Rhee. In her sister's eyes she saw both a vulnerability and a fierceness, and she thought again of guiding stars—burning bright, hot, alone. Josselyn had never felt more scared than she did now, but never more complete either. "We're going to give the people what they need," she said. She had to give Rhee what she needed too. There would be time for truths later. For now it was time to listen, and to do her best, and to serve her galaxy and her only remaining family.

EPILOGUE

WHEN he found her, she was standing at the window over-looking the crowd that had steadily gathered over the last twenty-four hours to see her coronation, her real coronation, live. Daisies hovered around them like bees around honey. Colorful lanterns hung from every balcony in the city, and fireworks shot into the sky.

Aly stood beside her. He didn't know what to call her—Kara? Josselyn?—she was both now. "Ready for prime time?"

"No." She turned around to face him, biting her lip. "What if this is a terrible idea?"

"You're a hell of a step up from the last guy who was in power."

"Way to set the bar." She swatted at him, but Aly caught her wrists and held on to them.

"You're brilliant, and you're fair, and you want to do what's right." He tried to tell her, with his eyes, how sorry he was. He tried to tell her that he didn't deserve her. "And you're forgiving. That's all I could ever dream of in a ruler."

"So you're saying"—Kara moved in closer—"that I'm your dream girl."

Before he could answer, Kara kissed him, a long, slow kiss that didn't feel as urgent as their last. It was unyielding, the way that ocean waves roll in. *You're my dream girl*, he said with his kiss. That's what the rhythm of it felt like, the ups and downs, the scary pull of the undertow that could drag you out and leave you adrift. He felt submerged in warm water, his mouth on hers, the silk of her dress as his hands gripped her rib cage and moved up . . .

"I have something to ask you," she said as she pulled away.

She fumbled in the folds on her dress and pulled out a small velvet box. Holding it between them, her smile was shy, her face red.

"Are you going to ask me to marry you?"

"No, you idiot." Kara glared at him. "Don't ruin the moment." She snapped it open. Inside the box was a small silver badge with the flag of Wraeta on it. "I'm asking you to be my Wraetan ambassador."

He didn't think he was into jewelry, but he was into *this*. It was the slickest pin he'd ever seen, and maybe the most beautiful gift anyone had ever given him. "There's no Wraeta, though," Aly said, suddenly feeling the sadness rush into his heart.

"Just because there's no Wraeta doesn't mean there are no Wraetans. You'll have to find them—wherever they are."

Aly felt his throat close up. It's what he'd always wanted—to be with Kara, and be with his people.

Her eyes crinkled when she smiled. "Are you *crying?*"

"No way. There's just something in my eye."

She pulled the pin out of its casing and threw the box over her shoulder. "Sort out your eyes, Ambassador Myraz," she said as she attached it to the rounded collar of his Kalusian-style suit. "You're going to be on TV."

"I've got plenty of practice." This time, he was the one to kiss her. It was the soft kind. It stopped and started, cascading into some new emotion so that their mouths, their breaths, their souls found new places to live inside one another. Every part of his body wanted to make contact with hers, and he leaned forward, and felt her hands under the hem of his shirt and up his back . . .

Aly thought his grin might split his mouth when he walked out onto the lower balcony, where Julian, Issa, Lahna, and Pavel had assembled to watch Kara's coronation. There was a wind at his back, and he swore he felt the ghosts of Vin, Jeth, and Dahlen—pushing him forward, to where he belonged.

"Looking sharp," Issa said, nodding to his new pin. Pavel extended a handkerchief and made a show of shining it.

Aly swatted him away. "You all too." They'd gotten Tasinn uniforms tailored, and they looked like the fiercest—and, sure, most random—assortment of bodyguards ever assembled. Julian reached out his hand and pressed his thumb into Aly's palm—a Wraetan greeting and a sign of respect, passed down from his Wraetan dad, probably. And Issa shimmied her shoulders to the beat of the horn blasts down below, confetti catching on the crown of her head.

"Look!" Lahna said, pointing up to the balcony. Rhiannon was smiling down at them. She lifted a hand to wave.

Then Josselyn emerged behind her. The wind whipped her hair up around her shoulders. The dress brought out the color of her eyes. She raised her hand to call for silence, and abruptly, the crowd went quiet. She opened her mouth to speak, and Aly thought to power up his cube. Lightning ran through him; it stung in a way that felt good, left him wanting more.

He wanted to remember this. From here on out, he wanted to remember everything.

ACKNOWLEDGMENTS

Jess Harriton, for your brilliance, kindness, and grace in navigating me through the chaos. Tiffany Liao, my partner in crime, for your editorial acumen and bottomless heart. Casey McIntyre, a Wonder Woman and publicist rolled into one, for all that you do. And Corina Lupp for a perfect cover. To Ben Schrank and all of Razorbill, thank you.

Alexa Wejko, my north star, this book has been shaped by you in countless ways—thank you for your friendship and genius. Lexa Hillyer and Lauren Oliver, for your guidance and expertise as we wrestled this story into something bigger than I'd imagined. Kamilla Benko, Tara Sonin, and Angela Velez for the positivity, love, and support. And to the rest of the Inkwell and Glasstown teams: Stephen Barbara, Emily Berge, Diana Sousa, thank you immensely.

To Adam Silvera, Dhonielle Clayton, and Ashley Woodfolk for letting me talk shop and craft all day and night. To the authors I have the honor of editing, and to the rest of my Imprint family, thank you. I'm a better writer because of all of you.

To my Ate, for reading all my terrible drafts and pushing me—and my characters—to get the things we want most. Jasy, Luis, and Alana: you're the points of constellation that guide me every day. Juan and Julian, for the home away from home. And Kuya, Ellie, Mason, and Logan, for being my constants.

And to Kyle for all the love you give.